Praise for the novels of Dale Brown

BATTLE BORN

"Is there anybody else out there who writes aerial techno-thrillers with the same explosive excitement and imagination as Dale Brown? If there is, I wish somebody would tell me. . . . a relentless pace and a satisfying conclusion . . . no matter the outcome of the battles in the air and the conflicts on land, the reader is always the winner."
—*Style Weekly*

"A gripping and entertaining novel that is hard to put down."—*BookPage*

"Brown fans will want to purchase this title."
—*Library Journal*

THE TIN MAN

"Dale Brown has the techno-thriller genre down cold. . . . Brown finely etches all the details, [and] the plot's tightly bolted together."—*USA Today*

"It's a page-turning start to a fresh new direction for both Brown and McLanahan."
—*Publishers Weekly* (starred review)

"A popular example of the techno-thriller form . . . a solid shoot-'em-up, with some clever technical apparatus that make this read a bit like SF."
—*Booklist*

BATTLE BORN

DALE BROWN

BANTAM BOOKS   NEW YORK

TORONTO LONDON SYDNEY AUCKLAND

BATTLE BORN

A Bantam Book

PUBLISHING HISTORY
Bantam hardcover edition / 1999
Bantam export edition / May 2000

ISBN 0-553-84030-4

Published simultaneously in the United States and Canada

Bantam Books are published by Bantam Books, a division of
Random House, Inc. Its trademark, consisting of the words
"Bantam Books" and the portrayal of a rooster, is Registered in
U.S. Patent and Trademark Office and in other countries. Marca
Registrada. Bantam Books, 1540 Broadway, New York,
New York 10036.

PRINTED IN THE UNITED STATES OF AMERICA

OPM   10   9   8   7   6   5   4   3   2   1

ACKNOWLEDGMENTS

Very special thanks go to two very special air warriors:

Thanks to Air Force General Mike Loh (ret.), former commander of Air Combat Command, for his inspiration, guidance, and suggestions. He continues to be this nation's strongest and most authoritative advocate for the heavy bomber, strategic airpower, and a strong national defense.

Thanks also to Colonel (BG selectee) Wil Fraser, former commander of the Twenty-eighth Bomb Wing, Ellsworth AFB, South Dakota, for his encouragement and support.

Thanks to Colonel Anthony Przybyslawski, commander, Twenty-eighth Bomb Wing, Ellsworth AFB; Colonel Tim Bailey, vice-commander; Colonel Richard Newton, ops group commander; Lieutenant Colonel Sloan Butler, Twenty-eighth Operational Support Squadron commander; Lieutenant Colonel Stephen "Taz" Wolborsky, Thirty-seventh Bomb Squadron commander; and Chief Master Sergeant Paul Hammett, Twenty-eighth Bomb Wing Senior Enlisted Adviser, for spending the time in explaining the employment of the B-1B and the mission of the Bomb Wing.

Thanks to all the Bomb Wing technicians and experts who demonstrated their skills, pride, and professionalism: Captain Scott Marsfield, Technical Sergeant Jerry Long, and Senior Airman Ryan Schod, life support; Staff Sergeant Robert "Chico" Cortez, weapons loader trainer; Master Sergeant Keith Malone, munitions; and to all the other men and women of the Wing for their time and assistance.

Special thanks to the crewdogs of the Thirty-seventh Bomb Squadron for hosting my spectacular flight in the Bone to Powder River: Captain Dave "Trooper" Johnson, aircraft commander; Captain Jason "PITA" Combs, copilot; Captain Chris "CK" Butler, OSO; and Captain Tom "Opie" Woods, OSO. These Tigers really showed me how lucky we are to have them on duty defending our country.

Last but certainly not least, very special thanks to Staff Sergeant Steve Merrill, Twenty-eighth Bomb Wing public affairs, for his expertise, attention, and professionalism in organizing and conducting a great tour of the Twenty-eighth Bomb Wing.

Thanks also to Michael Rascher and Nancy Dewey for their random acts of generosity and kindness.

AUTHOR'S NOTE

This is a work of fiction. Although some real-world names, organizations, and situations are used to enhance the authenticity of the story, any similarities to real-world persons, units, or situations are coincidental and all portrayals are purely the product of the author's imagination.

Please visit my Web site at www.megafortress.com for more information on *Battle Born* and on future works in progress.

CAST OF CHARACTERS

Kevin Martindale, President of the United States
Ellen Christine Whiting, Vice President of the United
  States
Corrie Law, chief of Vice President's Secret Service
  detail
Philip Freeman, General, National Security Adviser
Robert Plank, CIA Director
Jeffrey Hartman, Secretary of State
Jerrod Hale, White House Chief of Staff
Arthur Chastain, Secretary of Defense
Stuart L. Mortonson, Secretary of the Air Force
George Balboa, Admiral, Chairman of the Joint
  Chiefs of Staff
Victor Hayes, General, USAF, Chief of Staff of the
  Air Force
William Allen, Admiral, commander, U.S. Pacific
  Command

Terrill Samson, Lieutenant General, USAF,
  commander, High Technology Aerospace Weapons
  Center, Elliott AFB, Groom Lake, Nevada
Patrick S. McLanahan, Brigadier General, USAF
David Luger, Lieutenant Colonel, USAF
Hal Briggs, Lieutenant Colonel, USAF
Nancy Cheshire, Lieutenant Colonel, USAF
Adam Bretoff, General, Adjutant General, Nevada
  National Guard
Rebecca Catherine Furness, Lieutenant Colonel,
  NVANG, 111 BMS/CC

John K. Long, Lieutenant Colonel, NVANG, 111
  BMS/DO
Rinc Seaver, Major, NVANG, 111 BMS/DN
Annie Dewey, Captain, NVANG, copilot
Chris Bowler, Master Sergeant, NVANG, crew chief

REPUBLIC OF KOREA (SOUTH KOREA)
Kwon Ki-chae, President of the ROK
Lee Kyong-sik, Prime Minister
Kang No-myong, Minister of Foreign Affairs
Kim Kun-mo, General (Ret.), Minister of National
  Defense
An Ki-sok, General, Chief of the General Staff
Lee Ung-pae, Director of Agency for National
  Security Planning
Park Yom, Lieutenant General, Chief of Staff of
  Republic of Korea Air Force
Pak Chung-chu, former First Vice President of North
  Korea and interim Vice President of United Korea

DEMOCRATIC PEOPLE'S REPUBLIC OF KOREA
(NORTH KOREA)
Kim Jong-il, President of North Korea
Pak Chung-chu, First Vice President
Kim Ung-tae, Vice-Marshal, commander, Artillery
  Command
Cho Myong-nok, Lieutenant General, Chief of Staff
  of the Korean People's Army's Air Forces
Kong Hwan-li, Captain, commanding Nodong missile
  unit
Kim Yong-ku, Master Sergeant, Kong's assistant

PEOPLE'S REPUBLIC OF CHINA
Jiang Zemin, President of China
Chi Haotian, Minister of National Defense
Chin Zi-hong, General, Chief of Staff of the People's
  Liberation Army

Qian Qichian, Minister of Foreign Affairs
Xu Zhengsheng, Assistant Deputy Secretary of
    Cultural Affairs, Chinese embassy, Pyongyang
Zhou Chang-li, Ambassador to the United States

RUSSIAN FEDERATION
Yevgeniy Maksimovich Primakov, President of Russia
Dmitriy Antonovich Aksenenko, Deputy Foreign
    Minister

REPUBLIC OF JAPAN
Kazumi Nagai, Prime Minister of Japan
Ota Amari, Minister of Foreign Affairs

REAL-WORLD NEWS EXCERPTS

A CORNERED PYONGYANG COULD STRIKE OUT, WARNS U.S.
—Manila, Philippines (Reuters), May 21, 1997
The commander of U.S. forces in the Pacific said Wednesday that forcing famine-hit North Korea into a corner could drive it to attack its southern neighbor, resulting in heavy loss of life.

Adm. Joseph Prueher said the severity of the famine in the North remained unclear, but Washington's immediate concern was that Pyongyang "retains a considerable military capability to lash out."

"Should they try and conduct a full-scale assault they will not prevail, but it would nonetheless be a very difficult situation with a lot of loss of life because of the military capability North Korea maintains," he said. . . .

RIMPAC WILL ONLY INCREASE TENSION
—Pyongyang, June 6, 1998—(KCNA [Korean Central News Agency, official government news agency of the Democratic People's Republic of Korea])
Rimpac joint military manoeuvres involving the United States, Japan, South Korea, etc. will be reportedly held on the Pacific for a month from early July.

. . . The present South Korean regime, which styles itself a "government of people," is hell bent on confrontation and war preparations against the fellow countrymen in the north. It has frequently staged military exercises simulating an invasion of the north throughout South Korea under the pretext of "coping with the enemy's provocation of a limited war."

It is obvious that the participation in the joint manoeuvres by the South Korean puppets, who are aggravating the situation of the Korean peninsula with north-south confrontation and war preparations, is aimed at invading the north in league with outsiders. . . .

S. KOREA PLEDGES MILK TO THE NORTH
—Washington Post, July 22, 1998
South Korea, overlooking recent spy incursions by North Korean agents, is sending 781 tons of powdered milk to help the starving North.

N. KOREA MAY BE BUILDING NUCLEAR SITE; ACTIVITY RAISES CONCERN ABOUT ARMS PRODUCTION
—Washington Post, August 18, 1998
American intelligence is worried that some 15,000 North Korean workers are building a huge underground nuclear facility. The suspected activity runs counter to an agreement Pyongyang made to suspend nuclear weapons research in favor of massive amounts of aid dollars. The White House officially refused to comment on the matter, except to note that North Korea remains in compliance with the 1994 accord and the situation is being closely watched.

CONGRESSIONAL AIDES REPORT HIGH HUNGER TOLL IN N. KOREA
—Washington Post, August 20, 1998
Upwards of 800,000 North Koreans are dying from starvation or hunger-related illnesses. A group of bipartisan congressional staffers, following a week-long fact-finding tour of North Korea, said the country is in miserable condition and the situation is only getting worse.

PYONGYANG ROCKET 'CRASHED OFF ALASKA COAST'
—South China Morning Post, September 17, 1998
North Korea's missile test nearly reached Alaska. A piece of the rocket traveled about 6,000 km and splashed into the Pacific near the Alaskan coast.

N. KOREA REPORTED TRAINING PILOTS FOR KAMIKAZE ATTACKS
—Baltimore Sun, September 20, 1998
North Korea is reportedly training some 140 pilots for kamikaze missions against key South Korean targets, should war break out on the divided peninsula.

NK OFFICIAL SAYS WAR GROWING IMMINENT
—Pacific Stars & Stripes, October 1, 1998
North Korea's vice foreign minister, Choe Su Hon, said in a speech to the U.N. General Assembly that the danger of another Korean War is "getting even more imminent" because the peninsula remains divided. Choe said reunification would remove the danger but called the U.S. military presence in South Korea the major obstacle.

EXPERT URGES MISSILE DEFENSE
—Pacific Stars & Stripes, October 22, 1998
U.S. military strategist William Taylor warned Japan, South Korea and the U.S. are "totally naked" to missile attacks from rogue nations like North Korea. He urged that missile defense systems planning take priority in Washington, Tokyo and Seoul.

PENTAGON: NUCLEAR UPGRADE NEEDED FOR DETERRENCE
—Washington Times, December 4, 1998
A blue-ribbon Pentagon panel is urging the Clinton administration to improve the nation's nuclear forces for decades to come in the face of Russia's large arsenal and China's growing strategic force. The report by the Defense Science Board task force challenges key U.S.

arms-control policies, including the ban on nuclear testing, reliance on arms-reduction agreements and monitoring of nuclear-warhead reliability. A major finding is that the Pentagon lacks a long-term planning mechanism for nuclear-weapons programs.

JOINT 'MIND WARFARE' UNIT SET UP WITH U.S.
—*South China Morning Post, January 15, 1999*
U.S. and South Korean officials agreed to set up a joint psychological warfare unit that will attempt to win over North Korean civilians in the event of war.

PORTRAIT OF A FAMINE: STARVING NORTH KOREANS WHO REACH CHINA DESCRIBE A SLOWLY DYING COUNTRY
—*Washington Post, February 12, 1999*
As best they can, North Korean refugees drag themselves through snow and bitter cold to reach haven in China. Those who survive their personal exodus disclose horrifying tales of a slowly dying country, where famine is a continuing nightmare. . . . Aid supplies gathered by various agencies and sent to North Korea don't usually get to ordinary people, despite what international aid agencies proclaim. Most food and medicine is routed to families of the Workers' Party and the military. . . .

PROLOGUE

OVER NORTH-CENTRAL NEVADA
APRIL 2000

Get pumped, hogs!" the B-1B Lancer's pilot shouted excitedly on interphone. "We're coming up on the squid low-level. I'm ready to kick some ass! Let's show them who the top dogs are. I'm going to give us a few seconds on this way point, Long Dong. Thirty knots should do it. I want lots of room to rock and roll when they jump us. Power coming back to give us a few seconds' pad. I want some shacks!" He pulled the throttles back until the time over target matched the required time over target on the flight plan. Then he pulled off one more notch of throttle until he had a good twenty-to-thirty-second pad.

"Go for it, Rodeo," the B-1B's OSO, or offensive systems officer, responded eagerly. He glanced at his flight plan for the time over target, then at the time-to-target readout on his forward instrument panel. Being a few seconds late at this point meant they could fly faster on the bomb run itself, where the threats were likely to be heaviest. They fully expected to get jumped by fighters on this run, which meant they'd be running all over the sky trying to stay alive.

As he made the airspeed adjustment, the pilot strained forward in his ejection seat to look at his wingman, a second B-1B bomber in loose formation on his right wing. The B-1 "Bone" (few called it by its official nickname, "Lancer") rarely fought alone. If one B-1B supersonic bomber was a devastating weapon, two were triply difficult to defeat. They would need every possible advantage to win this battle.

Sure, this was only an exercise, not a true life-or-death struggle. But everyone in the B-1B was playing it as if it were the real thing. As someone once said, "The more you sweat in practice, the less you bleed in battle." Besides, in the eyes of these U.S. Air Force heavy bombardment crewdogs, getting "shot down"—especially by the U.S. Navy—was almost as bad as a real-life kill.

Naval Air Station Fallon was the home of the Navy Strike and Air Warfare Center and the new home of the "TOP GUN" Fighter Combat School. All aircraft carrier fighter and bomber aircrews were required to report to Navy Fallon before a deployment to certify their knowledge and skills in air-to-air and air-to-ground combat tactics. The Navy Fallon Target Range comprised over ten thousand square miles of an isolated corner of northern Nevada east of Reno, with some of the airspace restricted to all other aircraft from the surface to infinity, so the crews could practice live air-to-ground bombing, gunnery, and air combat maneuvers. Powerful TV cameras located throughout the range would score each bomber crew's attacks, and instrument packages onboard each aircraft sent electronic telemetry to range control stations, allowing great scoring accuracy in air-to-air engagements during post-mission briefings.

Because the Navy liked to mix it up with as many different "adversaries" as possible, the U.S. Air Force was frequently invited to "play" at Navy Fallon. For the USAF bomber crews, there was no greater thrill than to blow past the Navy's defenses and bomb some targets on their home turf.

Ever since the B-1Bs arrived in Reno, there had been a heated competition between the Air Force and Navy about who were northern Nevada's best military aviators. The competition would be even hotter today, because the B-1 unit in the box was the Nevada Air National Guard's 111th "Aces High" Bomb Squadron from Reno-Tahoe International Airport, just a few miles west on Interstate 80 from Navy Fallon. The 111th was one of only three Air National Guard wings to fly the sleek, deadly B-1B Lancer. Some serious bragging rights were on the line here.

"Get us some range clearance, Mad Dog," the pilot ordered.

"Rog," the copilot responded. On the discrete "referee's" radio frequency, unknown to the defensive players, he announced, "Fallon Range Control, Fallon Range Control, Aces Two-One flight of two, Austin One Blue inbound, requesting range clearance."

"Aces Two-One flight, this is Navy Fallon bomb plot," came the response. "Aces Two-One cleared hot into Navy Fallon ranges R-4804, R-4812, R-4810, Austin One MOA, Gabbs North MOA, and Ranch MOA routes and altitudes, maximum buzzer. Altimeter two-niner-niner-eight. Remain this frequency, monitor GUARD."

"Two-One, cleared into -04, -12, -10, Austin One, Gabbs North, and Ranch, two-niner-niner-eight, coming in hot and max buzzer, check," the copilot responded.

"Two," the second B-1's pilot responded. The less a wingman said on the radio, the better.

On interphone, the B-1's copilot announced, "We're cleared in hot, maximum buzzer."

"Let's go fry us up some squid, then!" the pilot

shouted again. There was no response. The rest of the crew was getting ready for the action.

Two systems operators, the OSO and the DSO—the defensive systems officer—sat behind the pilots in ejection seats in a small compartment just above the entry ladder hatch. As his name implied, the OSO handled the bomber's weapon and attack systems. The DSO's job was to call out threats as they appeared, monitor the system to make sure it responded properly when a radar threat came up, and take over operation of the defensive gear if the computers malfunctioned.

A tone sounded over interphone, a slow, almost playful *deedle . . . deedle . . . deedle.* "E-band early-warning radar, gang," the DSO announced. "Bad guys are searching for us. No height finder yet. Time to go low."

"Copy," the pilot said. On the interplane frequency, he radioed, "Trapper, take spacing. Keep it within eight miles."

"Rog, Rodeo," the wingman's pilot responded, and began a slight turn, letting the distance between the two bombers increase. Although they would both be flying the same route and attacking the same target, they would fly slightly different paths, separated by at least thirty seconds. This would hopefully confuse and complicate the defender's task. The two bombers also used air-to-air TACAN to monitor the distance between them, and they had emergency procedures to follow if the distance dropped below three miles and they didn't have each other in sight. "See you in the winner's circle."

"Radar altimeter set AUTO, bug set to 830, radar altimeter override armed," the copilot announced on interphone. "Both TFR channels set to one thousand hard ride. Wings full aft. Flight director set to NAV, pitch mode select switch to TERFLW, copilot."

"Set pilot." The pilot was flipping switches before the copilot read each step. The command bars on his center vertical situation display, or VSD, dipped to twenty degrees nose-down. "Twenty pitch-down command. Here we go." When he pressed the TERFLW, or terrain following, switch on his Automatic Flight Control System control panel, the B-1 bomber dove for the hard desert earth below like an eagle swooping in for the kill. In the automatic TERFLW descent, the 350,000-pound bomber was screaming earthward at over fifteen thousand feet per minute.

"Min safe altitude nine thousand," the OSO called out. "Looking for LARA ring-in." Just as he announced this, the low-altitude radar altimeter locked onto the earth. Now that the bomber knew exactly where earth was, it descended even faster. Dirt, dust, a piece of insulation, and a loose flight-plan page floated around the cabin in the sudden negative Gs of the rapid descent. The OSO felt like breakfast was soon going to follow, and he pulled his straps tighter.

Suddenly, the DSO shouted, "Bandits eleven o'clock, thirty miles and closing fast! Looks like a Hornet!"

"Shit!" the pilot cursed. He was hoping they wouldn't find them so early. "Hang on, crew." With his gloved right index finger, he pulled the trigger on his control stick to the first detent, then rolled the B-1 up on its left wing until they were almost sideways. The sudden loss of lift from the sleek, blended fuselage made the bomber plummet from the sky even faster.

"Passing twenty!" the OSO shouted a few seconds later, after pinching his nose through his oxygen mask and blowing against the pressure to relieve the squeezing in his ears. "Passing fifteen! C'mon, Sonny, let's get down there! Push it over!" The pilot didn't roll the bomber upside down, but he did increase the bank angle to well over ninety degrees. It roared out of the sky like a lightning bolt.

Just seconds before it would have hit the ground, the pilot rolled out of his steep bank with a fast yank of the control stick. The big but nimble bomber snapped upright with the speed and agility of a small jet fighter and leveled off less than a thousand feet above the ground. Its AN/ASQ-164 multimode radar displayed a profile of the terrain out to ten miles ahead of the aircraft on both pilots' VSDs. The B-1 punched through a layer of clouds at six thousand feet—and before their eyes was the high-terrain, snow-encrusted Dixie Peak staring right back at them, nearly filling the windscreen. "Damn!" the pilot shouted, banking left again to fly around the peak. "I hate letdowns over mountains!"

"That cumulogranite might've just put the fear of God into that squid pilot chasing us," the OSO reminded him. "Let him try to chase us now, with Dixie staring in his face!"

With the valley floor in clear sight, the rest of the descent went smoothly. The Offensive Radar System electronically scanned ten miles ahead and to both sides, measuring the width and height of the entire terrain and providing pitch inputs to the autopilot so the bomber would clear it by the selected altitude. The pilots first selected TF 1000 and accomplished a fast check of both redundant TFR system channels, then stepped the clearance plane down to its lowest setting of TF 200. They also selected "hard ride," which would command steeper climbs and descents over the terrain so they could hug the earth even closer.

Now that they were clear of clouds and could see the ground, after checking the TERFLW system for a few moments, the pilot deactivated automatic navigation and used visual contour procedures to guide the huge bomber. Instead of gripping the control stick, he pushed on the sides of it with an open palm, dodging and cutting down and between any significant terrain features while allowing the automatic TERFLW system to guide them over high terrain. Flying in a straight line only made it easier for defenders to find them. Hugging terrain contours while letting TERFLW keep the B-1B as low as possible was the best and safest tactic. "Where's that bandit, D?" the pilot shouted.

"Moving to four o'clock, twenty-five miles," the DSO replied. "He's not locked on . . . wait, he's got a lock! *Notch right,* reference heading two-four-zero!"

"Aces, notching right!" the pilot shouted on the interplane frequency. He then honked the B-1 into a tight sixty-degree bank turn to the right, changing course ninety degrees to their original track and placing themselves on the back side of Dixie Peak. Most modern-day fighters like the F-15, F/A-18, and F-22 used pulse-Doppler attack radars, which acquired targets based on relative speed. Turning ninety degrees to the fighter's flight path made relative speed equal to the fighter's speed, causing the fighter radar's computer to analyze the target as a terrain feature and squelch the target. The turn would also complicate the fighter pilot's attack geometry and give the bomber a chance to hide behind terrain. The B-1 descended to less than three hundred feet above the desert floor, flying over six hundred miles per hour.

"Lost the bandit," the DSO reported. "He's somewhere at five o'clock."

"Rog," the pilot said. He knew that Dixie Peak was between him and the fighter, and the longer he kept it there, the closer he'd get to his target before the next attack.

"Clear to the IP, pilot," the OSO shouted. "Center up, steering's good." The pilot started a left turn back toward the target area, drawing a mental picture of the air situation.

It was not a favorable attack setup for him and his crew, but these Navy air intercept exercises were usually one-sided affairs. Austin One Military Operating Area, or MOA, acted as the "funnel" of airspace that led to the three restricted areas where practice targets were attacked with live weapons. Navy fighters could chase a bomber all the way down as low as it could go in Austin One. Fighters could continue the chase in the restricted areas, but had to fly no less than a thousand feet above the ground to stay clear of bomb explosions. The Ranch MOA at the western end of the run was the "recovery zone," where the bombers and fighters had to disengage and establish safe altitude separation while the bombers turned around. The bombers were required to fly through the restricted area again and clear their bomb bays of all other weapons before they could exit the range complex.

The Navy pilots knew all this, of course, so all they had to do was wait at the bottom of Austin One for the bomber to enter the restricted areas. It gave the fighter jocks a little less time to intercept before bomb release, but they were almost assured of a kill. The first fighter they encountered was probably a young jock on one of his first fighter-intercept exercises, hoping to score an early kill while the bomber was at high altitude.

Well, the B-1B Lancer was not that easy to kill. It had almost the same agility as a jet fighter, it was just as fast, and it had one-half the radar cross section. Down low, no fighter in the world could keep up with a B-1—if it dared even to fly down close to the dirt.

The pilot released the trigger on his control stick, and the bomber made a relatively gentle thirty-degree bank turn toward the IP, or initial point, the start of the bomb run itself. The air-to-air TACAN read six miles—

just right, about thirty seconds apart. "Lead is two NAP from the IP," he radioed on interplane.

"Copy," the wingman replied. "We're seven NAP. We're popeye."

"Bandits at seven o'clock, no range," the DSO announced.

"Hold steady," the OSO called out. "Let me get my ACAL and get a patch."

"Range nine miles, five o'clock," the DSO shouted. "I think he's got a lock. Notch right, reference three-zero-zero."

"Got my ACAL, guys," the OSO said on interphone. "Clear to notch!" The pilot complied with a sharp right turn. Staying on a straight-line course for more than a few seconds with enemy defenders in the area was deadly for a bomber. The bombing computers needed accurate altitude data to compute bombing ballistics, and the OSO had to fly over a specific point on the route, usually the initial point of the bomb run, to calibrate altitude. There were several ACAL points on the route, but the one prior to the bomb run was the most important.

"AI's down," the DSO shouted. The fighter had turned off his radar, knowing he would disappear from the bomber's radar threat sensors. "He might have a visual on us!"

"ADF zero-three-zero, pilot!" the OSO shouted. The pilot turned hard left back toward the inbound track line to the target. By "ADF'ing" the course, he would return to the original inbound heading to the target, making it easier for the OSO to find the target on radar.

As soon as the pilot rolled out of his turn, the OSO switched to the target itself. Exactly as predicted, the first target appeared right under his cross hairs. "Got you, you bitch!" he crowed. "Pilot, give me twenty right, and I'll get a patch." When the pilot rolled out on his new heading, the OSO moved his cross hairs directly on the box, clicked the left button on his radar controller down twice, then clicked the button up.

The high-resolution synthetic aperture image on his digital display resembled a black-and-white photograph. The clarity was startling—he could actually make out the outline of a large tractor-trailer vehicle. "Hogs, I got a big mother trailer-sized vehicle—looks like a Scud missile reloading operation." He centered the cross hairs directly on the image. "You're cleared to the target! Let's nail that puppy! We're seven seconds late. Give me twenty more knots, pilot." The pilot goosed the throttles a bit more—they were now screaming inbound to their target at almost ten miles per minute. "TG twenty seconds."

"Bandits four o'clock, twenty miles and closing!" the DSO shouted. "Notch right!"

The pilot yanked the control stick right . . .

"No! TG fifteen! Wings level!" the OSO responded. "Stay on the bomb run!"

Suddenly, they all heard a faster-pitched *deedle deedle deedle* tone, no longer playful at all. "SA-6 up!" the DSO shouted. The SA-6 was a mobile Soviet-made medium-range surface-to-air missile system, widely exported all over the world. Its mobility, its top speed of almost three times that of sound, and its all-weather, all-altitude capability made it a deadly threat. The SA-6 fired a salvo of three missiles that were almost impossible to evade. "Three o'clock, within lethal range! Trackbreakers active!"

At the same moment, several white arcs of smoke traced across the sky, the thin white trails aiming right for the B-1, and the warning tone on interphone changed to a fast, high-pitched *deedledeedledeedle*. "Smoky SAMs!" the copilot shouted. Smoky SAMs were little papier-mâché rockets, no threat to the bomber by themselves, but signifying a missile launch against the bomber crew. It meant the crew hadn't done their job protecting their bomber.

"Simulated SA-6 launch!" the DSO shouted. "Uplink shut down! Chaff, chaff!" Clouds of thin tinsel shot out of canisters along the Bone's upper spine, creating a radar target several hundred times larger than the 400,000-pound plane itself.

"Hold heading!" the OSO shouted. "TG ten! Doors coming open!"

The copilot watched as one of the simulated SAMs passed directly overhead. Talk about the "bullet between the eyes," he thought grimly—if that had been a real antiaircraft missile, they'd have been dead meat. And he would have watched the final stroke all the damned way.

"Ready . . . ready, *now*! Bombs away!" the OSO shouted. One cluster bomb canister dropped free of the aft weapons bay. At the precise instant, it split apart and scattered the bomblets across the target area in a direct hit on the trailer.

"Bomb doors closed!" the OSO shouted. "Clear to maneuver!"

"Pump right, *now*!" the DSO shouted. The pilots rolled the bomber to the right away from the target area and pulled back on the control stick until the stall warning horn sounded, then released the back pressure. The DSO ejected more clouds of chaff behind them, successfully breaking the "enemy" radar locks and allowing the bomber to escape.

"That release looked good from back here, pilots!" the OSO yelled gleefully. "What did you see up there?"

"We saw our shit get blown away by a SAM!" the copilot yelled. "They had us dead-on!"

"I had the uplink shut down," the DSO protested. "No way that missile would've hit . . ."

"Well, then they used an optical tracker or they got lucky," the pilot said. "But they got us. If one of those smoky SAMs was a real one, we'd've gotten nailed. Shake it off, Long Dong. Nail the next one. These Navy pukes aren't playing fair anyway."

"Shit!" the OSO cursed into his oxygen mask. A perfect bomb run, a perfect release . . . and they got zilch. All that hard work for nothing. He angrily entered commands into his keyboard to sequence to the next target area. "Steering is good to the next target complex, pilot. We'll take out the next Scud missile site."

"What are the defenses in the area?" the copilot asked.

"SA-3s, SA-6s, and Zeus-23s," the DSO replied.

"All right. Shake it off, guys," the pilot said. "No more mistakes. Let's kick some ass this time."

"I've got another SA-6 and an SA-3 up," the DSO reported. "SA-6 is nine o'clock, moving outside lethal range. The SA-3 is at one o'clock."

"Where are the fighters?" the pilot asked.

"No sign of 'em," the DSO replied.

"Clearing turn coming up," the pilot said. "Back me up on altitude, co." He banked the B-1 up on its left wing, then strained to look aft up through the eyebrow windows for any signs of pursuit. When he had turned almost ninety degrees, he initiated a steep left turn. "I got it," he told the copilot. "Find the damn—"

"Aces!" they suddenly heard on the interplane frequency. It was their wingman, five miles somewhere behind them. "Bandit coming down the ramp! I think he's on you! You see him?"

Both pilots furiously scanned out their cockpit windows. Suddenly, the copilot shouted, "I got him! Two o'clock high! He's diving right on top of us! He's got us nailed!"

The pilot swore loudly, then racked the bomber into a steep right turn, jammed the throttles to full military power, pulled the pitch interrupt trigger to the first detent, and zoomed the B-1 skyward.

"What are you doing, Rodeo?" the copilot shouted.

"I'm going nose-to-nose with this bandit!"

"Are you *nuts*?"

"The best way to defeat a fighter on a gun or close-in missile pass is nose-to-nose," the pilot said. "I'm not going to let this Navy puke get a clear shot on us!"

Both pilots clearly saw the oncoming fighter as it plummeted toward them. It was a Navy or Marine Corps F/A-18 Hornet, the primary carrier attack plane, which also had a good air-to-air capability. The Bone's nose was thirty degrees above the horizon in the steep climb. All they could see was blue sky and the fighter diving down on them.

The sharp zoom maneuver was sapping their speed quickly. "Airspeed!" the copilot shouted—just a warning right now, not an admonition. The aircraft commander was still in charge here, no matter how unusual his actions seemed.

"I got it," the pilot acknowledged. He pushed the throttles forward into full afterburner power. "C'mon, you squid bastard. You don't have a shot. You're running out of sky. Break it off."

"We better get back down, pilot," the OSO urged him. "We're off our force timing!"

"Get the nose *down*, pilot," the copilot warned.

"You lost us, bub," said the pilot, addressing the pilot of the Hornet.

The OSO switched his radar display to air-to-air, and the ORS immediately locked onto the Hornet. "Range three miles and closing!" he shouted. "Closure rate one thousand knots! This doesn't look good!"

"Airspeed!" the copilot warned again. They were

now draining fuel at an incredible three hundred pounds of fuel per *second* and going nowhere but straight up.

"Pilot, we're off our force timing and three thousand feet high!" the OSO called. "We're inside the one-mile bubble!" For safety's sake, the rules of engagement, or ROE, at Navy Fallon prohibited any pilot from breaking an invisible one-mile-diameter "bubble" around all participants. "The ROE—"

"Shut up, co!" the pilot snapped. "We still got three seconds!" Breaking the ROE could put all the players in serious danger—and he was breaking rules one after another. "We're not going to show ourselves. *He'll* have to break it off."

"Get the nose down, dammit!" the copilot shouted again.

Then, seconds before the copilot was going to push his control stick and try to overpower the pilot, the fighter rapidly rolled right. They had lost almost three hundred knots of airspeed—and for what? They saved themselves from the fighter but were now in the lethal envelope for any surface-to-air missile battery within thirty miles.

"Ha! Where are you going, you wussie?" the pilot shouted happily. He was breathing as hard as if he had just finished a hundred-yard sprint. "Keep him in sight, co," he panted.

"This will work out perfectly, hogs," the OSO said. "This next target is a Zeus-23. We'll stay high and nail him! Center up."

The pilot started a left turn toward the next target. "Where's that fighter?" he asked.

"Eleven o'clock, moving to ten o'clock, way high," the DSO reported.

"Zeus-23 at twelve o'clock," the DSO reported. The real "Zeus-23," or ZSU-23/4, was the standard Russian antiaircraft artillery weapon system, a mobile unit with four 23-millimeter radar-guided cannons that could fill the sky with thousands of shells per minute out to two miles away—deadly for any aircraft.

"That's our target, crew," the OSO stated. He put his cross hairs on the Zeus closest to the preplanned target area. "Action left forty-five." When the pilot rolled out of his turn, the OSO took a radar patch on the target. "I got the patch. Steering to the target is good. Give me full blowers, Rodeo!" The pilot shoved the throttles back into max afterburner, and a few seconds later they broke the speed of sound.

"Bandit now at nine o'clock, ten miles and closing!"

"Stand by . . . bombs away!" the OSO yelled. The CBU-87 cluster bomb scored a direct hit.

"Zeus-23's still up," the DSO said.

"*What?*" the OSO yelled. "That run looked great! We were a little off, but well within the kill zone. Those squids are jacking us around, guys! That was a good kill all the—"

"Forget about it, Long Dong," the pilot interrupted. "Where's my steering?"

The OSO called up the last target in the third restricted-area bombing range. "Steering is good," he said. "Single Scud-ER transporter-erector-launcher with communications van. Supposed to be tucked in between some hills. Max points if we get this one, guys—it's worth more than all the other targets put together. Gimme a little altitude so I can see into the target area."

"Scope's clear," the DSO immediately reported.

It was clear to see why the OSO needed some altitude. The pilots couldn't see much more than a few miles ahead, and if they couldn't see, the radar could see even less. They were several seconds late too, and the faster speed meant even less time to spot the target.

"Get ready for a vertical jink," the pilot said. He reset the clearance plane switch to one thousand feet, and the bomber responded with a steep climb.

"I got . . . squat," the OSO reported. The cross hairs went out to a large section of blackness. There were no radar returns yet in the target area. His hesitant voice infuriated the pilots even more. "ADF a one-three-five track, pilots. Clear back down."

The pilot released the pitch interrupt trigger, and the bomber settled back down to its roller-coaster ride just two hundred feet above the blurred earth zooming by. "You got the target?" he asked.

"Not yet," the OSO responded. "The radar predictions said we won't see the targets until four NAP if we stay low—we'd need to go up to two thousand to see it sooner. Let's get back on planned track, and then give me another jink so I can get a better—"

"Bandits!" the DSO interrupted. "Eight o'clock, fifteen miles and closing! I think it's an F-14—no, *two* F-14s! Give me a hard left thirty!"

"I'll lose my look down the canyon!" the OSO objected. But the pilot rolled into a hard ninety-degree bank turn, rolling out just far enough to track perpendicular to the fighter. "Reverse as fast as you can!" the OSO said. "I need one last look down that canyon!"

"Clear to turn back!" the DSO said after only a few seconds. The pilot started a right turn. "Trackbreakers active! Bandits never turned. They're nine o'clock, nine miles."

"Give me a vertical jink now!" the OSO said.

"Negative!" the DSO interjected. "We'll be highlighted against the horizon! If the fighter gets a visual on us, he's got us!"

"I need the altitude!" the OSO cried. "I can't see shit!"

"If we climb, he'll spot us!" the pilot protested.

"Then center up!" shouted the OSO. "I'll try to get a lock close-in." He knew he'd have only seconds to see the target on radar before bomb release.

Sure enough, as they closed in on the target, all he could see on the digital radar screen was dark green, interspersed with flecks of white. The terrain was shadowing every bit of ground radar returns. Nothing showed up on the MTA display—no moving targets at all.

"Twenty TG," the OSO said. "Action left thirty. I need one thousand feet, pilot, and I need it *now*."

"All right," the pilot said. "You got about five seconds." He spun the clearance plane switch and they climbed. "You get your fix, Long Dong?"

The last climb did it. The cross hairs fell on a lone radar return in the very southern edge of the gully. When the pilot rolled out of the turn, the OSO snapped a patch image of the last target. "Got it! Steering is good!" he said. Damn, what a relief. His cross hairs were nestled right over a long, thin target, small and partially hidden. Magnifying the radar image showed a definite Scud transporter-erector-launcher on the move. A small, mobile target—max points if they hit it. "Let's nail this sucker! Fifteen TG! Ten . . . doors coming open . . . five . . . bombs away!" The pilots could see the target, a white trailer with an old sewer pipe strapped atop it, configured to look somewhat like a Scud missile. "Doors coming closed . . ."

"We got it!" the copilot shouted happily. "We nailed it!"

"Let's start a right turn to two-four-three," the OSO said.

But just as they zoomed past the target area and crossed over the southern edge of the gully, a flurry of smoky SAMs filled the sky. "I've got SA-3s, SA-6s,

SA-8s, and triple-A all around us!" the DSO shouted. *"Scram! Scram left!"*

The B-1 snap-rolled to the left so hard that the OSO's head hit the right bulkhead. Then he was thrown forward as the bomber quickly decelerated. He cried out in pain, his vision swimming with stars.

The pilot threw in forty degrees of bank and pulled on the stick to 2.5 Gs—almost tripling their weight—then pulled the throttles to idle to slow to cornering velocity.

"C'mon, Rodeo, turn!" the OSO shouted. "Pop the brakes! Go to ninety degrees bank!"

"We're restricted . . ."

"We're gonna get hosed if you don't get that nose around, pilot!" the OSO said. "Pop the brakes! You're VMC. Go to ninety degrees bank!"

"Speedbrakes coming out," the pilot shouted on interphone, then flipped the speedbrake OVERRIDE switches and thumbed them to decelerate even faster. The "scram" maneuver was an emergency turn designed to get away from ground threats as quickly as possible. It meant instantly slowing the B-1 bomber to cornering velocity, a speed that increased the turn rate but wouldn't normally sacrifice controllability.

"SA-8! Zeus-23! Eight o'clock, lethal range!" The electronic countermeasures system was ejecting chaff and flares as fast as possible, but the threats stayed locked on. The sky was suddenly filled with white lines—smoky SAMs, dozens of them, flitting around them like bees around a hive. Several of the little paper rockets hit the Bone, though there was no way they could do any actual damage—they weighed less than two pounds and were as fragile as a toy.

The pilot kept the back pressure on his control stick right at 2.5 Gs until the bomber had decelerated to their planned cornering velocity, then shoved the throttles to max afterburner. The maneuver worked. By the time he had plugged in the afterburners, they were headed virtually in the opposite direction. He pushed the control stick right to roll wings-level and thumbed the speedbrake control to retract the speedbrakes so they could recover their lost airspeed . . .

. . . except that the bomber never rolled upright. They were still in a steep bank. "Damn! Damn! Damn!" the pilot kept shouting. "What's happening here?" The TERFLW FAIL warning tone sounded, a continuous low tone signaling that the terrain-following system had failed. The system automatically performed a 3-G fail-safe pull-up, designed to fly the bomber away from the ground—but if it was in a steep bank angle, a fly-up would drive it into the ground unless the pilots intervened quickly. "*Shit,* what's going on?" yelled the pilot. "It won't roll wings-level! Mad Dog, get on your stick. I think my controls failed!"

"Get the nose down! Airspeed!" the copilot shouted as he grabbed for his stick. He tried to move it, but the bomber would not respond. He checked the flight control indicators. "Retract your speedbrakes! Spoilers are still up." The pilot thumbed the switch to retract them, but there was no change. "Check my OVERRIDE switches!" he yelled.

The copilot reached over to the center console and checked the switches. "Spoiler OVERRIDE switches are normal," he said. "What's going on?"

The OSO could feel a definite sink building—it felt like the bomber was mushing, on the verge of a stall. It was yawing to the left as well, as if the pilot had pulled back power on the left engines. "Roll out! Roll out!" he shouted on interphone. "TF fail! You got it, pilot? Altitude!" But he didn't have it.

The pilot saw his altimeter beginning to spin down faster and faster. He felt a weightless sensation, felt his

body floating in his straps. They were going in! Oh shit!
Oh shit!

No choice, no warning—the pilot put his hand on
his ejection lever, closed his eyes, and pulled.

Without warning, the upper hatch over each crew
member's station popped free, followed by a roar of
windblast and a cloud of debris and dust that enveloped
the aft compartment a split second before the rocket
motors blasted the pilot up the ejection seat rails. A
crushing blow slammed against his right shoulder, and
he felt his body tumbling hard through the sky as it was
snatched into the slipstream.

The last thing he remembered was seeing the sleek,
deadly looking B-1B slide underneath him, still in a
moderate left bank but with the nose up in a gentle
climb. The pain in his shoulder was excruciating. He
saw a tremendous fireball, a massive cloud of fire as big
as the mountains surrounding his home back in
Reno . . .

. . . and he saw two ejection seats, with partially
inflated parachutes, fly right into that hellish wall of
flames.

Seconds later he felt a sharp blow to his back and
head . . . and then everything went black.

WONJU AIR BASE, REPUBLIC OF KOREA
THAT SAME TIME

In recent months Wonju Air Base had been placed on
alert at least once a day, so when the Klaxon sounded
that night, the ROK crews assumed it was more of the
same. They ran to their planes and prepared to launch
their fighters with surprising calm.

Because Wonju was South Korea's northernmost air

defense installation, less than thirty miles from the De-militarized Zone and about one hundred miles from the North Korean capital of Pyongyang, it would always be one of the first to react to any incursion by North Korean attackers. Wonju had a mixed fleet of aircraft. The primary air defense weapon was the F-16K, a fighter license-built in South Korea by a conglomerate of Korean heavy equipment manufacturers. The fighters were designed to respond to a massive invasion force, so had only one centerline external fuel tank; but they carried two radar-guided AIM-120 AMRAAMs (advanced medium-range air-to-air missiles) and eight AIM-9M Sidewinder short-range heat-seeking missiles, plus 200 rounds for the 20-millimeter cannon. A minimum of twelve F-16Ks pulled round-the-clock alert at Wonju.

The base's fleet also included a number of French-built Mirage F1 fighters, American-built F-5 fighters for daylight intercepts—the North Korean Air Force was ill equipped to fight at night—and American-built F-4E Phantom jets for both bombing and air defense work. The alert fleet of twelve F-4Es was loaded with high-explosive and incendiary "firestorm" bombs specifically targeted for low-level, high-speed bombing raids of key selected North Korean targets, should the expected—many said inevitable—invasion from the North take place.

At the sound of the Klaxon, all alert crews went to their fighters and bombers, started engines, and monitored the air defense network. Even though they were in a heightened state of alert, no planes launched. A "launch on alert" could set off an uncontrollable military escalation between North and South in minutes. With engines running, the entire alert force could be in the air in less than two minutes. With planes taking off every fifteen seconds from the main runway and the two taxiways, twenty-four warplanes could be in the sky from this base alone in less time than it took a high-speed attacker to fly ten miles.

The crews listened and waited. Was it the actual invasion this time? Was this the big showdown between the Communists and the South here at last?

"Unidentified aircraft heading south at three-four-zero degrees bearing from Wonju, fifteen miles, you are in danger of crossing the Demilitarized Zone at your present heading and airspeed," the South Korean air defense controller warned. "This is your final warning. If you cross restricted airspace, you will be fired upon. Unidentified aircraft, turn north immediately or you will be fired upon." At that same moment, two green lights flashed on the flight-line ready board. The first two South Korean F-16s had launch clearance.

As soon as they were airborne, the lead pilot switched his wingman to the air defense controller's call-up frequency. "Sapphire Command, Tiger flight of two, passing three thousand, check."

"Two," his wingman replied.

"Tiger flight, Sapphire Command reads you loud and clear," the controller responded. "Switch to blue seven."

"Tiger flight going to blue seven now." After receiving a curt "Two" from his wingman—any good wingman will answer all calls with little more than his position in the formation—the two pilots changed over to a secure HAVE QUICK radio frequency. The channel "hopped" to different frequencies at irregular intervals, making it difficult for outsiders to eavesdrop. "Sapphire, Tiger flight with you passing four thousand, check."

"Two."

"Tiger flight, this is Sapphire Control, read you loud and clear," the air defense controller responded, his voice now slightly garbled by the computer-controlled frequency-hopping algorithm. "Say position from Solar."

The lead pilot flipped his navigation system to the Solar way point, an imaginary point from which they could give position reports without revealing their position to outsiders. "Tiger flight is zero-six-three degrees bearing and one-niner miles from Solar."

"Roger, Tiger flight. Fly heading two-niner-five and take base plus one-four." Base altitude today was ten thousand feet, so the F-16s started a climb to twenty-four thousand feet. A few minutes later, when they were less than twenty miles from the DMZ, the controller called, "Linear."

The lead F-16 pilot activated his APG-66 attack radar, and seconds later the radar locked onto a target directly off the nose. "Tiger flight is tied on, bogey bearing two-niner-seven, range thirty-two, low, speed three-zero-zero."

"Tiger flight, that's your bogey," the controller replied.

The F-16's APG-66 pulse-Doppler radar could track several targets simultaneously, but just for good measure the lead ROK pilot broke lock on the target and let the radar scan the sky again. No more targets. A lone invader from the North? The North rarely flew single-ship. A tight formation of many invaders? The Communist fliers were not known for their formation flying skills in daytime, and they rarely flew at all at night, much less in formation.

But the ROK pilot had learned never to rely on such assumptions. It was always better to assume there were numerous attackers out there. "Tiger flight, tactical spread, now."

"Two." The second F-16 left his leader's right wing-tip and spread out several hundred feet laterally and two hundred feet above, close enough to keep his leader in sight in the darkness but still be able to move and react quickly if the tactical situation changed. The Communist pilot might be able to see two targets on his radar screen—if he bothered to turn his radar on. So far, there was not one squeak from the threat-warning receiver, meaning he was not using his attack radar. Some of the North's advanced J-7 and MiG-29 fighters purchased from China had infrared tracking devices and infrared-homing missiles, so radar wasn't necessary close-in, but it was still very strange for an attacker to charge blindly into enemy territory without using radar.

The target continued across the DMZ without the slightest change in airspeed, altitude, or heading. The Communists had just committed an overt act of war, breaking the fragile truce between North and South.

The second Korean War was under way.

To the ROK pilot, this was not just an act of war—this was an act of barbarism. The two nations had been struggling for years to make peace and eventually re-unite their two countries. Covert probes by North Korean special forces and provocative but nonaggressive border "incidents," meant to trip the South into react-ing with force for propaganda purposes, were bad enough. But this was a deliberate air-attack profile.

There was plenty of mutual distrust to go around. The South was accused of building up an invasion force by buying or license-building American fighters, war-ships, antiaircraft systems, radars, and high-tech preci-sion-guided weapons. The North was accused of continuous spy missions and of deploying improved surface-to-surface missile systems capable of bom-barding Seoul with chemical, biological, or even nuclear warheads. Everyone knew the arms race between the two countries had to stop, but neither side wanted to make the first substantive move.

Both nations tried "baby steps" toward peace. The

North agreed to dismantle its breeder nuclear reactors in favor of light-water reactors, less capable of producing weapons-grade nuclear material. The West promised huge grants of cooking and heating oil so the North would not be tempted to trade weapons for oil from unfriendly Middle East nations such as Iran. The South canceled joint U.S. and Japanese military maneuvers, removed Patriot and Rapier air defense systems from the DMZ, and reduced U.S. military presence to less than ten thousand troops. But the distrust continued.

The ROK pilot wanted nothing more than to see the entire Korean peninsula reunited once again—under a Korean, not a foreign, flag. That had been the dream of all Koreans since the Chinese and Japanese occupations. But what he wanted didn't matter right now. Right now his homeland was under attack, and it was his sacred responsibility to stop it.

He scanned an authentication encoder-decoder card strapped to his left thigh. Even though the pilots and the controller were on a secure frequency and had already verified each other's identity, they were entering a critical phase of this mission. Careful coordination and verification was an absolute must. The card was changed every twelve hours and would provide positive command validation for all upcoming orders: "Sapphire Command, this is Tiger flight, authenticate Tango-Alpha. Over."

"Sapphire authenticates Alpha."

"Authentication received and verified. Tiger flight requests final intercept instructions."

"Stand by, Tiger flight," the controller responded. The wait was not long. "Tiger flight, you are ordered to attempt to make visual contact to verify the target's identity. If it is a hostile aircraft, or if identification is not possible, you are instructed to attempt to force the aircraft to land at a category Charlie, Delta, Echo, or Foxtrot airfield, military or civilian. If the hostile will not respond, or if you are approaching any category Bravo airspace, you are authorized to destroy the hostile aircraft." Then the controller read the current date-time group and authentication code, and it matched.

The F-16 lead pilot called up the coordinates of the closest category Bravo airspace, which happened to be Seoul itself. They were only fifty miles north of the edge of the thirty-mile Buffer Zone around the South Korean capital. At their current airspeed, the pilot had only about seven minutes to convince the Communist invader to turn around or land before he had to shoot him out of the sky.

He tried the radio first. In Korean, then in broken Chinese, he radioed, "Unidentified aircraft seventy-eight miles northeast of Seoul, this is the Republic of Korea air defense flight leader. You have violated restricted airspace. I have you in sight and am prepared to destroy you if you do not reverse course immediately. I warn you to reverse course *now*." No response. He tried the universal emergency frequencies on UHF, VHF, and HF channels as well as several known North Korean fighter common frequencies, but there was still no response.

It took two minutes for the F-16 pilot, with his wingman flying high cover position, to maneuver alongside the hostile aircraft. Thankfully, it was only a single plane, not an entire attack formation. It was easy to intercept the intruder visually because he had all of his outside navigation and anticollision lights on—and, the ROK pilot soon realized with surprise, he had his landing gear and takeoff flaps still down too! Incredibly, this pilot had launched and flown hundreds of miles with his gear and flaps down. He was sucking fuel at an enormous rate, and at over three hundred knots had probably overstressed them both to the breaking point. The ROK F-16s were equipped with three-thousand-candlepower spotlights on the left side of the plane, and when the pilot was close enough to see the plane's shadowy outline in the darkness, he flicked them on.

"Sapphire, this is Tiger flight lead, I have visual contact on the hostile," the ROK pilot reported on the secure HAVE QUICK channel. "It appears to be an A-5 Qian attack plane." The A-5 was a Chinese-made attack plane, a thirty-year-old copy of the ancient Soviet Su-7 attack fighter. It was a mainstay of the North Korean People's Air Army. "Configuration as follows: single engine, single pilot, small cylindrical fuselage, with short delta wings, large nose intake, and a small radome in the center of the intake. I see a red and blue flag of the Democratic People's Republic of Korea on the side, along with a tail code, 'CH,' and number one-one-four." The "CH" stood for Ch'ongjin, a North Korean air-attack base.

Ch'ongjin was known to have large stores of chemical and possibly nuclear weapons.

"The A-5 is carrying three external stores: one one-hundred-deciliter centerline fuel tank and another one-hundred-deciliter fuel tank under each wing." He steered the searchlight across the weapons, gulped in shock, then added in a barely controlled voice, "Correction, Sapphire, correction. The stores under the wings are not fuel tanks, repeat, *not* fuel tanks. They appear to be gravity weapons, repeat, gravity weapons. I see four purple stripes around the center of the starboard gravity weapon."

This was the worst possible news. The purple stripes around the bomb, a standard marking in both the Communist Chinese and the old Soviet military from which all of North Korea's weapons came, meant that they were thermonuclear bombs. They were the old-style

Yi-241 weapons, disguised to look like fuel tanks—the Chinese and Soviets had once even stored them outside secure areas to try to convince Western intelligence analysts that they were not nuclear bombs. But each of these "fuel tanks" had the explosive power of 600,000 *tons* of TNT—more than enough to level Seoul or any other city in the world. Because they were considered unreliable, two of them were dropped on a single target—if the first one detonated, the second would "fratricide" in the fireball.

There was a moment's tense pause. Then the controller ordered, "Tiger leader, this is Sapphire; you are instructed to attempt to divert the hostile away from category Bravo airspace in any way possible." The F-16 pilot could hear the quiver of fear in the controller's voice. "You must not allow the hostile aircraft to close within fifty miles of category Bravo airspace, but you are instructed to shoot down the hostile only as a last resort." The reasoning was clear: if the pilot put a missile into the A-5, at best the explosion would scatter nuclear material; at worst, the devices could detonate, causing widespread destruction. The ex-Chinese and ex-Soviet weapons did not have the numerous safety features of Western nuclear devices—they were designed to explode, *not* designed to safe themselves.

"Tiger flight copies," the leader acknowledged. "Check."

"Two copies," his wingman responded immediately. With the safety radius now increased to fifty miles, they had less than three minutes to get this intruder turned around.

The lead pilot shined the searchlight into the A-5's cockpit canopy from a distance of less than fifty meters. What he saw shocked him yet again: the North Korean pilot was not wearing a helmet! It looked as if he had simply climbed in the plane and blasted off without any of his flight gear. This was astounding, although it did explain why he never heard the radio or configuration warnings.

The North Korean pilot shielded his eyes from the searchlight—and, thankfully, turned away from the F-16. Good—they were no longer heading directly for the heart of the capital. The ROK pilot edged closer to the A-5 and again shined the light into the cockpit; again, the A-5 turned away. He was heading almost southeast now, well away from Seoul. This time the F-16 pilot flew slightly above and closer to the North Korean plane. As the A-5 descended and turned away, he saw that the pilot appeared to be screaming, gesturing wildly at the ROK plane while trying to shield his eyes from the blinding light.

The F-16 pilot called up a list of nearby category Echo airfields and found a deactivated military base, Hongch'on, less than thirty miles away. It was isolated; the nearest populated area was a small town over twenty miles distant. There was no time to search for a better choice.

The North Korean seemed to be weirdly single-minded, which worked to the F-16 pilot's advantage: if he steered away from the A-5, the Communist pilot tried to turn right toward Seoul, but if he crowded him, the pilot turned left, away from him. If he climbed over him, the Communist descended, but if he flew at the same altitude, the A-5 pilot would try to climb back to original altitude or maintain altitude. Good.

"Sapphire Control, this is Tiger lead, I have the hostile turned toward Hongch'on, and I will attempt to get him to land. Have security and special weapons maintenance crews standing by. Our ETA is fifteen minutes."

They were over Hongch'on in a little over twenty minutes. The airstrip was illuminated by several trucks shining their headlights onto the concrete; there was more than enough light. But herding the reluctant North Korean pilot to land on the nine-thousand-foot-long runway was proving more difficult. It was as if the North Korean pilot had finally realized what the F-16 was forcing him to do, and he kept trying to turn away from the runway. Finally, the wingman got on his left side, and they boxed the A-5 in. But when the leader tried to force it lower and along the runway centerline, the plane rolled hard left, striking the wingman's right wingtip.

"Damn! He midaired me! Tiger Two is lost wingman!" the second F-16 pilot shouted as he climbed away from the North Korean attack plane. "Lead, I have substantial damage to my right wingtip and number ten weapon station. I am climbing, passing five thousand."

"How is your controllability?" the leader asked. "Do you need an escort?"

"Negative," the wingman replied. "I feel a slight vibration from the damage area and I've lost some airspeed, but I have no warning or caution lights and my controls feel okay. I have safed and locked all my weapons. Still showing full connectivity on all stations except number ten. I am visually inspecting my right pylon . . ." The lead F-16 pilot knew his wingman was fishing a flashlight out of his flight suit pocket so he could see his wingtip: "I have lost my number ten weapon. Substantial damage to my right wingtip, but very little observed damage to my right wing."

"Good," the lead F-16 pilot responded with relief. "Stay above us at ten thousand feet until I end this intercept, and then I'll escort you back to base." The wingman had over an hour's worth of fuel remaining. More than enough.

The A-5 pilot was trying to turn back toward Seoul again. The lead F-16 moved in tight on his right side and fired its 20-millimeter cannon. The blaze of the muzzle flash made the pilot leap in shock, and he turned away exactly as before. The ROK pilot waited until the A-5 was almost in the direction of Hongch'on. Then he yanked the throttle, dropped back a few hundred feet behind it, kicked in a little left rudder, and fired a one-second stream of shells across the tail, being careful not to shoot below the wings at the thermonuclear bombs.

The shells ripped across the horizontal and vertical control surfaces, tearing them to shreds. Several rounds entered the engine exhaust, and the F-16 pilot could see sparks, then a fire spreading inside the engine compartment. The A-5's airspeed, already limited because of the hanging gear and flaps, was cut nearly to nothing as the engine slowly began to disintegrate. The fighter dropped like a brick.

Although the Communist pilot was obviously suffering from mental lapses evidenced by flying without his gear, his instinct and training took over as the A-5 began to die. The fire was extinguished as it fell, and the plane nosed over to help build up airspeed. As it did, the pilot was able to maneuver his stricken jet toward the runway at Hongch'on. Incredibly, he nearly managed to plant it on the runway. It was in a landing attitude, nose up slightly to try to preserve some airspeed, at the moment that it slammed into the ground about three miles short of the runway, digging into the soft peat surrounding the airfield. The F-16 pilot, trying to keep it in sight as long as possible, watched in horror as it flipped upside down in the soft earth, then spun across the ground. The bombs and fuel tank scattered. He couldn't see where they landed.

As the ROK pilot climbed away from Hongch'on, he thanked the gods that his own intended landing base was many, many miles away.

．　　　．　　　．

The provincial police evacuated the village of Hongch'on quickly and efficiently, and forces from the Republic of Korea Army base at Yongsan sealed off the area within twenty miles of the crash site. Village officials were simply told that a military plane had crashed, and that was good enough reason for them. Fortunately, the early morning winds were light, so the authorities anticipated no further evacuations for several hours, after the rising sun stirred the atmosphere again.

Slowly, deliberately, the Army nuclear weapons experts closed in toward the crash site. There was evidence of fire and debris everywhere, but they detected no radiation. The fires were small, probably because the A-5 had little fuel left in its tanks—just enough for a one-way suicide run over Seoul to dispense the cargo of death. There were no signs of explosion.

The wreckage of the fighter was found inverted, facing opposite from the direction of flight. The plane was almost intact, a tribute to its tough-as-nails construction. The centerline fuel tank was crushed up into the bottom of the fuselage, the cockpit canopy had been flattened—and the nuclear weapons were nowhere in sight.

While searchers fanned out to look for them, the pilot's body was pulled out of the cockpit. His head was crushed. He was wearing a dark brown wool flight suit ringed at the collar and cuffs with lamb's wool, typical of the North's Air Army, but he had no other flight gear at all—not only no helmet but no gloves, no survival gear, not even flying boots. How he survived the nearly one-hour ordeal in the freezing-cold cockpit was impossible to guess. There was no name tag. Some of his insignia, including the pilot's wings and flag of the Democratic People's Republic of Korea, had been partially torn off. Either he was trying at the last moment to hide his identity or country of origin—or he was ashamed to reveal it.

But the most incredible revelation was the pilot's body itself. It was as emaciated as a scarecrow. He could not have weighed more than one hundred pounds. His chest was sunken, his ribs were visible, and his skin was stretched taut across his bones. He looked like a concentration camp survivor, so skeletal that investigators guessed he might not have had a regular meal in months. The body was carried away from the crash site for further investigation.

Less than an hour later, searchers found both thermonuclear gravity bombs. By a remarkable stroke of fortune, neither had ruptured. One bomb's housing had cracked, but there was no spill and the basketball-sized globe of fissionable material was intact. The second bomb was fully intact except for its tail fins and several dents and scrapes. The weapons were carefully packaged in lead-lined caskets and carried away for analysis.

South Korea had now acquired its first two thermonuclear weapons. Unknown to it or to the rest of the world, the tiny nation would never be the same again.

CHAPTER ONE

MILITARY TECHNOLOGY SUBCOMMITTEE,
SENATE ARMED SERVICES COMMITTEE,
RAYBURN BUILDING, WASHINGTON, D.C.
SEVERAL WEEKS LATER

I hoped we'd never be facing this question again in my lifetime," the chairman of the Senate Armed Services Committee said, his voice serious. "But here it is. Looks like the devil's goin' to the prom, and we're praying he don't ask us to dance."

The main part of the morning's classified, closed hearing had already concluded; the scientists and comptrollers had packed up their charts and spreadsheets, leaving only the subcommittee members, several general officers, and a few aides. This was the open debate portion of the session, a "chat session" where everything was fair game and the uniformed officers had a last chance to persuade. It was usually more casual and more freewheeling than formal subcommittee testimony, and it gave all involved a chance to vent their frustrations and opinions.

"I'd say, Senator," Air Force General Victor G. Hayes, the chief of staff of the Air Force, responded, "that we've got no choice but to dance with that devil. The question is, can we keep him from only tipping over the punch bowl, or is he going to burn down the whole school gymnasium if we don't do something?"

"You characterize the attacks on Taiwan and Guam

as just a tipped-over punch bowl, General?" a committee member asked.

General Hayes shook his head and wiped the smile from his face. He knew better than to try to get too chummy or casual with these committee members, no matter how plain-talking and down-home they sometimes sounded.

This was the first time Victor "Jester" Hayes had testified before any committee in Congress. Although the Pentagon gave "charm school" classes and seminars to high-ranking officers on how to handle reporters, dignitaries, and civilians in a variety of circumstances, including giving testimony before Congress, it was simply impossible to fully prepare for ordeals like this. He did not feel comfortable here, and he was afraid it showed. Big-time.

The chairman of the Joint Chiefs of Staff, Navy Admiral George Balboa, was seated beside Hayes. The other members of the Joint Chiefs—General William Marshall, Army chief of staff; Admiral Wayne Connor, chief of Naval Operations; and General Peter Traherne, commandant of the Marine Corps, along with senior deputies and aides—were also seated at the table facing the subcommittee. Out of the corner of his eye, Hayes could see the barely disguised amusement on some of their faces. Balboa in particular seemed to be enjoying the sight of Hayes roasting a little in front of a congressional subcommittee.

Screw 'em all, Hayes told himself resolutely. I'm a fighter pilot. I'm an aerial assassin. These congressmen may be high-ranking elected government officials, but they wouldn't understand a good fight if it kicked them in the ass. Be yourself. Show 'em what you got. As far as Balboa was concerned—well, he was a weasel, and everyone knew it. He was virtually powerless, allowed to keep his position by the good graces of powerful opposition party members in Congress even though he publicly ambushed his Commander in Chief.

"Forgive me for trying to take some of the doomsday tone out of this discussion, Senator," Hayes responded. "After two days of secret testimony on some of the new 'black' weapons programs we've included in the Air Force budget, I thought it might be time for a little break. But I assure you: this is a very serious matter. The future of the United States Air Force, and indeed the fate of our military forces and the nation itself, will be determined in the next several years by the decisions we make today.

"I characterize the ballistic missile attacks on Taiwan and Guam by the People's Republic of China as a repudiation of thirty years of arms reduction efforts and a warning to the United States armed forces that we must develop a multilayered antimissile defense system immediately. We bargained away our antimissile capabilities in the 1970s, believing that nonproliferation would lead to peace. Now, in the face of renewed aggression, rearmament, terrorism, and the spread of small-scale and black-market weapons of mass destruction, I feel we have no choice but to rebuild our defensive forces. The days of believing that our conventional precision war-fighting capability obviated and obsoleted decades of nuclear warfare strategy and technology are history."

"Apparently so," one committee member said ruefully. "I for one am mystified and angry about this waste of time, money, and resources. We've spent hundreds of billions of dollars on these new 'smart' weapons, and now you're saying they won't protect us?"

"I'm saying that the rules are changing, Senator," General Hayes said earnestly, "and we must change with them.

"We gave away our defensive capability because we

kept a large, strong offensive force, including nuclear deterrent forces. We then dismantled those deterrent forces when the threat from other superpowers diminished. Now the threat is back, but we have neither defensive nor deterrent forces in place. That leaves us vulnerable to criticism at best and attack at worst. The China incident is a perfect example."

"That's all fine and good, General, but these budget numbers are staggering, and the path you want to embark on here reminds me of the nuclear nightmare times of Eisenhower, Kennedy, and Reagan," the senator went on, motioning to his staff report. "You're asking for billions more on some truly horrifying programs, like antiballistic missile lasers, space-based lasers, and these so-called plasma-yield weapons. What's going on, General? Is the Air Force so desperate for a mission right now that you'll even go back to 'mutually assured destruction' doctrines of the Cold War?"

"Members of the committee, I asked Secretary of Defense Chastain and Secretary of the Air Force Mortonson to give the Air Force a budget for the deployment of a new class of weapons not to shock or galvanize the Congress, but because I truly believe the time has long passed for us to be thinking about this kind of war fighting," General Hayes went on. "China's recent nuclear attacks on Taiwan; its suspected nuclear sabotage of the aircraft carrier USS *Independence* in Yokosuka Harbor; and its shocking, unprovoked, and horrific ballistic missile nuclear attack on the island of Guam, which all but wiped Anderson Air Force Base off the map three years ago, all are a warning to the United States."

"It's a warning, all right," another senator offered. "But it seems more a warning to avoid stepping up to the edge of that slippery slope. Do we want to start another nuclear arms race?"

It seemed as if most folks in America had all but forgotten what had happened only three years ago, Hayes thought grimly. In 1997, just before their "Reunification Day" celebrations, the People's Republic of China launched a small-scale nuclear assault on Taiwan, which had just declared full independence and sovereignty from the mainland. Several Taiwanese military bases were decimated; over fifty thousand persons lost their lives. At the same time, a nuclear explosion in Yokosuka Harbor outside Tokyo destroyed several American warships, including the soon-to-be-retired aircraft carrier USS *Independence*. China was accused of that unconscionable act, but the actual culprit was never positively identified. When the United States tried to halt the PRC's attacks against Taiwan, China retaliated by launching a nuclear ballistic missile attack on the island of Guam, shutting down two important American military bases in the Pacific.

The reverberations of that fateful summer of 1997 were still being felt. Japan had closed down all U.S. military bases on their soil and had only recently begun allowing some limited access to U.S. warships—provisioning and humanitarian shore leave only, with ships at anchor in the harbor, not in port, and no weapons transfers in their territorial waters. South Korea was permitting only routine provisioning and shore leave— they were allowing no weapons transfers within five miles of shore and prohibited staging military operations from their ports. It was the same for most ports of call in the western Pacific. American naval presence in the Pacific was almost nil.

And America's response to China's attacks was . . . silence. Except for one massive joint Air Force/Navy defensive air armada around Taiwan that all but destroyed China's Air Force, and an isolated but highly effective series of air raids inside China—largely attributed to American stealth bombers, aided by Taiwanese fighters—the Americans had not retaliated. It was world condemnation alone that eventually forced China to abandon its plan to force Taiwan back into its sphere of influence.

"I'm concerned about the path Russia, Japan, and North Korea are taking in the wake of the economic collapse in Asia and the conflict in the Balkans," Hayes went on. "Russia appears to be back in the hands of hard-liners and neo-Communists. Food riots in North Korea have led to the slaughter of thousands of civilians by military forces foraging for food. Japan has isolated us out of the Pacific and is proceeding with plans to remilitarize, all in an apparent attempt to shore up confidence in its government. I don't believe the United States sparked this return to the specter of the Cold War, but we must be prepared to deal with it."

"We are all shocked and horrified about all those events as well, General," the senator pointed out, "and we agree with the President that we must be better prepared for radical changes in the political climate. But this . . . this buildup of such powerful weapons that you're asking for seems to be an overreaction. What you are proposing goes far beyond what any of us see as a measured response to world events."

General Hayes swallowed hard. This was turning into a much harder sell than he had expected. While the world slowly went back to an uneasy, suspicious peace, President Kevin Martindale was roundly criticized for his inaction. Although China was stopped and an all-out nuclear conflict was averted, many Americans wanted someone to pay a bigger price for the hundreds of thousands who had died on Taiwan, Guam, and onboard the four Navy warships destroyed in Yokosuka Harbor. The hawkish President was slammed in the press for abandoning the capital onboard Air Force

One during the attacks on Taiwan, while failing to use most of the military power he had spent his entire career in Washington trying to build up.

No one could say precisely what Martindale should have done, but everyone was convinced he should have done something *more*.

"Then what is a 'measured response' to those attacks, Senator?" General Hayes asked. "The People's Republic of China devastated Taiwan and Guam with nuclear weapons, taking hundreds of thousands of lives. Our response was to secretly attack their last remaining ICBM silos. Although we caused a lot of damage and prevented China from launching any more attacks against the United States, that country still retains a tremendous nuclear force and is still a threat. Our best conventional weapons didn't work."

Army Chief of Staff Marshall spoke up to reinforce Hayes's point. "My concern," he said, "rests with other rogue nations that may want to use nuclear, chemical, or biological weapons against us. Intelligence reports say China has delivered nuclear warheads to North Korea via Pakistan in exchange for its missile technology. Combine that with North Korea's new long-range missiles and nuclear-capable aircraft delivery systems, and it could have a first-strike nuclear force in place in a few years, perhaps sooner. Iran, Iraq, Syria, and even Japan could be next."

"The question is, Senators, what does the United States do if another attack from one of these rogue nations occurs?" General Hayes asked. "Obviously, our conventional weapons superiority failed to deter China—it certainly won't deter any smaller nation. Do we use strategic nuclear forces? No American president would dare consider using a city-busting bomb unless the very existence of the United States itself was in jeopardy.

"Does this mean we do nothing, as the world thinks we did against China? That would be the safest move. But we look indecisive and weak, and I think that perception makes us appear ineffectual to our allies and ripe for more attacks by our enemies. South Korea and Japan think we abandoned them, and both are clamoring to renegotiate defense treaties to allow them to build up their military forces once again. As you know, Japan doesn't allow any more U.S. warships to homeport or even dock there. And they've concluded a multibillion-dollar defense deal with Russia for MiG-29 fighters because they're afraid of not being able to buy American jets.

"To the Air Force," Hayes went on, "the answer is costly and politically hazardous, but absolutely clear. We must put a multilayered aircraft, satellite, and ballistic missile defense system in place immediately and rebuild our rapid-response intercontinental heavy-strike forces. The cornerstone of the five-year plan we are requesting is early deployment of the airborne laser and additional funding for the space-based laser defense system."

"Well, let's get into the specific programs and their status right now, gentlemen," the subcommittee chairman said. The subcommittee members leaned forward in their seats; this was where the sparks would begin to fly. "I'd like to begin with the Navy. Admiral Connor, start us off, please."

"Thank you, sir," Connor said. "The Navy has vastly improved its air defense and ABM technology over the years and is now ready, with congressional support, to field the world's most advanced, most mobile, and most flexible antiballistic missile defense systems. The Aegis Tier One system is in service now and has demonstrated a credible ABM capability, but Aegis Tier Two, using components available right now, will increase its lethality tenfold. Aegis Tier Three will be the ultimate ship-launched air defense system, capable of defending the fleet and large sections of allied territory. We're on track and on budget to deliver both systems."

"General Hayes?"

"The Air Force is continuing development and acquisition research on the airborne laser, the nation's only air defense system designed to kill ballistic missiles in the boost phase rather than in midcourse or reentry phases of flight," Hayes said. "Mounted on a 747 airframe, ABL can rapidly respond to a crisis, can set up anywhere on the globe in less than twenty-four hours, and can give theater commanders an effective multishot missile kill capability."

"When can the ABL system be ready, General?" one senator asked.

"With continued funding support, ABL will reach initial operating capability with three planes by the year 2005 and full operating capability by 2007."

Hayes could see many of the senators shaking their heads—that was far longer than they recalled when the program was first introduced. "But Patriot and Aegis Tier One are ready now, is that correct?" one senator asked. "When can Aegis Tier Two be ready?"

"In two years, sir," Admiral Balboa replied proudly. "Modifications to the existing Standard missile, improvements on the Aegis radar system—all of which benefit fleet defense as well as improve ABM capability."

"Very good," the chairman said. "General Marshall?"

"The lead agency in antiballistic missile weapons technology has always been and will continue to be the U.S. Army," General Marshall began. "Our PAC-3 version of the Patriot missile is the only battle-proven antimissile system deployed right now. Our improved Patriot system, the Theater High Altitude Air Defense, or THAAD, system, is progressing and should be ready for initial operating capability in three years, providing we receive full requested-funding approval."

"But as I understand it," one senator said, "the performance of the weapon depends right now on the use of this so-called baby nuke. Is that a fair assessment, General Marshall?"

"No. That term is incorrect. The plasma-yield warhead is not a thermonuclear device, Senator," Marshall said. "It is a new technology high-explosive device that will increase the capability and effectiveness of all classes of theater or strategic antimissile defense . . ."

"Excuse me, General, but that sounds like doublespeak for a nuclear bomb to me," the senator interjected. "Would you mind explaining what these things do and omit the soft-soaping?"

"What plasma-yield weapons are, Senator," Marshall answered, "are the next generation of high-explosive weapons, designed to be small, lightweight, but very destructive warheads for antiballistic missiles, antiaircraft missiles, and cruise missiles. They are not 'baby nukes,' and I'm concerned that this characterization will deprive our arsenal of a very promising futuristic weapon. Although I'm not a physicist or engineer, I know enough about the process and the application of the device to explain it for the committee:

"Simply put, plasma is ionized gas—a cloud of charged particles, usually consisting of atoms that have had electrons stripped from them so their charge is unbalanced or dynamic. It is the most abundant form of matter in the universe—the physicists tell me that ninety-nine percent of all known matter is plasma. Because the gas is composed of charged particles called ions and not atoms or molecules as air and water are, plasma has unique properties. We don't really know how to contain it, but we do know a lot about shaping it—in essence, plasma can be programmed. We can control its size, shape, mass, and what materials it interacts with.

"Plasma-yield weapons give us added flexibility by giving smaller weapons and delivery systems more punch, until we can improve our missiles' accuracy enough to allow smaller conventional warheads," Marshall explained. "The weapons use a small fission reaction, not to generate a thermonuclear yield, but to generate radiation . . ."

"A fission reaction—as in a *nuclear explosion?*" one senator asked, his tone incredulous.

"A rapid but controlled fission reaction more like a nuclear power plant, generating heat rather than an explosion," Marshall responded. "We bring nuclear material together to start a fission reaction, but our goal is not to create the chain reaction that leads to an explosion. We're only looking for the intense radioactivity to develop for a very short moment—milliseconds in fact—and then the reaction stops. The radioactivity is concentrated along a magnetic field and hits a pea-sized pellet of nuclear fuel. This forces ions—positively and negatively charged particles—to be stripped from atoms, producing a bubble of energy called plasma. Because there is no explosion per se, we can precisely control the diameter of the bubble, making it as small as a few hundred feet or as large as a city block.

"There are two noteworthy properties of a plasma-yield effect," Marshall went on. "First, there is no large-scale release of radiation because the fission reaction is terminated gigaseconds after it starts. There is no nuclear chain reaction that produces the large explosion and release of nuclear particles and creates tremendous heat. The yield of this weapon is many times smaller than a thermonuclear detonation, and the levels of released radiation are far smaller than even the proportional size of the yield.

"The second property of this effect is that the plasma reaction cannot take place outside the field, or bubble, created by the explosion," General Marshall went on. "This is called the Debye effect. The plasma field basically consumes itself as it is created; it dies at the same time as it is born. The size of the field can be precisely determined, which is why plasma is used in such commercial operations as making microchips and drawing images in a plasma TV set. Outside the plasma field, there is no overpressure and very little heat or radiation. There is no shock wave as the plasma field is formed. The field grows to whatever size it's programmed to grow to, then stops. The weapon doesn't even make that much noise when it goes off."

"It doesn't make noise?" one senator asked, sounding startled.

"Some, but not as much as you'd expect for a small nuclear device," Marshall responded. "You see, the weapon doesn't explode as we all commonly think of explosions. It doesn't transform matter into energy and expanding gases, and it doesn't compress the air around itself. It simply changes matter—solid, liquid, or gas— to plasma, which is just another form of matter. As you know, there's no sound when ice turns to liquid or when liquid turns to gas."

"But there's got to be heat, light, flame, radiation, all that stuff," one senator pointed out. "Isn't that a pretty violent reaction? We're concerned about what the international community and the American people will think about our military forces using these weapons on missiles and bombs. How do we explain it, General?"

"We do tend to think of something changing properties as a violent process, Senator," Marshall explained, recognizing he was having difficulty getting his point across, "but in reality it's not. When a pond freezes over, it's not a violent thing. In physics, it's merely a transfer of energy—the molecules of water release energy in lower temperatures and don't bump around as much, forming a solid. Liquids boil when they turn to gas, but that's not a violent thing either—it's an atmospheric thing, the gases in the liquid flowing to a region of lower pressure when the absorption of energy separates water molecules. It's the same with a plasma field. Matter is transformed to another form of matter by absorbing energy."

"You make it sound so damned peaceful, so *natural,* like a flower blooming or a sunrise," a senator said acidly. "We're talking about a killer weapon here, General. Let's not forget that." He paused for a moment, then asked, "So what happens to the matter, the solids . . . oh, hell, you know, the buildings, the *people,* who get hit by this thing? What happens? Where do they . . . well, *go*?"

"They become plasma—that's the simple answer," Marshall responded. "The plasma field takes matter, absorbs energy, and converts it to ionized gas. The target is . . . well, the target's just not *there* anymore, at least not in a form that our senses can detect."

"You mean . . . vaporized," said one of the senators.

For a moment, Marshall's face was impassive. Then he nodded, looked the senator straight in the eye, and said, "Yes, sir. Vaporized. The target becomes a cloud of ionized gas, equal in mass to its original mass, but simply a collection of charged particles."

The committee sat in stunned, horrified silence. The members did not even look at each other—they simply stared at Marshall and the other service chiefs in utter disbelief. Finally, the committee chairman said, "This is incredible, General, absolutely incredible. And you are proposing that we actually deploy this weapon? You are asking this committee to write an amendment to the new budget to allow the military services to put this . . . this plasma-yield weapon on a missile? It sounds incredibly dangerous."

"One property that I didn't mention, sir," Marshall explained, "is that the plasma-yield weapon is more effective at high altitudes, because atmospheric pressure dilutes the plasma field. This makes it a good warhead to use in applications such as air defense, antiballistic missiles, and antisatellite weapons, and not as good with land- or sea-attack weapons. That's another reason the Army and Navy are using it in their ground- and sea-based antiballistic missile systems. Because we get a bigger bang, they can afford to use tracking and intercept systems that aren't quite as precise—or expensive."

"This is simply unbelievable," the chairman said, clearly shaken by what he had heard. "A weapon that can kill thousands silently, yet small enough to be put in a suitcase." As he looked at the others on the subcommittee, he shook his head. "I for one don't want to start traveling down this road without more facts. I think we should table this discussion until we review more scientific facts about this technology."

It was, General Hayes thought grimly, an urbane way of saying they didn't want to think about it any more. Apparently, everyone on the subcommittee shared the sentiment, because there was no dissent, no further discussion. Hayes was shaken. It seemed as though the vote had been suddenly, silently taken, and it was unanimous. No funding for the plasma-yield technology weapon—which probably spelled the end of the Army's THAAD program, and maybe the Navy's

Tier Two and Tier Three antiballistic missile programs as well.

Then, just as it appeared that the chairman was going to adjourn the hearing, a new voice spoke up. "Excuse me, Mr. Chairman. Permission to address the subcommittee?"

The Joint Chiefs turned toward Air Force Lieutenant General Terrill Samson, one of the aides supporting the Air Force chief of staff. The subcommittee chairman said, "The chair recognizes General Samson. Please be brief, sir."

"Thank you," Samson said. Terrill Samson, a large black man known as Earthmover to his friends, had risen through the ranks from high school dropout Air Force enlistee to three-star general and was the commanding general of the Air Force High Technology Aerospace Weapons Center, or HAWC, a secret research and test facility hidden in the deserts of south-central Nevada in an area known as Dreamland. "My group has been working with the Army in testing plasma-yield technology used in THAAD. Senator, the Air Force has an interim concept for a ballistic missile defense system that improves on THAAD and provides a near-term technology solution until ABL comes on-line in the next five to ten years. We call it Lancelot. Part of our budget request was for an operational Lancelot flight test in the next several weeks."

"Lancelot?" The subcommittee chairman flipped through an index, then turned to an aide, who scanned another set of files. "I don't see anything in here about a Lancelot program, General Samson."

"Lancelot was designed and built by one of our defense contractors, Sky Masters Inc., with help from my engineers at Elliott Air Force Base," Samson said. "With all due respect, General Marshall, we saw how poorly the THAAD and Tier Two programs were progressing and worked to address the difficulties. We used off-the-shelf components and shaved funds from some of our other programs, including our fixed operating budget."

"You mean, you just made up this weapon without any specific funding?" one senator asked. Samson nodded. "And now you're ready to test it, but you've run out of money; and besides, you can't fly it without approval from the Pentagon, right?"

"That's it in a nutshell, sir," Samson responded.

"Interesting," the senator remarked. He looked at General Hayes, noted his barely disguised discomfort, and asked, "General Hayes, do you know anything about this Lancelot program?"

Hayes took a deep breath, let it out, then said in an even voice, "General Samson was handpicked by the President and the secretary of defense to run the High Technology Aerospace Weapons Center, our nation's primary air weapons research center. In all honesty, sir, I did not know about Lancelot . . ."

"Neither did I," Admiral Balboa interjected hotly. "I know Dreamland is supposed to be a top-secret installation, General, but not from *me*."

"Quite frankly, sir," Hayes went on, "if General Samson waited to give me a detailed briefing and get my approval for every one of the hundreds of programs he manages every month out at HAWC, he'd never get any work done. We pay him to get results, not waste time in Washington giving briefings." He noted the irritated frowns on the subcommittee members' faces, grinned inwardly, and quickly went on: "If General Samson says it's good and it's ready to fly, then I support him. I'm sure General Samson enjoys the enthusiastic support of the White House."

Balboa had no response to that because he knew it to be true. After the successful counterstrikes against

China staged by weapon systems developed at Dreamland, Samson was the new golden boy at the White House. He and his senior staff members were far more popular than Dreamland's bombastic first director, Bradley James Elliott—who was missing and presumed killed in the attacks against China's intercontinental ballistic missile sites—had ever been.

"Good," the senator said, as if he expected no other response than that. "I'm sure GAO will have to look into the legality of General Samson raiding his budget for unapproved weapons research, but that's a question for some other committee. If it fails, you'll be the goat. If it works, you might be a hero."

"It'll work, sir," Samson said enthusiastically. "My troops and I believe in Lancelot so much that we've put our careers on the line to prove it'll work. If it doesn't, I'm sure General Hayes will be looking for a new director at HAWC. But we believe that won't happen, Senator. Lancelot will work. We can go into initial operational capability with one squadron, eight aircraft, within six months. Lancelot will give us a worldwide antiballistic missile, cruise missile, antiaircraft, and even antisatellite defense capability second to none until the airborne laser is deployed. We're betting our careers on it."

The members of the committee looked at each other, some with puzzled expressions. Then the subcommittee chairman said with a grin, "General Samson, General Hayes, I think that's a sucker bet. You come back to us with a working, deployable antimissile system, and I for one will enthusiastically support it. Until then, it's off the books and so not under our purview. Air Force will have to handle it from their existing budget—or scrap it. If there's no other business?" He waited one breath, then said, "This session is in recess." He rapped his gavel. A clerk immediately read a warning that the session was classified top secret and not to be discussed outside the committee chambers, and the meeting was over.

Joint Chiefs Chairman Balboa managed not to say a word until he and the other blue-suiters were out of range of any photographers or TV cameras that might be nearby. Then he exploded. "Goddammit, Samson," he swore, "you'd better start talking, and it better be good. What is this Lancelot thing? Why wasn't I notified of it?"

"It's a parts-bin project put together by my new deputy commander, sir," Samson explained. "He got some help from a military contractor buddy of his, Jon Masters." Balboa nodded—everyone in the defense business had heard of Jon Masters. That lent some credibility to Samson's case. "The thing works, sir. It's better than THAAD and it's ready right now, not five or ten years from now."

Balboa smiled as he felt the anger slowly drain away. He shook his head and said, "You've just been on the job a couple years, Samson, and already you're hanging it out. Shades of that bastard Brad Elliott." Samson's jaw tightened—Brad Elliott was a friend of his, and his mentor; Brad Elliott had sacrificed himself so guys like Balboa could look like leaders. "It must be the damned desert air, the isolation—it makes you HAWC commanders crazy, makes you do stupid things. Makes you put your asses and careers on the line."

He turned to General Hayes and said, "You're on your own, General. You want to blow your budget on this man's wet dream and embarrass yourself and your uniform, go ahead. But I'm not recommending any additional funding for this Lancelot program. Any money you need comes out of Dreamland's or ABL's budget. General Samson, let me warn you for the last time: you bushwhack me like that again in front of a congressional committee, and I'll can your ass on the spot. Is that clear?"

"Yes, sir," Samson responded quickly and loudly. But Balboa was already in the car and on his way.

The two Air Force officers dropped their salutes as soon as Balboa's car was out of sight. Hayes took a deep breath. "You know, Terrill," he said, "the only guy I knew who even dared joust with Balboa and lived to tell the tale is dead. I think that's the only way you'll stay out of that guy's bear trap." He paused, then turned to the big three-star. "Well, what the hell is Lancelot?"

"I'd rather show you than tell you, sir," Samson said. Hayes rolled his eyes in exasperation, about to protest, and Samson quickly added, "We need an extra pilot to fly a chase plane—perhaps you'd care to accompany me on a Lancelot test launch. I guarantee, sir, you won't be disappointed."

"Earthmover, be careful playing games—just when you think you're having fun, the real world has a tendency to jump up and bite you in the ass." Then Hayes shrugged. "What the hell—we're already chin-deep in the shit. We might as well show 'em something. Put it together. I'll get you your funding for one test, and I'll come out and watch this Lancelot thing in action. I need the flying time anyway. But it better work, my friend, or you'll be on the street so fast it'll make your head spin."

THE BLUE HOUSE,
REPUBLIC OF KOREA PRESIDENTIAL PALACE,
SEOUL, SOUTH KOREA
THAT SAME TIME

The presentation had just concluded; the full report was before each member of the Republic of Korea's National Security Council, the government's senior national defense policy-making board. Each member sat in stunned disbelief at what he had just heard.

"It is apparent that the crisis in the North has grown to dangerous, even epidemic levels, my friends," Kwon Ki-chae, the president of South Korea, said in a low monotone. "Now is the time for decisive action."

President Kwon had been elected to the presidency by the Election College less than a year ago, after the resignation of the elderly President Kim Yong-sam following a no-confidence vote in the National Assembly. Short and thin, younger than any of the others on the council by many years, educated in the United States, Kwon was a fixture in South Korean politics—but not because of his wisdom and insight into national and international politics. Kwon's power base came from South Korea's dominant private industries, which had groomed him from the start for the mantle of power he now possessed. He represented himself not as "the new South Korea," but as "the new Korea."

Kwon, the leader of the ultraconservative People's Democratic Party and a longtime National Assembly member, had won an uneasy coalition of support for his ideas on reuniting the Korean peninsula and for his get-tough policies regarding relations with North Korea. The thirty members of his State Council, including the members of the National Security Council, shared these premises. But until recently, there was little anyone in the South Korean government, even the powerful among them, could do to change the slow, dangerous course of the political, social, and military standoff between the two Koreas.

Now Kwon saw his chance. These men were scared to death and looking for guidance.

"Nuclear bombs, gentlemen," Kwon began, resting his hands on the council table and staring each of his colleagues in the eye. "No longer a supposition, no longer an intelligence estimate, but reality. Not only does the North possess nuclear weapons technology, but they have nuclear gravity bombs and the means to deliver them. This is the most significant and dangerous situation on the Korean peninsula since the Japanese invasion."

"Surely you exaggerate, Mr. President," Park Hyoun, leader of the United People's Party for Political Reform, said. The UPPPR was a small but rapidly growing opposition party; it had doubled its number of seats in the National Assembly in just two years. Although not yet a threat to Kwon's ruling party, Representative Park had been invited to sit in on this National Security Council meeting, along with the leaders of the other major Assembly parties, as a show of solidarity and of full disclosure. "Look at your intelligence reports. The North Korean pilot was starving to death; his aircraft was easily spotted and intercepted; and he had no fuel to complete his mission, let alone return, even if he had somehow avoided our air defenses."

"All valid points, Mr. Park," President Kwon acknowledged. "Perhaps it was nothing more than the desperate attempt of a starving madman for glory or suicide at someone else's hands. But I don't think that's all it was. I think we were fortunate—this time. The next attack could be a single Nodong rocket launch, or a dozen, or a *hundred*, all with nuclear warheads. We might be able to intercept a fraction of them with our borrowed American Patriot antiaircraft missile batteries, but even one nuclear warhead allowed to hit the capital would kill hundreds of thousands of our citizens."

"But what do you propose, Mr. President?" another party leader asked. "Peace talks have broken off again. The United States is delaying its next shipment of fuel oil and surplus wheat until the North resumes peace talks and agrees to inspection of the Yongbyon facility under construction . . ."

"Which are two conditions not a part of the original 1994 Agreement Structure," Kwon reminded them irritably. The Agreement Structure, a negotiated deal between the United States, the two Koreas, Japan, and other world powers, gave North Korea a trillion dollars of aid over ten years. In exchange, North Korea was to dismantle all of its old Soviet-style breeder nuclear reactors, the ones capable of producing weapons-grade nuclear material. The agreement had been plagued with problems almost from the start. "With all due respect to our powerful American allies, they are hampering peace by imposing these conditions on the North without consultation or negotiations. I feel these conditions were added purely for American political reasons. It was an unfortunate choice by our American allies.

"But now we have seen the error of our past policies of appeasement and delay," Kwon went on. "We have sent billions of yuan of cash, food, oil, and humanitarian supplies to the North, we allow increased family visits, we look the other way when their spies and minisubs wash up on our shores. And what do they do? They build two-thousand-kilometer-range ballistic missiles to sell overseas and to threaten us and our neighbors, and they have the audacity to test one of their rockets by firing it over our heads! Now we discover they have nuclear weapons, and their starving soldiers are so desperate that they will actually use them. The North is coming apart, and they threaten to tear our own country apart if something is not done immediately.

"The already tense political and financial situation in the North has obviously seeped into the military ranks, and that is a danger that far surpasses the former East and West Germany situation. Then East Germany was sufficiently encumbered by the Soviet Union that a unilateral military action was almost impossible. But North Korea has no such constraints. No one holds the North's leash. China and Russia have both disavowed any responsibility for the child they have spawned. Now their child has grown into an angry, starving, vindictive, and pathological monster. This monster must be stopped."

The members of the Security Council were silent. They knew President Kwon was right. They knew what must be done—but no one dared speak it or even think it. They left it up to Kwon to say the words and initiate the actions that could change their destiny.

"It is time to put our plan into motion, my friends," Kwon said. "Our military forces will be at their greatest stage of readiness prior to and during the Team Spirit exercises. In addition, we will have Japanese and American air and naval forces in our waters as well. That will be the perfect time."

"But will the North be ready?" the defense minister asked.

"I believe they are ready now," Kwon said. "But the burden will not only be on those in the North to act—it will be up to us to respond as well. When the time comes, we must be prepared."

"What about Pak?" another council member asked.

"Will Pak Chung-chu stand with you when the time comes?"

"Let us find out right now, shall we?" Kwon picked up a telephone and ordered the operator to dial a secure number in Pyongyang, North Korea.

OVER THE PACIFIC OCEAN,
WEST OF SAN CLEMENTE ISLAND
SEVERAL WEEKS LATER

'll tell you right now, Earthmover," said Air Force General Victor Hayes, "I hate surprises. I mean, I *really* hate surprises. And I'm really hating this already." Then he did an almost perfect aileron roll.

It had been years since Hayes, the Air Force's senior uniformed officer, had been at the controls of any tactical jet. He had reluctantly left his last tactical command, the legendary First Fighter Wing, Langley Air Force Base, Virginia, over ten years ago. His aviation incentive pay had been decreasing for the past five years, and now, with two kids in college, he could barely pay his phone bills on time. Yet even though he had been flying a desk for so long, he was still a fighter pilot through and through. Short in stature, astronaut-like in build, with broad shoulders tapering down to slender ankles, his piercing blue eyes forever seemed to be scanning the sky for any sign of "bandits."

He definitely had the feeling he was looking at a bandit right now.

"Don't send the kids to the showers before you've seen them play, sir," Terrill Samson responded, his deep, booming voice amplified over the intercom system. The two men were sitting side by side in the cockpit of an F-111 fighter-bomber, used by the Air Force as a photo "chase plane" on flight tests. They were flying a few hundred yards off the right wing of a black B-1B Lancer bomber, at an altitude of only two thousand feet above the Pacific Ocean off the southern California coast. Victor Hayes found it hard to believe Samson had managed to squeeze himself inside the F-111's rather small cockpit, but now that they were both strapped in, he was clearly right at home there.

"I usually don't go on a flight test without knowing more about what I'm getting into," Hayes said. In truth, he was enjoying the hell out of this flight—he got to fly so seldom these days. "You mind filling me in?"

"I was just going to get to that, sir," Samson said. His formation flying skills were excellent, Hayes had noted—he had chosen to hand-fly the big supersonic bomber the entire flight so far, and they might as well have been welded to the B-1's right wingtip. Very impressive—even with over ten thousand hours of flying time in over a dozen different military warplanes, Hayes doubted that he could fly as well, especially given all the years since he'd been operational in any tactical unit. "We've got about five minutes to go.

"As you know, sir," Samson went on, "my group at Dreamland helped test the Army's THAAD system. In fact, we launched some targets from that same B-1 . . ."

"I know," Hayes said. "Looks like THAAD is turning into a money pit. You find a way to fix it?"

"Not exactly," Samson said. "THAAD's supposed to be an improved Patriot system—to destroy ballistic missiles in the upper atmosphere, or in near-space, at least twice as high as Patriot. It's supposed to keep the warhead and critical pieces of the missile away from defended territory while staying as far away from the forward edge of the battle area as possible. But as you know from the Senate hearing, the technology to place a small antimissile missile close enough to a high-altitude, fast-moving target still isn't fully matured—it's literally a 'bullet hitting a bullet' from hundreds of miles apart. The problem is hitting a target in the midcourse or reentry phase of flight. THAAD can't do it except with the plasma-yield warhead, which increases the cost of the system tremendously. Well, I had my guys start trying some things . . ."

Beneath his oxygen mask and sun visor, Hayes winced. HAWC's first commander, Lieutenant General Bradley James Elliott, was famous throughout the Pentagon for "trying some things," mostly with exotic aircraft and weapons being secretly developed at Dreamland. Elliott had this knack for taking a weapons development program and turning it into a military marvel—or monstrosity. The truth was, his inventions were often successfully—and secretly—used in real emergencies all around the world to try to avert conflicts before they escalated into major shooting wars.

The problem was, Elliott sometimes sent his monstrosities off to war without letting certain key folks know about it—like anyone in the Pentagon, Congress, or even the White House. A conflict would be brewing somewhere in the world—China, Ukraine, Russia, the Baltics, the Philippines—and almost before anyone could react, Elliott's "creations" were on their way. He had been slapped down many times, even forced into retirement, yet he kept on coming back. As Hayes saw it, the curse of Brad Elliott now seemed to have fallen on Terrill Samson, former commander of Eighth Air Force, the command in charge of the Air Force's dwindling fleet of heavy bombers. There was no doubt that Samson was a protégé of Brad Elliott, especially in the development and deployment of the heavy bomber—and it certainly looked as though he was pulling some of the same tricks.

"So you built Lancelot—illegally, I might add," Hayes said. "You built it with money and equipment you didn't have, and now your ass is in a sling. I realize the fate of HAWC is tied up in this test, but what makes you think that Lancelot is going to be better than THAAD? You're using the same technology."

"Yes, it's the same technology, because no one has the money to build new stuff," Samson said. "But we attacked the problem from a different angle. We solved one major, fundamental problem with THAAD. My guys thought, 'If THAAD is too far away from the bad guys to intercept a target in the boost phase, why don't we bring THAAD closer?' "

"Closer to what?"

"Closer to the bad guys," Samson said. "The problem with THAAD is that it still relies on hitting a missile in the midcourse or reentry phase, when it's maneuvering, it's small, it's fast, it's probably over friendly territory, and it's high. Those are the two worst phases of flight if you want to do an intercept. The best time is during the boost phase—it's flying slowly, it doesn't try any evasive maneuvers, its propellants and airframe are under intense chemical and aerodynamic pressure, it has that big rocket plume behind it, it's still over enemy territory, and the warhead hasn't armed. But of course, getting an antiballistic missile close enough to the missile to destroy it during the boost phase was the problem—a big one.

"The aircraft-based ABL and space-based Skybolt laser systems were designed to kill missiles in all phases of flight, including boost phase, but they're still a few years from full deployment. So we've combined THAAD with ABL. We're going to launch an antiballistic missile weapon from a penetrating bomber."

"*What?*" Hayes exclaimed. "No shit!"

"Fireman flight, this is Neptune, two minutes," the warning message said.

"Fireman flight, roger, two minutes, check," the pilot of the B-1 responded.

"Two," Samson responded on the command frequency.

"Fireman flight, take spacing."

Again, the B-1 pilot acknowledged and Samson responded with "Two." Then he said to Hayes, "I've got the airplane," and took the F-111's control stick, giving it a shake to verify that he had control, then maneuvered the plane a few hundred yards away. "The launch is coming up. The Navy is going to launch one of several short-range Pershing test ballistic missiles from launch barges on and around San Clemente Island. We don't know which one."

Hayes motioned to the large multicolor display on his side of the cockpit. "So explain what I'm looking at," he said. "This is a great-looking display—pretty sharp. Where's it coming from? An observation plane?"

"We're looking at what the B-1's sensors are looking at," Samson explained. "We would ordinarily know through intelligence reports where the enemy's ballistic missiles are set up. If we don't, our system can integrate sensor information from many different sources through the Joint Tactical Information Distribution System—we can hook into AWACS or Joint STARS radar planes, satellites, other strike aircraft, or naval or ground forces. But for today's demonstration, we'll operate independently, using only sensors mounted on the B-1 itself.

"This is the first bomber to use LADAR—laser radar," Samson continued. "You're looking at a LADAR image. The smaller wavelengths mean a more high-resolution image. In addition, the LADAR emitters are so small, much smaller than a big radar dish, they can be mounted almost anywhere on the plane. That B-1 can look in all directions because it has LADAR emitters on the belly, on the fuselage, even in the tail."

"But you told the Senate committee you'd only used off-the-shelf components for Lancelot. If this is the first bomber to use LADAR, how can it be off-the-shelf?"

"LADAR has been in use in active-homing missiles and in artillery ranging and counterfire systems for years," Samson replied. "We just stuck it on a Bone, that's all. It has relatively low range for the amount of power it uses, but for attacking ballistic missiles, it's perfect."

"And the missile itself is off-the-shelf too?"

"Yep," Samson replied proudly. "We revived the old second-generation short-range attack missile and gave it the combined infrared and active radar terminal guidance system from the AIM-120 Scorpion air-to-air missile. We then put a fifty-pound high-explosive fragmentation warhead on it. That's Lancelot. We actually resurrected a project that Brad Elliott started eight years ago, after the SRAMs were taken off strategic alert."

The B-1 started a turn away from the launch area; a minute later it was heading the opposite direction from San Clemente Island. "All units, stand by," said the voice of the Navy range master.

A few moments later a warning tone sounded in their headphones. "Missile launch detection," Samson said. "The launch pad is on a barge out on the ocean. We're seventy-eight miles from the launch pad . . ."

"But SRAM-II had a range of . . . what? A hundred miles max? Aren't we a little far away?"

"Lifting our missile up to altitude with a carrier aircraft acts like an extra rocket motor, so we've effectively doubled the missile's range," Samson said. "Plus, by putting the uplink sensors aloft and closer to the target, we can provide our missile with more precise steering signals."

"Stand by," they heard the B-1's bombardier call. "Safe in range . . . missile counting down . . . doors coming open . . ." A warning tone sounded on the radio channel. As they watched, the B-1's forward bomb bay doors opened. ". . . release pulse, missile away, missile away." The Lancelot missile dropped free, fell for a few seconds, and then ignited its first-stage solid-rocket motor.

Hayes caught a glimpse of it as it fell. It was less than twenty feet long, with a triangular-shaped fuselage no more than eighteen inches in diameter at its widest point. It had no fins—Hayes remembered that SRAM-II used thruster jets for directional control. The missile streaked ahead, then began a sharp climb and arced backward on an "over-the-shoulder" trajectory. A few seconds later they heard a high-pitched *crrack-boom* as the missile broke the sound barrier, then another boom as the larger, more powerful second-stage motor ignited.

"Good launch!" Hayes said excitedly. "Go, baby, *go!*"

It was too high to see clearly, but seconds later they saw a flash of yellow-orange fire and a large puff of smoke. Range control gave them the good news moments later: "Target intercepted, T plus fifteen point seven seconds, altitude seventy-three thousand feet, twenty-nine point one miles downrange, velocity twenty-five hundred feet per second. Intercept circular error thirty-seven point four feet. Repeat, target intercepted. All participants, remain clear of Romeo-1402 for the next ten minutes to stay clear of falling debris."

"Thirty-seven feet! Incredible!" Hayes crowed. "With a fifty-pound warhead, that's overkill!"

"Fireman flight, range gives you clearance for secondary release," the launch controller radioed.

"Fireman flight copies range clearance, check," the pilot aboard the B-1 responded.

"Two," Samson responded in turn.

"Okay, Earthmover, what's happening now?" Hayes asked.

"The next part of Coronet Tiger one-plus," Samson explained. "You see, we're not satisfied with destroying the ballistic missile—we want to destroy the launch site and all the associated launch command facilities. Remember, we're over enemy territory, and we don't see any reason to be over enemy territory killing rockets if we can't do some more mayhem while we're there. The laser radar tracks the missile and at the same time computes the launch point and feeds it into the bombing computers. The B-1 has already computed the probable launch point using the launch detection signal and the radar track—all we need to do is attack."

A few moments later the aft bomb bay doors on the B-1 bomber opened, and a small missile dropped into the slipstream. It was much smaller than the Lancelot missile, with a fat forebody tapering quickly to a thin tail section and a star-shaped fin group aft. As it dropped, a pair of long, thin wings popped out from under the fuselage. It released a small puff of smoke as an engine started up, and soon the missile turned and descended. "Was that a JASSM cruise missile?" Hayes asked.

"Yep. A D-model AGM-177 Wolverine cruise missile," Samson replied. He reached over and hit some buttons around the edge of the large multifunction display on the right side of the instrument panel. The "God's-eye" image of the Lancelot missile launch was replaced by an aerial camera shot, so far showing only ocean. "The new and improved version of the joint air-to-surface standoff attack missile. Turbojet-powered, max fifty-mile range when launched at low altitude. Autonomous GPS and inertial navigation, autonomous target acquisition, autonomous millimeter-wave radar terminal guidance or imaging infrared terminal sensor with manual steering, with images fed back to us by satellite. It even has its own jammers and countermeasures. It has three bomb bays that can carry a mixed payload and actually make multiple attacks on several targets, or even do its own target damage assessment and reattack. The missiles we're using today only carry one warhead payload, however."

"A sensor-fused weapon warhead?"

"You got it, sir."

"Outstanding. I always enjoy watching an SFW take out a target."

"That's definitely the best part, sir," Samson said, the smile behind his oxygen mask evident in his voice. "Watch. The 177 will take a picture of the target after its pass."

The missile had descended rapidly—it was now skimming the surface of the ocean so low that Hayes thought one swell could easily reach up and snatch it out of the sky. A white box appeared on the screen, centered on a tiny black dot. "The inertial navigation system is steering the missile to the estimated coordinates of that Pershing launch barge, with coordinates dumped to it by the B-1's launch sensors," Samson explained. "At ten miles to go, it'll start searching on its own." He quickly reconfigured the large supercockpit screen so they could see both the missile's-eye view and a God's-eye view at the same time. The launch barge was a red triangle; the Wolverine missile was a white diamond streaking toward it.

Hayes could see three Navy ships surrounding the launch barge. Suddenly, blinking red boxes appeared from one of them, and a circle drew itself around the red box, enveloping the cruise missile. "Standard missile radar," Samson explained. "The circle is lethal range, based on type of radar and signal strength." Just then another red box and lethal range circle appeared around a second Navy ship. The red box began to blink. "The second Navy ship has launched on the 177," Samson said.

"Fireman flight, stand by for launch," the B-1 bomber crew radioed. Moments after Samson acknowledged the warning, a second Wolverine missile dropped free from the B-1's aft bomb bay.

"Two JASSMs!" Hayes exclaimed. "Now we really got a show going!"

"This is how we envision employing Coronet Tiger one-plus—in a hunter-killer role," Samson explained. "Obviously, the B-1 becomes an item of interest after it first launches an antiballistic missile missile and then attacks the launch site. Any area defenses will light up like crazy. That's when the bomber shifts from a rocket killer to SEAD—suppression of enemy air defenses—role.

"The B-1 can carry up to twenty-four Wolverine or Lancelot missiles internally, plus four more externally. A typical weapons load would be eight Lancelots and eight Wolverines on internal rotary launchers, and one internal fuel tank or eight more JASSMs. Externally, it can carry eight HARM antiradar missiles or twelve Scorpion air-to-air missiles, depending on support, range to the target, and the threat. The B-1 can carry up to one hundred and fifty thousand pounds of ordnance—as much as five F-15E Strike Eagles, with much greater range and equal speed."

"Scorpion? HARM?" Hayes asked. "The B-1 can carry antiradar or air-to-air missiles?"

"It always could, sir," Samson replied. "The B-1 has

four external hardpoints with a standard data bus—it can carry any missile, bomb, or sensor package in the inventory. It also has two external fuel tank hardpoints. But when the B-1 was disqualified from carrying cruise missiles because of the Strategic Arms Limitation Treaties, everyone seemed to forget about the hardpoints. Everyone except HAWC, of course. External stores destroy the Bone's stealth capabilities, but once the external stores and racks are used or jettisoned, it has full stealth capability again."

Hayes watched in utter fascination as the attack continued. Both Navy ships were launching Standard antiair missiles now. The Wolverines were skimming the ocean so low it looked as if they would crash into it any second.

The second Wolverine missile passed within one mile of the easternmost Navy warship. "That's a kill," Samson said.

"But it missed."

"It was programmed not to fly closer than one mile," Samson explained. "Range safety rules. It'll try to go after the second Navy ship now." But the missile's luck ran out. Because the first Navy ship was still "alive," it and the second warship bracketed the second Wolverine missile with a flight of four Standard missiles and shot it down long before it could approach the second ship.

"Not fair," Samson protested. "That first ship was 'dead.' "

"All's fair in love and ship defense," Hayes said.

"It's still unfair," Samson said. "But the first Wolverine missile has a live warhead. You'll see—it's going all the way to the target."

It did. Samson and Hayes watched as it streaked over the launch barge, the imaging infrared view of the barge flipping upside down as the IIR sensor stayed locked on the target. Three small cylindrical canisters appeared on the image, spinning under a small stabilizing parachute. Suddenly, all three canisters separated from the parachute, and moments later there were several bright flashes of light that completely obscured the barge. When the image cleared, the barge was on fire and half submerged.

"Man, I love watching those things," Hayes admitted. The BLU-108 "Shredder" sensor-fused weapon, or SFW, was the Air Force's new air-delivered antivehicle weapon. Each Shredder canister contained four copper skeets, aimed by an infrared sensor. As the canisters spin, they find a target, and at the proper instant they detonate. The explosion sends a molten copper slug out each skeet at the target at supersonic speed, fast enough and hot enough to cut even three-inch steel armor into Swiss cheese within a half mile of ground zero. Because the launch barge was the only target in the area, all twelve slugs hit the barge.

"Me too," Samson said. "I love the smell of molten copper slugs in the morning."

"Very, very impressive, Earthmover," Hayes went on, writing notes in a small notebook. "First a successful ABM test, then a successful counterattack test. Excellent. Interesting to think what it'd have been like if you'd had one of those plasma-yield weapons on a Wolverine."

Samson looked at Hayes, then hit the radio button on his throttle quadrant: "Fireman, this is Two, get us extended range clearance for second launch sequence."

"Roger, Fireman Two. Break. Neptune, Fireman flight, requesting extended range clearance for final launch sequence. Ten-mile minimum clearance all vessels."

"Roger, Fireman flight, this is Neptune control, the range is extended-radius clear. You are cleared hot for final missile series."

"Fireman flight copies extended-range clear, Fireman flight check."

"Two," Samson said. "Fireman, Neptune, stand by." He turned to Hayes. "Anytime you're ready, sir."

"Ready for . . . ?" Hayes stopped, dropping his oxygen mask in surprise. "You're shitting me, Samson. Don't tell me you've got a plasma-yield weapon onboard that B-1 right now?"

"No—I've got *two*," Samson replied. "I've got one Lancelot ABM and one Wolverine cruise missile armed with a THAAD plasma-yield warhead, ready to go."

"By whose authority?" said a stunned Hayes, his voice rising in fury. "Who the hell authorized you to do that, Samson?"

"Sir, as you said at that Senate subcommittee hearing, I did it under the authority given me by the President and the secretary of defense," Samson replied. "We developed the weapon, did some mating, release, jettison, and captive launch tests, and certified it ready for launch. It's never been tested before on a live launch. We own the airspace for two hundred miles in all directions; we've only got a couple of Navy ships in the area, and we've got a target. I think we should let 'er rip and see what we got."

"You're *crazy*, Samson," Hayes shot back. He was so red-hot angry that he thought he would explode. "You have got to be off your rocker. This is the most blatant form of insubordination I've seen since . . . shit, since Brad Elliott. You just think that you can load up a missile with an experimental subatomic warhead and shoot it into the sky anytime you feel like it? We can cause a major military crisis! We can cause an international incident! We can both lose our jobs and spend the rest of our lives in Fort Leavenworth! Goddammit, Samson, you scare me! I'm going to take a good hard

look at your suitability for your position and your continued service after we get on the ground!"

The tactical action officer, or TAO, aboard the U.S.
Navy *Ticonderoga*-class Aegis guided missile cruiser
USS *Grand Island,* who was acting as range controller,
attack officer, and supervisor for the morning's tests,
watched his electronic displays carefully. The Combat
Information Center—CIC—of the *Grand Island* had
four large multicolor electronic displays forward, which
integrated all electronic signals from ships, planes, and
shore stations, giving the TAO a three-dimensional picture of his "battlefield" for hundreds of miles in all
directions. He and his deputy sat in the middle of the
CIC compartment, surrounded by weapons officers,
sensor operators, and communications technicians.

He thought what he saw was a glitch in the two
displays that gave him horizontal and vertical plots of
the missile tracks. He turned to his radar technician and
asked, "Radar, what happened to those missile tracks?
What do you get?"

"Don't know, sir," the radar technician replied. "I
saw the target rocket launch, then the airborne missile
launch, then the cruise missile launch to attack the
launch barge, same as the first test sequence. It looked
like a good intercept. Then poof. Nothing. Both tracks
disappeared. No debris."

"Comm, did the zoomies broadcast an abort warning?" the TAO asked a communications technician.

"No, sir," the communications specialist confirmed.

"Damn Air Force weenies," the TAO muttered. "Too
embarrassed by a faulty flight to tell us they self-
destructed both missiles." He paused for a moment,
then asked, "Radar, you say you're not picking up any
debris?"

"No, sir," said the radar technician. "Usually, the SPY-1B will track debris pretty good, enough so we can clear a specific piece of airspace or ocean." The SPY-1B was the three-dimensional phased-array radar on the *Aegis*-class warships, powerful enough to track a target as small as a bird two hundred miles away. "Nothing this time."

"Humpf," the TAO grunted. Both missiles might have splashed down. He didn't know enough about either of them to know if they floated, if the warheads became more unstable in seawater, what they looked like when they broke apart, how to disarm a ditched missile—and a hundred other things he would've been briefed on if the Air Force had done its job correctly. "Comm, tell all vessels to stay east of the second launch barge. Radar, clear all aircraft out of the range via the shortest way possible away from the missile tracks. Then do a systems check, find out why we can't see their debris." On the intercom, he radioed, "Bridge, Combat."

"Go ahead." The TAO recognized the captain's voice.

"We lost track of the missile debris, sir, so we're clearing all aircraft away from the missiles' flight paths and terminating all activity. We're done for the day."

"Copy that. We'll form up and head back to the barn."

"What did you see up there, sir?"

"We saw . . ." There was a very long pause, then: "We don't quite know what we saw, Combat. We saw two good missile plumes heading toward each other, then . . . well, we're not sure after that. We saw a flash of light, and some of the lookouts say they saw a big silver globe. But we didn't hear or pick up anything. No explosion, no nothing."

"Checks down here, sir," said the TAO.

"What did it look like to you, Combat?"

"About the same."

"What about the cruise missile? Did it hit its target?"

"Stand by," the TAO said. "Radar, what have you got on the second launch barge? Did the zoomies hit it?"

"I . . . I don't know, sir," the radar technician stammered. "It's like the ABM intercept. It looked normal, heading right for the target, then . . . gone."

"Gone? The target? Gone like blew up? Gone like sunk?"

"Gone like . . . gone, sir," the technician said. "I pick up nothing. The missile has disappeared . . . shit, and the barge disappeared too!"

"What the hell are you talking about? Surface range thirty, high res," he demanded, and checked the short-range surface radar depiction. There was no sign of the barge.

"I've got a good radar lock on the first launch barge, sir," the technician said, "but zilch on the second. It must've broke apart and sunk like a stone."

"That barge was almost two hundred feet long, eighty feet wide, and weighed ninety tons. Those things do not just disappear," the TAO said aloud to no one in particular. Even the first launch barge, which was hit dead-on by the sensor-fused weapon dropped by the cruise missile, was still partially afloat. The TAO hit the intercom button: "Bridge, Combat. We don't have a fix on the second launch pad. It must've sunk. What kind of warhead did they have on that thing? It must've been a two-thousand-pounder at least."

"Negative, Combat," the captain responded. "We didn't hear or see any explosion."

The TAO looked at his CIC crew members in shock. "How is that possible, sir?" was all he could think to ask.

"I don't know," the captain said, feeling the anger rise in his throat. He had a suspicion that the Air Force had pulled a fast one on him—that they had tested a new weapon in the wide-open daylight skies and seas, in a well-used military weapons range that belonged to the U.S. Navy. To the officer of the deck, the captain said, "How long for us to get to that second launch barge's last position?"

"About thirty minutes at standard, sir."

"Officer of the deck, plot a course to the second launch barge's position," the captain ordered. "All ahead full. I want a full investigation on what kind of weapon sunk that barge. Air, water, electromagnetic, debris analysis, the works." He paused, then added, "And have the corpsmen prepare to do a full radiation scan as well."

The last order froze everyone on the bridge in their tracks. The captain was silent for a long moment, then said, "Get to it, gentlemen. Keep your damn eyes open."

It took less than twenty minutes for the two Air Force jets to fly back to Elliott Air Force Base. The base, ninety miles northwest of Las Vegas, was situated near a dry lake bed named Groom Lake. Anyone who viewed the lake bed—which would have been both difficult and illegal, since the airspace for fifty miles around the base was restricted from ground level to *infinity*—would have seen a roughly five-mile sheet of hard, sunbaked sand. But seconds before the planes touched down, sprinklers popped on and highlighted a long strip of sand-colored concrete in the lake bed. Less than three minutes later Terrill Samson had turned off the runway and the sun evaporated the water. The runway disappeared once again.

Bradley James Elliott Air Force Base was the name of the installation built next to the dry lake. It resembled a cross between a small, old, nearly abandoned air base and a modern industrial development facility. It had some old wooden buildings and many modern concrete buildings. Because it was so far from the nearest town, it had dormitory-style enlisted, officer, and civilian quarters. There were few amenities: a mess hall, only a small shopette instead of a full commissary and exchange, a little-used outdoor pool, and no base theater.

The roads were well maintained and the sidewalks were lined with cactus and Joshua trees. The roads had typical Air Force base names, honoring Air Force legends: military aviation pioneers like Rickenbacker and Mitchell, leaders like Spaatz and LeMay, Air Force Medal of Honor recipients like Loring and Sijan, and air combat aces like Bong and DeBellevue. Other streets had names that most people new at the base might not immediately recognize, like Ormack and Powell—names of dead test pilots who had been assigned to the base. About two thousand men and women worked at the base, typically four days on, three days off. They were either bused in convoys of air-conditioned Greyhound buses, making the 110-mile drive in under two hours, or flown in on unmarked jet airliners from Nellis Air Force Base north of Las Vegas in a matter of minutes.

The one difference between this base and dozens of other military bases resembling it around the world: Elliott Air Force Base did not appear on any map. There were no signs for it. It was not on any listing of active Air Force bases. No one could ask for an assignment there, and if someone did, he or she would be likely to come under secret investigation as to why the request had been made. Every person assigned there swore an oath never to reveal any details about the base or its activities. Most people took that oath very, very seriously—not because of the substantial legal penalties, but because they really believed that keeping their activities secret contributed to the strength and security of their homeland. By almost every conventional measure except physical presence, Elliott Air Force Base did not exist.

The base was the home of the High Technology Aerospace Weapons Center, under Terrill Samson's command. HAWC was officially Detachment One of the Air Force Operational Test and Evaluation Center headquartered at Edwards Air Force Base in California. Before any new aircraft or air-launched weapon began unclassified operational testing at any of the Air Force's test facilities prior to full-scale production and deployment, it flew at HAWC first. HAWC's pilots and engineers worked with aircraft and weapons years before the rest of the world ever saw them, and in many instances worked with weapon systems the world would never see. What would seem like the stuff of science-fiction novels were commonplace devices at HAWC. The secrecy and the weird sightings reported in the deserts of southern Nevada led many to believe the secluded area was harboring aliens from outer space and their spacecraft.

In reality, HAWC was simply a site for innovative, creative aerospace engineers. Although the days of unlimited "black" budgets were gone, free thinking—by engineers, pilots, scientists, and even the commanders—was encouraged and rewarded here.

Terrill Samson taxied the F-111 toward a row of twelve low hangars, all painted to blend in with the sand-colored desert landscape around them. As the plane approached, a hangar door slid open, and it taxied directly inside without stopping or even slowing down much. The hangar doors started to close long before the plane was fully inside—the less time the doors were open, the less chance that snooping eyes could catch a glimpse of whatever was inside. It had been preceded minutes before by the bomber that it had stayed with over the Pacific Ocean just a short while earlier, and parked next to it.

As soon as the F-111's engines were shut down, the crew chief and his assistant brought boarding ladders over to its side. But General Victor Hayes was still too stunned to remove his helmet and unstrap himself, let alone climb out of the cockpit. Samson took off his own helmet and released his straps, then sat in the cockpit, amused, quietly watching the Air Force chief of staff. A dozen heavily armed security policemen, maintenance crews, and engineers had descended on both aircraft on arrival, prepared to swarm over them and to gather electronically recorded information about the test launches. Now they all waited for Hayes and Samson to step out, perplexed but wisely keeping out of earshot.

"Well, sir?" Samson asked. "What do you think?"

The hangar was air-conditioned, but long before entering it Hayes felt a chill—especially when he thought about what he had witnessed that morning. "What do I think?" he echoed. "I can't believe it. That warhead is incredible. Talk to me, Earthmover. What the hell else have you got here? Whatever you're selling, I'm buying. I don't know how we're going to pay for it, but I'm for damned sure in the market."

"What I've got, sir, is a bunch of concepts and demo models," Samson said. "All a leftover of Brad Elliott's vision and leadership. He's got stuff here that would make James Bond shit his pants. I'm sorry I blew the poor son of a bitch off for so many years. We all thought he was just certifiable. It turns out he was a certifiable genius."

"The antiballistic missile stuff, Earthmover. Lancelot," Hayes said. "That's what Congress wants to field right now. What is it, how much, how fast can we get it in the field?"

"Let me show you what we've got, sir," Samson said. Hayes removed his straps at last and followed Samson out of the chase plane and over to the B-1 beside it. After their IDs were checked and verified by thumb and retina prints, they began a walkaround of the big, sleek bomber. "We call it the EB-1C Megafortress-2, sir," said Samson. "Prime-time example of taking a good strike aircraft and making it better. You won't notice too many changes outside, but Brad transformed this thing into a real tactical strike machine."

Hayes touched the big bomber, and his eyes narrowed in surprise. He was trying to identify what he felt. "That's not steel," he said.

"Fibersteel," Samson explained. "Same stuff as RAM—radar-absorbent material—but fibersteel is structural-strength. We've reduced the weight and the radar cross section and increased the durability by at least fifteen percent just by reskinning with fibersteel. A stock B-1 has ten times the radar cross section of a B-2 stealth bomber. This one has only three times the RCS."

He pointed to the bomber's broad, flat underside, between the nosewheel well and forward bomb bay. "There are the external weapons and fuel hardpoints. Best move we made was to bring those back. We can launch any weapon in the arsenal, including air-to-air missiles. Each external hardpoint can hold three AIM-120 Scorpion air-to-air missiles, two AGM-88 HARM antiradar missiles, four AGM-65 Maverick missiles, one AGM-84 Harpoon antiship missile, one Wolverine cruise missile, even one AGM-142 Have Nap TV-guided missile. We've even modified Lancelot as a low earth-orbit satellite killer."

"*What?*"

"Brad Elliott revived and perfected the old ASAT antisatellite program," Samson said proudly. "The B-1 can get a datalink from Space Command or use the LADAR, wait until an enemy satellite passes overhead, then fire an ASAT from an external hardpoint straight up. With a plasma-yield warhead installed, it'll kill a satellite up to two hundred miles in orbit; with a conventional explosive warhead, about one hundred miles. We haven't tested it, but all the computer models say it will work. And we can do it all now, sir."

"Amazing!" Hayes exclaimed. "I want to see that tested. Killing satellites two hundred miles in space— my God, what a capability that'll give us." He motioned to the long, pointed nose and asked, "That nose cone looks weird—almost like glass instead of fibersteel. What kind of radar did you put in this thing? Still the stock one, or did you soup it up too?"

"The EB-1 Megafortress uses LADAR—laser radar," Samson replied. "It's what I told you about just before the launch, when you were looking at the display. The emitters are tiny. They're in the nose, fuselage, and tail. They scan electronically in any direction, up or down, out to about fifty miles. In effect, the laser 'draws' a picture of everything it sees in a fraction of a second, in three dimensions and with terrific precision and definition. The system 'draws' a picture about twenty times a second, so the 'drawing' is updated as the bomber moves through the sky and the objects in each image become three-dimensional. The images are transmitted to the crew via helmet-mounted visors, and they change when the crew members move their heads—in essence, the crew can 'see' what the radar sees just by looking outside, even if the image is behind or underneath them.

To the crew, it'll feel as if they're floating in midair but able to see up to fifty miles all around them.

"Laser radar is not only more precise than standard radar, it can't be jammed, it can't be detected by standard radar detectors, and it's not affected by weather. We use LADAR for navigation, bombing, tracking—it's even precise enough for night formation flying. We retain all radar attack modes, including automatic terrain-following and radar bombing capabilities, and we've added long-range air target search, track, and weapons uplink."

"This thing's like a really big Strike Eagle or an F/A-18 Hornet," Hayes commented.

"But it has four times the weapons load, five times the loiter time, and six times the range of any other tactical strike aircraft in the world," Samson said. "The B-52 was number one until Congress made the decision to send 'em all to the boneyard. Now the B-1 is the most powerful bomber in the fleet. But we're changing the mission of the heavy bomber. We want big bombers to be able to do tactical missions—precision-kill, close-air-support, 'tank-plinking,' even air superiority, as well as antiship and saturation bombing."

They climbed the tall nose landing-gear strut entry ladder up into the Megafortress. Samson started to crawl forward, but Hayes immediately noticed the big change inside: "Okay, Earthmover," he called, "where are the systems officer positions?"

"Oh yeah. Missing, aren't they?" Samson grinned. "C'mon up to the front office and I'll show you."

Hayes crawled forward through the tunnel to the cockpit and slid into the open aircraft commander's seat on the left side. This looked very much the way he remembered a Bone's cockpit—but not the right side. Instead of the copilot's side being almost identical to the pilot's, it was now a sleek, uncluttered array of six large multifunction displays, with almost no analog round or tape instruments. "Made some changes, I see," he remarked.

"The Bone now joins the ranks of the rest of the bombers in the fleet that only have two crew members," Samson explained. "Meet the new automated Bone. I'd always heard that a B-1 is nothing more than a really big F-111 bomber—well, we took that description to heart and built exactly that. Like the B-2 Spirit stealth bomber, we combined the copilot and navigator-bombardier into the mission commander's position, sitting in the right cockpit seat. The big exception is, we use a pilot-trained bombardier as mission commander, instead of a bombardier-trained pilot."

"Why'd you decide that?"

"Mostly because of my deputy commander, chief program director, and chief of flight operations—a navigator, of course," Samson responded.

"McLanahan."

"The very one," Samson said proudly. "He's the one who conducted today's tests and dropped the weapons you saw. He knows what he's talking about, and when he talks, everyone listens." Victor Hayes merely nodded. Samson's deputy commander was indeed well known and highly respected within the Air Force and throughout the U.S. government. Patrick McLanahan had almost attained the status of legend, like HAWC's first commander, Brad Elliott.

"The mission commander controls everything with voice and touch-screen commands and a trackball," Samson went on. "Two CD-ROMs have the entire mission, weapons ballistics, and computer software, along with maps and terrain features for the entire planet, and it's all fed into the strike computers before launch. Everything's completely automatic, from preflight to shutdown.

"But we went one step further, sir," Samson continued. "The two-person crew isn't exactly alone. We use real-time high-speed satellite communications and datalink technology to create a 'virtual crew' onboard the EB-1C Megafortress . . ."

"A what? You mean, a robot crew, like an autopilot or computer?"

"Not exactly," Samson said. "The bomber crew and the plane are tied into a ground-based cockpit by satellite. We have a pilot, an engineer, a weapons officer, and a tactics officer on duty, linked to the crew. They see and hear everything the crew does. They have access to all the bomber's systems and can spot problems and take corrective action if necessary. They can advise the crew on tactics, keep an eye on systems, and sort of look over the crew's shoulder all the time—even fly the plane for them if absolutely necessary, although the system probably can't react fast enough to survive while under attack.

"What's more, this 'virtual cockpit' is transportable by cargo plane and can be set up in remote locations and run off a standard jet aircraft's power cart. It's the same technology we've been using for decades on manned spacecraft—we've just adapted the concept to manned bombers. And for bomber defense, we've replaced the ALQ-161 defensive management suite with the new ALR-56M and ALE-50 systems . . ."

"Speak English, techno-geek."

"Yes, sir. Bottom line: fully automated, more maintainable, and overall a better electronic jamming and self-protection system, with a towed decoy system," Samson said. "Antennas on the bomber still pick up enemy radar signals and process them, but now jamming signals are sent out via a robot emitter that's towed several hundred feet behind the bomber. It's a target decoy. It's only a foot long and three inches in diameter, but it has an electronically adjustable radar and infrared cross section. The system automatically changes the electronic 'size,' depending on the threat. If the bomber's just being scanned, the towed emitter is almost invisible. But if the enemy gets a lock-on and fires, its radar and infrared cross section can be changed to hundreds of times larger than the bomber.

"The B-1 carries eight decoys on tail fairings. It can still transmit jamming signals and drop expendables if the towed decoys all get shot down, but the system makes it more survivable in a high-threat environment. We've replaced the standard chaff and flare expendables with tactical air-launched decoys, or TALDs, which are tiny electromagnetic emitters that work far better than chaff or flares in decoying enemy missiles. And since the new system is fully automatic, we simply eliminated the DSO's station."

"Incredible, Earthmover, just incredible," Hayes exclaimed. "I can't believe we had anything in the budget to make design changes and upgrades like this."

"It's been tough, sir," Samson said. "We've eliminated the B-52 and grounded one-third of the B-1B fleet to get the money to make any upgrades at all. Give us a budget, and we can field a squadron of B-1 rocket killers in less than twelve months."

"Less than a year?" Hayes echoed. "How in the hell is that possible?"

"Because HAWC has turned into scrounger's central, sir," Samson explained. "We suck up every gadget we can get our hands on. Everything we have on this beast is off-the-shelf, and in some cases the shelf the stuff came from is mighty dusty. It's what we're forced to do nowadays to build new weapon systems—instead of designing an antiballistic missile killing system from a clean sheet of paper, HAWC looks at what we've got lying around the boneyard and depot warehouses. Beyond that, it's just the raw talent and imagination of the troops we have around here."

"So what's your proposal going to look like, Earthmover?" Hayes asked, excited now.

"I propose the formation of a rapid-response antimissile squadron," Samson responded eagerly. "I'm looking for at least ten B-1B Lancer bombers sent here to Elliott Air Force Base, one per month. We modify the planes and train the crews simultaneously. My suggestion: get the B-1s from the National Guard, and use National Guard crewdogs. We train them, reequip them, then send them back to their home states to stand ready. That way, we have low acquisition costs, low personnel costs, and low upkeep costs.

"But the trick," Samson went on, "is going to be finding the right combination of crews to man these Megafortress-2s. The bombers'll be operating behind enemy lines all the time, right in the bad guy's face. They have to be hunters. They'll have to hang around the forward edge of the battle area, expose themselves when a ballistic missile lifts off, then drive right down the enemy's crotch to cut off his balls before his erection goes away. We need to pick the most aggressive, most fearless crewdogs in the service. I mean, they have to be real hard-core mud-movers."

For the first time that day, Hayes seemed concerned. "I don't know if that kind of flier exists nowadays," he said, "especially in the bomber force. Their entire career field has been raped so badly over the past six years that if we've got any heavy-iron aerial assassins anymore, it'll be a miracle."

"Oh, they're out there, sir," Terrill Samson said confidently. "Let my deputy loose and he'll find exactly who we're looking for. They might seem ugly and unruly and not poster-child material, but they'll happily drive a two-hundred-ton Bone down a bad guy's throat and all the way out his asshole any day of the week. We'll see to that."

The feelings of strength and urgency that had begun coursing through Victor Hayes when he stepped into the chase plane's cockpit that morning now turned overwhelming. They came from the sense of direction, purpose, and urgency created by Terrill Samson and the men and women in this isolated, secret desert airfield. These people weren't afraid of getting into trouble, rocking the boat, or busting the budget. All they cared about was doing the job. They identified a problem, devised a solution, and built the right weapon for the task. They never gave a thought to how what they did would look on an effectiveness report, evaluation, news article, or budget analysis.

"Do it, Earthmover," Hayes said excitedly. "Get started ASAP. I don't know how I'll find the money, but I'll find it. Get your guy to find the hardware and the crewdogs, and I'll back your play. I think we're about to set the ballistic missile weenies of the world back on their asses big-time."

NEVADA AIR NATIONAL GUARD TRAINING
CENTER, RENO, NEVADA
LATER THAT DAY

Tall, athletic, with dark brown eyes and brown hair, Lieutenant Colonel Rebecca "Go-Fast" Furness, commander of the 111th Bomb Squadron, Nevada Air National Guard, had the intelligence of a physician, the spirit and determination of a police officer, and the looks of a model. But her life had always revolved around flying. Men, career, a decent living, and excitement were all good things to have—but flying was her one and only true love.

She had graduated from the University of Vermont with an Air Force ROTC commission and attended Air Force flight school at Williams Air Force Base, Arizona, graduating in 1979 at the top of her class. All top pilot graduates, including women, had their pick of assignments—just as long as the women didn't choose any combat flying assignments. As a subtle sign of protest, Furness requested the FB-111A Aardvark supersonic bomber, but accepted the KC-135 Stratotanker aerial refueling tanker with the Strategic Air Command—she knew the bomber was never an option. She set out to show she was worthy of the best assignment and quickly proved her exceptional flying skills and dedication. She cross-trained to the coveted KC-10A Extender tanker-transport, the military version of the DC-10 airliner, and tore up the program there too, quickly becoming a flight commander and instructor pilot.

It was Desert Storm that changed her life. Rebecca Catherine Furness was in command of a KC-10 tanker flight over Saudi Arabia when a call came in about an F-111 bomber suffering massive battle damage. The bomber had numerous fuel leaks, and its crew was only minutes away from having to eject over Iraq. Furness took her KC-10 more than a hundred miles inside Iraq, dodging fighters and surface-to-air missile sites to refuel the bomber, and gave its crew the chance it needed to fly into friendly airspace.

As a reward, Furness achieved her lifelong dream—she became the Air Force's first female combat pilot. She accepted a Reserve assignment with the 394th Air Battle Wing, Plattsburgh, New York, flying the RF-111G Vampire reconnaissance/attack fighter-bomber. Her unit was the first to see action in the Russia-Ukraine conflict when the Vampires were deployed to

Turkey to help defend Ukraine from Russian imperialists seeking to reunite the old Soviet Union by force. She earned her nickname, "Go-Fast," as a result of her tenacious, fearless flying over Turkey, the Black Sea, Ukraine, and Russia, including an attack on Moscow itself.

The Air Force grounded the RF-111 bombers shortly thereafter, but they didn't dare try to ground Rebecca Furness. She sat still long enough to complete Air Command and Staff College and the Army War College, then went after her next career dream—a flying command of her own. She commanded a B-1B Lancer flying training squadron in Texas, then was offered command of a T-38 Talon flying training wing in Arizona. That didn't suit her one bit. She had had enough of training units and wanted a combat command.

She found one in the Nevada Air National Guard. When the unit traded in its C-130 Hercules transports and became the third Air National Guard B-1 bomber unit in the United States, she applied for a job. She was by far the best-qualified applicant, and the state of Nevada made her ambition reality. In a very short time, her unit had won the Proud Shield Bomb Competition and was recognized as the best bomber unit in the United States military. Until now.

"Well, well," Lieutenant Colonel John Long exclaimed as he and Furness entered the B-1B Part-Task Training Facility with six crew members—two new ones, one DSO and one OSO, and two simulator operators. "Look who's here, boss. Ejection boy."

"What?" Furness took a look at the man in the pilot seat of the simulator cab and felt her heart pounding.

"We should welcome his ass back from the hospital," Long said sarcastically. The air-conditioned room grew frostier still.

Furness hesitated, happiness, concern, and fear tearing at her all at once. Here she was, her dreams of becoming the Air Force's first female combat pilot and achieving a combat command not only realized but at the very finest level—and it had all begun to crumble. In the weeks since the B-1B bomber crash that took the lives of three good men, the 111th Bomb Squadron of the Nevada Air National Guard was tearing apart—and sitting in the simulator cab before her was the man they blamed for it.

Major Rinc "Rodeo" Seaver was dressed in full flying gear, flight suit and boots, his short-clipped hair the only visible indication of his four weeks in the hospital after his ejection from the B-1B in April.

"Hi, boss," Seaver said. He did not stop what he was doing. "Okay, Neil," he said on the intercom, "reset me back to the third target and get ready to plug in faults G-seventeen and E-twenty again."

"What the hell are you doing in here, Seaver?" Furness demanded. "You're not due back from sick leave for another two weeks. And what are you doing in the sim? You weren't on the schedule."

"I feel pretty good, boss," Seaver said. He flexed his right shoulder experimentally, trying hard not to grimace from the pain. His right shoulder had hit the edge of the upper escape hatch during the ejection sequence, causing him to tumble wildly as he left the stricken aircraft. The tumble had made him lose precious altitude during ejection. The rocket motor blasted him down instead of up, and he had hit the B-1's right elevator at the attach point to the vertical stabilizer. Luckily, his steel ejection seat took most of the force of the collision, and his chute still opened properly. He underwent reconstructive surgery, three weeks of rest, and one week of in-hospital physical therapy; he was still undergoing daily physical therapy and doing as much swimming as his body could stand. But he was ready and anxious to get back on flying status.

"I got tired sitting on my butt," Seaver explained. "I couldn't stand being cooped up in the house one more day. I called Neil and he said the box was free for a couple hours, so I thought I'd play around. We've been experimenting with various malfunctions that I think occurred on my last flight, and I think I got it."

John "Long Dong" Long, Furness's squadron operations officer and second-in-command, looked daggers at Seaver. Arrogant as always, he thought.

It was one way, and not an uncommon one, of seeing Rinc Seaver. He was tall, thin, wiry, with bony features and vivid green eyes, a second-generation American, born in Nevada, whose family had emigrated from Wales during the Depression. Seaver's entire military career was a study in perseverance and raw determination, a series of ups and downs that would have crushed a lesser man. From childhood, his dream had been to fly the hottest military jets in combat, to lead a squadron of attackers to fight in a decisive battle that would decide the fate of nations and defend his homeland. Movies like *Midway* and TV shows like *Baa Baa Black Sheep* cemented that idea firmly in his head. He visualized strapping himself into his futuristic jet, lifting off a runway as the sneak attack was under way, then battling through waves of enemy defenders until the enemy command center was in his bombsights. He went to the annual Reno National Championship Air Races, where the dozens of vintage World War II fighters roaring overhead reinforced the thrill of flying, the thrill of the hunt, the thrill of victory.

Rinc Seaver decided the road to fulfilling that dream was a civilian pilot's license, so when he was fourteen, he began working to raise the money for flying lessons. He received his pilot's license on his sixteenth birthday, and it was the happiest moment of his young life. But no one told him until it was too late that the way to the hot military jets was through good grades and good SAT scores, not hours in a logbook. Ask him any question about aerodynamics or FAA commercial pilot regulations and he could write a book or teach a class on it; ask him about elementary calculus and he was lost. His average grades and average SAT scores—he took the test three times—denied him his hope of admission to the Air Force Academy.

Now desperate to make up for lost time, Rinc enrolled in the University of Nevada at Reno and graduated with a degree in electrical engineering. He turned down dozens of offers from companies all over the world—a young engineer with a commercial pilot's license was rare indeed—and applied for and won a place at the Air Force Officer Training School at Maxwell Air Force Base, Alabama. After that came a pilot training slot, one of only a handful awarded to OTS "ninety-day wonder" graduates.

He graduated with honors and was one of the first Air Force second lieutenants to be selected to fly the coveted FB-111A Aardvark supersonic bomber for the Strategic Air Command. The FB-111 was an elite showpiece assignment—there were fewer than fifty line Aardvark pilots in the entire U.S. Air Force. But the SAC version of the F-111 fighter-bomber never went to fight in the 1991 Persian Gulf War, so Seaver never saw any combat. And his FB-111 assignment ended less than two years later, when the Aardvarks were retired from service, a victim of budget cutbacks.

There were no other flying slots open during the steep force drawdowns of the early nineties, so Seaver transferred to the Aeronautical Systems Division, Special Projects Office, at Wright-Patterson Air Force Base, Ohio, working as a project officer and weapons design engineer for the B-1B Lancer bomber. He helped develop a series of high-tech, almost science-fiction-like weapons for the bomber, earning accolades and high-ranking attention throughout the Air Force as a forward-thinking, innovative designer. But the Lancer was in danger of being unceremoniously retired as well, and funding for advanced weapons and upgrades was slashed. Seaver's job was eliminated virtually overnight. He attended Squadron Officer School and was promoted to captain, but his prospects were looking poor for the career in the military that he longed for.

Without a regular commission or any recent flying experience, the young captain left the active-duty force, went home to Reno, and transferred to the Nevada Air National Guard. The Guard unit in Reno was one of the last to fly the RF-4 Phantom tactical reconnaissance jet, and Seaver saw his opportunity to fly a fast-mover once again. But he was a victim of the same old pattern that had dogged him before: the aged RF-4 was soon doomed to retire. When the Reno Guard got C-130 Hercules cargo planes, Seaver, disappointed but thankful to be back in the sky once again, accepted a part-time pilot assignment, flying one or two missions a week out of Reno-Tahoe International Airport.

In between, he worked as a flight instructor and charter pilot in Reno, earning his Airline Transport Pilot rating and quickly accumulating more commercial flight time. He piloted every charter assignment that came his way, got as much sleep as he could, then worked equally hard as a C-130 "trash-hauler." He completed Air Command and Staff College and received his master's degree, both achievements very unusual for National Guard officers. Everyone thought he was crazy for chasing an unattainable dream: to someday be called back to active duty and fight in the mythical air battle he still dreamed about.

But Rinc Seaver proved them all wrong. When the Reno Air National Guard transitioned from the C-130 to the B-1B Lancer bomber, he applied and was immediately accepted for pilot transition training and a full-time Guard assignment. He was back in his element, and his star quickly rose. He was promoted to major three years below the zone and became the squadron's senior standardization/evaluation pilot. To top it all off, he led the fledgling 111th Bomb Squadron in winning the LeMay, Dougherty, Ryan, Crumm, and Fairchild Trophies in Air Combat Command's biennial long-range Bombing and Navigation Competition. "Aces High" became the first Air Force Reserve Component unit in history and only the second B-1B unit to win the coveted Fairchild Trophy.

But Seaver's promotion and success did not sit well with most of the other Reno Air Guard crewdogs. Although he was clearly the most technically knowledgeable flier in the squadron—his pilot skills rivaled those of some of the veteran aircraft commanders—almost everyone saw him only as a young, cocky, know-it-all junior major with no life other than flying. What made him think he was so great? He had relatively little total military flying time, very little Bone time, and no combat experience. Some of the pilots he gave evaluations and check rides to had thousands of hours and many more years in service, and had flown combat missions in Desert Storm and even earlier conflicts, such as Operation Just Cause over Panama. As far as they were concerned, Rinc Seaver was an outsider and would always be one—forget that he was a native Nevadan and one of the first members of Aces High. Even after winning Bomb Comp, the old heads still considered him a mere systems operator, not a real aviator.

Rinc Seaver's answer to them was simple: go piss up a damned rope. He worked hard to be the best. He did his job with skill and dogged determination, just as he did everything else in his life, and he took no crap from anyone regardless of rank or flying time. Even in the Nevada Air National Guard, where politics, influence, and family name meant almost as much as skill and dedication, Rinc Seaver—the name meant "determined warrior" in Welsh—took a backseat to no one. He developed a reputation as a brash, determined loner who liked to push the envelope as much as possible at every opportunity.

Now he sat in the B-1B Part-Task Trainer, a computerized B-1 flight simulator, with a pilot and OSO/DSO compartment side by side in nonmoving but otherwise fully realistic cabs, ignoring Long's glare. "Watch this," he said to Furness, about to recap the doomed flight. "Okay, Neil, hit it." Furness suppressed her irritation and nodded to him to continue. The PTT had full visual displays out the cockpit windows and a worldwide radar and threat display database, so the crews could fly anywhere in the world and get realistic terrain and geographic displays and readouts. A control console was manned by two instructors and a computer technician. The instructors could program thousands of different scenarios into each simulator session, re-creating the simplest orientation flights or the most complex wartime emergency procedures scenario imaginable. The simulator operated twenty hours a day, six days a week. Like most military units in this age of steep budget cuts, the simulator had more "flying" time than all of the unit's aircraft combined.

The computer-generated visual display out the cockpit windows showed a vast expanse of desert, dotted with tall, jagged, rocky peaks. "Here we are at the Scud-ER target at Navy Fallon," said Seaver. "We hit two targets, but the damned squids jerked our chains and kept the emitters on and didn't simulate a kill, so we thought we missed. Chappie is ready to spit nails because he thinks he shut down all the threats, which he did, but the Navy kept on transmitting like they never got hit, the bastards." Chappie was Al Chapman, his dead defensive systems officer.

"Seaver . . ."

"Hold on, boss," Seaver said, pushing on. "We're yanking and banking and jammin' and jivin' our asses off. Everyone's pissed at me because they thought we missed the first two targets and because I wasn't doing enough for bomber defense. That's bullshit too—we shacked all three targets—but . . ." He stopped, ashamed that he had patted himself on the back and then said something negative against the dead. He could feel the icy stares on the back of his neck and knew the others, Furness too, resented it.

"Anyway, we nail the third target. Dead-on. We fly right into a SAM and triple-A nest on the other side of the ridge. A shitload of SAMs and triple-A—the smoky SAMs are everywhere, a couple dozen of 'em. We scram left away from the trap. We're at two hundred hard ride. I put the spoiler override switches into OVERRIDE, pop the speedbrakes and pull 'em into idle power, and start our two point five Gs pull to cornering velocity. Speed comes down nicely. Override switch back to normal, speedbrakes down. Now watch."

The visual display showed the steep bank, with more and more earth replacing sky in the cockpit window. Seaver pushed the throttles to max afterburner and pulled the stick right, but nothing happened—the steep bank stayed in, and they dipped earthward. Seconds later the simulator crashed with a sound resembling Wile E. Coyote hitting the ground in a Road Runner cartoon.

"Seaver, I don't know what you're trying to prove . . ."

"I know why we crashed, boss," he said. "Look: over ninety degrees of bank, airspeed slowing . . ."

"You cross-controlled your jet," Furness told him. "You know you're not supposed to do over ninety degrees of bank while TF'ing."

"But look at the speedbrakes," Seaver said insistently. "Just like the Powder River accident a couple years ago. Low altitude, steep bank angle, tight turn, and the speedbrakes are still extended. Sink rate builds up . . ."

"But you said you retracted the speedbrakes."

"They had to be still extended, boss," Rinc said.

Long rolled his eyes in disbelief. "So you say."

"I know I did," Rinc said. "Either they didn't retract, or they stuck extended. But they didn't retract."

"CITS said they did," Long told him. CITS, the Central Integrated Test System, was a monitoring, recording, and troubleshooting device on the B-1 bomber that acted like a flight data recorder. The CITS was heavily armored and designed to withstand a crash. They had recovered the stricken bomber's CITS module, and its memory was successfully retrieved and analyzed by the Air Force.

"I think something happened, something that prevented the speedbrakes from retracting, or retracted them too late," Rinc insisted. "The smoky SAMs were all around us—it's possible one of them got stuck in the spoiler wells. In that case, CITS would report them retracted even though they were still deployed. But that's the only way that crash makes any sense."

All he saw were blank faces staring back at him hostilely.

Seaver knew his arguments were falling on deaf ears. Since he had initiated the ejection sequence and punched everybody out long after the Bone had departed coordinated flight, they were putting the blame squarely on him.

Several long awkward moments passed. Then Rebecca Furness turned to the systems officers and simulator operators behind them and said, "Excuse us for a minute, guys."

Seaver got to his feet. "If you'll excuse me for a minute, boss, I'm going to take a leak, and then I'm going to get all the sim data together and upchannel it to Air Combat Command. We'll need to independently verify what we found and give this information to the accident board."

"Save your own butt by blaming the dead, huh, Seaver?" Long said under his breath, but loudly enough for the other squadron members to hear. Furness scowled.

Seaver inwardly winced at the remark but simply said, "It happened, John. It was some kind of technical malfunction. We can prove it." Looking about, he saw no sympathy in the faces around him.

Within a few moments, everyone had departed but Furness, Long, and Seaver. "So. You saw the flight surgeon today?" Furness asked. "What did he say?"

Seaver proudly produced a sheet of paper. "He signed me off for flying," he replied. "I know the squadron is getting ready for the pre-D. I realize I have a bunch of training to catch up on, but I know I can get back up to speed in time to recertify along with the rest of the squadron."

Furness examined the paper with a rueful shake of her head. The flight surgeon had given Seaver full medical clearance for flight duties, even though he was still undergoing physical therapy. The sign-off usually meant that the crew member was off all medications and was observed to be free of any apparent psychological or emotional difficulties as a result of the crash.

More important, for Seaver, was the sign-off that allowed him to train for the predeployment certification, or pre-D.

The pre-D was the unit's biggest gauge of its combat effectiveness. Air National Guard bomber squadrons were "replacement" units, not frontline combat-ready units. In the event that the bombers were needed, the squadron would be "federalized," or transferred from the command of the Nevada state adjutant general to the Air Force and "gained" by an active-duty bomb wing. The Guard aircrews would be tasked to ferry the aircraft to the deployment base, either in the United States or overseas; and the best crews might fly actual combat missions if there was a shortage of active-duty crews. In order to prove they were ready for full integration into the active force, twice a year the squadron was sent either to Ellsworth AFB in South Dakota or Dyess AFB in Texas to undergo a grueling two-week drill to demonstrate their combat readiness.

Fail the pre-D, and you could be dismissed from the squadron. If too many crews failed, the entire unit could be decertified. The unit already had one big black mark against it—Seaver's crash. Having even one crew fail a pre-D could bring the entire squadron down.

Furness put the paper aside, glancing at Long. "You know you're not supposed to go to the flight surgeon or ask him for any sign-offs without asking me first," she said to Seaver.

He narrowed his eyes quizzically. "No, I didn't know that, boss. I must've filed that piece of info in the 'Like I give a shit' folder when the President briefed it."

"Don't be a smart-ass, Seaver."

"But I didn't go to the doc to ask for a sign-off—I went for a scheduled rehab follow-up. He asked me how I felt, poked and prodded, and then said I looked okay enough to go back to work. He did the sign-off. I didn't ask him for shit. If he's out of line with you, that's his problem, not mine." He looked hard at his squadron commander, then asked, "It sounds like maybe you don't want me flying or participating in any pre-D work-ups. There a problem here, boss?"

"I don't know, Seaver," Furness said. "I don't like seeing you in here when you're supposed to be recuperating, that's all."

"I'm all right, Beck," Rinc said. "I'm ready to get moving." He looked at her, then at Long's scowl. "What else, guys?"

"Start by telling us the *real* reason you lost it, Seaver," Long said acidly.

"Excuse me?" Seaver asked incredulously. "What the hell is that supposed to mean?"

"You heard me, Seaver," Long retorted. "The wreckage and the bodies are still warm and you already want another crew and another plane . . ."

"Those 'bodies' were my *friends,* Long Dong," Seaver said bitterly.

"They were my friends too," Long said. "But I for one don't think you deserve another chance until you fully explain what *really* happened out on the range."

"Like I told you and the accident board," Seaver said, "we were in trouble. We were scramming away from the SAMs. I popped speedbrakes to get us down to cornering velocity. I admit I went over forty-five degrees of bank, but I had the TERFLW paddled off and I was flying it visually—if we were in the clouds, I would've kept TERFLW on and done forty-five. But we were under attack, dammit! I tried to roll out but couldn't straighten her out. I knew something was wrong, so I gave the command to eject—"

"Bullshit you did," Long said.

Seaver looked angrily at Long and finally nodded. "Okay, maybe I didn't give the command," he said.

"But the plane was in a bad skid, a high angle-of-attack, a steep bank, and we were still at two hundred hard ride with TERFLW doing an inverted fly-up. I was trying to fly it out, but I lost it. When I couldn't get it back, I didn't think. I just reacted."

"You're damned right you didn't think. You screwed up," Long shot back. "Did you ever think to give us a yellow light?" There was a yellow PREPARE TO EJECT and a red EJECT light that were manually activated by the pilots in a controlled ejection situation. Normally during a flight, the crew's ejection mode switches were set to AUTO, which allowed either the pilot or the copilot to eject the rest of the crew. Even on the ground, Long and most other crew members couldn't actually say the word "eject," as in the "red EJECT light." He and every other flier knew it was a command that demanded an instantaneous response. Seeing the red EJECT light was the same as issuing the "Eject! Eject! Eject!" order verbally.

"No. There was no time."

"There could have been, if you didn't have your head so far up your ass," Long said angrily.

The memory of his dead fellow crewdogs hit Rinc Seaver hard, and the anger welled up out of his body like air out of a popped balloon. Seaver had been training both Chappie and his wife, Daphne, to fly—Daphne had already soloed and was just a night cross-country from her check ride. Rinc was godfather of one of their kids, even though none of them were very good Catholics. They were the closest friends—no, the closest *family*—Seaver had. Chappie left his wife and two kids, a son and daughter, behind.

"You're damned right. No one else went. No one else even initiated the sequence," Long said bitterly. "You know what I think, Seaver? I think you couldn't handle it. You were getting hosed by the Navy, you were confused, you were disoriented, and you were scared, so you panicked and hit your handles!"

"We were in a skid, we were headed down, and I thought I could save it."

"That crash was *your* fault, Seaver!"

"No it wasn't," he cried out. "I proved what happened. I tried to fly it out, but the left bank was still in and we never leveled out. I knew I lost it, and I went. I did the best I could."

"You caused that accident, Seaver! There was no reason for that crash except for *your* stupidity."

"John . . . ," Furness said softly, as if trying—not very convincingly—to tell Long to stop arguing.

"You oughta be grounded, Seaver," Long dug in, jabbing a finger at the OSO. "You oughta be kicked out of the Guard. You oughta be kicked in the fucking *ass*!"

"You don't have the balls to try it, Long!"

"Enough, John," Furness said, forcefully this time. She looked sternly at John Long, her second-in-command. "We're not going to solve anything here. The accident board will have its report in a couple days, and then we'll all know for sure." Then she looked grimly at Rinc and shook her head. "But our problem right now is one of trust, Seaver. Even if you're found not responsible for the accident, who's going to trust you? Who's going to fly with you? And if you're grounded, who's going to trust you to properly plan a mission or give a tactics briefing?"

"What the hell do you mean?"

"I mean, you're going to have to prove to this squadron that you can handle it, that you can follow orders, that you can be part of a team and not think about yourself."

"I damn well can be part of this squadron, Beck!"

"Shut up and listen," Furness broke in angrily. "I'm not going to fire you unless directed by higher headquarters or unless I feel your membership here is dragging this unit's performance and morale down. Both situations are out of my control. It's going to be up to you to prove that you can fly with Aces High."

Furness grabbed the flight authorization form, scanned it, then signed it. "You can fly again, Seaver—we can't spare the manpower to keep you sitting on your ass for another two weeks. I want you to do a full annual check ride, including open-book, closed-book, orals, sim, pubs check, and flight evaluations."

"No sweat, boss," Seaver said confidently. "I've already talked with Scheduling, and I got a crew and a plane penciled in. I'll be ready for a flight check by the end of the week."

"You better be," Furness warned. Long shook his head and snorted as if saying "No way," but they both knew that if any member of the squadron could be ready for a flight check in less than seven days, it was Seaver. "If you pass, you can accompany us to our pre-D work-up—but I'm not going to let you try to requalify until I'm positive your head is on straight and you're ready to do your job."

"Hey, boss, give me a break," Seaver said. "I'll be mission-ready and up to speed before we go to pre-D. All I ask is for a chance to qualify."

"I'm not worried about you, Seaver," Furness said bitterly. "I'm worried about the morale of this unit if we fail the pre-D. I choose the crews that qualify, and right now I don't think you'll be ready in time."

"But . . ."

"Do me a favor, Seaver, and shut up and listen. This entire unit has been through hell the past several weeks. We're all hurting, not just you. But what do we see? You're in here cooking up wild excuses for the crash."

"They're not wild excuses, boss. I think I know . . ."

"You don't get it, do you? You might have the answer, you might not. But it doesn't matter. Right now we don't want to find out that someone screwed up. We all just need to know it's gonna be okay, and everyone needs to pitch in, including you. You should start thinking about ways you can help this squadron pull itself together, rather than worrying about clearing your precious reputation."

"What the hell am I supposed to do, boss?" Seaver asked hotly. "Give everybody a big hug? Serve tea and cookies and explore everyone's feelings? Flog myself with a horsehair whip?"

"You do whatever you have to do to make this squadron believe you're one of us, Seaver," Furness responded. "If you do it, everything will eventually get back to normal. If you don't, we'll be on our way to being disbanded. Think about it. Now get the hell out of here and go home."

There was silence for a long moment. That was Seaver's indication that he was dismissed.

After he left, Long shook his head. "Fucking weasel," he said. "He's sticking to his lame-ass story."

"Ease up on him, Long Dong," Furness said. "Whether he's going to make it or hit bottom, let him do it on his own. I just hope that if he doesn't make it, he doesn't pull this unit down with him."

OFFICE OF THE SECRETARY OF THE AIR FORCE,
THE PENTAGON, WASHINGTON, D.C.
LATER THAT SAME DAY

I am getting ready to go overseas for a major military exercise," Secretary of the Air Force Stuart Mortonson raged, "and now you drop this on me. General

Hayes, you'd better have a real good explanation." This, Mortonson thought, was definitely one of those times when being the chief civilian officer of the nation's youngest military service was a totally thankless job.

Mortonson, formerly a dean at Stanford University and lieutenant governor of California, got his post in the Pentagon as a gift for helping win California in the last presidential election. The position meant a boost for California's aerospace industry and lots of grant money for California institutes and universities, which were two good reasons why Mortonson was being groomed to run for the Senate or for governor of California. But except for making a few speeches or visiting a few bases, no one ever saw or recognized the secretary of the Air Force—unless something went wrong. Then everyone knew your name.

First, it was the B-1 bomber crash in Nevada back in April. Technically, it was a Nevada Air National Guard plane, not an Air Force plane, but that kind of hairsplitting was useless from day one—it was and always would be an Air Force problem. The Navy squawked about how reckless the crew was, complained about all the violated rules of engagement, and demanded the Air Force clean up its act. Mortonson took the scolding from the secretary of the Navy and the chief of Naval Operations, got the third-degree stare-down from the secretary of defense, and loudly promised everyone to get to the bottom of the incident and kick some butts.

But now a new controversy had surfaced, and again it involved the Navy. During a scheduled antimissile weapons test over the Pacific Ocean, some very odd things had happened, and the Air Force guys on the scene, including the Air Force's chief of staff, were being very, *very* closemouthed about it. The Navy, which had some ships in the area, squawked again, accusing the Air Force of testing a new warhead—possibly even a nuclear device—on a Navy range with Navy personnel in close proximity without informing anyone or setting up proper safeguards.

Air Force Chief of Staff Victor Hayes fired off an e-mail message to the secretary of the Air Force less than an hour after the test, asking for an immediate secure video- or phone conference. Mortonson was out of the office and didn't have access to a secure phone. Hayes arrived back at the Pentagon just a few hours later, asking for an immediate face-to-face meeting with the secretary and with Major General Gregory Hammond, director of the Air National Guard Bureau. Hammond was in charge of the office that interfaced the secretary of the Air Force and the chief of staff of the Air Force with the governors and adjutant generals of the states that had Air National Guard units. But by then the shit from the Navy had hit the fan, and Mortonson changed his schedule and took this meeting.

Of course, all this was going on in the middle of one of the biggest military exercises of the year: Team Spirit 2000 was going to kick off in less than two months. Often the controversial political football in peace negotiations between North and South Korea, Team Spirit 2000 had become the largest joint war game in the Pacific. Land, naval, and air forces from the United States, South Korea, and Japan were going to participate in the three-week-long exercise, practicing and demonstrating joint military maneuvers over a broad conflict spectrum and geographic area.

This was the first year that Japan was going to be a full participant instead of an observer or support entity. Because it was in the midst of near-collapse, with a severe government downsizing and financial reorganization program in effect, and still suffering the aftermath of the nuclear detonation in Yokosuka Harbor three years earlier, everything possible was being done to include Japan in major Asian defense events so as to try to keep that nation from sliding back into isolationism or extreme anti-American nationalism. Its ban on all combat-armed American warships in its territorial waters and its threat to close all U.S. military bases were ominous signs that such fears were valid.

About a year after the explosion—which had killed and injured only a handful of Japanese citizens and caused very little damage to Japanese property—Japan had begun buying frontline high-tech surplus military equipment from Russia as if it were dollar day at the Goodwill store. Ex-Russian MiG-29 fighters and Sukhoi-33 fighter-bombers were now flying alongside American-made F-15 fighters in the skies over Japan. It was a clear message that Japan wanted to rearm and assume more of the responsibility of defending itself—and it wanted to do so *now*. The threat of an economically unstable, ultranationalistic, and rearmed Japan was a serious concern to Washington.

To try to present a unified front, the Vice President of the United States, Ellen Christine Whiting, accompanied by several of the service secretaries and chiefs of staff, was going to tour some of the foreign players' military bases in the region. Of course, that was not the only reason Mortonson was going along; his main task was to try to talk the Japanese out of buying so much Russian hardware and into buying more American equipment. Mortonson was armed with joint development contracts, licensing agreements, incentives, loan packages, and grant money—everything short of an out-and-out bribe to try to get Japan to buy American again.

The pressure was already on. He didn't need his own troops adding more gray hairs, wrinkles, and bags under his eyes.

"I've got the secretary of defense, the President's national security adviser, the director of Central Intelligence, and the chief of Naval Operations ready to shit on my desk!" Mortonson shouted after the door to his office was closed. "What in hell went on out there, General?"

Hayes told him—and Mortonson was scared. Stunned, angry, incredulous, yes—but mostly scared.

The secretary of the Air Force was a politician and bureaucrat by trade, not an engineer, scientist, or soldier like some of his predecessors. The politician in him said this was so damaging to the administration, not to mention the Air Force, that the President's opponents might not even wait until the November elections—they could all be out of a job within days. At a time when the threat to America's security was at its greatest, and the perceived readiness and ability of the military to fight a major conflict was very low, the last thing the White House or Pentagon needed was an unauthorized test of some unknown weapon.

"General Hayes, I hope you realize the consequences of what you did," Mortonson said ominously.

"Of course I do, sir," he said. "I'm also prepared to brief you with results of our tests."

"Are you prepared to lose your job? Have your career destroyed?" Mortonson asked. "Because that's what's going to happen to you, and most likely to me, when I report this to the rest of the Joint Chiefs and the White House. They're going to blow a gasket."

"Sir, the thing works," Hayes said. "The Air Force's antimissile hunter-killer system works. Forget the plasma-yield warhead for a moment, sir. No harm, no foul. The Navy still doesn't know what kind of warhead we used, and in my estimation they'll never figure it out unless someone tells them."

"You're giving me this 'no harm, no foul' nonsense,

Victor?" Mortonson asked incredulously. "You expect me to go in front of the Joint Chiefs and the President and say something like 'no harm, no foul'? Are you crazy?"

"Sir, what I'd prefer you say is that we have the antiballistic missile system the White House and Congress have been clamoring for," Hayes said earnestly. "Lieutenant General Terrill Samson at HAWC demonstrated an air-launched antimissile system that is almost as effective as the airborne laser program but that we can field in just a few months. You told me to find a way to fit ABL into the budget—here's how we do it. I respectfully suggest, sir, you tell the Navy to stuff it."

"I think we will be fighting to keep from getting *our* asses stuffed, General," Mortonson said. He paused, staring across the room for a moment. Then: "It was our range, right?"

"The range is administered by the Navy, and a naval officer was the controlling authority," Hayes said, "but we were paying for it." Mortonson closed his eyes and shook his head in exasperation. Hayes was indignant. "Sir, we *paid* for that range and everything in it. We paid for those ships, we paid for the target rockets, we paid for the antiair missiles, we paid for security, and we would've paid any claims in case of an accident. The Navy insisted we accept responsibility for everything. In my mind, that gives us the right to use the range however we want.

"The Navy never gave us any limits on what weapons we could use, only that we not overfly any of their ships with our missiles. We briefed which weapons we'd use and we used what we briefed—except for the plasma-yield warheads. All of the Navy ships were well outside the warheads' kill radius, which we knew with great precision because that's a property of the weapon. The Navy knows all about the weapon because they intend to use it on their Aegis Tier Two and Three antiballistic missile weapons. It was perfectly safe. No Navy personnel were in any danger, and they know it."

"You're deluding yourself with that argument, General," said the secretary of the Air Force. "They are going to nail our hides to the wall over this. What was the closest detonation to any ships?"

Hayes checked his notes: "The rocket intercept was thirty miles downrange and at an altitude of seventy-four thousand feet—that's over twelve nautical miles high," he replied. "The launch barge was over nine miles from the nearest warship. The explosions didn't cause a ripple in the water. They didn't detect any radiation until they sailed right over to ground zero and recovered a piece of the barge, and radiation levels were well below danger levels. The closest nonmilitary vessel was twenty-three miles."

Hayes was heartened to see Mortonson stop to think again. Good, he thought, maybe he wasn't ready to concede defeat over this. "All right, General," Mortonson said finally. "I'll back your play. I'm going to need a briefing file on the plasma-yield warhead and on the missiles you launched. I'm sure we'll all take a few turns roasting on the spit, but I think I can keep us from getting completely cooked."

"Thank you, sir," Hayes said gratefully.

"Don't thank me yet, General—if the CNO or the White House wants someone's ass, it'll be yours, mine, and Samson's. We're not out of the woods by any means. All this means is you have an advocate. It may not do us a lick of good."

"Then, if you'll permit me, I suggest you don't go in there with your hat in your hand, sir," Hayes said.

"You have something else in mind, General?"

"Sir, we did a successful boost-phase antimissile test this morning," Hayes said. "We built the weapon they wanted us to build. We have a victory, not a failure. I think the Navy and the Army both know it, or at least suspect it. Let's capitalize on it. We are ready to begin operational tests of the new 'Coronet Tiger.' "

Secretary Mortonson shook his head in some confusion. He was very familiar with the program—he had almost lost his confirmation to be secretary of the Air Force because of his overwhelming support of the expensive, controversial weapon system. "Coronet Tiger" was the classified code name of the Air Force's new antiballistic missile defense program, starting with the airborne laser and continuing on to the new Skybolt space-based laser system.

But in this day and age of military "jointness," every branch of the service had to be involved or nothing would ever get approval. The airborne laser was the Air Force's one and only contribution to the new fifty-billion-dollar antiballistic missile program; its designs and plans—and funding—for the space-based laser were all transferred to the Navy.

"I don't understand, General," he said irritably. "Coronet Tiger is dead."

"You can blame Lieutenant General Samson at HAWC for this one too, sir," Hayes said. "The air-launched antiballistic missile system was Samson's lab's invention. He wants to put the Lancelot ABM system on a dozen B-1 bombers and create an antimissile attack squadron. Lancelot is teamed up with cruise missiles to destroy not only enemy rockets but the launchers as well, and Lancelot even has an antisatellite capability. Fast, deployable, survivable, and effective. I've got a full report, and I can brief you and the Joint Chiefs whenever you'd like."

"Forget it, General," Mortonson said. "There is no way that's ever going to be approved now. Even if I can keep all our asses out of the fire—which I'm not confident I can do—there's no way in hell the Department of Defense will authorize funding for a new squadron of B-1s to carry these weapons. Hell, we'll be lucky if they let us keep Dreamland open, let alone allow us to keep those missiles."

"Samson has already drawn up an organizational chart and preliminary budget proposal," Hayes said. "He suggests we fund and equip the unit through the Air National Guard. We share the cost of the conversion, training, upkeep, and basing with the Guard. He's got it laid out pretty well, sir. I think it's worth a look."

Mortonson scowled at Hayes, then glanced at General Gregory Hammond. "You seen any of these numbers, Greg?"

"Yes, sir," Hammond replied. He shrugged noncommittally. "It's workable. It's certainly cutting-edge, so the states might actually *compete* to get such a unit. Kansas, Georgia, Nevada—they can all afford to invest in the conversion. A popular, needed technology, lots of deployments, maybe a training center in the future for the first unit that gets the weapon—the states see an opportunity for big revenues from this. And each state has nationally known congressmen, so interest and visibility will be very high."

"Who has the best package?"

"Hard to say exactly, sir, but—no pun intended—I'd put my money on Nevada," Hammond replied with a slight smile. "They have two possible facilities other than the Reno-Tahoe Airport: Tonopah and the old Tuscarora Air Force Base near Battle Mountain. Both have first-class runways, taxiways, construction areas, and weapons storage facilities—they just need major work on buildings and infrastructure, which the state would fund to our specifications."

"The Nevada Air Guard, eh?" Mortonson remarked. "The Reno B-1 bomber unit? Not only do they *not* deserve an upgraded unit, they probably deserve to be *disbanded*. What's the latest on that crash investigation?"

"The investigators are now saying crew error and possibly a dummy missile hit them," Hammond replied. "The crew was performing a 'scram' maneuver, which is a tight turn to get away from a ground threat. The finding is unofficial right now because we have a lot of new information, but it's been demonstrated in two different B-1 simulators."

"How did it happen?"

"A flight manual procedural 'Warning' violation," Hammond responded. "The final report will be out in a few days, sir, but it appears the pilot initiated a steep bank turn over sixty degrees during a high-G low-altitude maneuver—in fact, he may have exceeded ninety degrees. The bank automatically causes the terrain-avoidance system to do a fail-safe fly-up. At the same time, the crew is trying to slow the bomber down . . ."

"Slow it down? Why? Isn't going slower dangerous?"

"No, because the B-1 turns faster at a slower speed," Hayes explained. "It's called cornering velocity. Every crew computes that speed for the altitude and gross weight it'll be at during the bomb runs. If they decelerate to cornering velocity, they can turn faster without fear of stalling." He paused, considering, then added, "They'd have the bomber at max Gs and throttles idle. This crew popped their speedbrakes to slow down faster. Deploying speedbrakes also decreases roll efficiency, which is why bank angles are limited by procedure to forty-five degrees."

"The theory presented by the unit said that several of the little papier-mâché rockets the Navy uses to simulate surface-to-air missile launches flew into the speedbrakes, causing them to not fully retract," Hammond went on.

"And?" Mortonson asked.

"It was confirmed by Navy range officers," Hammond said. "They didn't expect the B-1 to make that tight turn, thinking they were firing well clear of the plane. Several of the rockets came close enough to the bomber so that they might have hit it. Combine that with low speed, crossed-up flight controls adding more drag, and low altitude, and you have your accident. The papier-mâché rockets would leave no trace, so there was no evidence at the crash scene. Engineers are going over this scenario, and so far we think it's the most likely explanation."

"The bottom line is, our crews screwed up," Mortonson repeated bitterly. "That is unacceptable. Totally unacceptable."

"It happens to the best crews, sir," General Hayes said somberly. "In the heat of battle, the crews react. Most times their training takes over, and they come out of it okay. This time it didn't happen."

"That doesn't cut it, General," Mortonson said. "Losing planes in combat is one thing. Losing a two-hundred-million-dollar bomber in a training exercise in good weather is not acceptable."

"Fly low and fast, and even one small mistake can be deadly," the chief of staff said. Hayes had lost too many good friends in aircraft accidents—he knew that it could happen even to the best of the best. "The crews train hard. And these were the best Air National Guard bomber crews in the force—and one of the best in the entire world. They were aggressive . . ."

"They screwed up, General," Mortonson emphasized. "I don't care how aggressive they were or how many trophies they've won. Something happened. Someone lost it. In war, I can understand that—but in peacetime, no. We have rules, don't we, General? We have rules of engagement? The crews are briefed not to push it to the edge, right? Train hard, I know, but they aren't encouraged to be unsafe just to win a training exercise, are they, General?" When Hayes hesitated, the secretary of the Air Force looked as if he was going to explode in rage. "Well? Are they?"

"The crews are briefed on the rules of engagement, yes, sir," Hayes responded. "But both sides play it as if it's the real thing. They use every bit of their skills and experience to win . . ."

"So I noticed," Mortonson said. "Reminds me of you and Samson, pulling that stunt today with that plasma-yield weapon. You do anything you think you need to do to win. Well, I think you've screwed yourselves this time with that kind of thinking.

"General, this is not a failure of our crews—it's a failure of our training, which is a failure of command," Mortonson went on. "After the stunt you pulled out in the Navy test range, I'm not surprised that our crews have the same attitude. Win at all costs, right, General? Forget the regulations as long as the bombs are on target, right?"

"Sir, I am the senior uniformed officer of the United States Air Force," General Hayes said. "I am responsible for each and every man and machine under me, and I include the Air Guard and Reserves. If you need a sacrificial lamb, sir, I'm your man."

"General, I goddamn guarantee that all of our necks are on the chopping block right now," Mortonson said. "Your head will just be the first one to roll." He knew he should fire Hayes right now, do it before Congress and the White House questioned why he waited so long. But he realized he couldn't do it. Hayes was wrong, dead wrong . . . but he was wrong for all the right reasons.

And he did have Coronet Tiger. The real antiballistic missile systems—the airborne laser, the Navy's Aegis Tier Three, and the space-based laser called Skybolt—were all many years in the future. Congress was so frustrated with the delays, failures, and cost overruns that they were ready to either cancel the entire program or, worse, buy an inferior system.

This Lancelot system might save their bacon, even from something as serious as setting a subnuclear device off in the Navy's face.

Mortonson thought for another moment, then asked, "Why a Guard unit, General? Why not an active-duty unit?"

"Money, sir," Hayes replied. "Right now this project is totally off the books, buried in HAWC's black research budget. Brad Elliott bounced enough checks and wrote enough IOUs to get a handful of his creations flying—it's the way he always did things. But Terrill Samson doesn't want to play it that way. He knows it's not his job to create tactical units—his job is to test hardware. If he gets full authorization, he'll turn over his technology and weapons to whatever unit we want and provide training for that unit. Otherwise, he'll put it all back on the shelf where it came from."

"If we decided to deploy an active-duty antimissile squadron, we would need to either convert a unit or stand up a new unit, both of which will take time and money," said Mortonson.

"With the Air National Guard, we use the states to help fund the program, sir," Hammond pointed out. "The states will pay the bulk of the costs—the physical plant, the personnel costs, and the cost of daily training and upkeep. We give the states the planes, pay for the upgrade equipment, and we pay the costs of certifying each unit to our standards. If the President federalizes the unit, we pay the states a fixed fee. It's a good deal all around."

"But the main reason General Samson suggested using the Air Guard is performance," said Hayes. "The bottom line is, the Air Guard guys are good. Their personnel are as well trained and as knowledgeable as any active-duty unit. The unit that lost the plane won the last Bomb Comp trophy. They are the best around."

"Why the hell is that?"

"It's a completely different world in the Air Guard, sir," General Hammond said. "Flying for the Guard is treated as a special privilege, like belonging to a special club. It's more competitive because there are fewer slots, so they only take the best of the best. Each candidate is handpicked by the adjutant general and the governor. To weed out candidates, most units require their members to be longtime residents of the state, so you really have to make a long-term commitment to the unit. Some Guard members serve with the same unit and fly the same planes for years. They don't get uprooted every few years or worry about promotion or reassignment like the active-duty troops do. They have to compete every year to keep their jobs, so they're aggressive. They take pride in their units on an entirely different level than the active-duty force does, because they represent their hometown and their state."

"You know about all the criticism we're getting about Guard and Reserve units flying these planes, don't you?" Mortonson asked Hayes. "Part-timers can't handle sophisticated war machines. What do you think? Should we do away with the Air National Guard bomber program?"

"You know that talk is all bullshit, sir," Hayes replied. "These guys are only replacement units, not frontline fighters. They train hard and work hard, but they're not the equivalent of the active-duty force. They exist to give us a reserve fighting force that can be mobilized and ready to fight in a matter of weeks or months. It's a trade-off. We don't spend as much money keeping their men and machines in the inventory, but we don't have those forces available quickly or at such a high state of readiness."

"You've given me the politically correct reply, Victor," Mortonson said, "but I want to hear what you *think*. Is it a good idea to let part-timers fly the fast jets?"

"They've been flying the fast jets for years, sir," Hayes replied. "The Reserve forces account for about one-third of all the missions flown by the Air Force. In some missions, like air defense, they account for *one hundred* percent. There's only two weapon systems they don't fly, the stealth bomber and stealth fighter, and that's because we don't have that many of those to begin with."

Mortonson glared at Hayes. "Dammit, General," he said, "are you ever going to give me a straight answer? Do you think it's a wise move, a wise investment, to have the Guard and Reserves flying planes like the B-1 bombers?"

"Yes, sir, I do," Hayes replied resolutely. "I believe in the concept of the citizen soldier. I'd rather see talented, highly trained crews get out of the active-duty force and fly in a Guard or Reserve unit for a few years than be sucked into the civilian market where we can't use their skills. The Guard and Reserves preserve a good bit of the hundreds of thousands of training dollars we spend per crewman—if he didn't fly in the Guard or Reserves after active duty, we'd waste all the investment we made."

Mortonson carefully considered that argument. "Point taken," he said, nodding. "That's too big an issue to handle right now anyway. General, I'm not going to consider your antiballistic missile squadron idea at this time. We're going to have our hands full trying to convince the Joint Chiefs, SECDEF, and the President that we're not a couple of maverick nutcases ready to plunge the world into a nuclear holocaust . . ."

"Sir, before you say no, here's what we have right now," Hayes said quickly. "We've got weapons, avionics, training materials, and spares ready to equip two more planes. The gear is already bought and paid for. If Terrill Samson gets authorization and funding, he can put together two more Lancelot planes within three months, and ten more within a year. Let's find a couple of airframes and some crews and give it a shot. If it doesn't work, we haven't wasted anything. If it does work and you want to proceed, we're already in motion."

Mortonson hesitated—another good sign, especially for a guy known to make snap decisions. "These will be Air National Guard assets?"

"We've already got several candidates lined up," General Hammond said, "and we can begin the selection process immediately. All we need is a go-ahead."

Mortonson hesitated once again, then nodded. "All right. Put it together for four airframes only. But be prepared to put it all back on the shelf if SECDEF or the White House says no." Both Hayes and Hammond nodded. "Speaking of the Air National Guard, what's the current status of that Nevada Guard unit?"

"They are fully operational, with five manned planes, one plane without a full crew, and one spare," General Hammond responded. "The five crews are reserve mission capable, which means they can be called up, used as replacements, or trained to full combat-ready status within sixty days. They begin their unit requalification course in a few weeks."

"If they pass it, they stay—if they don't, we pull the

plug on them," the secretary of the Air Force said flatly. "We don't have the money to waste on ineffective units, even if the state is putting up a bunch of money to support them."

"Sir, I think this Nevada Air National Guard unit might be exactly the guys we're looking for with this new antiballistic missile intercept squadron," Victor Hayes suggested. "The mission demands an experienced and hard-charging crew . . ."

"No way, Victor," Mortonson interrupted, waving a hand in dismissal. "Frankly, I'm hoping for the sake of our budget that they *don't* pass their requalification test. Putting seven B-1 bombers on ice will save us billions per year. It might send a message to the rest of the force too—shape up, or you'll find yourselves unemployed."

"I think it'll definitely send a message, Mr. Secretary," Hayes said. "I think the message will say, 'Don't be aggressive, don't risk it, because if you screw up, you'll be shit-canned.' Sir."

"My message about shaping up or you'll find yourself unemployed applies to the commanders as well as the airmen, General Hayes," Mortonson said acidly. "It should probably go double for you and General Samson. You take risks, you'd better be prepared to accept the consequences. That is all."

CHAPTER TWO

Although the Nevada Air National Guard had a very nice all-ranks dinner club in Reno—in fact, one of the finest in the nation—few of the members of the 111th Bomb Squadron used it except for official social functions. Years earlier, back when the Air National Guard flew the RF-4 Phantom, the squadron members had "adopted" a run-down little bar and casino on South Rock Boulevard near the old Cannon Airport, now the Reno-Tahoe International Airport.

The bar's real name was the Quarry, because it had been built near a small quarry used to provide sand and gravel for the concrete for Reno's new airport's runways, but no one used it. It was known to all as Target Study. It provided a convenient and convincing excuse or explanation to someone asking about a squadron member's whereabouts, as in "He's at target study" or "I'll be at target study for the next couple of hours." Because it was close to the airport, it also made for a fine place for crew members to wander up onto the roof and watch the planes come and go.

It was the first time since his accident that Rinc had been back in the place. Out front, there were six tables, a few booths, a couple of card tables, a few slot machines and video poker machines, and the bar. The place had become decorated over the years with photos, memorabilia, books, signs, and other items from the Air National Guard flying units in Reno, and from visiting flying units from around the world. Every new guest was required to sign his or her name on the walls—most chose the bathroom of the opposite sex. Signatures and messages at the bar itself were reserved for VIPs or high-ranking officers. Anyone uninformed enough to wear a tie or bring a hat into the place had it snipped off or removed and tacked up on the rafters, and there was a huge collection of these trophies overhead.

Behind the bar, up on the shelf next to the expensive liquors, Rinc knew there was a full set of B-1B tech orders, and he had no doubt they were in inspection-ready condition. There were also tech orders of all the planes the Nevada Air Guard had ever flown since its inception in 1946: P-39, P-40, P-51, T-33, and F-86 fighters, RB-57, RF-101, and RF-4 tactical reconnaissance fighters, and C-130 Hercules cargo planes, all in equally perfect condition. In the back was a billiard room with slot machines, movies, newspapers, and computers. It was off limits to all but Aces High personnel of all ranks.

Martina—no one knew her last name—was out front behind the bar as usual. She virtually came with the place, and she was most definitely in command here. Martina weighed more than 260 pounds and could have just as easily been the bouncer. Rumor had it that pilots paid off big bar tabs by sneaking Martina onboard their planes. She supposedly had over a hundred hours in the RF-4 Phantom, although it seemed impossible she could ever have squeezed herself into the seat.

"Hey, Rodeo," she said, greeting Seaver as if she had

just seen him the day before. She poured him a large glass of diet cola. Martina knew the flying schedule just as well as the crews did, and she always knew when a guy was within twelve hours of a sortie and would stop serving him alcohol. Woe to any flier who tried to argue with her.

Rinc was looking the place over, drinking in the welcome atmosphere. There was no air-conditioning, and it was stuffy and musty-smelling, but it still felt cozy, much like his dad's old ham radio room in the basement of their house when he was a kid.

His eyes were drawn to the back of the bar and the "Snake Eyes" board. Fifty-three years of photos of dead members of Aces High were pinned up there—and yes, he saw they had added the pictures of his dead crewmates to the array. In fact, it was a crew photo, their Fairchild Trophy shot taken in front of their plane . . .

. . . with Rinc's picture cut out of it.

He was frozen in place. It was logical that he be cut out of the picture—after all, *he* wasn't dead—but they had left the pictures of the surviving crew members, and why his squadronmates had chosen that particular photo to use on the memorial wall made him uneasy. All the other pictures were individual shots, even in cases where multiple crew members had been lost. It was as if he were worse than dead—he was excluded, ousted. They had made a point of eliminating him, as if to remind him that he had survived an accident that he had no right to survive.

Rinc hadn't yet selected a seat, but Martina made the choice for him by bringing his cola and a bowl of pretzels over to a booth. She picked the one farthest from the door to the back room. He looked at the closed door, then at Martina. Her expression answered all his questions: yes, some members of Aces High were back there; yes, the commander, Rebecca Furness, was there—and no, he wasn't welcome.

"Don't worry about it none, Rodeo," she said in her raspy, cigarette-scratched voice. "Give 'em time. They'll take you back."

"Time is the one thing I don't think I have, Marty," Rinc said.

"You don't worry about nuthin' 'cept your check ride tomorrow," she told him. She had the flying schedule pinned down as well as if she were on the operations distribution list. "You jes' show 'em what you got. You ain't a member of Aces High 'cause they let you in the back. You a member because you got what it takes."

She noticed Rinc glancing over toward the Snake Eyes board again. "Fergit 'bout dat too, Rodeo." But she didn't offer to take it down. She couldn't even if she'd wanted to. The Snakes Eyes wall was like a shrine. However hurtful or even vindictive a posting, no one, not even Martina, could mess with it.

"Did that asshole Long Dong put that up there?"

"Long Dong's sho' enough an asshole. Don't let him git under your skin none." He noticed she didn't actually answer him. "You listen good, boy," she said, pointing a sausagelike finger at him. "You hold your head up like a man and don't never be ashamed of anything anyone ever says about you—even if it's a damned lie. You remember that." And then she left him alone.

Rinc got out his flight manuals, charts, and target study notes and tried looking them over, but the words and pictures blurred before his eyes. He left all of it on the table—Martina would see to it that no one touched it—grabbed his glass, went outside, and climbed up the freshly painted wood steps that led to the roof. There he put on his sunglasses and sat down on a metal bench. The sky was ice-blue. The air was cold, but the sun felt warm. There were clouds piling up over Mount Rose to the west, and the Sierra Nevada mountaintops above eight thousand feet still wore a thin blanket of snow.

The winds were calm, so the tower was using the northbound runways. As he watched, two B-1B bombers pulled out of their parking spots and taxied to runway 34 left, a Reno Air Boeing 727 following them. It was easy to visualize the passengers straining to look out the windows as they taxied past the Air National Guard ramp and catching a glimpse of the sleek, deadly warplanes. At the end of the taxiway, the Bones turned right onto the "hammerhead," a section of the taxiway with a high steel wall on the runway side, to make way for the commercial flight to pass. The warplanes were soon followed by the SOF, or supervisor of flying, an experienced pilot whose task was to do a "last chance inspection," a drive around the B-1s to check that all streamers were removed and the planes were ready for takeoff.

The steel revetment wall in the hammerhead was supposedly there to protect commercial flights in case any weapons accidentally dropped on the runway and exploded. These days, almost all B-1 missions carried practice bombs, either small "beer can" bombs or concrete-filled bomb casings. But because it was only a replacement unit, Reno had no stockpiles of real weapons. All the weapons they might be called upon to use were stored at the weapons depot near Naval Air Station Fallon, and would be delivered to the base by rail. The steel wall was only window-dressing anyway—a two-thousand-pound Mark 84 would take out any aircraft and almost anything else above ground within a half mile of the blast.

A few minutes later, after the commercial flight had

departed, the first Bone taxied into position and ran its engines up to full afterburner takeoff power. Watching a B-1B Lancer on its takeoff roll was just as thrilling to him now as it had been the first time he saw one more than ten years ago. The bomber looked huge on its long, spindly legs with its wings fully extended, but when the pilot pushed those throttles up to full afterburner, it leaped down the runway like a cheetah.

The noise was not too bad—loud, like the old Boeing 727 that had taken off just before it, but not irritating. But when the afterburners were plugged in, the sound was deafening, a low, piercing harmonic rumbling that you could feel in the middle of your chest from two miles away. Surprisingly, there were few noise complaints. When they took off to the north, the Bones flew within a half mile of the Reno Hilton and right over John Ascuaga's Nugget Hotel and Casino, and they must certainly rattle the windows in those hotel towers! But Rinc had often seen hundreds of people gather outside the casinos to watch the Bones launch, especially during the rare nighttime launches when the bombers' afterburner plumes stretched a hundred feet across the sky. It was like a mini air show several times a week. The Bones were part of the city's attractions, like the glittering neon lights, the brothels, and the National Bowling Center. Eerie, a little ominous, yet curiously welcome. Nonetheless, takeoffs and landings between nine P.M. and seven A.M. were allowed only on weekends and only using military power, which produced about the same amount of noise as a commercial airliner.

Rinc must have been temporarily deafened after the Bone blasted off because he never heard her approach on the rooftop.

"Hello, Rodeo."

He turned, startled. There before him was Lieutenant Colonel Rebecca Furness.

He got to his feet, but as he stepped toward her, he sensed her body stiffening. "Rebecca, I . . . It's good to see you," he stammered.

Her eyes hardened, her jaw was set taut—and then she rushed into his arms. "Damn you to hell, Rinc," she whispered, pulling him tightly to her and kissing him hard and hungrily. Tasting her lips, Rinc felt like a man on the verge of drowning who had just taken a deep gulp of sweet, fresh air.

They kissed for a few lingering moments. He sat down on the bench and tried to pull her next to him, but she remained standing. "I've missed you so much," he said.

"Why didn't you call me?" she asked him, the hurt evident in her voice. "Why didn't you call to tell me you got back on flying status?"

"I was going to that night," Rinc said. "But the way you acted in the sim—I thought it was too early, maybe not right . . ."

"You're a real jerk sometimes, Rinc," Rebecca said angrily. "I love you. I care about you. You can't just cut me out like that. I've hardly heard from you at all since you got out of the hospital. You've never returned my calls, never called me . . ."

"I tried."

"Trying doesn't help. It hurts too much. And then to see you in the sim, duplicating the crash—that was worse. You were well enough to hunt for a different cause for the crash, but not well enough to want to see me. I decided the best I could do was let Long Dong chew on your butt for a while."

Her words sliced into Rinc's very soul. "Oh God, Beck, I am so sorry," he cried. "If I could, I'd trade my life for all of them. You know that, don't you?"

"Dammit, Seaver, don't you understand?" she said hotly. "No one wants you to trade your life for anyone

on your dead crew. No one wants to see you dead—
that's the *last* thing anyone wants. Especially me. We
want you to be one of us again. It's *you* that has this
chip on his shoulder. What you don't seem to get is that
we're all hurting . . . dammit, *I'm* hurting. I want you
back. I want you with me, the way it was before."

"The way it was before?" Rinc interjected. "What
was so great about that? Sneaking around? Not allowed even to come near each other in public for fear
someone might see us? Nothing but a series of one-
nighters . . ."

"Look, Rinc," she answered. "You know this was
the way it had to be. We talked it out when we first fell
in love—that we'd rather have each other part-time
than not at all. I am your squadron commander and
your superior officer. If anyone in this unit learned we
were sleeping together, I'd lose my job and you'd lose
all credibility. There wasn't any possibility of a normal
relationship. There still isn't—not until and unless we
both decide, together, that we're willing to make a serious career change—either you leave the Guard, or I do.
But you know all this—my God, we've hashed it out
over and over. What's the point of bringing it up again?
We're stuck with the decision we've made—to stay in,
and to see each other whenever and however we
could."

He started to speak but she cut him off, the pain
evident in her voice. "Listen, Rinc," she told him,
"however difficult it is, this still doesn't give you the
right to ignore me, to cut me out when I needed to
know that you were all right. It killed me to think that
you were in pain or needed my help. And after you
came out of the hospital it hurt even worse to be worrying that maybe you didn't want me anymore."

"You know that's not true," Rinc said. He took her
hand, and she raised it to her lips. "Oh, Beck, I've been

so lonely. I've missed you. I've missed your body tight up against mine, making love to you under the stars . . ."

"I'm here, Rodeo," she said. "I've missed you too, and I want you more than I can ever tell you." She paused, waiting. God yes, she wanted him, wanted him inside her *now*. But he needed to invite her. She wanted him to ask for her. When she was younger, she'd had plenty of men who just wanted sex, release. But no more. She was too old to simply provide a warm place to put it. She needed to love and be loved, and being loved meant being asked.

Still, she was not above doing a little prompting, especially for this man. She smiled at Rinc, took his hand, and ran it down the front of her body, letting it graze her breast and his fingers just barely tug at the waistline of her blue jeans. "Rinc?"

"I'd . . . I'd better get a little more studying done," she heard him say. He was watching her, watching for the hurt that he knew would spread across her face. "Hey, Beck, I'm sorry. It's just the check ride coming up, you know . . . it brings back some memories. The crash, the accident . . . I don't think I'd be much company."

"I understand—although I'm horny enough to do you right here on this rooftop, big guy." She smiled at him mischievously. "I'd be just as happy to talk with you and be with you if you'd like. Well, not *just* as happy, but it would be fine."

"I'm not sure if I want to talk about it, Beck. Ever."

"I know," Rebecca said sympathetically. But then she let her voice and her body harden. "People die in airplanes, Rinc," she told him. "It's a dangerous business. I know you, and I know—knew—Chappie and Mad Dog. We're all alike. We push the envelope hard.

That's how we survive—and sometimes don't. That's why we're the best."

"Then why does everyone blame me for the crash?" Rinc asked angrily. "Because I survived it? Why doesn't anyone believe me when I tell them that I'm not responsible for the crash?"

Rebecca reached out her hand to stroke his face. "I believe you, Rinc," she said.

"Like hell you do!" he shouted. "You're like everyone else—I punched out, so I must've either chickened out or caused the crash. That's bullshit. You and all the rest of this damned squadron can kiss my ass!" He pushed her hand away. "Leave me the hell alone, Colonel ma'am. I'm off the clock."

Furness choked down the sudden, gut-wrenching pain and found she was furious. "Fine with me," she said. "Whatever's eating on you, I hope you enjoy it—alone. Good-bye, Major, and I hope you go straight to hell."

He sat alone on the bench, steaming, looking down at his clenched fists. Minutes later there was the sound of footsteps coming up the stairs. It was a guy he'd never seen before. "Who the hell are you?" he barked.

"Sorry," the guy said. "I didn't mean to disturb you. I was looking for Lieutenant Colonel Furness. Thought she might be up here."

"You thought wrong."

The guy didn't move. Rinc was deciding whether to ignore him or chase him off the deck when he was surprised by a question: "You're Rinc Seaver, aren't you?"

"Who wants to know?"

"My name's McLanahan. Patrick McLanahan."

"So what?" The name registered somewhere in the back of Rinc's mind, vaguely connected to when he was just starting out in the active-duty Air Force, but he was too angry and too dejected to pursue it. "You can see Furness's not here, and I don't feel like company."

"It's tough, losing a crew. The guilt will stay with you the rest of your life."

Alarms went off in Rinc's head. Who was this guy? He knew way too much. All thoughts of losing Rebecca Furness as a friend and lover vanished, replaced by an intense wariness.

He got to his feet and sized up the stranger. This McLanahan was not too tall, not too short. He looked solidly built, like he worked out—most crewdogs these days were thin, so Rinc doubted he was a flier. His hair was blond with graying temples, cut shorter than Air Force reg 35-10 required. He wore an Air Force issue– brown leather flying jacket, with no rank or insignia on it, over his civvies. Rinc stepped closer and noticed that McLanahan didn't react—didn't back off, but didn't go on guard either.

"What'd you say your name was?" Rinc asked.

"McLanahan."

"Military?"

"Yes."

He didn't say his rank, which meant he was proba- bly a very low- or very high-ranking commissioned or noncommissioned officer. But by the way he acted, Rinc thought, the man most likely outranked him. What was going on here? "What unit?"

"Air Force headquarters. Office of the chief of staff."

Definitely outranked, Rinc decided—he was proba- bly a light colonel or colonel, maybe even a one-star. That explained a lot. He'd heard that the place was crawling with inspectors, investigators, and evaluators for weeks after the crash; in fact, he had been visited by a few of them while he was in the hospital recovering. But by the time he was out of the hospital, the investi- gation was just about wrapped up. It was one of the main reasons he felt such an urgency to get back on his feet and explore some alternate theories of the crash on his own in the simulator—he hadn't had a real opportunity to present his side of the story and time was short. And now that he was trying to get back in the cockpit, the investigators and evaluators were back—gunning directly for *him* this time.

"Don't tell me; let me guess. You're flying with me day after tomorrow," Rinc said. The guy was probably an ex-crewdog, tapped by someone in the chief of staff's office or some other Pentagon staffer to decide his fate. The only bright spot was that it meant the brass probably hadn't already made their decision. "You're going to do my evaluation for the squadron. You're also here to see what kind of shape my unit's in, whether we're ready to do the job or ready to be disbanded."

McLanahan nodded. Seaver's insight and honesty impressed him. "Exactly."

"We get just one day of mission prep before you decide my future? I don't get a Guard evaluator from my own unit? No sim ride with you first? That sucks."

"Major Seaver, if you think the process is unfair, you know you have only one recourse—you can vote with your feet," McLanahan said coldly.

"Everyone would like that, wouldn't they?" Rinc snorted. "You ever fly the Bone before, sir?"

"Yes." But before Rinc could ask the obvious question—when and where—McLanahan asked, "Are you in or out, Major?"

Rinc looked at McLanahan quizzically. A little evasive perhaps? Did this guy have a past, one he didn't want to talk about? Curiouser and curiouser. He shrugged. "I'll play it any way Air Force wants to play it. Sir," he replied.

"There you go," McLanahan said. "Proper attitude

adjustment achieved. I'll meet you at the squadron at six A.M. tomorrow, and we'll talk about your ride. If I think we'll need one, I'll schedule the simulator." Rinc knew the simulator was booked up for the next three weeks, but he had no doubt this guy could rearrange the schedule. "I'll tag along when you mission-plan with your crew at oh eight hundred."

"Fine by me."

"See you tomorrow, then." McLanahan headed for the stairs, then stopped and turned around. "There's a lot more healing to be accomplished beyond the hospital and the check ride," he said, looking down the stairs toward the parking lot where Seaver's dead partner's wife used to run. "You left the team when you punched out of that Bone. You've got to prove that you can be a part of it again."

"So I'm a putz because I survived, huh?"

"I guess you will be, if you believe you are," Patrick said.

"You think I caused that crash?"

"That's for the accident board to determine, not me," McLanahan replied. "I'm not here to pass judgment on what happened in the accident, Seaver—I'm here to judge if you're still able to be a combat-ready Air Guard B-1B aviator. But you can ace this check ride and still be on your way out. There are a hundred ways to do it."

"I know, sir," Rinc said. This was a very smart guy. It was tough to realize that his skills, knowledge, dedication, and experience suddenly meant nothing—that his fate was in the hands of someone else, plain and simple.

"I think you've got the picture. Get some rest—you'll need it. Tomorrow, oh six hundred." And he left without looking back.

· · ·

The big woman behind the bar gave Patrick an evil look as he stepped back inside. Both the place and the bartender had the same tough, hard-shelled atmosphere of the biker bars in his hometown of Sacramento that he had reluctantly tangled with in recent months, but the feel was completely different. Like the biker bars, this place sought to exclude strangers—but he sensed it also seemed to welcome future friends, especially military types.

Patrick walked over to the woman, about to ask where he could find the commander of the Air National Guard squadron, when she wordlessly jerked her head to the right, indicating a hallway. Well, she was consistent—she hadn't said anything earlier when he said he was looking for Seaver. But the nod had a kind of implicit warning to it—she's that way, but watch your step.

He followed the hallway. The two doors on the left were the rest rooms. One of the doors on the right looked as if it led to the storeroom or kitchen; the other door had a sign reading "Private." Patrick had had enough of going into strange rooms in the back of redneck locals-only taverns, but duty called. He took a deep breath and entered.

Patrick always hoped to find a place like this when he was in the military—maybe he hadn't looked hard enough, or maybe he really didn't want to find it or believe one even existed. In any case, it was a crewdog's idea of paradise.

Along with pictures of jets and models all over the walls and ceiling, the room had its own bar stocked even better than the one out front, slot machines, video games, old-fashioned pinball machines, a PC with flight simulator hardware installed, and card tables. It was a bigger room than he'd expected, and he saw half a dozen guys in flight suits, two of them sitting at the bar playing liar's dice, the other four playing cards.

"Who the hell are you?" asked one of the guys at the table.

"I'm looking for Lieutenant Colonel Furness."

The guy looked Patrick up and down, noting the flier's jacket. Didn't mean a damn—anyone can get one of those by mail order, lots of wannabes had them. "You didn't answer my question, ace. Who are you?"

"I'm Colonel Furness's two o'clock appointment," Patrick said.

The guy put his cards down and got up off his chair. He apparently knew nothing of the appointment and was clearly perplexed, even angry. "You should meet up with her in the squadron . . . sir," he said. He had suddenly turned much more polite—apparently realizing it was a good idea to be a bit more sociable until he learned exactly who the newcomer was. He noticed the guy wasn't surprised when he said Furness was a "her." "We can show you where the squadron is—it's on the other side of the airport. I'll page Colonel Furness immediately and tell her you've arrived. May I tell her your name and organization, please?"

"No," Patrick replied. "We can talk just as well here." He maneuvered around the guy and began to survey more of the room. The other squadron members stared at him in surprise.

The cardplayer decided to drop a bit of his nice-guy routine. "I'm the colonel's operations officer and second-in-command, and I don't know anything about a meeting this afternoon. Are you sure the meeting with Colonel Furness was for today?"

"Yes, Colonel Long."

John Long blanched. Shit, he thought, he knows who I am. "The colonel is probably back at the squadron right now, sir," he said. "Perhaps you'd better head on over there." He motioned to one of the guys at the card table. "Bonzo, take this gentleman to headquarters. I'll page the colonel."

"I don't have an appointment with you or anyone else today, sir," came a woman's stern voice, "and I'd appreciate it if you'd be a little more candid with my men. The colonel asked your name. You can tell us, or you can get out."

Patrick turned and found Lieutenant Colonel Rebecca Furness standing right behind him. She was every bit as attractive as her official photos, but that took away none of the iron in her voice. Back when she was flying the RF-111G Vampire reconnaissance/attack planes as a flight leader and the Air Force's first female combat pilot, Furness had earned the appellation "the Iron Maiden." Patrick could see right away that it was deserved.

"We need to talk, Colonel," Patrick said, allowing his eyes to survey her body.

Furness didn't react—but John Long did. "Hey, asshole," Long said angrily, "the lady said scram. You better leave or we'll *help* you out." A few of the squadron members started to move closer to the stranger.

"Colonel Long, sit down and relax," Patrick suggested, continuing to stare at Furness. "We're going to be working together for a long time—if you're lucky." He turned, went over to one of the slot machines, put in a quarter, and pulled the handle. A ten-dollar winner dropped a satisfying tinkle of coins into the tray. "Looks like I'm pretty lucky. You guys aren't. Or maybe that's *all* you guys are—just dumb lucky." He left the money in the tray.

"Who the hell are you?" Furness demanded.

"My name is McLanahan, Colonel. Brigadier General Patrick McLanahan. From Air Force headquarters.

General Hayes's staff." There was a startled silence in the room at the news that a one-star general had walked into the middle of their "unit training session."

"I see," Furness said. "Do you have ID, General? Orders?"

"Yes," McLanahan replied. He withdrew a set of orders and his green Air Force ID card.

Furness checked the card and scanned the orders, her eyes narrowing in confusion. They were the shortest set of TDY orders she'd ever seen. She handed them to John Long. "These orders don't say shit," Long said. "It's just a bunch of account codes."

"I'd like something that tells me what you want with my squadron on my base, sir," Rebecca said.

"Okay." Patrick reached into his pocket, pulled out a tiny cellular telephone, and tossed it to Furness. She caught it in surprise. "Speed-dial one for General Bretoff in Carson City." Adam Bretoff was the adjutant general of the state of Nevada, the commander of all Army and Air National Guard forces in the state. "Speed-dial two for General Hayes at the Pentagon. Speed-dial three for the secretary of the Air Force. Speed-dial four for the secretary of defense."

Furness looked at the phone, then opened it and looked at the keypad. "Who's speed-dial five?" she asked flippantly.

"Try it and find out, Colonel. But be *very* polite."

Furness glanced at McLanahan. "I'll call your bluff, General," she said, then hit some buttons. She was surprised to hear the beeps of a digital scrambler. A moment later she heard "Bretoff here and secure. Go ahead."

Furness swallowed in disbelief, unable to control her surprise. She recognized the adjutant general's voice immediately—the call went right to the secure phone on his desk, not to the comm center, his aide, or a clerk.

This guy was carrying a *secure* cell phone—she didn't even know they existed! "Colonel Furness here, sir."

"Problem, Rebecca?"

No pleasantries, no chitchat. She decided that the other speed-dial buttons on the phone were too hot to even *think* about right now. "Just verifying the identity of the gentleman who was sent over here this afternoon."

"Are you secure?"

Furness stepped as far as she could away from the noisy video poker machines. "Yes, sir," she replied.

"McLanahan, Patrick S., brigadier general, Air Force," Bretoff said. "Came from the chief of staff's office. Identity verified. Is he there already?"

"Standing right in front of me now, sir. I'm using his cell phone."

"You'll get a classified memo first thing in the morning informing you about his arrival," Bretoff said. "Frankly, I'm not sure what he wants, but whatever it is, give it to him."

"His written orders don't say anything about what he's doing here."

"He doesn't need any other written orders. He'll brief you on what you need to do. Give it to him. Anything."

"Say again, sir?"

"I said, give the general anything he wants," Bretoff repeated. "Treat him like the inspector general."

"What's his clearance?"

"Colonel Furness," the adjutant general said with exasperation in his voice, "am I not making myself clear? Whatever the man wants, he gets. Full access. Full authority. Whatever he says, goes. He's got a clearance you or I have never heard of. Two hours ago I had the governor in my office and the secretary of the Air

Force on a conference call. *They* don't even have this guy's security clearance."

"Sir, I understand what you're saying," Furness said, "but it's damned irregular. I'd like written confirmation of my orders."

"Written orders have been red-jacketed and placed in your personnel file, Colonel—and in mine," Bretoff went on. "If you want, you can come down here to the vault and look at them. In the meantime, do whatever the man says. Understand?"

"Loud and clear, sir."

"Good. And, Colonel?"

"Sir?"

"Don't let anyone in the squadron go anywhere near the back room of that bar, the Quarry or whatever it's called, the one you guys hang out at near the airport, until this guy departs," Bretoff said. "The last goddamn thing we need is for a high-powered scalp hunter like McLanahan to see how depraved you characters are. In fact, I don't want any of you near that entire establishment until he leaves. Try showing your faces in the SANGA club for a change. We don't have all-night poker or play dollar-a-ball eight ball, but you might actually enjoy yourselves there anyway. Got it?"

Furness grimaced, and McLanahan smiled, as if he could hear everything. "Yes, sir." The line went dead after another chatter of digital descrambling beeps. Furness carefully closed up the phone and handed it back to McLanahan.

"You don't want to try any of the other numbers?" McLanahan asked. "It's not too late to call Washington."

"Boss? What's the story?" Long asked, dumbfounded by the expression on Furness's face.

"This is Brigadier General McLanahan, boys," Furness said. She made introductions to all of the squadron officers in the room. "He's going to be with us for a while. You are to extend him every courtesy and comply with each and every request as if it was an order from the adjutant general himself."

"We should show him a *little* more courtesy than that," someone said *sotto voce*.

"Knock that shit off, gentlemen," Furness said, her amused eyes studying McLanahan. "Please excuse that remark, sir. Some of my crew have been on edge. We've had a lot of investigators and other unwanted attention lately . . ."

"Yes indeed—a dead crew and a smoking hole in the desert," Patrick said. The smiles and whispered comments vanished, replaced by angry glares. He looked around and added, "Good to see you're taking the accident and the corrective action seriously."

"Of course we are. But you can't just order men to forget about the deaths of their friends and fellow crew members, General," Rebecca answered. "It takes time. Please understand—this unit has been through a lot lately. We all deal with grief differently."

"I see. Well, I can help you through some of your turmoil a little, Colonel. I came here to administer a requalification check."

Furness frowned in confusion. "Yes, sir," she said formally, neither agreeing nor disagreeing. "We can set up an orientation flight for you. Major Seaver isn't currently qualified to fly the B-1, but . . ."

"I know that. I will administer his requalification checkout. Emergency procedures check in the sim tomorrow, then a flight ASAP."

"I see," Furness said, again noncommittally. "I would prefer that his requal ride be done by someone in the Nevada Guard. I would also like to know your qualifications, sir. Are you qualified to fly the Bone?"

"Doesn't matter now, does it, Colonel?" Patrick replied.

Furness looked furious but held her anger in check. "Very good, sir. Well, this ought to be fun." She slapped her hands together in mock excitement. "Well then, we've got a lot of work to do. Why don't we get you set up in a hotel, schedule a meeting to review Seaver's paperwork and fitness reports, and—"

"You don't seem to understand, Colonel," Patrick interjected. "I'm not here just to give Seaver his flight check, and I think we'll all be too busy to worry about hotel rooms."

"Then what the hell *are* you . . . pardon me, sir, but what are you here for, then?"

Patrick reached into his jacket pocket and withdrew an envelope. Furness saw the code "A-72" on it. Her eyes bugged out and her breath caught in her throat. He handed her the envelope. "You've just been notified, Colonel, that your squadron has seventy-two hours to put bombs on target and then deploy to a remote operations base to begin simulated long-range bombardment operations. Your unit's predeployment evaluation has just begun. The clock is ticking, and as of right now, *I* am keeping score."

"*What?*" Furness exploded. She grabbed the envelope and tore it open. Sure enough, it was a standard Air Force warning-order message, stamped "Confidential," directing an air strike against simulated targets in the Nellis bombing ranges in southern Nevada. The strike would be followed by a deployment of not more than two weeks to an undisclosed location to conduct night and day bombing operations from a bare-base location. "This has got to be a joke!" the squadron commander shouted. "I don't know you! I can't generate seven Bones on your say-so only!"

At that moment, John Long's cell phone beeped. He

answered it immediately, listened, then closed it up. "Boss, the airfield operations manager just got a fax from Bretoff's office, notifying them that intensive Air Guard operations will commence this afternoon."

"That message was supposed to be secret," McLanahan said. He shrugged. "You've got a good intelligence operation here, Colonel, I'll give you that." It was common courtesy for evaluators to give a "heads-up" to certain folks, such as local air traffic control facilities, before an exercise kicked off. It was also common for air traffic control facility managers to slip a heads-up call to the military guys when an exercise was about to commence, even though the information was supposed to be kept under wraps to enhance the shock and surprise element of the exercise.

"Also, Reno Approach Control reports a KC-135 twenty miles out, call sign 'Blitz Nine-Nine,' " Long went on. The "99" suffix was a common one used by evaluation teams. "RAPCON says he's parking at Mercury Air for two weeks and is requesting COMSEC procedures in effect for the Air Guard." That, too, was typical of the kickoff of an exercise. From now on, under COMSEC, or communications security procedures, all movements of Air National Guard aircraft except for safety-of-flight concerns were not to be reported on open radio or phone lines.

Furness looked at McLanahan with a combination of irritation and surprise, then eased up. The predeployment exercise was usually conducted at another B-1B bomber base, usually with the unit flying out and beginning there—but nothing in the regs said it couldn't start right at home base with a no-notice deployment generation exercise and Furness, like most good fliers, hated surprises.

But she also loved challenges, loved excitement, loved action. Exercises involving recalls, generations, en route bombing, and deployments were right there beside actual combat on the list of things that made Rebecca Furness's blood race. McLanahan saw the fire ignite in her eyes. He was pleased.

"Long Dong, initiate a squadron recall," Furness ordered. "Get Dutch and Clock's sorties back on the ground on the double. The battle staff meets in fifteen minutes with their checklists open and ready to go, and I will personally kick the ass of the man or woman who is not in their seat ready to go by the time I get there. Notify Creashawn on the secure line, have them start a recall, and get ready to move live weapons for the entire fleet on my orders." Creashawn Arsenal was the large weapons storage facility near Naval Air Station Fallon where live weapons for the B-1s were stored. "Then call Bretoff secure and inform him I'm generating my fleet for combat operations. Reference General McLanahan's written orders and his own verbal orders."

As Long got on his cell phone to initiate the recall, Furness turned to McLanahan, a mischievous smile on her lips and a malevolent glow in her eyes. She looked him up and down, then said, "McLanahan. I once heard of a McLanahan from a friend of mine, the chief of staff of the Lithuanian Army. He told some pretty extraordinary stories about him. Any relation, sir?"

"Maybe."

"Interesting." Furness grinned. "This McLanahan was in charge of some pretty cosmic stuff, real Buck Rogers high-tech gear, made for bombers." There was no response. She nodded, then asked, "You ready for this, General McLanahan? We move pretty fast around here."

"I'll be with you the entire way," Patrick said. "When the sorties launch, I want to be manifested with Seaver as copilot. He'll be number two in your flight."

Furness glared at McLanahan in surprise. "I can't do

that, sir," she said. "I'm not going to put an unqualified person in the right seat during a live weapons mission. It's unsafe." She looked at him warily. "Or are you going to pull rank on this too?"

"Yes, I was," Patrick said, "but I'll make you a deal: I'll fly in the copilot's seat with Seaver in the sim. If you don't think I know my shit well enough, you can kick me out. Deal?"

"Deal," Furness said. "Have fun flying in the DSO's seat, sir."

"Don't bet on it, Colonel," Patrick said with a smile. He glanced over at John Long and added, "Put Colonel Long in my OSO's seat."

"Whatever you want, sir," Furness responded. Then she shouted to the rest of the squadron members, "Get your asses moving, you grunts! That's the last time I want to see any of you hogs standing around with your thumbs up your asses! Now *move!*"

THE WHITE HOUSE OVAL OFFICE,
WASHINGTON, D.C.
THAT SAME TIME

It's good of you to come, Minister Kang," the President of the United States said. He shook hands warmly with Minister of Foreign Affairs Kang No-myong of the Republic of Korea. With him in the Oval Office were Vice President Ellen Christine Whiting, Secretary of Defense Arthur Chastain, and White House Chief of Staff Jerrod Hale. Official White House photographers took photos of the handshakes; no reporters were present.

"Mr. President, Madam Vice President, Secretary Chastain, Mr. Hale, may I please introduce the South

Korean minister of defense, retired general Kim Kun-mo," Minister Kang said in broken but very under-standable English. General Kim bowed deeply, then shook hands with each American. His Korean transla-tor was also introduced, and all were led to seats around the coffee table in the Oval Office. As refresh-ments were served, the photographers snapped a few more shots of the leaders making small talk, then de-parted. The visitors looked around the famous White House Oval Office, as wide-eyed and awed as any con-gressman's constituent on a "photo opportunity" visit. Jerrod Hale remained standing in his usual place behind and to the right of the President.

"This is an unexpected but certainly welcome visit, gentlemen," President Martindale began politely. "We all knew that you were both in our country visiting military installations and preparing to address the United Nations. I'm glad we have this chance to get together." The Koreans bowed in thanks.

Unexpected, yes—welcome, no, the President thought. Nearing the end of a tumultuous first term in the White House, following two terms as Vice Presi-dent, the fifty-one-year-old divorced Texan, a former state attorney general, U.S. senator, and secretary of defense, was in the midst of the greatest fight of his long political life. He was knowledgeable in foreign and mil-itary affairs, but it seemed that almost every foreign policy decision he had made in recent years, especially those involving his military forces, had cost him dearly at home. And having Asian political and military lead-ers pop in on him at the White House was never good news.

"We thank you most profoundly for the honor of meeting with you in person, Mr. President," Minister Kang said formally. Kang was pudgy, with thick glasses and greased-back straight black hair. He was a sharp contrast to General Kim's wiry body, chiseled face, and cold, steady eyes. Nonetheless, despite Kang's disarming features, Martindale knew he was an expert strategist and businessman, the former head of one of the most powerful oceangoing shipping companies in the world.

As impressive as Kang's background was, General Kim's was even more so. He had risen through the ranks from conscript to chairman of the chiefs of staff of the South Korean military. He had survived innumerable purges, dismissals, and outright assassination attempts, only to emerge stronger and wiser after every encounter with his foes. Kevin Martindale stared into Kim's eyes and saw the general staring unabashedly right back at him, unblinking, challenging.

What was it like, Martindale asked himself, to live in a country like South Korea? The entire peninsula had been a pawn in an Asian chess match spanning many centuries. Like so many other world hot spots today—Iran, Iraq, Kuwait, Germany, Africa, Israel, the Balkans—his country was spawned out of the ashes of war, trampled, blood-soaked land divided up between conquering invaders. But because the lines drawn on a map rarely take into account the social and cultural differences of a nation, the warring never ended for countries like South Korea. Kim's country had known either foreign occupation or political and societal schizophrenia for centuries. What was that like? It sounded like an unending civil war.

Martindale noticed Kim give him a subtle smile and a nod before resuming his unblinking stare. It was as if he knew what Martindale was thinking and was thanking him for trying to understand. Although the President did not show it, Kim gave him the creeps. There was a war raging in that man's head as well as in his homeland, the President decided.

Jerrod Hale noted Kim's defiant gaze. He shifted his position slightly. It had the desired effect: it caught Kim's attention. "I hope you're finding your tour of our military installations informative, General Kim," Hale said when Kim looked at him, his voice neutral, neither friendly nor challenging. The translator passed along Hale's words; Kim bowed deeply in response but remained silent. The two men looked at each other unblinkingly. But Jerrod Hale, a former Los Angeles County prosecutor and police commissioner and a longtime political ramrod, took intimidation from no one. As he stood by the most powerful man in the Western world, in the most prized hall of power on earth, General Kim respectfully averted his eyes.

"Mr. President, I wanted to personally deliver to you some very disturbing and alarming evidence that we recently acquired," Minister Kang said. He withdrew a folder from a briefcase. "I apologize if these pictures offend your sensibilities, Mr. President. I only offer them because of the enormous gravity of the situation they portend."

Martindale studied them, his eyes narrowing in shock, then wordlessly passed them along to Vice President Whiting. She swallowed a gasp when she saw the photograph of the mangled, emaciated corpse of the North Korean fighter pilot. "Please explain, Minister Kang," Martindale said.

"This starving, near-frozen man was at the controls of a North Korean attack jet that was shot down over South Korea," Kang responded. "He was en route to Seoul."

"An attack jet?" Secretary Chastain asked.

"A fighter-bomber on a one-way suicide mission, carrying two gravity bombs," General Kim said via the translator. "Two *nuclear* bombs."

Whiting's mouth opened in surprise; Chastain and

the President exchanged shocked expressions. "My God!" the President gasped. "Were they live weapons? Fully functional? What yield?"

"Older but fully functioning weapons of Chinese design, in perhaps the six-hundred-kiloton-yield range," Kang replied. He handed Chastain a folder. "Here is an analysis of the weapons, as conducted by our military intelligence division. It is in effect a standard Chinese medium-range ballistic missile reentry vehicle warhead, modified for gravity bomb use. A rather dated design, not very efficient or reliable. Discarded many decades ago by Communist China because of a lack of safety features, large design, and heavy carriage weight."

"Were the weapons destroyed when you shot down the aircraft?" Chastain asked.

"No."

"Then you recovered them?" Kang nodded. "Were they intact?"

"Yes, sir," Kang replied. "The weapons have filled in many vital pieces of a giant puzzle that our intelligence agencies have been investigating for years. We have suspected the presence of nuclear weapons in the North, but now, after examining the components of the bombs, we have pinpointed the locations of several bases and facilities that manufacture these and other weapons of mass destruction.

"What we now know, Mr. President, is that the Communists have nine key bases, mostly in the north close to the Chinese border and in the central part of the country," Kang went on. "They not only manufacture and stockpile nuclear, chemical, and biological weapons, but they are also staging bases for air and rocket attacks using these weapons against targets in the South, against Japan, and against American bases as far away as Alaska. The evidence is incontrovertible."

"Jesus," the President murmured. He turned to Hale.

"Jerrod, get Admiral Balboa and Director Plank over here immediately." Hale was dialing his staff before the President finished the order.

"We would like to examine these weapons as soon as possible and assist in destroying them," Secretary Chastain said. "We would also like to examine your intelligence material, allow us to update our own records, and verify your data with our own intelligence assets."

The President noted that, after the translation, General Kim seemed agitated, as if barely controlling his rising anger. Minister Kang hesitated uneasily for a moment, glancing at Kim nervously, then replied, "I have provided all the pertinent information on the incident and the weapons in that file, Mr. President."

"Does that mean you don't want to let us see those weapons, Minister?" Martindale asked.

Again, Kang squirmed uneasily. "Mr. President, we will of course gladly provide you and your intelligence staff with anything you request." Hearing the translator's version, General Kim seemed irritated at the equivocal statement, but he said nothing. Kang went on: "But I have been instructed to beg you for your advice and assistance in dealing with the threat from the Communists in the North once and for all. The threat to our peace and security is real, and it is at the breaking point. My government feels it must act."

"Act? How? In what way? What do you want us to do?"

Kang took a deep breath, then said, "Mr. President, we plan to invade North Korea and destroy all of the bases identified as attack staging locations. We want the attack to begin immediately, within the next two or three days."

"*What?*" Martindale exclaimed. "You want to *attack North Korea?* That's insane!"

"Mr. President, the inevitable fact is that one of two

things will happen," Kang explained. "Either North Korea will be emboldened or provoked into attacking my country, or it will collapse under the sheer weight of its corrupt, bankrupt, and morally wasted system of government. A revolution or coup is impossible; President Kim is far more ruthless than his father. The North will not shed communism like East Germany because it is more isolated politically, geographically, and socioeconomically than the European Communist nations."

"It will also not shed communism because of the influence of China," the President interjected, "and that's a major reason why any military attack against North Korea will result in disaster—China will certainly come to North Korea's aid. At best, an attack will ignite another war on the Korean peninsula. At worst, it could start a global nuclear war."

"If I may speak frankly, sir," Kang said, referring to recent events all too vivid in the President's memory, "the world's opinion was that an attack by any nation against an American aircraft carrier, or against such a strategically important territory as the island of Guam, would be immediately met by a full thermonuclear retaliation. Yet this did not happen . . ."

"We don't know the *Independence* was attacked by China," Secretary of Defense Arthur Chastain retorted, almost apologetically. "It could've been any number of terrorist groups . . ." But then he fell silent. The follow-up to that was obvious: there was no doubt about who had attacked Taiwan or Guam.

The President held up a hand. "Arthur, no need to try to come to my defense," he said. "Yes, I suppose I had every right to order a full nuclear retaliation against China. I suppose if I had, few would have said I acted rashly or without sufficient provocation. Our nuclear forces had been fully mobilized, and the location of China's ICBMs and nuclear bomber fleet was pin-pointed. And it is true that we've spent trillions of dollars developing a force to deter such an attack, but when deterrence failed, I did not use those forces."

The President leaned forward, looked Kang in the eye, and said, "The world might very well believe ours is a hollow force, that if we can't protect our own forces and won't avenge an attack against a vital territory, we certainly won't come to the aid of a foreign ally. Is that what South Korea believes now, Minister Kang? Do you feel that the United States won't protect you? Do you believe we're so impotent?"

Before Kang could respond, Martindale glanced at General Kim and got his answer: absolutely. Kim clearly believed that the United States would not risk war with China if North Korea invaded the South.

"Of course not, Mr. President," Minister Kang replied, looking Martindale in the eye in return. "The United States is a valuable and trusted ally, and it will always be so. But there are many in my government who feel that the time for reckoning is upon us and that we gain the upper hand by taking the initiative."

General Kim spoke, sharply and resolutely. Kang did not even attempt to stop him. The translator said, "The general says, 'The threat is real, Mr. President. We have a definite set of targets before us, and we have the resources and the will to strike a swift, crippling, but surgical blow. You must support us, sir. You must. We may not be so fortunate to stop the Communists' next desperate attack.' "

"Let us see your data and verify it," President Martindale said. "A few more weeks, perhaps after the Team Spirit exercises are concluded—North Korea's forces will be on high alert anyway, and I don't think you'd want to start a fight with all of their forces poised for war. If what you say is true, let us work together to . . ."

General Kim opened a folder and angrily tossed it on the coffee table in front of the President and his advisers. The interpreter translated his angry words: "The general says, 'Here is our evidence, sir. Three bunkers in Kanggye, Chagang province, loaded with Vx nerve gas warheads suitable for surface-to-surface missiles. Verified. The main Western Air Combat Command air base at Sunan, with twenty-four F-4 fighter-bombers on alert loaded with Vx and anthrax munitions. Verified. The new naval and air base at Hungnam, with eighteen Scud-B missiles on alert loaded with biological and chemical warheads, plus six Scud-C missiles *with nuclear warheads*. Verified. Also at Hungnam, the frigate *Najin,* with long-range high-speed SS-N-9 antiship missiles with nuclear warheads, not old SS-N-2 missiles as we once believed.' "

Secretary of Defense Chastain was thunderstruck. He examined the photographs, scanned the translations of the field agents' reports and observations. "This is . . . this is incredible," he stammered. "I had no idea North Korea had so many WMDs in their possession."

"All the same, General, even if we verify all this evidence, we can't rush into anything," Vice President Whiting said. "We need to confront the North in a global forum, show the world the evidence, and gauge the reaction of China, Russia, and the other Asian powers. There may be a way we can defuse this thing peacefully."

"This will also give us a chance to start organizing our own forces," Secretary Chastain said worriedly. "If you start a war now, with a lot of our forces ready to participate only in an exercise, we'll be scrambling to respond if a general war breaks out. If we move forces into the region slowly and gradually, we can have a sizable force in place and ready to prevent the conflict from spreading and to give you maximum assistance— and we won't look like we're itching for a fight."

As the translator finished, it was obvious that General Kim didn't like what he heard. As the translation progressed, he had lowered his head so that his emotions were concealed.

"I promise you, General Kim, Minister Kang," the President said, "that I will use all the forces in our arsenal to protect and defend the Republic of Korea. But an attack against the North is out of the question. The risk of China entering the conflict and retaliating with special weapons is too great. They've already proved their willingness to use them outside their borders. I think they would use them against anyone who dared stage a preemptive attack on North Korea."

General Kim spoke again, and the translator said, "The general has asked Minister Kang to explain about our special forces apparatus, already in place."

"What special forces apparatus?" the President asked.

"I have not been authorized to divulge this," Minister Kang explained nervously. But General Kim barked at him in Korean, which everyone guessed meant, "Go ahead, damn you, tell them." Kang swallowed hard and went on, "The general speaks of our newly formed Reconnaissance and Operations Department. It is a mirror group to North Korea's Reconnaissance Bureau of the General Staff. It is composed of Regular Army soldiers and elite special operations forces, trained"—he swallowed hard again—"trained by Russian intelligence officers."

"*Russians!*" Chastain exclaimed. "You have a clandestine military organization trained by *Russians?*"

"Why in the world would you do that?" Vice President Whiting asked incredulously. The President was silent; the appearance of the two famous silver locks of hair curling across his forehead was the only sign of his anger and concern. "What makes you think the Russians aren't passing along information on this group to the North Koreans?"

"Because we pay them far more than the North Koreans could ever possibly hope to," Kang replied matter-of-factly. "The Russians gave North Korea billions of rubles' worth of training, equipment, and expertise in setting up their infiltration, sabotage, subversion, and terrorist network, and they were given nothing in return. We now get even better assistance from the Russians, and they receive millions of dollars' worth of aid in return."

"We . . . we knew nothing about this," Vice President Whiting exclaimed. "This should have been approved by us in advance, Minister Kang. This could compromise all of America's intelligence operations in Asia—perhaps even all over the world."

"We have also used our new sources and agents to back-check and cross-check the North Korean government," Kang responded. "I assure you, no American or allied intelligence sources or methods have been compromised. No information on the Reconnaissance and Operations Department exists in North Korea . . . or China."

"China?" Chastain asked. "You've infiltrated China too?"

"At the highest levels, civilian and military," Kang said. "We know the exact disposition of Chinese military forces within a thousand miles of the Korean peninsula, and we know exactly the chain of command, communications routing, codes, and procedures for relaying orders from Beijing to the field units. We can shut down the Chinese command and control system and all links to North Korea in a matter of minutes."

Kang turned to President Martindale, true excitement building on his face. "Sir, we have operatives spread throughout North Korea and China, in the most sensitive and valuable locations. Over the past several months, they have created a vast network of informants, activists, propagandists, and agents in every level of society, government, the universities, and the military. It is not merely meant to destroy and kill, although we can do this if we wished. It is primarily meant to reassure our North Korean brothers that we are ready to help them unify the peninsula and the Korean people.

"What we have determined is that the people of North Korea are with us," Kang went on. "The revolution is growing. It is not just a political revolution, but an ideological, cultural, and religious revolution as well. It is repressed, of course, because of the oppressive Communist regime, but as in the former Communist East Germany and Russia, it is alive and spreading. All it needs is a spark. That spark is the Republic of Korea, and the time to ignite it is *now*."

"This is incredible, absolutely astounding," Chastain said. "It'll take time to assess this extraordinary news . . ."

"Time is a luxury we cannot afford, Mr. Secretary," said Kang. "The North can launch a devastating attack at any moment."

"I'm sorry, Minister, but we can't afford to act rashly," the President replied. As the interpreter translated for General Kim, it was obvious the Korean commander was growing angrier by the second. Martindale went on, "We need to analyze the information from your Reconnaissance and Operations Department, verify it independently, discuss it here in Washington, formulate a plan, then present it to our congressional leaders for funding and approval." General Kim barked something in Korean at Kang, then glared at him impatiently. Kang kept his eyes on Martindale, not reacting; but it was obvious that the two Koreans were not receptive. "You have something on your mind, Minister Kang," the President said warily. "Let's hear it."

"We have, as you say, placed all our cards on the table, sir," Minister Kang said. "I understand your concerns and your desire to study and discuss this information. We do not wish to inconvenience you any longer with our presence. I thank you for your time and attention. I would be happy to convey your concern and thoughts to my government."

"We would like to hear what General Kim has to say, Minister," Martindale said stonily.

Kim shook his head sharply. Kang seemed relieved. "The general seems to have nothing more to add, Mr. President. Therefore, I thank you again for—"

"Hold on a minute, Mr. Minister," the President said. Addressing Kim directly, he said, "If you have something on your mind, General, now's the time to say it."

Kang got up. "Thank you for your hospitality, sir."

Suddenly, Kim exploded. He shot to his feet, firing words at Martindale, at Chastain, at Kang. Kang shouted something in return, but Kim would not be stopped.

"What did they say? Translate!" the President ordered.

"General Kim says that you have become too timid in the face of the Chinese," the interpreter said. "He says that you are too concerned with your image and your reelection to risk it all by defending democratic Korea's peace and freedom. He says you," turning his head to Chastain, "counsel caution and 'wait and see' in safety while free Koreans worry about a nuclear holocaust. And he says that Minister Kang has not the courage to tell the Americans that if they will not help us, we will do what we must to protect our homeland. Minister Kang ordered the general to be silent or he will see to it that he is relieved of duty. The general says he will lead his forces to victory over the Communists whether or not he gets any help from the weakling Americans."

The angry voices had penetrated outside the Oval Office, and at that moment Secret Service guards burst inside, automatic pistols leveled. Two plainclothes officers reached for the President, ready to shield him with their bodies. "No!" he shouted. "Wait!"

Kang shouted something at Kim, but Kim was already headed for the open door. More plainclothes and uniformed guards were ready to tackle him. "Let him go," the President ordered. He turned to Kang. "Minister Kang, I want to talk with President Kwon immediately. If you're considering war with North Korea, you must wait until I have had a chance to talk with him."

"I assure you, Mr. President, we are not contemplating war with the North," Kang said. "Many in my government are gravely concerned, but we agree that the best hope we have is calling the world community's attention to the North's aggression, backed up with the power and influence of the United States of America. But we must have assurances that America will support my country in our efforts."

"I'll tell President Kwon that he will always have the full protection and support of the United States," Martindale said. "But listen carefully: we must not be blindsided or railroaded into war because some hotheads in your government like General Kim think they can ignore the Chinese and can whip the North Koreans into submission overnight. We'll fight by your side, but we want this to be a partnership. I can't sell it to the American people any other way."

Kang looked deeply hurt at that, hurt that the President had to "sell" the idea of protecting South Korea to the American people. His face was grim as he said, "I see, Mr. President." He bowed deeply. "I am very sorry to have disturbed you and disrupted the peace of this eminent place. I personally apologize and take full responsibility for General Kim's behavior. If you will excuse me." And with that he left, neither looking up nor shaking hands.

Martindale, Whiting, Chastain, and Hale looked at one another as if in a daze. "What the hell was *that*?" Chastain asked incredulously.

"Let me hear it, folks—are the South Koreans planning anything?" the President asked. "Will they actually attack these targets?"

"I'd want to get some briefings from Central Intelligence," Chastain offered, "but offhand, I'd say the Korean government is certainly leaning toward taking some kind of action. Kim seemed ready to charge across the DMZ by himself right this minute."

"There is no way on God's green earth that President Kwon can actually believe he could successfully stage an attack against North Korea unless we were totally behind him and ready to step in," Vice President Whiting said. "He knows he wouldn't stand a chance. North Korea's military outnumbers his forces three to one. And China must have more cooks than Kwon has troops in his entire military. I think this incident with the nukes just spooked them. Kim's was the voice of the hotheads wanting revenge—Kang's was the voice of moderation. I don't see a war happening."

"Don't guess, Mr. President," Jerrod Hale said. "Call President Kwon. Ask him point-blank. Tell him how you feel. If you find he wants war, tell him to wait and suggest a peaceful alternative. If he still cares about one."

At that moment, Joint Chiefs of Staff Chairman Admiral George Balboa and Director of Central Intelligence Robert Plank entered the Oval Office. "That looked like South Korea's foreign minister leaving the White House," Plank said. "Was he here?"

"He was here—and he dropped a bombshell on us," the President said, returning to his desk. "I want a full rundown of the military situation on the Korean peninsula, including a complete accounting of all of South Korea's forces, and I needed it an hour ago." Then he picked up the phone, called the White House Communications Center, and ordered a call placed to President Kwon Ki-chae of South Korea.

CHAPTER THREE

111TH BOMB SQUADRON RAMP,
RENO-TAHOE INTERNATIONAL AIRPORT,
RENO, NEVADA
TWO DAYS LATER

Impressive as hell, Muck," said Dave Luger. "That's it in a nutshell. Very damned impressive."

Patrick McLanahan took a sip of coffee and raised an eyebrow in surprise as he sat in the back of a large blue StepVan, used by his evaluation team as their mobile headquarters. It was a couple of hours before dawn, right at the twelve-hour safety-of-flight crew rest time limit prescribed by regulation for all fliers. It was damned early, much too early, but Patrick was determined not to let his team leaders—who certainly had had much longer days than he—see how tired he was.

With him inside the van were Patrick's old friend and partner Lieutenant Colonel David Luger, acting as chief of the maintenance and weapons inspection team; Lieutenant Colonel Hal Briggs, chief of the security and administrative inspection team; and Lieutenant Colonel Nancy Cheshire, chief of the command and control and services inspection team. They were parked on the Air National Guard ramp, just outside the entry control point of the long aircraft parking ramp. The line of sleek, deadly B-1B bombers, illuminated in the harsh yellow glow of overhead "ball park" lights, filled the place with excitement. Maintenance vehicles and crews moved around purposefully. To this unit, this was no exercise—it was the real thing. Aces High was going to war, and every man and woman in the small unit, from the airman basic cook in the in-flight kitchen to the commander, knew it.

"All of the planes came up with only minor squawks," Luger went on. Dave Luger was a tall, lanky Texan, a former B-52 navigator who now worked as chief project engineer under Patrick McLanahan at the supersecret Dreamland research facility. "Seven bombers fully configured and ready to fly. The biggest hitch was getting weapons from the Navy depot at Creashawn, but once they showed up, they uploaded them without any deficiencies."

"None?" Patrick asked incredulously.

"None," Dave assured him. "Seven B-1s with mixed payloads—twenty-eight Mark 82 AIRs in the forward bay, a rotary launcher with eight GBU-32 JDAMs in the mid bay, and ten CBU-87s in the aft bay—all went up on time without a major glitch. I'm going to have to nitpick to find something to ding 'em on.

"The place is amazing, Muck. You know how you can tell how a unit is going to function as soon as you walk in just by looking at the floors? I knew these guys had their shit together the minute I walked in there. The floors are so clean you can eat off them. They look like they *polish* their weapon-jammers and tow bars, not just clean them."

"Every unit spit shines their gear when an inspection team's on base," Patrick pointed out.

"But you can usually tell if the spit shine is cosmetic, done once a year, or if it's done regularly—and around here, it's obviously done a lot," Dave said. "Besides, this was a no-notice inspection—there was no time to spit shine every tool, every shop, every workbench, every rack. It was already done. And remember, this unit thought they were on their way to Ellsworth or Dyess for their pre-D. Why clean every piece of equipment *before* dragging it all off station?

"A big help around here is the crewdogs," Luger went on. "The flight crews are right there with the maintainers, assisting and checking. Their attention to foreign-object damage control is the best I've ever seen—we can take some lessons from them. They aren't afraid to go up to an inspector and get on his case for dropping a pencil or not checking vehicle tires for FOD."

"Good." Patrick knew that was true. A buck sergeant had admonished him—politely but firmly—for placing a checklist clipboard down on the ramp. The nearest running engine was at the adjacent parking spot almost three hundred feet away, but the danger of having a gust of wind or a vehicle push the checklist close enough to get sucked into a seven-million-dollar jet engine was too great to take a chance. "So we've got seven birds uploaded and ready to fly?"

"Seven in the green, fueled, armed, and ready," Luger replied. "These guys pull together well. They'd be hard to distinguish from an active-duty unit. I have no doubt they can surge their birds for as long as we want."

"Overall rating?"

"Excellent," David replied. "In critical mission-essential areas, I rate them an 'outstanding.' "

"Very good." Patrick turned to Hal Briggs. "What have you seen, Hal?"

"Ditto," Briggs replied. He was a wiry black man who always seemed in perpetual motion, always animated and excited, with dark dancing eyes and a quick smile. But Patrick had also seen him kill with equal joy. Until the death of his mentor, Brad Elliott, Hal's favorite sidearm had been a rare .45-caliber Uzi submachine gun—now it was Elliott's ivory-handled .45-caliber Colt M1911A1 Government autopistol.

"As you know, me and a couple of my white boys and girls arrived a couple of days ago to poke around and do some security probes," Briggs said. "We tried everything—the janitor routine, the telephone man routine, the sneak-and-peek routine, everything but a full commando assault. For a unit located on a commercial civilian airfield, their security is pretty damned good. They practice good COMSEC procedures all the time. Airport security is typical—lousy—but security tightens quickly as you get closer to the Guard ramp. Good K-9 unit, good use of manpower, good rotation procedures, good challenge and response and use of authenticators.

"I found a few unlocked doors and open gates and was able to get close enough to hand-toss some fake grenades at a plane in a fuel dock. We found one bag of shredded classified material in a Dumpster, but it was confetti-shredded and unreadable—still a violation, but not a serious one. Never got access to a plane, never got near their command post or their classified documents vault. Couldn't hack into their classified computer server. Bought lots of drinks, but we couldn't get one single Guard guy in a bar to talk about anything even remotely approaching classified topics—even had one guy report his contact to Furness, who filed the report with the adjutant general, state police, and Air Force Office of Special Investigations at Beale Air Force Base. Rating: 'above average' overall, 'excellent' in critical areas."

"Good," Patrick said. "What do you have, Nance?"

"I sound like a broken record, Patrick, but I give them an overall 'above average' and an 'excellent' in mission-essential areas," Lieutenant Colonel Nancy Cheshire replied. Cheshire, a petite dark-haired woman in her late thirties with large doe eyes and a little button nose, was one of the Air Force's toughest and most talented test pilots. She was the first female pilot to fly the B-2A Spirit stealth bomber, but her real accomplishments had come as Dreamland's first and greatest female test and combat pilot, flying three secret missions in experimental B-52 bombers over the past several years. Now she was the chief test pilot of the High Technology Aerospace Weapons Center.

"It was a pleasure to watch these Guard guys go to work," she continued. "The battle staff, operational support squadron, and command post performed flawlessly in all the scenarios. Good security procedures, good time control, good use of checklists and command doctrine. One overdue situation report and one brainfart with a radio frequency that broadcast a coded message on an open frequency prevented them from getting an overall 'outstanding.'

"I was primarily concerned about the mobility line, but that's where this unit really earns an 'outstanding' score. It must be the unit's recent history with C-130 transports, but these guys run a mobility line more efficiently than anyone I've ever seen. Excellent use of computers, with most programs custom-written for this unit. Almost no wasted time. But the key is the folks going through the line, and I've got to say that this unit has got the procedures down cold. Everyone had updated records, everyone had current vaccinations, everyone had their required gear. This unit was *waiting* for their transportation to arrive. It's a small, close-knit unit, true, but these folks are revved up and ready to fight."

"They can generate, they can pull alert, and they can mobilize," Dave Luger summarized. "The big questions now are . . ."

"Can they fight, and can they deploy and *then* fight?" Patrick finished for him. "Maybe it's time to load 'em up a bit and see how much mayhem they can take."

Nancy Cheshire gave an evil grin. "You gonna make it hurt, Muck?"

"This is not a training situation here," Patrick replied. "I want to see what they got. It might hurt a little." He nodded to all of his staff officers around him. "Thanks for all your hard work, guys. Unclassified summary reports in my e-mail box by sixteen hundred hours today; classified summaries by tomorrow morning. I'll see you at Tonopah."

Suppressing yawns, they all left the StepVan except for Dave Luger. "How are preparations for Lancelot progressing back at the home drome?" Patrick asked.

"General Samson has got the Lancelot modification kits ready to go for the first two planes—we just need the planes and we're ready to go," Luger replied. "He received authorization for two more kits. By the time we're ready to fly one and two, we should be starting work on three and four. Leaving one for a ground training article, that should leave us with three operational birds in two to three months." He paused for a moment, then added, "From what I've seen so far, we might be looking at our best candidates right here. The birds are in excellent shape; the maintenance guys are top-notch; they have good facilities and good support. What do you think?"

"I don't know, Dave," Patrick replied uneasily. "I agree, the machines are in good shape—it's the aircrews I have a problem with. These guys have a real cocky attitude. Furness delights in telling everyone to go to hell, and it's rubbed off on her troops. They were mouthing off at the adjutant general right to my face, all of them. Rinc Seaver is the worst of the bunch—the best, but the worst." Patrick got up, stretched, then told their driver to head over to the squadron building.

"The force is different from when we were pulling a crew, Muck," Dave said. "Since the Strategic Air Command's bombers were absorbed by the Tactical Air Command, all the crewdogs are like fighter jocks—they're cocky, tougher, more aggressive, more competitive, and lots smarter. The force is smaller and leaner, which means that only the best of the best get to fly. And the Air National Guard is all that and more. They're like a pack of wild starving wolves fighting over who's going to kill the caribou. I don't think we need to straighten *them* out—I think it's *us* that needs to realize what the modern-day force is like."

"Maybe so," Patrick said grumpily, suddenly feeling very old. "But some of them can still use a good dose of whup-ass."

Luger watched his longtime friend stifle a jaw-breaking yawn. "You ready to fly, partner?" he asked with a smile. "It's been—what, five years, six?—a long time since you've been in a B-1."

"I'll be fine, Dave," Patrick said. "I know the Bone like the back of my hand—"

"I'm talking about *you,* partner," Dave interrupted. "It's been about a year since you ejected out of the Megafortress. Are you ready to start flying again?"

"I *have* been flying for the past year or so, Dave . . ."

"I don't mean flying prototypes, simulators, test beds with a bunch of engineers, or the BERP suit—I mean flying a real sortie with a real crew, as *part* of the crew," Luger interrupted again. "You don't have to do this, you know. Nancy can give Seaver an evaluation, and I can certainly let you know if these guys are the real deal or just hot dogs. Besides," he added with a serious expression, "you old guys need more sleep."

Patrick scratched his nose with an uplifted middle finger, making sure Luger got the message, then clasped him on the shoulder. "I'll be fine, partner," he said. "This will give me an opportunity to get back into the real world. I'm looking forward to this."

Dave nodded. "Then go get 'em, Muck," he said. "I'll be on the SATCOM if you need me." Patrick nodded, successfully stifling another yawn. They were silent for a moment. Then: "You can always take command of the squadron," Dave said.

If Patrick had been a bit drowsy a moment ago, he now looked as if he had been blasted awake by heaven's trumpets. He stared at his partner in utter surprise and asked, "What did you say, Dave?"

"Don't tell me you haven't thought of it already," Luger said, grinning. "If Furness can't control her troops, she deserves to get taken down a peg or two. She's treating this squadron like her own personal plaything, true, but the operative word is 'her.' Take it away from her, even for a short time, and then see what kind of commander she is. If she straightens out, good. If she doesn't, you've saved the state of Nevada the task of removing her, and you've still created a better unit. Plus, you get your first command."

"Dave, my job is to give this evaluation and report back to Samson, not pirate an Air National Guard command," Patrick said. "Besides, I've got a job. I've got a dozen projects that need my attention. I can't just leave—"

"Ah, the first sign of mental illness—thinking that you're indispensable," Dave said. Patrick scowled at him, then shook his head, laughing it off. "Muck, I know you. You're not a desk jockey. You're a crewdog. You've always been one and you'll always be one, no matter how many stars you wear. But you're also a one-star general in the United States Air Force, and that means you command. This Lancelot unit is going to be your creation—why not take command of it?"

"Dave, the idea is nutzo," Patrick said, shaking his head. The StepVan pulled up in front of a squat concrete building. Patrick grabbed his flight gear and manuals and headed for the door. "I'm not here to replace Furness or kick her ass or teach her how to fly the Bone—I'm here to observe and report. That's all I'm going to do, and then I want to go home to my wife and son and my work that's piling up back at Dreamland."

"Yes, sir," Luger said, obviously not believing a word of it. "Have a good flight . . . commander."

A security guard posted inside the front door of the squadron building called the squadron to attention as Patrick walked in. "As you were," Patrick responded as he showed his ID armband to the guard. Even with a major exercise going on, someone still thought about calling the unit to attention when a senior officer entered the building. Just as his staff said in their preliminary exercise report—impressive.

Patrick found Lieutenant Colonel Rebecca Furness in one of the squadron mission planning rooms a few minutes later, writing a schedule on the whiteboard with felt-tip markers of various colors. "Morning, Colonel," he said.

"General," Furness responded. "Briefing in fifteen minutes. Coffee's in the Casino. I'll get one of the guys to help you find things."

"I'll find it," Patrick said. He walked back to the "Casino," the squadron's lounge, found a guest coffee mug, and poured himself a cup. Cripes, Patrick thought, even each squadron member's coffee cup was clean—he never remembered seeing such a spotless coffee bar back at his old B-52 base. There was beer on tap—with a pair of fuzzy dice tied around the beer tap handles, signifying that the bar was closed. There were a few slot machines, some pinball and video games—all unplugged—and a big popcorn maker, with all the fixings for jalapeño popcorn, where they mixed chopped jalapeños in with the cooking oil. There was a "crud" table, which looked like a regular billiard table except there were no pool cues around, meaning that the balls had to be propelled by hand as the players raced around the table in a sometimes physical free-for-all. Over the bar, the squadron's "Friday" name tags were on display, with each flier's call sign on the patch instead of his first and last names.

Like all of the TV sets Patrick saw all over the base, the lounge's TV was on and tuned to CNN. As it had been for the past several weeks, the international news was about North Korea. One of the planet's last Communist states had barely come through last winter intact. Hundreds of thousands of citizens had died of starvation, sickness, and exposure because of a lack of heating oil, food, and medicines. There had been yet another unsuccessful attempt on President Kim Jong-il's life; the perpetrators had been arrested, publicly tried, and publicly executed by firing squad, all of this shown around the world on CNN. President Kim then executed several military officers on charges of conspiracy, treason, and sedition. Food riots were commonplace; all were harshly, even brutally, repressed by government forces.

But at the same time, North Korea continued a massive military buildup that surpassed all other Asian countries'. They had tested another rail-garrisoned Daepedong-1 intercontinental nuclear ballistic missile, firing it over sixty-five hundred miles across the Pacific, and were promising to make it operational within the year. An advanced longer-range version of the missile, the Daepedong-2, reportedly had a range of over nine thousand miles, making it capable of hitting targets in the continental United States. They had deployed the Nodong-1 and Nodong-2 rail-mobile nuclear ballistic missiles, capable of hitting targets all over Japan, including Okinawa. They had hundreds of short- and medium-range ballistic missiles, some carrying chemical or biological warheads; and some of their nine-thousand-plus artillery pieces and howitzers were also capable of firing nuclear, chemical, or biological weapons shells. In a country with a population of only twenty-four million, a per capita income of less than nine hundred dollars, and a negative growth rate, North Korea was spending a staggering *thirty percent* of their gross national product on defense.

What was equally puzzling was South Korea's reaction to the North's huge military buildup. Instead of calling for a larger military buildup of its own, or for increased help from the United States, the South Korean government was actually *increasing* aid and outreach programs to the North and simultaneously erecting roadblocks to a greater American presence on the Korean peninsula. The United States had fewer than ten thousand troops stationed in South Korea, almost all of them observers, advisers, and instructors, not combat forces. Compared to North Korea, the South's military forces were much more modern, but a fraction of the size. Yet while the South's defense budget barely managed to hold steady year after year, its budget for economic aid, humanitarian programs, cultural exchanges, and family reunion programs with North Korea was rapidly increasing.

Was this part of the Korean mind-set? Patrick wondered as he watched the news piece on the growing North Korean crisis. Help your enemy even though he wants nothing more than to crush you? Or was South Korea naïvely assuring its own destruction by feeding and supplying its sworn enemy? Every time another spy ring or cross-border tunnel was discovered, South Korean aid to North Korea increased. When Wonsan was nearly destroyed by a nuclear device three years earlier, reportedly by China in an attempt to divert world attention from its attempt to conquer Taiwan, it had been South Korea that sent money and equipment to rebuild the city.

He returned to the mission planning room and studied the schedule Furness had put on the whiteboard. It had been copied from a page from a three-ring binder, part of the extensive array of "plastic brains" the squadron used to do every chore, from turning on the lights to going to war. "Good idea," Patrick remarked as he reviewed the contents of the binder. "No need to remember how to organize for a mission briefing—it's all in here."

"No need to reinvent the wheel on every sortie," Furness said. "Everyone does it the same, so there're no surprises. If something gets missed, someone will know it."

Every step of mission planning was organized to the exact minute: show time, overview briefing, intelligence briefing, the "how d'ya do?" briefing—a short meeting to check everyone's mission planning progress—the formation briefing, mass briefing, crew briefing, step time, life support stop, weather and NOTAMS briefing, flight plan filing, bus time, time at aircraft, check-in, copy clearance time, start engines time, taxi time, and takeoff time. Each crew member in the formation had a job to do—everything from preparing flight plans, to getting sun positions during air refuelings and bomb runs, to getting lunch orders, was assigned to someone. He or she would return to the mission planning room and drop off the paperwork for the flight leader to examine, and then check off the item.

Patrick's task written on the whiteboard was a simple one: "Hammer on Seaver."

At that moment, Rinc Seaver walked into the mission planning room. "Morning, General, Colonel," he said formally. Furness did not respond.

"Good job on that EP sim ride, Major," Patrick said. He had decided to give Seaver an emergency procedures simulator evaluation, loaded up with a fairly demanding scenario, to see how he could handle stressful situations. What Patrick had really wanted to do was duplicate the fateful Fallon mission, to see how it could have been done differently. But as he told Furness and the others, he wasn't there to investigate the crash. "I like the way you delegate the radios and checklists. Shows good crew coordination, good situational awareness."

"Thank you, sir."

"I thought you were a little *too* aggressive," Furness said. At Patrick's request, Rebecca Furness had flown in the evaluator's seat, while two systems officers operated the SO's side of the weapon systems trainer; terrain-following systems would only work in the sim if the SO's cab was powered up too. He also asked Furness to administer his closed-book and emergency procedures written test. "Why ask for CITS codes and the expanded tech order text?" she went on. "It got distracting. You were juggling too many balls in the air at once."

Rinc looked at Patrick, who nodded. "She's right," Patrick said to Seaver. "You obviously know your stuff, but you did get a couple steps ahead of the crew as they ran through the troubleshooting matrix, and it was distracting. You had a handful of broken jet to fly." He turned to Furness. "Good call, Colonel. Anything for me?"

"You're rusty, you don't know local procedures that

well, and you don't verbalize enough," she replied. "But you got the job done and brought your crippled jet back home. I'd fly with you. You'd fly anyway, I suppose, even if you were picking your nose the whole time, right?"

"Right. But thanks. I'll give my official critique to General Bretoff, but I rated Seaver's performance an 'excellent.' Good job, all of you."

"Thank you, sir," Seaver said. Furness offered no congratulations. Seaver copied some notes from the whiteboard, then departed.

"I gotta tell you, Colonel," Patrick said as he watched Furness work, "I'm very impressed with the squadron. Everyone's doing an exceptional job."

"You say that like you expected us to be a bunch of drunken slobs," Furness retorted.

"No. But it's certainly getting tough to explain how you lost a jet and a crew."

"I don't suppose you believe in plain old bad luck, do you?"

"Sure I do," Patrick replied. "You think it was bad luck?"

"Yep. Shit happens. You fly jets long enough, something bad happens. It's a dangerous business."

"True," Patrick admitted. "But I've noticed in the sim and looking over the accident records . . ."

"I thought you weren't here investigating the crash, sir."

"I'm not, but I'd be an idiot if I didn't get some background on the accident, wouldn't I, Colonel?" Patrick retorted. "Most of your bomb runs are level radar bombing, right?"

"*All* of our bomb runs are level radar," Rebecca replied. "The Joint Direct Attack Munition will give us a little more flexibility, but without precision-guided bombs or imaging sensors like LANTIRN or Pave Tack, we pretty much do it the same way strategic bombers have been doing it since the beginning."

"But your squadron flies very aggressively," Patrick pointed out. "Maybe too aggressively. Some might say recklessly. If all your bomb runs are the same, why all the gyrations?"

"My opinion, sir, is that we're asked to do more with less," Furness replied. "We have fewer bombers, smaller budgets, and more taskings over more dangerous battlefields. We don't set up the threats. We do whatever it takes to destroy the target against whatever threat we encounter."

Furness regarded Patrick for a moment before continuing: "You're a bomber guy, sir." Patrick had no response. "I remember hearing a little about you, back when I flew tankers and later when I got into the RF-111s. You know how bombers used to fly—low, fast, and alone, mostly with gravity nukes or SRAMs. Well, it's not done that way anymore. We fly as packages. We go in high, or low, or slow, or fast, depending on the threat and the weapon we employ.

"But we don't train that way. We still train like you and I did years ago—alone against the threats, the area defenses, and the target. Instead of having a cruise missile or stealth bomber take out the threats from standoff range followed by Bones with fighter cover, we drive a couple of Bones through a gauntlet of fighters and SAMs. It's unrealistic. We'd never do that in the real world. But that's the way we train because it's cheap and it's easy.

"Our job is to destroy the target, no matter what the threat," Furness went on. "That means pushing ourselves and our machines to the limit. The Bone has the payload of a BUFF but the speed and agility of a Strike Eagle. We've got the horses, so we're going to use them."

"Well, what do you think about Bones going in alone?" Patrick asked. "Are they capable? Or do they need a package to do the mission?"

"Of course we're capable," Rebecca replied hotly. "When you flew BUFFs, you flew against every threat in the book without any support. True, in the SIOP missions, you expected to go in long after the initial ICBM laydown, so most of the threats would be taken down for you. But if that's true, why did BUFFs and Bones and Aardvarks and even B-2 stealth bombers start going low? Why did we start training in ranges with fighters and SAMs and triple-A? Because we were expected to fly against any target, any threat, whether there was a strike package or nuclear laydown preceding us or not.

"We can do the same thing again—but we need better tools. Give us a standoff capability, like JSOW or SLAM or TSSAM, and we can take out our own threats as we encounter them, like a HARM shooter such as an EA-6 or F-16CJ. Or give us an imaging infrared or TV capability, and we can hunt down our own targets like an F-15E or F-16 Block 50. The Bone can do all that. We can carry four or five different weapons at the same time. I guess it's politically better to build fighters and deploy carriers. But we're still training like we did in the seventies and eighties. We should train like we're going to fight."

Patrick nodded, pleased with the way this woman was thinking. He knew he was on the right track—he knew his plan would be accepted by the crews. Now he just had to make it work and then sell it to the brass.

"What's everyone got against Rinc Seaver?" Patrick asked. "He's a good stick, a good systems operator, a good crewdog. Is he a good team player or more of a loner?"

"No one has anything against the guy," Furness said.

"You ever lose a crew and a plane in your unit before, sir?" Again, Patrick had no answer, so Rebecca assumed the answer was no. "It tears the unit apart like nothing you'd ever believe. But we're still technicians, pilots, systems officers. We need to find a reason for the accident . . ."

"You mean someone to blame?"

"We're human too," Rebecca said. "Maybe part of the healing process is assigning guilt, blame, responsibility. Rinc is it. He had the controls, he was the commander, he pulled the handles, and he survived, and all that makes him culpable. It's shitty, but it's the way it is."

"How do *you* feel about Rinc Seaver, Colonel?" Patrick asked.

"I told you. He's a good crew member, a good OSO. But he had the bad luck to survive this unit's only training mission crash. It'll take some time for him to work his way back into the unit." Patrick hesitated, looking carefully into her eyes, expecting her to add something a little more. "If you have something to say, sir, please say it."

"No," Patrick said finally. "Forget it. Completely unrelated." He spotted Rinc Seaver and a few other crew members drifting back and forth in front of the open door, wondering if it was safe to enter, so Patrick decided to back off. They had a mission to prepare for, and everyone's attention had to be focused on the task ahead. The room filled up quickly with crew members and technicians ready to start the briefing.

Furness began precisely on time; she dinged one crewdog two dollars for showing up just as she was starting to close the door and gave him a warning glare, then began:

"This is the initial flight briefing for Aces Two-Zero flight of two." She put the first of a small stack of overhead slides on the projector. "Everyone is present. I am the flight lead, and Rodeo is second-in-command in Aces Two-One. We are the first strike package for our unit pre-D. Intelligence briefing."

A technical sergeant stood up and put his first briefing slide on the projector. It was marked "Confidential (Scenario Unclassified)." "Good morning, ladies and gents," he said. "The following is classified 'confidential,' with a fictional exercise scenario; the real-world briefing is available in the intel shop if you're interested.

"Two days ago the godless Communist dictatorship of North Kimchee moved eleven armor and infantry brigades to the border of the God-fearing democratic pro-American nation of South Kimchee, and stepped up fighter and antiship patrols over the ocean around its borders." Patrick always found himself struggling not to smile when the intelligence techs recited the fictional exercise scenarios; they were prepared with a vivid imagination and a good sense of humor. "The National Command Authority responded by ordering the full mobilization of all long-range bomber units, in case the North Kimchee Army decides to invade, and warned North Kimchee that we were guaranteeing the peace and sovereignty of South Kimchee and would use force to back our promise up. The warning order directed us to prepare to execute an attack-then-deploy bombing mission against North Kimchee ground units along the border. One Navy carrier battle group was already in the area when the warning order was issued, and another is en route."

As the briefing continued, Patrick was amazed at the level of detail. When he kicked off the exercise, he had given the squadron a simple notification order, a short message explaining the exercise scenario. The intelligence and operations support divisions had gleaned a massive amount of follow-up information from his exercise referees, then devised an entire realistic play-by-play mission profile based on the exercise scenario. He had no doubt that this was exactly what the real briefing would look like if this were an actual combat situation—with real-world country names, of course.

"In response to our mobilization," the intelligence technician continued, "North Kimchee moved a large number of antiaircraft weapon systems into the area. We have received fairly good data about the types and numbers of systems, but since they're mobile systems, it's been difficult to pinpoint them. Then, early this morning, North Kimchee declared our actions tantamount to war, formally declared war against the United States and South Kimchee, and crossed the border with eight divisions, leaving three in reserve. We received the execution order this morning, and we expect the launch order in about six hours.

"Our primary job is to blunt the invasion by destroying as many enemy vehicles as possible," the briefer went on. "Our prestrike satellite reconnaissance can tell us fairly accurately where the troop and vehicle concentrations are, so we'll plan saturation bombing and minelaying operations against them. The problem is, we don't have a very accurate picture of what the antiair defenses are, and we can't risk any manned aircraft to find out.

"So the plan is to have a large salvo of Navy Tomahawk surface- and sub-launched land-attack cruise missiles lead the mission. The cruise missiles will be going against fixed targets farther north, not against the divisions that are going across the DMZ. But the cruise missiles will certainly draw a lot of fire. The Air Force will send electronic reconnaissance aircraft to try to pinpoint the locations and types of enemy antiaircraft that will try to shoot down the cruise missiles. We're hoping that the recon planes will detect and pinpoint most of the surface-to-air missile sites during North Kimchee's response to the first salvo of cruise missiles, and pass the position info back to us. We hope they'll do a good job, because we'll be coming in right behind them, before North Kimchee gets a chance to reload and regroup.

"So our secondary mission is to destroy as many targets of opportunity as possible so we can clear the way for follow-on sorties. We'll use two-thousand-pound JDAMs for plinking targets of opportunity. We can expect to receive target coordinates in a multitude of ways, so part of our tasking on this mission is to see how carefully we can monitor all of the data sources for target info."

The intel briefer put up a new slide with all of the various communications systems, their security authentication routines, and times of operation. "The primary source of target information will be via SATCOM hookup between us and the theater commander, which for the exercise will be simulated by the exercise referees. But we must also maintain listening watches on HAVE QUICK, VHF, UHF, and even HF for data relays by radar planes, mostly via the E-8 Joint Surveillance Targeting and Reconnaissance plane. We can get target info through a list of geographic coordinates that we can plug directly into JDAM, or receive a set of grid coordinates where we can look for targets on the attack radar. We also have to be prepared to upchannel any target coordinates we mensurate ourselves."

Next came another slide, this one of area enemy defenses and threats. "We can expect everything in the book out there," the briefer continued. Patrick liked the way he said "we," as if he were going along on every sortie—which, judging by the way this unit pulled together, was figuratively true. "North Kimchee has an extensive list of Soviet and Chinese antiaircraft systems, from long-range modern stuff like the SA-10 and SA-12 to low-tech, optically guided antiaircraft artillery. They're playing it smart, keeping their radars shut off and their units on the move, so we may not be able to detect or pinpoint these systems until close to your target times. Therefore, expect extensive last-minute in-flight replanning and retargeting.

"After the attack, we will be deploying to a bare-base location in southern South Kimchee, approximately five hundred miles from the border. Weapons, fuel, equipment, and supplies have already been moved there under cover of darkness, so we feel fairly certain that we can conduct operations from there for at least two days before the bad guys realize where we are and start counteroffensive actions. We can expect to conduct three-per-day surge bombing sorties from this location. By that time, the Navy will have moved two carrier battle groups and more cruise missile shooters into the area to help out.

"Our sources tell us that, although not involved right now, the People's Republic of Chowdown may support North Kimchee's war effort by sending fighters and bombers to harass or even attack us during our deployment," the intelligence briefer concluded. "Of course, if we fail to stop North Kimchee's advance, we may come under direct attack by North Kimchee artillery. Therefore, supplies and support might dwindle. We'll learn more later. Questions?" There were a few; after they were answered and discussed, Furness took the podium again.

Before she began, she wrote the acronym "BOTOTCHA" as item number one on the list of objectives of the mission. "Our overall objective on this mission is, as always, 'Bombs on target, on time, come home alive,'" she said. "Our primary objective is to stop or blunt the North Kimchee invasion by destroying as many high-value strategic targets such as artillery sites, rocket sites, air defense sites, armor and vehicle concentrations, and vehicle marshaling areas as possible. Our secondary objective will be to destroy targets of opportunity transmitted to us by reconnaissance and intelligence sources. Our subobjectives, as always, are: no withholds due to crew or switch position errors; no unreacted-to threats; and clear communications and transmission of threat and intelligence information.

"Each sortie has two assigned targets, which will be attacked using Mark 82 AIRs from the forward bomb bay and CBU-89 cluster bomb dispensers from the aft bay. The Mark 82 attacks will generally be against armored-vehicle marshaling areas, vehicle and troop concentrations, and enemy weapons and supply depots inside South Kimchee. The CBU operations will generally be against air defense sites, artillery emplacements, and vehicle and troop concentrations inside North Kimchee, since we don't want to hamper friendly vehicle movement with our mines.

"We will then withdraw to a refueling anchor area and await any follow-on targets transmitted via SATCOM. Follow-on targets will be attacked using JDAMs from mid- or high altitude. These can be any type of target, deep inside North Kimchee or over South Kimchee. You hit as many as you can, then withdraw to the forward operating location.

"The forward operating location for us will be Tonopah Air Force Base, Nevada," Rebecca went on. "The Operational Support Squadron, Civil Engineers, and the Air Base Group have already deployed. After you arrive, you'll reload with Mark 82s and CBU-89s, go on crew rest, and get ready to accept new strike packages."

"What!" John Long exclaimed. A loud, surprised

murmur of voices in the room echoed him. "We're going to fly strike missions from a *bare-base* location?"

"Shut up, all of you," Furness broke in hotly. "I know this isn't standard. Our usual scenario is to turn our birds over to a forward-deployed active-duty unit that has already been set up in the forward location. Well, we're not doing it that way. The bare-base operation at Tonopah will be ours—our gear, our spares, our planes, our staff, our plans. We can expect to do this for as long as ten days, so I hope you brought your toothbrushes and gave your honeys the full monty, because it's going to be us in the sand with the bugs for a long time."

Rebecca pointed to the list of tasks on the whiteboard. "Here's your jobs, here's the schedule. We'll have a 'how d'ya do?' in thirty minutes." She paused, then glanced at Patrick. "I suppose you all know that we'll be having an evaluator aboard Rodeo's flight. General McLanahan will be in the copilot's seat, so I guess that makes him invulnerable to SAMs, right, sir?" No response from Patrick. "Remember, we follow peacetime safety-of-flight rules," Furness concluded. "We play it by the book. Any questions?" No reply. "Rise."

As Rinc Seaver headed for the door, he placed several piles of papers on the table in front of Furness, then began checking off items on the whiteboard. "What's this, Rodeo?" Furness asked.

"Got all these things done already," Seaver replied.

"What? How? I just got the info myself an hour ago."

"I got it an hour ago too," Rinc said, "and I finished the planning. Computer target predictions, fly-through simulation, threat assessment, sun position, terrain analysis—it's all there. I'll get the latest intel briefing materials and plug 'em into the flight plans."

Furness looked very irritated. She glanced up at Mc-Lanahan, who instantly got the message and stepped out of the briefing room. When he was out of earshot, Furness said angrily, "You better not have busted crew rest, Rinc."

"Not that you know about," Rinc shot back. Furness looked as if she was going to explode. "Lighten up, Beck. The general was already out on the ramp. I saw Heels coming out of the in-flight kitchen when I was going to the command post, so she was obviously on base before five." Captain Annie "Heels" Dewey, one of the 111th's three other female Bone crew members, was Furness's copilot for this mission. "I showed up at the command post at five after five to get a copy of the frag order. They said you already picked a copy up—*twenty minutes* before me. Let me know when you're ready to bust your own ass—I'd like to see it for myself."

Rinc stepped closer to Furness, looked her right in the eye, and said in a low voice, "This is *my* requal check ride, Beck, my first evaluation after losing my crew and my friends. Let me sink or swim on my own. You do your job and let me do mine, and we'll see if I got what it takes to keep my wings. If I don't, I'm outta here."

"No one wants to see you flunk, Rinc." She lowered her voice a bit, then added, "Especially me. But we're all under the gun here. We've got to do it like we always do it, by the book and *together*." But Furness could see that Rinc wasn't about to believe anything she said right now. "Rodeo, get together with the other crews and see if they need some help."

"I've got a better idea, Colonel," Patrick said from just outside the door. He reached into a flight suit pocket and pulled out a small stack of envelopes. Fanning them out like a deck of cards, he held them up to

Furness. "Pick a card. Any card." Furness looked puzzled, then selected an envelope. Patrick opened it, read it quickly, then nodded. "Good one. Very good." He left the room with a smile on his face.

"What was that about?" she wondered.

"Change in scenario," Rinc said. "He must've seen us arguing and decided to shake things up a bit."

Sure enough, a few moments later the intercom buzzed, summoning Furness to the senior controller's desk in the ready room. The ready room was filled with crew members scurrying around, collecting information and getting ready for the mass prestrike briefing in a couple of hours. "What is it, Scarecrow?" Furness asked the senior controller, Major Sean "Scarecrow" Asterman.

"Just got a note from the exercise referee," Asterman said. "ACC wants to send three bombers straight to the forward operating location ASAP, without doing bomb runs. Battle staff will be meeting in five minutes."

"Shit, shit, *shit*!" Furness exclaimed. That meant that the four remaining bombers would have to take up the target list of the three scratched bombers. And that meant a complete replanning—new weapons loads, which would take time, all new frags, all new target times, all new intelligence briefings, all new mission tapes. And they had less than six hours in which to do an entire day's worth of planning.

Furness's eyes scanned the room and found Brigadier General McLanahan talking on his secure cellular phone. Patrick looked up, saw her glaring at him, then smiled and waved the envelope—the one Furness had picked! It was the change of scenario! McLanahan must've noticed that the mission planning was going so well that he decided to throw a major monkey wrench into the works.

"I'm on my way," Furness told Asterman. "Notify

the crews and tell them to stand by to start replanning."
When Patrick walked up to her, she said in a low voice,
"This isn't realistic, General. We're less than six hours
from launching. Air Combat Command would assign
the new sortie to another unit that hadn't finished generating its sorties. We have to replan, download weapons, deconflict all our tracks . . ."

"Then I suggest we get on over to the battle staff
meeting and find out what we need to do," McLanahan
said. "But the change stays. Or do you want to throw in
the towel now? You have that authority."

Furness gritted her teeth and mumbled a low, growl-
ing "No way, sir," then spun on her heel and headed
for the door. Patrick had to trot to keep up with her.

NEAR SUKCHON, DEMOCRATIC PEOPLE'S
REPUBLIC OF KOREA
SEVERAL HOURS LATER

The tactic was simple: Do what the North Koreans
had been doing for years—only deadlier.

One hundred and sixteen feet long and displacing
only 275 tons submerged, the *Yugo*-class midget sub-
marine looked like a sophisticated but comical toy. Its
top speed was twelve knots, but it was usually restricted
to three or four knots because its temperamental diesel
engines couldn't stand the strain—some ocean currents
around the Korean peninsula could easily outrun it. It
was one of approximately forty-five midget submarines
used by the North Korean Spetznaz special operations
forces to infiltrate South Korea and land commandos
and spies near its most important military bases.

But several Yugos had been captured intact over the

years, and now they were the property of the Republic of Korea Marines.

Eight Yugos captured by the South Koreans had been towed by the South Korean Navy from their base at Cheju Island in the East China Sea to the naval special operations base near Inchon, refueled and rearmed, then sent on their mission. Staying at least three miles offshore, diving only when acoustic or electromagnetic threats were detected around them, they made their 150-mile trek across North Korea's west coast in twenty hours. Before crossing into North Korean waters, two Yugos had to drop out of the formation because of massive engine or electrical malfunctions. But the men aboard the remaining subs considered the 75 percent survival rate a real bonus.

The last twenty miles to Sukchon, traveling into the mouth of the Yengyn Inlet, were made completely submerged. Using its passive sonar detection system to clear the area of nearby enemy ships first, the lead sub raised a global positioning system satellite navigation receiver on a retractable mast just two feet above the waves to get a position fix. Once the vessels reached their preprogrammed initial point, they bottomed themselves into the thick mud of the inlet about two thousand yards off the shoreline and waited.

Every spring, the Sukchon delta region falls victim to killer floods, so the area had recently been extensively rebuilt, with assistance from Chinese military troops and engineers. At least, that was the story most of the world knew. Those Chinese engineers had made other improvements as well: they had rebuilt nearby Sunan People's Army Air Base into the new secret Military Command and Coordination Facility of the Korean People's Army. In just two short years, Sunan had been transformed from a minor supply and transportation air base into North Korea's main war-fighting nerve center.

The region was also the home of two full Army corps infantry commands, a mechanized corps command, nine artillery brigades, and five special forces brigades—over 100,000 troops stationed at three Army barracks in the immediate area. These served as the main reserve forces for the defense of the capital, Pyongyang, only thirty miles to the south. The air base facilities had also been beefed up: Sunan was the new home to one full air combat command, including a light bomber regiment, two ground-attack air regiments, five interceptor regiments, ten transport regiments, and three air defense regiments. Between one main and two auxiliary airfields nearby, more than three hundred aircraft were assigned to Sunan.

Sunan had other key forces as well. It was the new home of the Fourth Artillery Division, comprising eighteen medium-range and ten long-range ballistic missile batteries. The short-range FROG-5 and FROG-7 missiles had nonnuclear warheads, designed to blast any South Korean forces who dared move north of the Demilitarized Zone, just 120 miles to the south. Four medium-range mobile Scud-B missile batteries, designed to hit targets inside South Korea, carried chemical and biological munitions, mostly Vx nerve gas and anthrax agents. The other six longer-range rail-mobile Nodong-1 batteries, housed in concrete aboveground shelters covered with earth to camouflage them from spies, carried ten-to-one-hundred-kiloton nuclear warheads and had sufficient range to reach Seoul, Taegu, even Kwangju—effectively, over 90 percent of South Korea.

But the Command and Coordination Facility, or CCF, was the most important target at Sunan, and possibly the most important in all of North Korea, for reasons beyond its aircraft, infantry, armor, or even its deadly missiles.

It served as the main command and control facility for all of the military bases in North Korea, the Defense Ministry in Pyongyang, the Central Committee of the North Korean Politburo, and with Beijing. In times of conflict or heightened alert, the bases were linked together through the CCF so that the general staff could issue orders to all facilities at once, through one central coordinator. Although most of the world did not know it, Sunan was the tip of the spear, the key to the destruction of the Republic of Korea and the Communist occupation of the entire Korean peninsula.

That's why Sunan had to be neutralized.

At the prearranged time, the minisubs lifted from the thick silt bottom and began cruising at minimum steerageway speed toward shore. At periscope depth, about six feet below the surface in the tiny vessels, a hatch popped open on each sub and eight commandos rose to the surface, gave each other an "okay" sign, then swam for their infiltration point. One sub's hatch could not be reseated, and it had to be scuttled. Its crew had no choice but to swim for shore and either hide or try their best to make it back to friendly territory on their own. There was no emergency rescue plan for this one-way covert operation.

The leader swam slowly, using a minimum-effort stroke that placed him under the surface during all but a few seconds out of every minute. He stopped frequently to check his bearings, listen for danger, and check his troops. Every time he came up, the first thing to break the surface was the muzzle of his Heckler & Koch MP5K submachine gun.

It took twenty minutes for the team of forty-eight commandos to swim to shore and reach the wharf that was their landfall. They secured their swimming gear to the bottom in black nylon bags, climbed up a dockside ladder until they could get up inside the framework of the wharf, then made their way ashore. They found a dark, secluded area between two noisy ventilator units and stopped to dole out equipment and to rest. While the leader checked in via satellite to his headquarters, his men began to unpack their equipment.

Twelve commandos carried the waterproof weapons bags for all of them. Each man was armed with a submachine gun, with a shoulder harness and five-cell pouch system that strapped onto his calf, plus a 9-millimeter SIG Sauer P226 autopistol carried on the shoulder harness. The leg pouch contained three thirty-round magazines of subsonic ammunition plus the sound suppressor for the submachine gun.

Twelve other commandos, two per squad, carried the electronics, including target markers, radios, remote-control detonators, and night-vision equipment. Two commandos carried radios; two others carried medical gear. Six commandos were the "mules," carrying the explosives—an assortment of plastic explosives, shaped cutting charges, antipersonnel mines, incendiary explosives, and Primacord, plus detonators and timers. When they were all loaded up, checked, their timing established, and their objective identified on the map and compared to their surroundings, they set off.

Sunan was actually a conglomeration of several bases, spread out over most of western Pyongan Namdo province. In peacetime, all the facilities were independent, run by several different branches of the military. Two South Korean commando squads were detached from the group and dispatched to set charges and electronic target markers on several other key targets on base, including the early-warning and fire control radars, surface-to-air missile sites, and the Scud-B and Scud-C missile sites. Another squad was dispatched to set explosives that would act as diversions and create panic and confusion in other areas of the base.

The CCF was the commandos' main target. The remaining three squads, twenty-four highly trained commandos, moved toward this important objective.

The CCF compound was a sprawling one-hundred-acre site with a drab gray bunkerlike building in the center. Sneaking onto the compound itself was simple. The outer-perimeter security was in poor repair and had already been broken down by bands of roving citizens looking for food or trying to sell food to starving soldiers, or by soldiers on base sneaking supplies off base to sell to local black marketers. Ironically, the best place to penetrate the outer security zone was right in front. Since heavy road traffic from the main base often set off the motion and trembler alarms, they were usually deactivated during base-wide alerts when there was a lot of vehicle traffic. A few silenced gunshots took care of the lights they could not avoid. They saw signs indicating canine patrols inside the outer security ring, but they knew there were no dogs on duty—the soldiers on base had long ago sold or butchered the guard dogs for food.

The Command and Coordination Facility itself was a squat steel and concrete building, two stories aboveground but four belowground. A long concrete tunnel controlled access to the entrances, so a frontal assault was next to impossible. The guard tower on the roof and the two guard towers around the building were dark, but the commandos could not assume they were unmanned—in fact, they had to assume that a response team was already on the way, so speed was imperative. A short chain-link dog fence protected a twelve-foot-high electrified fence. There was no doubt that the fence was on—the deadly current flowing through it could be heard and felt from ten feet away, like waves of heat from a nearby furnace.

They were hamstrung—they could not go forward unless they blew the electric fence apart, nor could they retreat. The leader hunched down with his second-in-command, set to discuss their dilemma . . .

. . . when suddenly they heard a noise ahead of them. In a matter of moments, several dozen heavily armed soldiers rushed out of an access tunnel on the north side of the squat concrete structure before them, headed right for the South Korean commandos.

And the mission had barely begun . . .

RENO-TAHOE INTERNATIONAL AIRPORT,
RENO, NEVADA
THAT SAME TIME

Even in his earliest days as a B-52 navigator and bombardier, Patrick McLanahan never remembered moving this fast. Was it because these young guys just liked to hustle, or because the schedule was that compressed? It *couldn't* be a function of age—or could it?

Precisely at the prebriefed time, the crews loaded up the old bumpy two-gear blue school bus (at least that hadn't changed—it seemed like the same old noisy school bus he had ridden in on the way to the B-52 flight line almost twenty years ago) and headed off. First stop was the life support shop, where they grabbed their flight and survival gear and checked oxygen masks and night-vision goggles. Rinc Seaver helped Patrick find his stuff and showed him how to operate the NVG tester, but they couldn't dawdle because Rebecca Furness, her copilot, Heels Dewey, and the other crew were out the door and loading up. The next stop was base operations, where the crews received a weather briefing, filed their flight plans, checked Notices to Airmen, verified the maintenance status of the planes, got their box lunches from the in-flight kitchen, and took one last nervous pee.

This was the first opportunity Patrick had to take a breather and check out the other crewdogs as they made last-minute preparations before heading out to the flight line. The differences in the modern-day military kept surprising him. They made him feel a little—check that, a *lot*—out of place and, well, pretty goddamn old.

Because the first thing he noticed was how young these guys were. Even though the Air National Guard usually employed veteran aviators, and this unit was definitely top-heavy with field-grade officers, these guys still looked damned young. Their slang and references—mimicking characters like Bart Simpson, Austin Powers, and Beavis and Butt-head seemed to be the big thing—made them seem younger still. They all had very short haircuts, wore perfectly clean flight suits and spit-shined boots, none of them smoked cigarettes (cigars, yes—even the women), and none of them used vulgarity routinely in conversation. They ate like ravenous wolves—all but Heels ordered two box lunches, one to eat in base ops and the other to take along on the flight—but they all seemed trim and fit, so lean, most of them, that they bordered on the anorexic.

Rinc Seaver was not typical of the new breed. While the others were chatty, chummy, and casual, Seaver was quiet, businesslike, and not very sociable. While the others had *Playboy* pictures downloaded off the Internet stuck under plastic page protectors in their checklists, Seaver did not.

What was it with this guy? Patrick wondered. He didn't need to give Seaver a full-blown check ride to know he was more than competent—he was an expert in every aspect of the Bone. The other crew members in the squadron certainly didn't resent him or resent his expertise, and it was plain that despite the crash, the feeling of detachment, of ostracism, even outright anger toward Seaver was pretty much in Seaver's own mind. The other crewdogs didn't resent anyone as long as he pulled his weight and supported the unit.

Furness motioned to Patrick, and they walked out into the hallway to talk without being overheard. "With all due respect, sir—this really sucks," Furness said. Her voice was low but angry. Well, at least the *crews* didn't use vulgarity as a part of normal conversation; the commanders were different. "My guys worked damn hard to gin their birds up on time without a glitch, and then you reward them by forcing everybody to replan. It's unfair to my troops."

"Relax, Colonel," Patrick said. "We take all this into account when we tally the score. But you know as well as I do that flexibility and replanning are standard operating procedure. 'Flexibility is the key to air power.'"

Furness nodded, though her face was still rigid. "My boys will do fine, General, no matter what you toss at us."

"That's what I want to hear, Colonel . . ."

"But if I or any of my troops feel that any of this violates crew safety, I'm calling it off, and then I'll gladly go nose-to-nose with you on who's right," Furness said. "Rank or no rank, no one endangers my crews."

"My first concern is always crew safety, Colonel—but I'm also authorized to run this exercise any way I choose in order to fully evaluate your unit's performance. That means I set the limits here, not you. I'm risking my own career by doing what I'm doing. If you squawk, you'd better be prepared to risk your career over it too. Clear?"

"No, sir, it's not clear. Not one bit."

"Things will become clearer to you as we go on, Colonel," Patrick said.

Rebecca Furness squinted at the one-star general, trying to piece together what she had just heard. "General, what in hell is going on here? This isn't about a pre-D or a check ride for Seaver, is it?"

"Don't try to second-guess me, Colonel," Patrick snapped. "This is my exercise. You do it my way, or you prepare to give up your command over your protest. Do you understand?" Furness had no choice but to agree. "Good. I suggest you let the game proceed, even though it might weird you out. Don't turn your back on anything until you're sure you have nothing to learn from it." Furness did not argue, did not agree—she only looked more confused, although a tiny hint of intrigue and curiosity began to creep over her face. "Carry on."

"Yes, sir," Furness said. "We penetrate, decimate, and dominate. We never give up."

"Ho-rah," Patrick said, not smiling. They went back into the room, and he said, loudly enough for everyone to hear, "The unit is looking real good so far, Colonel. I'm looking forward to shacking some targets today. Anything else for me?"

"No, *sir*," Furness said, spitting out the "sir" from deep in her belly. Patrick noticed a lot of straight backs and serious expressions when she started the formation briefing. "Okay, hogs, listen up." She opened up her checklist and said, "Someone get a time hack. Formation brief . . ."

The excitement level began to build as they headed out to the flight line several minutes later. Security was tight, but once the security guards checked line badges and inspected the crew bus with dogs and mirrors, they seemed just as keyed up about the upcoming mission and deployment as the aircrew members. Even the young airman-first-class bus driver gave them a "Go kick some ass, sir," as they stepped off the bus at their aircraft parking spot. In the "old days," when Patrick pulled a crew, the "sky cops," the maintainers, the support specialties, and crewdogs all lived in separate worlds. Even though everyone respected one another's work and knew that they all played for the same team, they knew little about what anyone else on base really did. There was always a certain degree of ambivalence and even resentment.

Not here. It felt to Patrick like a pro football team, where offense, defense, special teams, coaches, trainers, and fans all cheered equally loudly before, during, and after every play.

Furness, Dewey, and Seaver stepped off the bus and quickly carried their gear to their plane. But Patrick couldn't help but stop and admire the plane itself. He had a couple of hundred hours' flying time in the Bone, including second-in-command time, plus another few hundred hours in various simulators and procedures trainers, but he looked at this one as if it were the first time he'd ever seen a B-1B Lancer.

The best phrase to describe it was "deadly-looking." He had always used that term to describe his EB-52 Megafortress bomber, the experimental high-tech B-52 Stratofortress bomber that he had worked on and flown into combat for many years. With the Bone, however, that phrase really stuck. The EB-52 was a souped-up B-52 with a pointed nose and other aerodynamic enhancements, but it still had the bulk, the huge thick wings, and the presence of a big, lumbering bomber—the various enhancements worked very well, but they definitely looked "tacked on," retrofitted.

The B-1 looked sleek and deadly because it had been

designed that way from the beginning. Unlike the B-52s, nothing was hanging off the wings or the fuselage. All weapons were carried internally, and the wings were thin, supercritical airfoils that swept back for high-speed flight. From its long, pointed nose to its gracefully swept "lifting body" fuselage, to its thin wings, to its swept and pointed tail, it looked fast even sitting on the ground. But it was every bit as large as the EB-52, and it could do far more things.

The rising sun spilled over the Sierra Nevada and began to shine on the flight line, surrounding Patrick's Bone with golden light. It was then that he knew his future was going to be with this war machine. He had worked on many different high-tech planes and weapons at Dreamland, but none of them had the potential that the B-1 had right now. He realized that he was looking at the new Megafortress.

Brad Elliott had created the EB-52 Megafortress. That was his legacy. This plane was going to be Patrick McLanahan's legacy.

He quickly rejoined his crew at the base of the one-story-tall nose landing gear, and Rinc Seaver began reviewing and briefing the Form 781 aircraft logbooks, going over any recent problems and making sure all the required sign-offs were there. Patrick met the crew chief and two assistant crew chiefs, remarking again to himself how young they were as well. The crew chief, Master Sergeant Chris Bowler, was a fifteen-year veteran, but his assistants, one buck sergeant and one staff sergeant, looked fresh out of tech school. In reality, they had twenty-five years of B-1B experience between them.

The first order of business after reviewing the 781 and briefing the crew chiefs was a "FOD walk," where the flight and ground crews walked out from the wheels along the Bone's taxi path to check for anything on the ground that might get sucked up into the engines when they taxied. Every bit of the aircraft parking ramp was meticulously swept and checked for FOD twenty-four hours a day, and the chance that the flight crew, who were busy mentally preparing for their upcoming mission, would actually find anything on the concrete was fairly remote.

But this was a "crew" thing, something the crews did together for their bird. The aircraft "belonged" to the crew chiefs until the aircraft commander signed the 781, at which point the aircraft "belonged" to the flight crew until the crew chief signed the 781 after the maintenance debrief and took control of it again. The FOD walk was a kind of symbolic act, something they did together for the mutual benefit of "their" war machine. For a brief period of time, they were not officers or enlisted personnel, not fliers or ground-pounders—they were Aces High.

Once they parted after the FOD walk, shaking hands, giving high fives, flashing their squadron "gang sign" at each other—three fingers jammed downward in a dunking motion, signifying the 111th—and shouting their squadron motto, "Aces High: Penetrate, Decimate, and Dominate," they became "flight" crew members and "ground" crew members again. But the bond between them would never be broken.

Patrick followed the crew offensive systems officer, or "O," John Long, as he did a preflight of the Bone's three weapon bays. As briefed, the bomber was fully loaded. It was as exciting for Patrick to be out here now, preflighting a bomb bay filled with live weapons, as it was years ago when he was the bombardier in charge of all the explosive power in the B-52 Stratofortress and later in the EB-52 Megafortress.

Long counted the bombs in the forward bomb bay. "Twenty-eight Mark 82 AIRs, ready to go," he said. The bottom of the bomb bay was ten feet overhead, so there was nothing for him to do but count the weapons and check for any obvious malfunctions or damage.

The five-hundred-pound Mk82 was the second smallest high-explosive bomb carried by the Air Force and the smallest weapon carried by the B-1. Its basic design hadn't changed since the 1950s; in fact, many of the more than one million Mk80-class weapons still in the inventory were leftovers from the Korean and Vietnam conflicts. The Bone's Mk82 AIRs (air-inflatable retarded) were modified for low-altitude delivery with the BSU-49/B Ballute tail unit, which was an air-inflatable mushroom-looking canvas parachute that would slow the bomb down enough to allow the bomber to escape the detonation and blast effects without damaging itself.

The weapons were loaded onto slanting racks in a confused-looking array, with bombs tightly stacked atop one another. It seemed impossible that those racks could fold and flip out of the way before the bombs above them released, Patrick thought. Twenty-eight five-hundred-pound bombs safely leaving the bomb bay, separated by only one-fifth of a second. Amazing. He knew precisely how they worked, of course—but studying the engineering on paper was much different from actually seeing the bomb bay jammed with more than five tons of explosive power.

"These are my babies here," John Long said proudly as they reached the center, or intermediate, bomb bay. This bay held a rotary launcher loaded with eight inert two-thousand-pound GBU-32 JDAM (Joint Direct Attack Munition) guided gravity bombs, the deadliest nonnuclear weapon in the Bone's arsenal.

Although radar level bombing from the B-1 had always been very accurate, JDAM gave the Block D Bone its only near-precision bombing capability. Target coordinates were fed to a global positioning satellite/inertial navigation system computer strapped onto each bomb, either by manually entering the geographical coordinates by computer keyboard or by feeding the coordinates from the Bone's bombing computers and attack radar. When the bomb was released, it would steer itself to the target coordinates, using movable control surfaces on its tail. The Bone's rotary launcher could spit out eight JDAMs in a little over sixty seconds.

Using only its strap-down inertial navigation system, JDAM was normally accurate to within two hundred feet, even if released from an altitude of thirty thousand feet. But if the bomb could lock onto at least three GPS navigation satellites as it fell, its accuracy increased to sixty feet. If it locked onto eight satellites for at least seven seconds, which it could do if released from high altitude, the bomb's accuracy increased to less than twenty feet—and with a two-thousand-pound bomb, that was guaranteed to wipe out any target smaller than a three-story house.

What's more, the bomb could glide as far as fifteen miles if released from high altitude, so it was not necessary to release it at a specific point in space. That meant that the B-1 could fly anywhere within a fifteen-mile diameter "basket," from any direction and at any speed, and start pumping out JDAMs as fast as the rotary launcher could go—and each bomb would automatically find its own target, even if the target was *behind* it. On a large target complex such as an airfield, military base, city, or weapons storage area, eight different targets could be attacked on the same bomb run by one bomber within sixty seconds, with accuracy second only to laser- or TV-guided bombs or missiles, day or night, in any weather or battlefield conditions.

"You like JDAM, do you, Colonel?" Patrick asked.

"If it wasn't for JDAM, I think we'd be out of business," Long replied. "Every other attack plane in the inventory except the Bone and the B-2 stealth bomber has a precision-guided bombing capability—even the lousy little F-16 can launch Maverick missiles. Even with all its payload, range, and speed advantages, what good would a Bone be if it took three bombs to destroy a target that one bomb from an F-15E or F-117 stealth fighter could destroy? With JDAM, we come close to pinpoint bombing accuracy without having to use a datalink, forward-looking infrared, or laser."

Patrick nodded, appearing to agree—though it was all he could do to keep quiet. The Joint Direct Attack Munition was indeed a good weapon. It was cheap, it worked well, and it modernized the huge supply of one- and two-thousand-pound bombs still in the inventory. But there were a dozen next-generation weapons available for the B-1B bomber, and at least another dozen weapons Patrick and his teams at Dreamland were working on, third- and fourth- and fifth-generation stuff, that made JDAM seem as effective as cavemen throwing rocks. Patrick only wished he could tell this young bombardier about the innovations they were about to unleash.

They moved to the aft bomb bay, which was loaded with ten CBU-87/B CEM (Combined Effects Munition) dispensers. This was the primary wide-area antiarmor and antipersonnel bomblet used by the Bone. Each dispenser carried over two hundred two-pound bomblets. When released, the dispenser would spin rapidly, scattering BLU-97 bomblets over a wide oval-shaped area. The bomblets would float down on a tiny inflatable parachute, then detonate at a preselected altitude above ground.

The kill-and-hurt pattern of this tiny two-pound bomblet was enormous. A shaped charge warhead, capable of penetrating four inches of steel, would shoot straight down, designed to cut through the light armor atop a tank or armored vehicle. At the same instant, a hundred tiny steel fragments would shoot outward, capable of shredding light vehicles within fifty yards and injuring soldiers over a hundred yards away. Finally, a ring of sponge zirconium would ignite, scattering burning pieces of white-hot metal over two hundred yards away and igniting brush, fuel, buildings—or humans—with ease. One CBU-87 could cut a swath of death and destruction the size of eight football fields.

After Long completed his inspection, they climbed up the steep ladder behind the tall nose landing gear into the crew compartment. Patrick followed right behind. He had to keep from grinning like a kid stepping onto a roller coaster. He couldn't believe how excited he felt. After all the bomber missions he'd flown—*why?*

Go with it, he told himself, and he broke out into a big shit-eating grin. It was exciting because it *is* exciting. It felt fun because it *is* fun! Yes, it was dangerous. Yes, this crew had a mission to accomplish, and Patrick was their judge, their jury—and, in a very real sense, their executioner. But they were also going to fly one of the deadliest planes in the world and drop enough real live no-shit high-explosive material to wipe out an entire brigade of enemy armor. It was the ultimate job, the ultimate game, the ultimate kick in the pants.

Savor it, Patrick told himself. For once, forget about the responsibility and the mission and savor the excitement you are about to experience.

Despite the fact that the B-1B was over 140 feet long and its max gross weight exceeded 230 tons, there was just enough room inside for four crew members in ejection seats plus a little storage space. Rinc stowed his jacket in a cubbyhole above the entry tunnel and his gear in a little step built behind the center console, preflighted his ejection seat to make sure it was safetied, then sat down and began running his power-off and before-APU-start checklists.

Patrick stuffed his jacket in the "bunk" behind the copilot's seat, his helmet bag of extra booklets and "plastic brains" in the space beside his seat, then preflighted his seat. He checked that the four seat safety pins were in place, the ejection handle lock was down, and the ejection mode switch was in MANUAL, meaning that if either pilot's seat malfunctioned or was inadvertently activated, it wouldn't automatically eject anyone else's seat. Then he climbed in and started strapping in.

The last bomber he had any time in at all was the EB-52 Megafortress—and that was cavernous compared to the B-1 cockpit. Patrick was unaccustomed to wearing a big, bulky survival vest, and threading all the seat straps around it and finding the right clips and fasteners was harder than he expected. You didn't just sit in a B-1 bomber—you wore it. He had to leave the shoulder straps as loose as he could and push his arm with his opposite hand to reach switches. Even adjusting the seat took a few moments to relearn.

"How're you doing over there, sir?" Rinc asked, a trace of amusement on his lips. "Finding everything okay?"

Patrick felt a bit self-conscious as he finally got straightened around and settled in. He wrapped the Velcro strap of his checklist around his left thigh, a small metal kneeboard around his right thigh, and opened the checklist to the "Before APU Start" checklist page. He capped it off by slipping on a new pair of Nomex flight gloves, working the fingers down tight, then punching a fist into his palm excitedly, just as he used to do before starting engines years ago as a young crewpuppy. "I'm doing fine, Major," Patrick replied. "Don't be afraid to kick my butt if I'm not keeping up with you."

"You're doing fine so far," Rinc said. "It took me three tries to find all my harness straps without help."

The first order of business was starting the APU, or auxiliary power unit. The APU was a fifth small self-contained jet engine, mounted in the B-1's tail, which provided electrical, hydraulic, and pneumatic power to the aircraft without starting one of the big turbofans or relying on external power carts. With the APU, the Bone was completely self-sufficient—it did not need ground power equipment for any flight-line operations. Once the B-1's APU was started and supplying electrical power, the crew started to turn on their equipment and run power-on and before-engine-start checklists. At precisely the briefed time, the crew began the engine-start and after-engine-start checklists. It took only a few moments to get all four engines running.

Things happened quickly after that. The pilots ran a series of checklists, testing every system, backup system, and function aboard their plane. The TACAN radio receiver was not passing its self-test, but the avionics maintenance "Red Ball" team had a spare part out to the aircraft and installed in record time. They certainly could've launched without a TACAN receiver—with all the sophisticated inertial and satellite navigation gear on board, the old TACAN was seldom used except on precision instrument approaches—but it was a required piece of equipment. Furness's flight checked in precisely at the prebriefed time. Patrick copied the mission clearance and command post clearance, then began to taxi out.

Except for a sudden brief loss of the nosewheel steering system in Rinc's plane, which was corrected immediately by recycling the system, the flight taxied out without incident. A large crowd of onlookers was up on the roof of both commercial airline terminal buildings at Reno-Tahoe International, watching the two-ship of

B-1B bombers taxiing out for takeoff. All the commercial flights had been cleared onto the parallel runway to make way for the military flights, but several stopped to watch the Bones parade by. Almost everyone based at Reno International knew that the 111th Bomb Squadron was getting some sort of evaluation, and a few knew that these planes carried live weapons, so they recognized that this was something special.

They received a "last chance" inspection at the end of the runway by the supervisor of flying behind the steel revetments in the runway hammerhead. "Looks like you got a nick in the left nosewheel tire, Rodeo," the SOF radioed via the maintenance officer's intercom cord. "Must've happened when your nosewheel steering cut out."

"Any cords showing?" Rinc asked.

"I see two cord belts."

"Shit," Rinc muttered. That meant an abort to change the tire. A Bone near max gross weight with a bald spot on a nose gear tire was not a good place to be. "Screw it. We'll take it."

"You sure about that?" Patrick asked.

"The book says we can take up to three cords—"

"But at gross weight?"

"It doesn't give a gross weight restriction, sir," Seaver pressed. "Besides, we're forty thousand *under* gross right now. Three cords peacetime, five cords wartime. We can probably get a waiver for five. We should—"

"We're going off station to a forward-deployment base that probably won't have the gear we need to change tires," Patrick said. "Better to get it changed now rather than take a broken bird to a forward bare-base."

"This is our pre-D launch, General—we're talking about Probability to Launch and Survive points," Rinc emphasized. "PLS isn't a factor once we get to our deployment base. But if we lose PLS points due to a late launch, we get hammered. We'll be okay with two cords missing. You should know that the tires have twelve cord belts, and even with five gone we've got a wide safety margin. We're still legal. Let's get the hell outta here and go drop some iron." Patrick hesitated. Seaver added irritably, "Unless you're going to order me to get it changed."

"You're the boss," Patrick said.

"SOF, I'm taking the plane," Rinc said, nodding to his guest copilot. "Finish up and clear the runway for launch."

"Roger dodger, Rodeo," the SOF said. He finished his drive-arounds and found nothing else wrong with any of the planes. "Aces Two-Zero flight, pins and streamers pulled, doors closed, and you appear to be in takeoff configuration. Penetrate, decimate, and dominate. SOF is clear. Break. Reno tower, Aces SOF, clear me on three-four left for a last-chance runway inspection."

"Aces SOF, Reno tower, clear on three-four left, report when off." The SOF sped down the runway, making a last inspection for anything that might cause damage to the Bones during takeoff. Once the SOF cleared off the runway, it was time for departure.

Patrick had forgotten what a takeoff in the B-1B was like. He had flown lots of different aircraft, including supersonic bombers, but there was something different about the raw power meshed with the physical size of the Bone that made takeoffs even more spectacular in this plane than in any other.

As soon as Rebecca Furness in Aces Two-Zero started rolling, Rinc Seaver lined up on centerline, locked the brakes using his toes on top of the rudder pedals, then started to feed in power. The sound was muted, silky smooth, with no trace of rattle or "burping" as in the G-model B-52s Patrick used to fly. Rinc moved the throttles up to military power, paused to let all four engines stabilize, then cracked the throttles into afterburner range. He watched as the eight afterburner initiator lights illuminated, then released brakes and pushed the throttles to max AB.

Acceleration was rapid but not very dramatic in military power—but when those four huge afterburners lit and power was moved to max AB, the thrust and acceleration snapped Patrick's eyes open. The ejection seat felt as though it came up and smacked him in the back of the head. He had felt afterburner kicks plenty of times, but usually it was just that—a kick and nothing more. In the Bone, a constant, steady pressure that forced him deep into his seat followed that nice hard kick. It was like flying in a rocket ship headed for earth orbit. Patrick hadn't felt G-forces like that in a long time. The pressure and acceleration made his head spin—it seemed as if the deck was inclined at least forty-five degrees.

Seaver's little "departure show" routine didn't help Patrick's stomach. Rinc lifted only about one hundred feet off the runway, pushed the nose over to hold that altitude, then raised the gear and flaps and swept the wings back to twenty-four degrees. He accelerated to well over four hundred knots—at max afterburner, it only took a few seconds—then, as he blasted between the twin towers of the Nugget Casino and the Hilton Hotel Casino, he wagged the wings twice before lifting the Bone on its fiery tail. Their 400,000-pound bird suddenly did become a rocket ship, headed skyward at almost ten thousand feet per minute. Rinc didn't revert to a more conventional climb-out until passing twelve thousand feet, when he pulled back to military power at

350 knots. They leveled off at twenty-one thousand feet in no time.

John Long reported "tied on radar" and fed continuous position information on the flight leader, and the formation quickly joined up. After closing to tight wingtip formation to check one another out, Rinc extended to loose route formation so he could perform their checklists without having to concentrate too much on formation flying.

"How you doing over there, General?" Rinc asked.

"Fine," Patrick replied.

"Heard some heavy breathing on interphone. Thought you might lose some of your box lunch."

"Not a chance," Patrick responded. "I'll be with you on the TERFLW checklist in a minute. Crew, I'll be on secure SATCOM. I'd appreciate it if no one monitors that channel until I let you know. Copy?"

"Sure," Rinc replied. "Monitor GUARD and interphone, report back up. I'm starting the TERFLW checklist."

"O."

"D."

"Thanks," Patrick said. "Copilot is clearing off to SECURE."

Patrick set the referee's SATCOM channel into the satellite communications thumbwheels, clicked his communications wafer switch to SECURE, then keyed the mike button: "Firebird, Firebird, Aces Two-One."

"Two-One, this is Firebird." Patrick instantly recognized Luger's voice on the scrambled satellite communications channel. "Authenticate Foxtrot-Uniform."

There was a moment's pause while Patrick looked up the response in his AKAC-1553 code book for the familiar "F-U" challenge: "Two-One has 'Tango.' Is this Amarillo?"

"Sure is." Dave Luger was from Amarillo, Texas,

and Patrick, from California, usually never let him live it down. Only months of concentrated Russian brainwashing and years of working as a Soviet bomber design engineer in Lithuania, where he was known to the Central Intelligence Agency as an American defector code-named "Redtail Hawk," had made Luger lose his thick Texas drawl.

"Then authenticate Alpha-Hotel, amigo," Patrick said. The "A-H" was another endearing authentication used by parties known to each other.

"Firebird authenticates 'India.' "

"Loud and clear," Patrick said. Both parties were required to double-check authentication, even though they were on a discrete, secure satellite channel available only to them. "How's it going, partner?"

"All bombers are away, the last of the squadron will be loaded up in a few hours, and we'll be right behind them," Dave said. "Be advised, bud: I was with the SOF during the launch, and I got a good look at your nosewheel. I think you got more than two cords cut—looked to me more like five or six. If you land with weapons onboard, be careful. I understand these guys wanted to max out PLS points, which they did, but they might have violated peacetime safety-of-flight rules by taking a broke bird into the air. I think they should have at least gotten a maintenance supervisor out there to look. Just so you know."

"Copy that, Amarillo." Patrick shook his head, hoping Seaver was eavesdropping.

"How did your takeoff feel, sir? Didn't fill up a helmet bag, did you?"

"Felt just great," Patrick said. "I forgot what a zoomer this baby is. I think I left part of my gut back on the runway. If I lose it, it'll probably be low-level."

"You mess up, you clean up, sir," Luger reminded him. "That was quite the show your AC put on. I'll bet the folks in those casinos got a great shot. You could see the windows rattling from the ground. Hey, listen, Muck. I got a call from the home drome." The home drome in his case was Dreamland. "We're getting ready to monitor the Chinese and North Koreans during the first day of Team Spirit bombing exercises in South Korea."

"Everything okay so far?"

"Normal activity from the DPRK and China—not so normal for the ROK," Dave said.

"How so?"

"I dunno. Just—busy. Everyone is supercharged. It sounds like it's the big finale day of the exercise rather than the first supercautious ramp-up-slowly day."

"Lots of high-powered visibility in this one," Patrick pointed out. "Lots of VIPs, including Japan. Our cutie Vice Prez is out there too." He hesitated for a moment, thinking hard. Something inside his head was saying the news from Luger had to be investigated. He didn't know why, but it had to be checked out. No matter what other disasters were happening, he never went wrong when he listened to that tiny, almost drowned-out little voice in his head. Patrick keyed the mike: "What do we got overhead?"

"I'll have to double-check," Luger said. "Overhead" meant satellites. Through their contractors, Patrick had access to several kinds of sophisticated photo, communications, radar, and electromagnetic reconnaissance satellites, all of which could be steered over the Korean peninsula in a matter of hours if needed. Since Dreamland was not an active combat base—at least, not one that most of the rest of the government knew—Patrick and his staff did not get normal access to CIA and Defense Department satellite imagery, so they relied on their own. "You want to take an unofficial peek, Muck?"

"Let's get a Carter and a Ford over the peninsula and start matching up origins and destinations of all that comm traffic," Patrick said. The reconnaissance satellites designed, built, and launched by Sky Masters Inc., one of the Air Force's smallest but more important contractors, were all named for American Presidents. The Carter series were communications eavesdropping satellites capable of detecting, tracing, and analyzing radio, TV, cellular, microwave, Internet, and satellite communications. The Ford series of satellites were millimeter-wave radar reconnaissance satellites, capable of detecting, pinpointing, and identifying objects as small as a car almost anywhere on earth—even underground, hidden in buildings, or under camouflage or underwater. All were inserted into low earth orbit so they needed very little power to send their signals back to earth. Launched by boosters carried on commercial airliners, a constellation of these small satellites, called NIRTSats ("Need it right this second" satellites) could be set up in a matter of hours.

"You got it, Muck," Luger said. "I think we have a few assets in place right now we can tap into."

"Good. I've got checklists to run, Amarillo. Talk at you soon."

"Go kick some butt, D," Luger said. "I'll meet you at Tonopah. Firebird clear."

Patrick flipped back to interphone. "Crew, D's back up interphone. Clear to switch SATCOM to primary monitor channels."

"We need to get going on these checklists, sir," Seaver said. "We're waiting on you."

Yep, he was behind already. Things happened fast in the B-1B. "Sorry about that, gang. Got busy on SATCOM. I'm ready."

"Let's not be late, co," Rinc said, taking a swig of orange juice and giving his guest copilot a mock disapproving scowl, then a friendly, easy smile. He was taking great delight in needling the one-star general sitting in his cockpit. "Let's not be late."

KOREAN PEOPLE'S ARMY MILITARY COMMAND
AND COORDINATION FACILITY,
SUNAN, DEMOCRATIC PEOPLE'S
REPUBLIC OF KOREA
THAT SAME TIME

Y ou are late."
The South Korean commandos relaxed and lowered the muzzles of their MP5Ks. The two groups approached each other. The South Korean team leader saluted the ranking officer. "Lieutenant An Sun-hun, team leader."

The North Korean returned the salute. "Major Hong Song-ku, chief of security. Welcome to the People's Army command center. Follow me." Lieutenant An dispatched one squad to set explosives at several other key sites on base. What he didn't tell his North Korean contact was that the commandos would also place electronic target markers on the CCF itself. In case their plan did not work, the CCF was going to be demolished with concentrated aerial and rocket bombardment until it was nothing more than a hole in the earth.

The upper two levels of the Command and Coordination Facility, which were mostly administrative offices, were virtually deserted. The ground-floor security desk was manned, with the five-ton vaultlike upper-access door secure, but the guards on duty did not register the least bit of surprise when the twelve South Korean commandos were escorted through.

The commandos quickly descended the staircase to

the first subfloor level. This level housed the facility's security forces—two full infantry companies, over two hundred specially trained and heavily armed soldiers. A security station at the bottom of the stairs was deserted too. On the other side of the security officer's desk was another vault door, which led to the command center. On either side, angled away so there would be no cross fire from security troops, were the two access hallways leading to the barracks of the two infantry companies. The North Korean security commander led the South Koreans to his office along one of the corridors.

"We were afraid you would not come," Major Hong said. "You were not spotted by any of our patrols until you entered the outer perimeter." He smiled wryly. "I suppose that does not look very good for our security here—we knew you were coming, and still we could not detect your presence. My congratulations."

Lieutenant An bowed in thanks. "We must contact our headquarters as soon as we have secured this facility, or else it will be attacked."

"What must I do?" Hong asked.

"We must take the command center itself immediately," An replied. "What is the situation, sir?"

"Full staffing in the command center, communications, and intelligence cells," Hong replied. "Thirty-seven officers and fifty-three noncommissioned officers, all loyalists." Lieutenant An's face fell—that was a very large complement of Communists, and even if they weren't all battle-hardened soldiers, it was going to be tough to take them all. "The vice-marshal in charge of the Artillery Command and the commander of the Air Forces are here as well, along with their personal security teams. They are here to monitor your Team Spirit bombing exercises."

Hong added, "They ordered both security companies activated to double the guards, so I have my full force of two hundred and eleven men on duty. We have fifty men in the command center, ten in the communications and intelligence centers, and the rest spread out inside and around the building. They are more than enough to subdue all the loyalists. All are under my sole command."

Hong noticed An's second-in-command shift his feet uneasily. "Do not worry, Sergeant," Hong said with a reassuring smile. "Not all of my men are conscripts, but most are, and the rest are not full party members—only officers and senior noncommissioned officers are accorded full party status."

"Are you a party member, sir?" An asked.

"My parents were both party members, and so I was enrolled in the Young Patriots Corps and then awarded a commission," Hong replied. "But my mother was killed trying to cross the frontier. She was accused of illegal travel and treason. She committed suicide in prison. My father and I were stripped of our party affiliations, and I was reduced in rank and given a noncombat post. I have been an outcast ever since. My father died of pneumonia eight months ago because he was not given any medical treatment. He had not had one regular meal or any heat for his apartment in over a year.

"Not one of us nonparty members, myself included, have been paid in more than six months, nor do we expect to be paid until perhaps next spring, if ever. Our families are starving. Our children have no clothes, no education, nothing. Only full party members are allowed to buy food at the base commissary—the rest must beg, steal, scavenge, or starve. Yet our government spends billions of won on weapons to destroy the very people whose unity we hope will bring us salvation."

He looked at the South Korean commandos and added somberly, "The time for mistrust is over. We are on our knees. We must stop the Communist war machine from destroying us. We will start now. Every true Korean patriot is behind us." He pointed to a stack of boxes in a corner of his office. "There are ponchos you can wear to cover your uniforms."

"Not necessary, sir," Lieutenant An said. With that, his commandos withdrew their own ponchos—which looked identical to North Korean–issued ones.

"Very well," Hong said, smiling approvingly as he donned his own poncho. "Let us then march into history—or oblivion—together. I have everything ready. Follow my lead."

"Tell me what your plan is," An said.

"It would be better if I did not," Hong said. "Your surprise will help the ruse. Trust me. Do you have ear and eye protection?" An nodded, then looped his flash-bang goggles around the back of his neck and hid them under his poncho. Hong did the same to his pair. "Good. Follow me." With that, he shouted an order to his men in the hallway, issued an order on a handheld radio, then marched purposefully out into the corridor. Although An still felt that old chill of mistrust and fear, he could do nothing else but follow along. He and his men, and the nation behind them, were already too far down the path to look backward.

Hong stepped in front of the large steel door leading to the command center and pushed a CALL button. "Identify yourself" came the reply on the speaker.

"Major Hong."

There was a confused moment's silence. The person at the other end was the assistant to the senior controller, in charge of access to the command center. "State your business please, comrade Major."

"Status inspection. Several security systems are not in order. I want to inspect them myself and then report to the senior controller personally. I am also bringing down six cases of food, electronic parts, water, and publications. You should have received the invoices for them already. Lieutenant Wu is with me."

"Stand by, please." A moment later, after receiving permission from the senior controller, the heavy steel door motored open. By design, the elevator was big enough for only three or four persons, and only two persons after they loaded the six crates of supplies onboard. Lieutenant An hid his MP5K and backpack under his poncho and squeezed inside the tiny elevator with Major Hong. The elevator moved at only two meters per minute on its way down the ten meters to the command center. It had been designed that way to prevent a massive, rapid enemy assault.

Five minutes later the elevator doors slid open, and Lieutenant An found himself staring at a room he never truly believed he would ever be allowed to see—the Korean People's Army Military Command and Coordination Facility. The entire North Korean military machine was directed from this very chamber. It was exciting to be here—and also a bit of a letdown. It was much darker, gloomier, and smellier than Major Hong's intelligence reports had said.

"Lieutenant," Major Hong said in a sharp, officious voice just as the doors slid fully open, "take the top two boxes to the galley immediately."

"Yes, sir," An replied. He hoped this was some sort of ploy or diversion, because he had no idea where the galley was. An picked up the top two boxes . . .

. . . and, just as he took a step forward, he felt a tear at the bottom of the second box, and the bottom popped open, spilling bags of rice, cans of cooking oil, dried meat, tea, and other foods onto the floor of the elevator. The two-gallon cans of oil and the bags of rice split open, scattering rice everywhere, and the floor was slippery from the oil oozing from the cans.

"Lieutenant, what in blazes are you doing?" Hong shouted. The North Korean major whirled around and struck An sharply across the face with his open hand. "You idiot! Can you not follow one simple order without creating a disaster?"

"What is going on over there, Major?" a voice from the gloom asked.

Hong turned and bowed into the darkness. "My apologies, comrade Vice-Marshal Kim," he replied. "My clumsy assistant has spilled some supplies in the elevator. It will take only a moment to clean it up."

"If any of those electronic components are damaged, Major," another voice said, "I will hold you personally responsible."

"They do not appear to be damaged, comrade General Cho," Hong replied.

"Relax, General," Kim said. "We are all under enormous stress. Get it cleaned up immediately, Major. We cannot afford to have our only service access elevator down too long. And it is not the sign of a good commander to physically strike a subordinate in public, no matter how much stress one is under. Remember that next time."

"Yes, sir, comrade Vice-Marshal," Hong said. "Lieutenant, get out of the way."

Lieutenant An swallowed hard as he maneuvered clear of the elevator, ready to help Hong in any way he might indicate. He realized Hong had been talking to Vice-Marshal Kim Ung-tae, the commander of the Artillery Command, himself. Vice-Marshal Kim was in charge of all of North Korea's rockets, ballistic missiles, air defense missiles and artillery, and coastal defense missiles and artillery. He was also responsible for all of North Korea's nuclear, chemical, and biological warheads that could be delivered by rockets or artillery. He was the third most powerful man in the North Korean armed forces and reported directly to Marshal Chang Song-u, the commander in chief of the Korean People's Army, and to Supreme Commander and Beloved Leader President Kim Jong-il.

The other man was probably Lieutenant General Cho Myong-nok, the chief of staff of the Korean People's Army's Air Forces. General Cho was responsible for approximately one-fifth of North Korea's weapons of mass destruction—the warheads carried on his bombers and strike fighters. Together, these men commanded four-fifths of North Korea's deadliest weapons. They held one of the two keys necessary to unleash those forces; the Beloved Leader, Kim Jong-il, held the other key.

It was generally believed, however, that Vice-Marshal Kim and General Cho had full authority and standing orders to launch an attack, especially if South Korea struck first—President Kim would immediately authorize a counterstrike with special weapons without any hesitation or question. That meant that Kim and Cho had extraordinary powers that few men on earth commanded.

Lieutenant An quickly realized the purpose of the spilled supplies in the elevator. Because there was only one elevator to the command center, because it moved so slowly, and because it could only hold three or four persons at a time, it was constantly in use. No one could leave or enter now.

As An's eyes adjusted to the gloom, he could make out more details of the command center. It resembled a theater, with a wooden stage, an "orchestra" section at which computer and communications technicians worked, and behind them seats for the defense ministers, senior commanders, and their aides in a semicircle. There were several conference rooms and cubicles behind the commanders' stations, a circular access aisle, and then more support staff areas. Up onstage, old-fashioned greaseboards and mark-and-erase maps and flow charts, updated by communications technicians with tissue paper and grease pens, dwarfed a few electronic computer screens. It was all much smaller and much less sophisticated than An had anticipated. But security guards were everywhere. Vice-Marshal Kim and General Cho each appeared to have one armed aide with them at all times, and another armed bodyguard was roaming the aisle off to the side so he could observe the entire room.

"Take that box up to the plotter's station, Lieutenant," Major Hong said in a loud voice, "and if you make another clumsy mistake, I will do much more than embarrass you before your fellow officers. Now *move*." Lieutenant An bowed and picked up the box Hong indicated. He didn't know where he was supposed to go, and Hong didn't give him the slightest indication. The only thing that looked like a plotter was up on the stage, in front of all those high-ranking commanders. Swallowing hard, he turned and started down the access aisle to the front of the command center. When he reached the floor, he simply went up the nearest set of steps. Then, once he reached the stage, still without any guidance, he started across to the center of the stage.

Just as he reached the center, he heard Major Hong shout, *"Lieutenant, what in the name of the gods in heaven are you doing?"*

An stopped and turned to face Hong, somewhere in the back of the command center. Every face on the command center floor, from Vice-Marshal Kim to the lowliest clerk, was looking at him. "Major, I . . ."

Just then the world exploded in a blinding flash of white light and an ear-splitting *ka-bang*. Anyone whose eyes were open and without vision protection, including

An, was instantly blinded and paralyzed from the two-kilo flash-bang grenade in the box that Major Hong had set off by remote control.

Lieutenant An awoke a long time later, sprawled in a chair on the stage. His poncho was still on, which he removed, and he still wore his MP5K on its shoulder harness sling. When he looked behind him, he noticed several officers and enlisted men, bound wrist and ankle with nylon handcuffs, their mouths wrapped in nylon too. A few were shouting muffled curses, but most were still. Major Hong handed An a canteen of water, which he poured over his face. The cool water felt wonderful—his face felt as if it had been badly sunburned.

"Welcome back to the land of the living, Lieutenant," Hong said with a reassuring smile. "Are you all right?"

"I still can't see very well," An replied, "but I think I am unhurt."

"I do believe you are the first one ever to have a two-kilo flash-bang charge detonate in his hands," Hong said. His voice was louder than normal because he knew An's ears would still be ringing from the blast. "Good to see it is not fatal—at least not when it's pointed away from you." He paused, then said, "Time had run out, young sir. Several status checks had been missed; reports were being radioed directly down to the command center instead of through my office. I had to act immediately—there was no time to tell you to don your protective gear."

"I understand, sir," An responded. He looked around him through blurry eyes. "Are the officers secure?"

"Secure or dead—it was their choice," Hong said matter-of-factly. "I have taken twenty officers and forty-one enlisted men captive. Ten officers and ten enlisted men pledged their support to a united Republic of

Korea. They sealed their promise by desecrating their flag before the vice-marshal and General Cho. They offered to man the consoles and communications systems and try as long as possible to maintain a normal communications pattern. I do not think it can be done for very long, but we will try."

"Can you trust the men who pledged loyalty to your revolt?" An asked. "If they are on the communications panel, they can radio for help."

"Lieutenant, all I have to rely on is trust and my own intuition," Major Hong said. "I trust your government to support me and my men, before and after the revolt. Besides, there is very little anyone can do even if the whole world knows of what we have done. This facility is not impregnable, but it is self-sufficient and it can withstand a very large assault. And if they do destroy it, they destroy their own national military command center, which will paralyze their command, control, and communications systems." He smiled a faint smile. "But if our brothers in the South fulfill their part of the bargain, it will not matter. The revolution we are praying for will still take place."

Lieutenant An nodded. "I have been praying for unification all my life, sir," he said. "I am proud to be standing with you here this day. What shall we do now?"

"We continue operations as long as we can and make it seem as normal as possible," Hong replied. "When the fun starts, we shall do everything we can to delay, confuse, and disrupt the Communists' response, and then we shall pray that our brothers to the south are successful. In less than six hours, we shall see what kind of world we have created together here today."

KOREAN PEOPLE'S ARMY FOURTH ARTILLERY
DIVISION READY ROOM,
SUNAN, DEMOCRATIC PEOPLE'S
REPUBLIC OF KOREA
A SHORT TIME LATER

What in blazes is going on!" thundered Colonel of
Artillery Forces Cho Mun-san, commander of the
Fourth Artillery Division at Sunan People's Army Base.
"You had better start talking *now*, Captain!"

"Sir!" The duty officer, Captain of Artillery Kong
Hwan-li, a former missile battery commander, stood at
ramrod attention as the division commander entered
the ready room. Kong was a young, dedicated Korean
People's Army officer, groomed to be a military officer
since the age of twelve. He had been promoted to serve
in headquarters after only six years in the field, first as a
missile launch officer and then as assistant company
commander. Now he was the night division headquarters senior duty officer, in charge of the entire artillery
division at Sunan—three brigades of short-, medium-,
and long-range surface-to-surface missile units, aimed
at South Korea and the region just north of the Demilitarized Zone. It was a high honor for a young captain.

To Kong Hwan-li, this assignment and his previous
assignment as a missile launch officer were the most
important ones he could ever hope to have. With his
skills and knowledge, he would be the first to strike
against the capitalists to the south. It was a sacred
honor and a sacred duty. The state was in a constant
condition of alert and readiness, and the sooner war
came, the better.

This situation was a perfect example. Either this was
a joke, a no-notice exercise, or the beginning of the
long-awaited war with the capitalists. To Kong, it

didn't matter—his duty was clear no matter what was going on. It was he who had had to make the decision to wake up the division commander, and now he had to have all the answers. "Sir, I must report a serious error in our routine communications checks with headquarters," Kong said.

"Spit it out, Captain."

He produced the duty officer's logbook, which contained a page detailing the communications procedures that must be performed every hour. "I sent a routine hourly continuity check message to the Command and Coordination Facility. My last message was properly acknowledged by the computer, except that the authentication was made using last hour's code. I know the assistant controller at the CCF, so I . . ." He swallowed nervously, then went on: "Sir, I took it upon myself to phone him to reprimand him for using the old code."

"That is what you got me out of bed for, Captain?"

"No, sir," Kong hurried on. "I was unable to reach the CCF by phone. I sent a communications check message, and it acknowledged properly, but again with last hour's date-time group and authentication code. I then sent an operational security warning message to the—"

"A *what*?" Colonel Cho shouted. "You sent a *what*?" Captain Kong handed the colonel a sheet of paper, which Cho snatched out of his hand in total disbelief. "You *idiot*!" Cho shouted. "An operational security warning message is only sent by the division commander to notify the CCF that his designated missile batteries cannot respond to attack orders!"

"I am aware of that, sir," Kong explained. "I thought such a serious violation of secure communications procedures warranted such a message. But when I received the reply . . . well, sir, this is what I received."

Colonel Cho looked at the acknowledgment message in disbelief. The Command and Coordination Facility *acknowledged* Kong's message and ordered him to keep all of his missile forces at the ready but take no further action. The CCF did not countermand or ask for clarification of the warning message, did not call Kong or Cho directly, did not send a security team out to the corps headquarters to ask what was happening or to arrest Cho and Kong for scaring the living hell out of the commanders in the CCF. Instead, they ordered him to *stand by*!

"What in blazes is this?" Cho muttered. He picked up the hot line telephone that rang directly to the CCF senior controller. No answer. "You have had no other contact with the CCF, Captain?"

"None, sir," Kong replied. "Only the invalid computer-generated acknowledgment messages."

Cho was confused. The only operational contact he was permitted was through the Control and Coordination Facility. He spoke quite often with Korean People's Army headquarters in Pyongyang, but only for administrative and doctrinal purposes. Well, this was an emergency. It was better to wake up a few general officers than sit on his hands and look like an idiot for doing nothing.

"All I ever wanted," Cho muttered angrily to no one, and especially not to Kong, "is to preserve my family's name and accept an honorable retirement and pension. Is that too much to ask for a loyal servant of the fatherland? I realize I might not get much of a pension, the state's economy being what it is, but I expect and deserve an honorable retirement. Yet it seems everyone is conspiring against me and my simple wishes." He glared at Kong and added, "Especially the snot-nosed young captains, the ones who think they will conquer the world."

Muttering a curse, he picked up the telephone and dialed. "Captain, this is Colonel Cho, Fourth Artillery Division commander. I want to speak with General Li." Captain Kong swallowed hard. General Li was the commander of First Corps, the People's Army's largest and most powerful military headquarters, and Colonel Cho's superior officer. Colonel Cho looked at the phone in exasperation, then said, "Well, then I will speak to his deputy, Colonel Ban . . . I know all calls outside normal duty hours are to be routed through the CCF at Sunan, Captain, but I have lost normal voice communication with the CCF. Perhaps you should try to contact the CCF yourself . . . I don't mean a routine ops-normal connectivity check, but a simple phone call . . ."

The colonel went back and forth with the headquarters duty officer for a few more minutes, then was placed on hold. Captain Kong dared not ask the colonel if he wanted tea, if he wanted him to hold the line, anything—he just waited, realizing that headquarters seemed equally as confused as he did. Finally, after nearly fifteen minutes on hold, Colonel Cho shouted, "At last! What is the meaning of keeping me on hold so long, Captain? . . . *What?* My apologies, General . . . Yes, sir . . . Yes, sir . . . Right away, sir." Colonel Cho lowered the phone back on its cradle, a shocked expression on his face.

"Was that General Li, sir?" Kong asked timidly. Cho did not answer, only stared blankly across the room. It was then that Kong realized something was very wrong, something strange was happening. "Sir, what are your orders from headquarters?"

"My orders were . . . my orders were to stand by," Colonel Cho said woodenly. He frowned, deep in thought and confused. "General Li apparently was unable to reach the CCF either."

"What does this mean, sir?" Kong asked. "Is it not dangerous to lose direct contact with the CCF for so long? We have no way of receiving instructions. Our forces are vulnerable to—"

"I am well aware of the impact on our forces, Captain," Cho snapped. "My orders are to stand by. Stand by . . ." He thought for a moment longer; then: "We have no choice but to do as ordered."

"Sir, the last valid communications check with the CCF was ninety-eight minutes ago," Kong emphasized. "Two other computerized messages received from the CCF since then, but neither valid. Three voice checks, two over direct secure lines—none received." Kong noticed his commander's hesitation. "Sir, this is very serious," he protested. "We must assume that all our communications to the CCF are compromised. I say we must also assume that the CCF itself may be destroyed or overtaken by enemy forces."

"*What?*" Cho asked incredulously. "How can you make such an assumption? Are you mad?"

"That is the only safe assumption you can make," Kong said. "Either that, or this is an exercise, a test. Either way, sir, you must respond as if we are under attack. You must order the division to disperse and prepare to attack immediately."

"You *are* insane, Kong!" Cho shouted. "I am going to do no such thing!"

"Then we will fail this test—and fail our fatherland," Kong said. "Sir, you must—"

"Be silent, Captain," Cho scolded his duty officer. But the thought that this could be a secret no-notice test of his readiness—and possibly his loyalty—resonated. That could be the only reasonable explanation. And if it was, his most proactive response would be an alert dispersal. He had the authority to move his forces, and he had the authority to launch all but a nuclear attack if he felt his forces were threatened. He had the authority. If ever he should decide to use it, it would be now.

"All I really want is my retirement and for my good name to last at least one generation," the colonel muttered again, shaking his head. But there was no choice. "Very well, Captain. Implement a division-wide alert. Brigade commanders and battle staff members will report to the battle staff command center in fifteen minutes. All regiments are to deploy to L-1 positions and await further instructions. On my authority."

"Yes, *sir*!" Kong replied enthusiastically. "Sergeant!" he yelled to his communications chief. The noncommissioned officer ran in from the comm center, startled by the tone of the captain's voice. "Issue a division-wide alert immediately, recall the battle staff and brigade commanders, and order all regiments to deploy immediately to . . . to L-1 positions." The sergeant blanched, then nodded and turned back to the comm center. It was the order he always knew he would relay one day—and the order he had always dreaded.

An L-1 deployment was an attack-in-place directive. All of the division's 240 FROG, Scud, and Nodong missiles were mobile to some extent. The FROG series and Scud missiles were road-mobile rockets, mounted on either wheeled or tracked vehicles; the Nodong-1 was a rail-mobile missile, resembling a standard railroad boxcar when in the road-march configuration. The missiles were designed to be deployed with Army units and dispersed throughout the countryside. Normally, they would be transferred from Fourth Division to whatever Army unit needed them, and that commander would deploy them and give the order to launch. In fact, one-third of Fourth Division's weapons were already tasked to other infantry or mechanized brigades, mostly arrayed within fifty miles of the Demilitarized Zone, ready to move south and attack.

But in case of a sneak attack, Colonel Cho had plans in place for the missiles still at Sunan to quickly move to presurveyed launch points throughout the country-side, where in effect he became a field commander in charge of a massive array of firepower. The L-1 directive ordered all missile batteries to quickly march to preselected launch pads, anywhere from two to fifty miles away, set up, and prepare to launch. The wheeled FROG-7 rockets and Scud-B missiles could travel at highway speeds over most terrain, so they were dispersed farther away. The older FROG-5s on their tracks took much longer, so they were dispersed just a few miles, mostly inside the base. The nuclear Nodong ballistic missiles could take several hours to prepare to move, but they could be dispersed anywhere in the country. Mixing in with the regular commercial rail traffic would create a type of "shell game" to confuse the enemy and decrease the chance they could be destroyed by a sneak attack. The L-1 directive was a last-ditch effort that gave Cho's valuable forces a chance to survive and perhaps even strike back at the enemy.

Captain Kong took his seat at the duty officer's desk and retrieved the checklist book for the L-1 directive and for a division-level battle staff meeting. He worked swiftly and efficiently, a product of years of training and countless exercises, but his heart was jackhammer-ing in his chest. He knew this was no exercise. Some-thing or someone had cut off communications with the outside world, and his commander had just ordered his forces to get ready to attack.

It was what he was trained for. It was inevitable: the clash between good and evil where the world was destroyed but eventually made way for a new, peaceful world. The capitalist society to the south was corrupt, an American puppet. The Americans fostered the North-South split, fearing that a reunited Korea would not want anything to do with them. Peaceful reunification was theoretically possible, but the Americans wanted to use their weapons and military might because that's what their corrupt government, propped up by money-hungry military industrialists, wanted. So as long as Americans were on Korean soil, war was inevitable. It was essential to force all foreigners off the sacred peninsula so reunification under communism could take place.

The winner, then, would be the first to strike. Now Fourth Artillery Division took one more step toward making that glorious honor theirs.

Kong opened the checklist book and began making the phone calls, activating the division recall roster and setting everything in motion. A few more calls, and it would roll forward on its own momentum, like a runaway locomotive. Finally, the war would be under way—and the North would strike first and win.

CHAPTER FOUR

MASTER CONTROL AND REPORTING CENTER,
OSAN, REPUBLIC OF KOREA
SEVERAL HOURS LATER

Welcome, Madam Vice President, Admiral Allen, and our other distinguished guests," the Korean Air Force officer began in excellent English. "It is a pleasure to welcome you to the Republic of Korea's most advanced tactical air control facility on the opening day of the free world's largest multinational air combat exercise."

Vice President of the United States Ellen Christine Whiting bowed amidst a polite round of applause. Attending the briefing along with Vice President Whiting was Admiral William Allen, commander of U.S. Pacific Command, the officer in charge of all American military forces between North America and Australia. Accompanying them were a few aides and the chief of the Vice President's Secret Service detail, Special Agent Corrie Law.

After walking around the facility and meeting a great number of the men and women working there, the distinguished visitors were led through the heavily guarded hallways and the massive vaultlike steel doors to the master command room itself. A thin, fit but older South Korean general officer stepped before them, bowed deeply, then began: "My name is Lieutenant General

Park Yom, and I am chief of staff of the Republic of Korea Air Force. It is my very great pleasure to welcome you and conduct this tour of our newest and best command and control facility, a technological marvel and a true sign of friendship and cooperation between our nations in the defense of the free people of the Republic of Korea.

"We are in the Master Control and Reporting Center, which is the main joint American and South Korean military air traffic control center for South Korea. All military flights over the Korean peninsula are handled from this place. In case of war, this would serve as the main command and control center for military air operations. We are sixty feet underground, protected by a total of twenty feet of reinforced concrete, one foot of steel, three inches of Kevlar armor, and over thirty feet of earth. The center can withstand all but a direct nuclear hit. It is impervious to the effects of a nearby nuclear blast, and it can filter out massive quantities of biological and chemical warfare toxins. There is enough generator power for two weeks, enough emergency battery power for seven days, and enough air, water, fuel, and food to sustain two hundred occupants for two months."

General Park motioned to the twelve large full-color digital displays on the wall behind him, covering a four-hundred-square-foot area. "We combine data from radar sites, airborne radars, and warships into a composite image of all air traffic covering over three million cubic miles of space, including over the Yellow Sea, the Sea of Japan, the northern East China Sea, the entire Korean peninsula, and parts of Japan, China, and Russia."

Then the guests were seated in a small auditorium-like area behind two rows of radar controllers at their consoles. "You are seated at the battle staff area," General Park went on. "The senior controller and the deputy senior controller sit there, as well as assistants and communications officers. The senior controller's position is rotated between American and Korean senior field-grade officers. On one side of the battle staff is the Tactical Control Operating Team section, which are the American Air Force officers in charge of American military flights, and on the other side is the Korean Air Combat Control Team, which is in charge of all Korean military flights.

"Behind you are the workstations for thirty staff officers, representing all the American and Korean military services, the United Nations Command, and many government and civilian defense-related agencies, who take reports from field commands and units and pass them to the senior controllers. Behind the staff area is the support staff area, including weather forecasters, security, communications technicians, and so forth. Above you is an observation room, which can be manned by myself or any other high-ranking officials and where directives can be passed down to the senior controller. We shall go up there in a moment to observe the opening battles of today's exercises."

Vice President Whiting nodded. A former Miss America runner-up, an attorney, a former state treasurer, and former governor of Delaware, the forty-eight-year-old mother of two was comfortable and knowledgeable in every aspect of government and public affairs—except what she thought of as the military stuff. President Martindale was the military freak. Her job was to formulate budget policies and communicate with the people, and she did both very well. Guns, bombs, and radar just confused and frustrated her. She relied on a thorough prebriefing and common sense when dealing with military men, who always thought the world revolved around them.

"Very impressive, General," Whiting commented. "It is very similar to the military command centers in the United States, but yours is much more modern and up-to-date."

"As the Republic of Korea has been in a state of war almost since our beginning, Madam Vice President," General Park responded, "we keep this place and all of our control centers and reporting posts in a high state of readiness and modernization at all times. It is a heavy price we pay to maintain our freedom and sovereignty in the face of the Communist threat, but a price we gladly pay."

"Of course," the Vice President said. She had a way of disarming men's hearts with a simple look or a special lilt of her voice, designed to completely captivate, deflate, or gain empathy from those she encountered. But it rarely worked with senior military officers. Empathy, like defeat, was not in their emotional or professional lexicon.

"Our twelve ground-controlled intercept officers monitor and control all military traffic throughout South Korea's airspace," General Park went on. "Each controller is responsible for a sector. There are seven major sectors, one through six plus the North Zone. All military aircraft flying within South Korea need a clearance from us before they can even start engines."

"I notice that the airspace we see doesn't extend all the way to the Demilitarized Zone," Whiting pointed out. "There is also a blank area around Seoul itself. Why is that?"

"In addition to the air traffic sectors, there are separate Korean controllers that monitor and control all traffic within the capital airspace complex, the Korean Buffer Zone, and the Korean Tactical Zone," General Park replied. "The Korean Tactical Zone, otherwise known as Prohibited Area 518, is the area north of the air traffic sectors to the Military Demarcation Line, and it is the area from which Korean air defense units will respond to any border incursions first. The Buffer Zone is a five-mile-wide strip of airspace south of the Military Demarcation Line that acts like a 'warning track' to aircraft operating near the DMZ. The capital airspace complex is two rings, ten and five miles radius, centered on the Blue House. Warning shots will be made on unidentified aircraft that enter the outer ring, and any aircraft not cleared to enter the inner ring will be attacked without further warning and shot down. Although American forces can enter these areas, they are under the control of separate Korean-only controllers."

General Park noted the Vice President's troubled expression. "It is a small but significant token of our national sovereignty, Madam Vice President," he said. "We depend on the United States for so much of our security. Both Americans and Koreans, working side by side, handle all other military air traffic and command and control functions. But as a matter of national pride, we have insisted that control of the frontier between North and South be held strictly by us. The control center is at Taegu, with auxiliary centers at Seoul and Chongju. I will be happy to show it to you at any time."

"Forgive me if I seemed a bit concerned, General," Whiting said apologetically. "I don't mean to suggest that the United States must and should be involved in every facet of Korean defense. But after seeing almost everything else relating to defense in this country so 'joint,' it seemed unusual to see a Korean-only command center. I'm sorry to be so . . . so bigoted."

"Not at all, madam," Park said. Somewhat embarrassed, Whiting thought she detected a look on Park's face that seemed to say "Yes, you are bigoted," but she thought it best to ignore it.

"Today's exercise will involve mostly the Republic of Korea Air Force, with a few American and Japanese air defense units participating as well," Park went on. "Our objective is to try to blunt a sneak attack by the North as they mount a massive incursion into South Korea. The attack will commence just after dawn along the flatlands of the Han River estuary, the coastline, the Uijongbu highway, and the Munsan highway south toward the capital.

"However, this will be a feint. At the same time, a second sneak attack will be mounted by a simulated North Korean strike force in the east, traveling down the coast highway toward Kangnung. Therefore, the success of our forces will depend on discipline. They must not be distracted by the initial, obvious attack toward the capital and must remain vigilant along the entire frontier for signs of enemy invasion.

"The air attacks will take place in target complexes set up here, in Restricted Area 79 southwest of Osan, Restricted Area 124 in the Yellow Sea, and in Restricted Areas 30 and 31 northwest of Kangnung," Park went on. "Each of these target complexes is surrounded by a military operating area and an air combat maneuvering area that are set aside to allow simulated air-to-air attacks. The South Korean bombers will have to rely on their fighter protection to clear a path for them into the ranges. Although every bomber will be able to attack a target in the range—after all, this is a training exercise—the exercise scorekeepers will determine which sorties would have actually survived the enemy air defenses and made it to their targets.

"A probability-of-damage score will be computed for each attacker, and the individual and composite scores will be presented at the mass debrief session at the end of the day. These scores will be used to determine what the scenario will be for the next day. If our forces do well, the enemy may be forced to throw more firepower at us. If our forces do poorly, we may lose bases and equipment. Although this is just an exercise, we will make it as realistic as possible so we can get some authentic, true-to-life training out of it."

Park pointed to one of the large digital screens with a small laser pointer. "Here are our air bases from which we will launch the air attacks in the west," he said. "Seoul, Suwon, Chongju, and Kwangju will each launch a sizable fleet of F-16, F-4, and Hawk fighter-bombers, along with F-5 escort fighters, against the enemy forces in the west. Japan has deployed a number of its MiG-29 and F-15 fighters to Suwon and Seoul, and they will provide air cover for our bombers as well. They are far more capable than our F-5 fighters. The American forces are not participating in today's battle."

"May I ask why, General?" Vice President Whiting said.

"The scenario we devised is based on actual American force doctrine," General Park said, his tone flat. "This doctrine states that American air forces may not act except to defend themselves or by direct order of the President of the United States, no matter what happens to South Korea. In this scenario, no American forces will be threatened. We assume Washington would take time, at least a day, perhaps two, to analyze and respond to the attack. So involvement of U.S. forces in the first day of the Communist offensive is never factored in."

Whiting turned a shocked face to Admiral Allen, silently asking "Is this true?" Allen looked at his Vice President with a pained expression, then said, "I believe the decision to commit our forces would come much, much sooner than that. But the general is . . . technically correct." He added quickly, "However, our on-scene commanders do have considerable latitude to—"

"Depending on how well his forces do, our on-scene commander may choose to commit forces from Kangnung, Taegu, Kunsan, and Ch'unch'on to the western front," General Park interrupted, cutting off Allen's strained effort at conciliation. "If he does, he will not be able to stop the real enemy offensive in the east. The commanders have not been apprised of this scenario—it will be a true test of their discipline, skill, and professionalism."

"How many aircraft will you launch today, General?" Vice President Whiting asked.

"The Air Force will launch almost half of our fleet of bombers and fighters—over three hundred planes," Park replied. "The Army will launch perhaps one-third of its helicopters, another one hundred aircraft. The Navy will launch several P-3 Orion and S-2 Tracker patrol planes and a few dozen helicopters."

"I'd say that's pretty amazing," Admiral Allen commented. "Our biggest war games launch perhaps half that number of aircraft."

"What do the North Koreans think about you launching so many warplanes all at once?" the Vice President asked. "Aren't they alarmed?"

"Of course," General Park replied with a sly smile. "They warn us every year that conducting these exercises is tantamount to a declaration of war. Weeks ago, they announced that they have mobilized their forces, called up their Reserves, and are prepared to fight to the death."

"That sounds serious to me."

"We do not completely ignore these threats," Park said, "but they are only threats. We are prohibited by treaty from loading weapons on more than half our planes, and we have United Nations observers at every base who count how many planes are loaded and report that number to the Security Council. But it actually makes little difference to the Communists. In years past we have completely canceled these exercises, yet the North still threatens war and refuses to negotiate a lasting peace. We have decided that preparing for war, demonstrating our readiness, and providing realistic joint training are far more important than the fear of inciting the Communists.''

"Everything we do seems to incite North Korea," Admiral Allen agreed. "Besides, almost all of South Korea's military forces are geared up for Team Spirit. It would be a bad decision to go to war now."

"We are always 'geared up,' as you say, Admiral," General Park said somberly. "But your point is well taken. We are always prepared for a sneak attack by the Communists, but tactically speaking we think now would be a foolish time for them to do so."

General Park turned to Whiting and added, "As you may have noticed, Madam Vice President, after our national anthem is played at reveille and at retreat, we also recite a prayer for peace. Some airmen drop to their knees on the tarmac as they pray. But they will then climb into their planes and be just as anxious and just as fervent in their desire to kill the enemy and defend their homeland. That is the struggle we live with every day."

"I've noticed," Whiting responded. She wondered why Park had mentioned that. "General Park, how do you feel about war with the North? Do you want the peninsula reunited? If so, are you willing to go to war to do it?"

Park Yom hesitated, obviously uncomfortable with the question. "Please excuse me, Madam Vice President," he said, "but I am not permitted to speak openly about such matters."

"Anything you tell me will be in the strictest confidence, I assure you," Whiting said.

Park gave her a wry smile. "I know enough about politics and government, madam," he said, "to know that nothing a general says to a foreign leader could be held in confidence. It is your job, your duty, to divulge such things." Park was right, of course. If something happened, or if Martindale asked her, Whiting would recount the entire conversation word for word. But she tried again.

"General, I really want to know—will South Korea go to war?" Park remained stone-faced. "It's vital that we work together to protect your country and deter any aggression, General," she went on. "Unilateral action can only lead to disaster."

"War is certainly not desirable, Madam Vice President," Park said. "True warriors abhor war." There was a long, very uncomfortable pause. Then: "Do not be concerned, Madam Vice President." Whiting felt a chill go down her spine.

Admiral Allen motioned to the computer screens. "It looks like some launches have already taken place," he said. They all turned to the screens. Several white lines began tracking northward across the digital maps from the southernmost South Korean bases—Kwangju, Kunsan, and Taegu. "I didn't think the exercise was kicking off for another hour or so."

At that moment, Secret Service Special Agent Corrie Law answered a secure cell phone call, then told the Vice President that a call was coming in from Washington. General Park escorted the Vice President, Admiral Allen, and the others upstairs to the staff observation area, a large room whose windows overlooked the command center below, and left them alone. Corrie Law stood guard inside; a plainclothes U.S. Marine Corps sergeant stood guard outside the door.

"Professor here and not secure," the Vice President said into the phone. It was a secure cellular telephone, and they were in a room at least partly owned and operated by the United States, but Whiting harbored no confidence that the room was clear of listening devices.

"Hello, Professor. This is Paramedic." It was Director of Central Intelligence Robert Plank. The White House Communications Center must be stuck on job names this month, Whiting thought. "Enjoying your trip?"

"You know how much I enjoy military technology and the ever-present scent of impending war," Whiting replied sardonically. "What's up?"

"I hate to put you on the spot like this," Plank said, "but we're picking up some unusual communications activity. I don't mean for you to act as a trained analyst or anything, but is anything . . . out of the ordinary there?"

"You're right—it is pretty tacky of you to ask me a question like that, knowing that I'm a guest of the South Korean government and standing in their own high-security command center," Whiting said. "But to answer your question—no, I haven't noticed anything unusual. What kind of activity?"

"It's probably all related to the Team Spirit exercise," Plank said, but she could hear worry in his voice. "Lots of coded communications traffic that our military guys couldn't decode—if it was part of the exercise, I'd think we would be able to decipher that. But it's what we're not getting that's just as interesting as what we're getting."

"Which is?"

"Which is nothing much from *North* Korea," Plank said. "Every South Korean military base is jabbering away using a new code, lots of activity everywhere—including lots of activity from units not involved in Team Spirit—but nothing from the North. Usually, the activity between the two is the same—one starts talking, the other reports it, the other reports that report, the other makes new reports, and so on until it finally subsides. Now South Korea's comm traffic has substantially increased, but the North is virtually silent. Only simple 'ops-normal' messages from their command centers. A few units belonging to First Corps on the move here and there, nothing big. Just unusually quiet."

"Well, everything seems to be 'ops-normal' around here," Whiting said, looking around the observation room and trying to make sense of all the data displayed on the large computer monitors. She shook her head and gave up. "Anything else, Paramedic?"

"Have you seen President Kwon yet?"

"I'm not scheduled to meet with him until later," Whiting replied irritably. "He wanted to give a little pep talk to some of his troops before the big mass take-off. General Park has been showing me around."

"Can you let me know when President Kwon arrives?"

This was quite enough. "Listen, Paramedic, I'm not in the mood for playing spy for you today. Everything looks normal around here. I'll tell you as soon as possible if I notice anything unusu—"

At that moment, the door to the staff observation room was flung open, and the U.S. Marine guard, stunned but apparently not badly hurt, was pushed inside. Several South Korean soldiers rushed in after him, M-16 rifles at the ready.

PEOPLE'S ARMY BASE,
SUNAN, DEMOCRATIC PEOPLE'S
REPUBLIC OF KOREA
THAT SAME TIME

Why is that train stopped?" Colonel Cho Mun-san shouted. "Never mind, I don't care why. I want it moved within the next ten minutes or I will get some soldiers in here who can. Now *move!*" But even more black smoke poured out from under the locomotive pulling Unit Twenty, and Colonel Cho renewed his furious tirade each time another officer crossed his path.

It was not the first time Captain Kong Hwan-li had ever seen a Nodong-1 missile up close, but it always thrilled him to be so close to his country's ultimate weapon. Although the missile was still in its canister in rail-march configuration, Kong could sense its power.

Unlike the missile he had been trained on, the old ex-Soviet 8K14 Scud-B, the Nodong-1 was North Korea's first truly accurate land-attack ballistic nuclear missile. The FROG series rockets were unguided spin-stabilized weapons; the Scud series used simple gyroscopes, little more than toys, to keep the missiles pointed at their targets. Neither missile had an accuracy better than a thousand meters, and most times they were lucky to have it hit within two or three miles.

Not so the Nodong-1. It had a true inertial navigation system, which used computer-controlled accelerometers to actually sense the motion of the earth to help improve its accuracy. In fact, the warhead of the Nodong-1 had a better stabilization and steering mechanism than the most modern Scud model. Although the Nodong was still a liquid-fueled rocket, like the Scud, it used less corrosive and more stable propellants and was easier to service in the field. The Nodong-1 was carried aboard a railcar, loosely disguised to look like a standard commercial cargo container. A single locomotive pulled the launch car, a reload car that carried two more missiles, a maintenance car, a command car, and a security car.

Captain Kong marveled at the Nodong's simple yet elegant design. He had trained on the Nodong-1 back at Cheung-son, North Korea's nuclear development and training base, before he got his new assignment to Fourth Artillery Division headquarters. North Korea was developing even more powerful rockets, like the Daepedong-2—a rocket that could hit targets in North America with a fifty-kiloton nuclear warhead—but the Nodong was currently their best deterrence against capitalist aggression.

Unfortunately, this particular unit was not performing well at all. All of the Nodong rail units were assembled inside a huge covered shelter, along with a number of decoy units that were sent out onto the commercial rail system all at once. But just as Unit Twenty had cleared the shelter, a brake booster system failed. Trains were not easy things to stop once they got started. It was deemed too dangerous to try to back the unit into the shelter if the brakes were inoperative, and it would take several minutes to get another locomotive hooked up. So this unit was now exposed to the world, available for any enemy reconnaissance or surveillance satellite passing overhead to get a good look.

In fact, it appeared that most of the missile units deployed over the past few hours had irritating minor problems, which really disturbed Kong. Normally, the men of Fourth Artillery Division were the best of the best. Over the past several months, however, the quality of their performance had markedly decreased. Of course, morale was already at an all-time low because of the poor economy. While the military usually got the best, far better than the civilian population, these days even the elite units were suffering. This meant morale was bound to suffer still more, even among the best-trained and most highly motivated troops. This was the absolutely worst possible time to suffer a malfunction like the one they were witnessing.

"Weaklings," Kong muttered. A bunch of malcontent soldiers bellyaching about not being paid. The People's Army provided the best the country could offer. Everyone had to make sacrifices. Didn't they realize who was responsible for the shortages and poverty? The capitalists in South Korea were deliberately sucking the life out of the North, to weaken it enough to make an attack easier and less bloody. How could the People's Army soldiers *not* want to do their part to save their homeland—to strike back at those who were responsible for their families' pain and hardship?

At last another locomotive appeared outside the thick steel security gate. There were not enough rail sidings to move the malfunctioning locomotive out of the way, so Kong assumed the new one would simply be hooked up to the existing engine and go on its way. He pulled out his walkie-talkie and keyed the mike button. "Taepung, this is Seven," Kong radioed, using Colonel Cho's call sign. *Taepung* meant "typhoon." "I request permission to go to Unit Twenty to inquire about the new engine. I shall report to you what I find."

"Proceed," Colonel Cho responded. "*Ppalli*. Report back to me in five minutes."

"*Ne, Taepung*," Kong replied, and hurried over to the command car to talk with the battery commander. But when he was just a few meters away from the command car, Kong slowed, then stopped. Something was wrong here. There were no guards on duty. Thirty security guards were assigned to each Nodong battery, and four of them were assigned to patrol outside the command car while it was stopped. What in blazes was going on here? He sped over to the entry hatch and, as he reached it, heard several gunshots from inside.

Kong pulled his walkie-talkie from its holster and shouted, "Gunshots! Gunshots! Inside the command car!"

Just then the heavy steel entry hatch to the command car swung open, and several security guards and technicians jumped outside. One of them was shouting gleefully, "Freedom! Freedom!"

"*What are you men doing?*" Kong yelled. "Why aren't you on duty?"

One of the guards shouted at him, "Don't try to stop us now, lackey!" raised a pistol, and fired at Kong. He flinched as he felt the bullet whiz by his left shoulder, spun around, and threw himself on the muddy ground. He reached for his holster, finally controlling his trembling fingers enough to lift the flap and pull out his Type 68 automatic pistol. But the soldiers were long gone by the time he raised the pistol to return fire. Or had he moved slowly on purpose, hoping the security guards would think the shot had wounded him and leave? He didn't want to think he had been cowardly . . . no. He was alive, and that was the most important thing.

"Attention! Attention!" Kong radioed on the walkie-talkie. "There has been an attack on Unit Twenty's command car! All security forces, seal off the area and allow no one to leave or enter! Taepung, Taepung, please report to the Unit Twenty command car!"

Pistol raised, Kong made his way to the command car. It was wide open and completely unguarded. Cautiously, he made his way inside. There was a small chamber inside the outer hatch, big enough for two or three men. This was the chemical/biological warfare air lock and decontamination chamber that would alternately spray a soldier with decontamination fluid and then blow his body with compressed air to remove traces of toxins or radioactive fallout. He was shocked to see that the inner hatch was open too. Even after what had just happened to him, all Kong could think about was how serious a breach of security and anticontamination procedures this was—both hatches open while . . .

He could smell it before he saw it in the gloom of the command module. It was the stench of violent death: the putrid smell of feces and urine, the coppery smell of fresh blood, all mixed with the acid smell of gunpowder. The battery commander, his deputy commander, his noncommissioned officer in charge, and the communications technician—all were dead, still in their seats, with bullet holes in the backs of their necks just under the edge of their helmets.

"What in the name of heaven?" Colonel Cho shouted, arriving breathlessly at the command car, a Type 64 Browning pistol in his hand.

"Traitors," Captain Kong said. "Traitors to their uniform and their fatherland. The security troops appear to have turned against us. They slaughtered the battery commander and the command car crew."

"In the name of Tangun, help us," moaned Colonel Cho, invoking the name of the mythical warlord of ancient Korea.

Kong saw he was frozen in confusion and said, "Sir, we must establish contact with the rest of the division immediately." He stooped down and retrieved large silver keys from around the commander's and deputy commander's necks. Thankfully, the traitors hadn't thought to remove the missile launch keys from their victims. He gave one to Cho, who held it the way a child holds a fuzzy caterpillar for the first time—both scared and fascinated. "This uprising could have been organized throughout the command," Kong warned.

"We must make contact with as many missile batteries as possible and assess our operational status."

"I . . . I do not know . . . We must contact headquarters . . ."

"There is no time!" Kong shouted. "Our first priority is to preserve our missile batteries from the enemy—especially if the enemy is within our own ranks. We must contact the division."

Cho seemed utterly bewildered. Kong ignored him and started dragging bodies out of the command car, shoving Cho out of his way as he did so. The colonel did not protest. When he finished the bloody task, Kong went back to the battery commander's seat and got on the scrambled command net: "To all Fourth Artillery Division batteries, to all Fourth Artillery Division batteries, this is Taepung." Again, there was no protest from Cho when he heard Kong use his call sign. "We have been attacked by traitors and spies. All brigades, report status."

It took little time for the reports to filter in because very few units responded. Kong estimated he did not hear from one-half to two-thirds of all companies. He was stunned. More than 180 missile batteries, representing one-sixth of the offensive and defensive might of the Democratic People's Republic of Korea, were off the air.

Kong soon found out why. When he switched over to the division security net, which linked the security forces of all deployed missile units, he heard: "Now is the moment to rise against your oppressors, fellow Koreans! Brothers, strike now! Your comrades to the south are moving to join you in your struggle for freedom and unity, once and forever! The borders are open, comrades! There is no longer a Demilitarized Zone. Korea is free! Korea is one! Now strike! Rise up against any who oppose peace, freedom, and unity. Strike against any, no matter what uniform or title they wear, who continue to oppress and starve their own in the name of mindless ideology. Disable all weapons of mass destruction, carry your personal weapons for self-defense, and march on the capital and bring down the repressive outlaw regime once and for all! You are not alone! Hundreds of thousands of others throughout Korea are with you!"

Captain Kong Hwan-li was horrified. Capitalist propaganda—right on the division's security network! He switched channels to Unit Twenty's brigade command net and heard the identical broadcast. To his astonishment, the message, obviously on a continuous-loop broadcast, was being sent over several communications networks, both secure and nonsecure.

No . . . not a recorded message. Several times the message was interrupted by live broadcasts. Units he could identify, all within Fourth Division—even some officers whose voices he could recognize—were reporting that they had taken control of their companies or battalions and were disabling their weapons and moving toward Pyongyang. Hundreds—no, *thousands*—of soldiers were defecting. He heard no officers higher in rank than captain. Some of them bragged about killing Major this or Colonel that—battalion and brigade commanders. There was talk of moving on the capital . . .

Kong shut off the radio. This was impossible. It had to be the South, somehow broadcasting propaganda messages on the secure division comm net and persuading the soldiers to defect or to desert their units en masse! Kong refused to believe that the soldiers were acting of their own free will, or in the hope that they might actually unify the peninsula. There had to be some hidden signal in the broadcast altering the men's minds, brainwashing them into actually killing a superior officer and leaving a nuclear or biochemical missile on the field.

"What is happening, Captain?" Cho asked, as if awakening from a deep slumber.

"The capitalists have somehow brainwashed our soldiers into believing the borders have been thrown wide open and they should kill all the commanders and storm the capital," Kong replied. "I heard reports that several high-ranking division officers were killed or imprisoned by the traitors."

To Kong's surprise, the old colonel's shoulders started to quiver. "We must get away," he said, sounding on the verge of tears. "We . . . we should take a civilian vehicle and . . . No, we should take a military vehicle, go cross-country, try to make it to the Ministry of Defense or to First Corps headquarters. We will find help there." In between sobs, Kong heard him mutter, "My name . . . my good name . . . what is to become of me? . . . my retirement . . ."

Kong was repelled. All the old fool could think about was his pension and his reputation—whether his name would be remembered, forgotten, revered, or defiled in the minds of future generations.

"It might be dangerous to go to Pyongyang, sir," Kong said. It pained him to call this man "sir." Instead of commander of a twenty-thousand-man ballistic missile division, Cho had turned into a trembling, fearful old man. "If the reports of traitors marching on the capital are true, we won't make it. Our best bet is to try to head north, away from the capital, to Sinuiju or even Kanggye." Sinuiju was the capital of the province of Pyongan Pukdo; it was right on the Chinese border, and there, Kong reasoned, they would find plenty of support and help from Communist Party supporters and the Chinese Army itself. Kanggye was the capital of Chagang Do province and the headquarters of North

Korea's nuclear, chemical, and biological weapons facilities, probably the most secure and defensible base in North Korea. "If we can find an all-terrain vehicle, we can stay off the roads in case we encounter more deserters."

"Very well, Captain," Cho said. "Find us a suitable vehicle with fuel and weapons. And deal harshly with anyone who tries to stop you."

Well, that was the first bit of backbone the old fart has shown in a long time. "Of course, sir," he said. "But first, we must deactivate the missiles. Unit Twenty has one missile in its erector-launcher and one reload; Unit Seventeen is just a few kilometers away. It will be easy to—"

"No!" Cho shouted, his eyes spinning in fear. "We will leave right away!"

"Sir, we *must* deactivate the Nodong missiles," Kong said. "If this is part of an invasion, we cannot let our live missiles fall into enemy hands. That would be a complete disaster!" He saw Cho was going to continue arguing, so he quickly added, "Sir, all I have to do is activate the missile's thermal battery without processing a launch command. In just over five minutes, the battery will discharge, the missile's onboard computer will be rendered useless, and no one will be able to launch it. The battery cannot be recharged—the missile must be completely dismantled to charge the battery. Impossible to do in the field. It is the fastest way to keep a live missile out of enemy hands, so it cannot readily be used against us."

Cho still looked dazed. Deciding to act, Kong jumped off the deck of the command car to head for the launcher. He heard a weak "Wait, Hwan!" behind him—the first time that he could remember Colonel Cho using his given name—but kept moving. Gunshots cracked behind him. He hunched down automatically and dodged left toward the side of the command car for cover, then turned. The shots were coming from Colonel Cho—the idiot was shouting and firing at the sky! Kong couldn't tell what he was yelling over the noise of the gunshots and the roar of fighter jets . . .

Fighter jets! Kong looked up to where Cho was blasting away just as a small, sleek, single-engine fighter roared overhead. To Kong's shock, it was not a Chinese or Soviet-made fighter—it was an American-made F-16 fighter-bomber! It was low enough for Kong to see it was heavily laden with all sorts of external weapons; he could make out two large fuel tanks, two large missiles, racks of smaller gravity weapons, smaller missiles on the wings, jammer pods or datalink pods under the fuselage, and smaller missiles on the wingtips. Seconds later several more F-16s that looked similarly equipped streaked by a few miles farther east. The jets were flying no more than a few thousand feet above the ground— but well out of range of Colonel Cho's futile pistol shots.

Of course, Kong knew exactly what they were—they were well briefed on South Korean military hardware: F-16C/Js, the capitalists' newest and most formidable weapon system. Each one carried two antiradar missiles that would home in and destroy surface-to-air missile-tracking radars. They also carried cluster bombs to destroy the missile launchers or any other soft targets they might encounter. Once their air-to-ground weapons were expended, each F-16C/J could transform into an air superiority fighter, with its 20-millimeter cannon and two radar-guided and two heat-seeking air-to-air missiles. The fuel tanks gave the F-16 very good range and loiter time.

But what Kong found most disturbing in the sighting was that all the F-16s still had all of their antiradar missiles onboard. They were over a hundred miles north of the Demilitarized Zone—they had probably overflown the capital, Pyongyang!—yet they had not fired their antiradar missiles. How was it possible for all those enemy fighters to fly so deep into North Korea yet not have to fire one attack missile or drop a single bomb?

Then came several loud explosions in the distance. He'd jumped the gun—the F-16s were indeed attacking. Kong didn't know what the target was, but it appeared to be on the main base itself, on the west side—possibly division headquarters. From the sound, they were using five-hundred- or thousand-pound bombs, not cluster munitions. It was almost certainly the headquarters building. Cut off the communications, and the division was instantly deaf, dumb, and blind. They could easily . . .

Wait. What if all communications weren't yet cut off? Just because the division's comm nets were being disrupted by the traitors didn't mean the entire People's Army defense network was shut down! There might still be a chance . . .

Kong ran back to the command car. He had tried all the division nets, trying to communicate with the brigades and battalions and assess the status of the division. He never tried "Fire Dragon." Fire Dragon was the nationwide command channel direct to People's Army headquarters in Pyongyang and rebroadcast throughout the country by extreme low-frequency transmitters that were immune to the electromagnetic pulse generated by nuclear explosions. Fire Dragon had one main purpose: to transmit the execution order for a nuclear, chemical, or biological warfare attack.

As he suspected, Fire Dragon was still on the air—and it was indeed in use. Kong heard a long string of letters and numbers. He pulled out a decoding book, listened, and waited. He must not start copying a coded message until he was sure he was copying from the beginning. When he heard the words "All units, all units, I say again . . ." he started copying. At the end of the long message, he pulled out the decoder documents, found the proper date-time group page, and began decoding.

As he suspected, it was an execution order. Pyongyang was ordering its forces to attack. The decoded message contained the launch order, a launch authenticator code for the computer—and a warhead fusing enable code. The order was simple: all units, all weapons, fire at will, reload, fire at will, reload, fire at will. He hurriedly rechecked his work, but he had done hundreds of launch decoding exercises and had never made a mistake with such a deadly, dreadful task.

Kong retrieved the commander's checklist. He wiped out all awareness of the stench of death and the treason he had heard, and set to work. The panel was undamaged, and full power came on instantly.

Moments later Colonel Cho came running into the command car. "The missile! The missile!" he screeched. "The launcher has been raised! It appears to be in firing position!"

"It *is* in firing position, old man," Kong said. With a shaky finger, he dialed in the launch authenticator code. It was immediately accepted, and the three-minute countdown commenced. He also immediately received a fault message, telling him the hatch to the command car was open—as a safety measure, the computer would not process a launch until the command car was secure. The countdown would continue, but if the command car wasn't secure, no launch would take place, and after five minutes the missile would dud itself. "Come in and close the door, Colonel," he ordered.

"What are you doing, Captain?"

"I am preparing to launch my missile," Kong replied.

"I have received a valid launch order. I intend to launch all of Unit Twenty's missiles, then proceed to all of the units I can find and launch their weapons too."

"I ordered you to find me a vehicle so we can escape to Kanggye," Cho said. "Forget about firing the missile. That is not our responsibility."

"Our nation is under attack, Colonel," Kong shot back. "I have received a valid launch message, and I intend to carry it out. I need you in the deputy commander's seat, Colonel. You must help me launch the missiles. Just do as I tell you and—"

"And I order you to stop this nonsense and find me a vehicle!"

In a fit of rage, Kong leaped out of his seat, grabbed Cho, punched him in the stomach, threw him into the deputy commander's seat on the other side of the console, then closed and latched both hatches. Only momentarily did he feel a flash of regret and shame for striking or even touching a superior officer and an elder—acts that went against everything Koreans were taught from birth. But this nation's survival and defense were more important than the whinings of a gutless old man.

"Colonel, you must—you *will* help me carry out the attack order," Kong said. He inserted the commander's and deputy commander's launch keys into the locks, then pulled Cho up so his face was right next to the key switch. "When I give the word, you will turn the launch key. You must do it at the same instant as I do, within a fraction of a second, or the missile will dud itself." After the countdown was initiated, as a security and safety measure the keys had to be turned within two seconds of T minus zero, and they had to turn simultaneously. Launch crews spend time every week practicing this procedure. It was very unlikely that this whimpering old man on the verge of a breakdown could do it properly.

Cho, half collapsed against his seat, sobbed like a child. "Do you understand, Colonel?" No response. Kong pulled out his sidearm and aimed it at Cho's head. "Do it, Colonel, or I will put a bullet in your brain and end your miserable, cowardly life right now."

"I can't . . . I won't do it," a weeping Cho protested. "I want to get out of here. I want to go home . . ."

"Your home—*our* home—is being destroyed by the capitalists and their American puppet masters right now," Kong shouted. "The only way to save our homeland is to stop the South, and the only way to stop them is with our missiles. Now put your hand on the key and turn it when I give you the signal!"

"No! No, I cannot—"

"*I will kill you if you do not do as I say!*" Kong burst out, the muzzle of the gun quivering. "Put your hand on that key!"

"Kill me!" Cho shouted. "Kill me! If I cannot go home, you may as well end my miserable life right now!"

Twenty seconds to go. Time was running out. Kong had only one thing left to try. "Sir, I neglected to tell you," he said, his voice now calm and soothing. "Headquarters left a message for you. They are ready to award you a fine pension and recognize your value to the fatherland. They are going to retire you with full military honors, sir."

"A . . . a pension?" Cho said weakly, finally turning toward Kong. "A full pension? Upon my retirement?" Color began returning to his face, and he straightened up in his seat. "I am to be awarded a pension and a full retirement?"

"With full military honors," Kong said, "as befitting

a commander so loyal and dedicated to the fatherland."
He motioned to the code book, with the decoded
launch execution and weapon pre-arming codes in it.
"This is the last order you will be given, Colonel. Your
last official act. Do as I say, and the Glorious Leader
himself will pin the Star of Honor on your chest. He has
even authorized a passport and travel if you wish: Hong
Kong, Ho Chi Minh City, Tripoli, even Havana." Kong
glanced up at the countdown clock—shit, less than ten
seconds to go! "Ready, Colonel? Your last act before
your retirement. Turn the key to the right when I tell
you. I will say 'Ready, ready, *now*' as I bob my head,
and when I say *now*, you turn the key. Do you—"

Suddenly, a tremendous series of explosions shook
the command car, followed by the sound of a jet fighter
screaming overhead. The string of bombs sounded as if
a giant were running toward them, and then one of the
giant's boots kicked the command car. A five-hundred-
pound bomb exploded just a few feet outside it, sending
both men flying into the bulkhead from the impact.
Cho screamed.

Kong picked himself off the deck and looked over
just as Cho shouted, "Damn you all for condemning me
to obscurity forever!"—and turned the launch key.

Kong's hand shot out to his own key switch. It
would not be simultaneous but . . . He turned the
key. It worked! The missile launched! The roar of the
Nodong-1 was a hundred times louder than the bomb
that had just exploded outside. Kong checked the system readouts and was pleased—they showed a fully
pre-armed warhead and a fully aligned heading and
navigation system. The missile was alive and tracking
perfectly. He had done it! He immediately hit the
PRELOAD command switch, which automatically moved
the transporter-erector-launcher assembly to its preload
condition and also commanded the second Nodong

missile to raise up to load position, then he hurried outside.

The Nodong missile was long gone by the time Kong made it outside the command car—all he could see was a trail of white, acid. It arced across the sky toward the southeast, so he knew it was on course. Then he checked the progress of the reload and knew he would be launching no more missiles. The nearby bomb explosions had damaged the car containing the reload missile; white and orange smoke—the missile's fuel and oxidizer—was beginning to billow out. By the time the reload missile itself was visible, its corrosive fuel had all but leaked out. It would set itself on fire, perhaps even explode, in minutes. Unit Twenty was effectively dead. Nothing else to do but find another missile—or escape into friendly hands.

"We did it!" he heard behind him. Colonel Cho leaped off the steps of the command car and ran over to Kong. "We launched her! You and me, Captain! Our job is finished. We obeyed our orders and did as we were told, and now it's time for our reward."

"Yes, sir," Kong said. "Time for your reward." He pulled out his pistol and put two bullets into Colonel Cho's chest, then one more into his brain after he hit the ground.

MASTER CONTROL AND REPORTING CENTER,
OSAN AIR BASE, REPUBLIC OF KOREA
THAT SAME TIME

Special Agent Law's mini-Uzi was in her hand in an instant, but before she could reach the Vice President or level her weapon, several South Korean special forces soldiers burst into the observation room. All of them carried M-16 rifles at port arms—at the ready, but not leveled or aimed at anyone. General Park was right behind them, standing in the middle of the doorway. He now had a sidearm strapped to his waist, but the weapon was not drawn. Law raised her weapon . . .

"Wait, Corrie," Vice President Whiting shouted. "Don't shoot!"

Everyone froze. Corrie Law could have easily mowed down every South Korean in the room—with the soldiers' weapons visible, the threat was clear and present, but there was no way they could defend themselves in time. They could see the cold, dead look in Law's eyes: no fear, no hesitation, no mercy. Her gun muzzle did not waver. If the Vice President gave the order, they knew she would open fire and put a three-round burst into each one of them before they had the chance to get into a firing stance.

"Put your weapons down on the floor *now* or I will fire," Law shouted.

"What's going on there, Ellen?" CIA Director Plank asked on the cell phone.

"Don't, Corrie . . ."

"I said, put your weapons down!" Law repeated. She raised the Uzi so she could use the sights; the muzzle tracked every movement of her eyes as they caught the slightest motion of the soldiers. Law maneuvered herself between the soldiers and the Vice President, then positioned her back behind a console so no one could get a clear shot at her. Summoning the only bits of Korean she knew, she shouted, "*Mit ppali!* Down quickly!"

"What's going on here, General?" the Vice President asked. She held the cell phone behind her back, pointed outward against the chance Plank might pick up the conversation. "Why do you have soldiers in here? Are we your prisoners?"

"No, Madam Vice President," General Park replied. "You are our guests, and a witness."

"Witness? Witness to what?"

"Close your telephone connection with Director Plank and I will tell you," said a new voice. And Kwon Ki-chae, the president of South Korea, entered the room. He ordered the soldiers to lower their weapons and leave; General Park remained.

Vice President Whiting raised the still-active phone to her lips. "I'll call you back, Bob."

"What in hell's going on there, Ellen?"

"President Kwon and General Park want to have an urgent parley with me, in private. I'll call you back." "Urgent parley" was a code phrase for "The situation here is tense; have help standing by." She pushed a button on the phone, closed it, and slipped it into an inside jacket pocket.

General Park issued some instructions by radio in Korean and then turned to Whiting. "All wireless communications from this facility will be jammed now, Madam Vice President," he said. "It is for our protection." It was obvious he knew that the Vice President had activated a function on the phone that kept the line open and transmitted a locator signal.

"Jamming our locator signal could be considered a hostile action, General," Whiting said evenly.

"Discussing activities inside our country's most secret command and control facility with the Central Intelligence Agency could also be considered a hostile act," General Park said. "As you Americans might say, that makes us even stephen."

"Please be seated," President Kwon said, motioning to a chair. He gave Park an order, and the Air Force general immediately unbuckled his holster and handed the weapon over to Special Agent Law. "I promise, we mean you no harm."

Law immediately went over to the door and tried it, keeping both Kwon and Park covered with her mini-Uzi; it was locked. "So we *are* your prisoners," Whiting said. "We can't communicate, and we can't leave."

"You will be free to leave in a very short time," President Kwon said. "But first I invite you to watch history in the making, unfolding right before your eyes."

"What are you talking about?"

"May I?" Kwon asked, motioning to the large windows overlooking the command center to indicate to Law where he was going to move. He went over to the windows with Whiting. General Park took a seat behind the communications console. "The culmination of years of planning, a year of intense preparation, months of espionage and infiltration work, and hundreds of billions of won. The expense almost bankrupted us, especially with the financial downturn throughout Asia in recent years. We lost many fine men and women to the Communists, on both sides of the DMZ. We are about to witness the fruits of their sacrifice."

"Mr. President, what's going on?" Whiting asked. "What are you planning to do?"

General Park said something in Korean, and Kwon nodded with a broad smile and what sounded to her like a muttered prayer. "Our first units are approaching the coastline," Kwon told Whiting. "The Eleventh Patrol Squadron out of Inchon has the honor of leading the attack. Their call sign is 'Namu.' The counterjammer aircraft will be inbound sixty seconds later. Their call sign is 'Pokpo.' "

"*Attack?*" Admiral Allen exploded. "What attack? You mean the exercise attack?"

"The Eleventh is an S-2 Tracker maritime patrol unit, flying one of the slowest and most vulnerable planes in our inventory," General Park said. "However, these planes have been modified as tactical jamming aircraft. They will shut down all of the Communists' search radars between Haeju and Kaesong. They are being followed by F-16KCJ aircraft carrying HARM antiradar missiles. Any Communist radar that attempts to counter the jamming will be destroyed. A similar attack is commencing from the west toward Nampo and Pyongyang itself, from the east toward Hamhung and Hungnam, and from the south at Kimchaek and Ch'ongjin."

"This is crazy! This is suicide!" Vice President Whiting exclaimed. "Won't the North Koreans see those planes coming or see the jamming on their scopes and warn the rest of their defenses? They might start a retaliatory strike the second they notice all this happening. They might be starting an attack of their own at this very second!"

"In fact, Madam Vice President," General Park said, "the Communists issued the first attack warning over fifteen minutes ago."

"*What?*"

"It is virtually impossible to fly anywhere within two hundred miles of North Korea without some Communist radar site detecting you, whatever your altitude," General Park said calmly. "The Communists start tracking our aircraft almost from the moment they are launched. When our planes were within ten minutes' flying time of their airspace—the amount of time it takes the slowest North Korean fighter pilot to get off the ground—the early-warning radar sites issued a warning to all other air defense sites throughout North Korea. The warning was relayed to the Military Command and Coordination Facility at Sunan, near Pyongyang."

"But if the North Koreans know you're coming, *why in heaven's name are you doing this?*"

"Because, Madam Vice President," President Kwon

replied, "the North Korean Central Command Facility issued instructions to all installations to continue to monitor the aircraft but to take no further action. They then issued an 'ops-normal' message to military headquarters in Pyongyang."

"How do you know that?"

"Because, madam, it was a United Republic of Korea officer who issued those orders. Or, to be more precise, a North Korean patriot, working together with South Korean military assistance officers. The North Korean military command and control headquarters at Sunan, such as it is, belongs to North Korean patriots who desire nothing else but the reunification of the peninsula under a free, democratic government. They have decided to shut down the Communists' military machine and allow us to assist them in destroying the most dangerous elements of it."

At that moment a Klaxon went off in the observation room, and red revolving lights started blinking everywhere. On the public-address system they heard: "For Namu Two-Five, for Namu Two-Five, and for Pokpo Three-Eight, for Pokpo Three-Eight, this is Airedale, Hot Dog Hot Dog Hot Dog. Turn to heading one-five-zero immediately. Acknowledge."

Both General Park and President Kwon started to chuckle. "I have always thought that was very amusing," Kwon said. Whiting stared at him. Total chaos was breaking out in the command center, and these two men were laughing through it! "The code words you Americans invent for serious situations such as this are very comical. What a refreshing sense of humor you people have."

"What is going on?"

"Perhaps you do not know what this Hot Dog message means?" Kwon was surprised. "How little you know of the things you have put in place in our country that we rely on every day for our lives and our freedom. The Hot Dog warning is issued whenever an aircraft violates the Buffer Zone. It is supposed to warn our aircraft of unintentional overflight. 'Airedale' is the senior American battle director, whom you met down below in the command center.

"The warning is actually issued quite frequently, usually due to radar anomalies, jamming or decoying by the Communists, or by accident—an overzealous pilot, a new pilot trying to find landmarks, or one who is distracted from his work. Many innocent causes. The North calls them all preludes to war and declarations of war and demands an apology and reparations. Such demands are ignored, of course."

They heard the Hot Dog call repeated many times, with several more call signs. Then there was a commotion on the floor of the command center, and they saw South Korean soldiers enter and head for several of the American officers and technicians.

"What's going on down there, President Kwon?" Ellen Whiting asked. "I demand to know."

"The American officers in charge of protecting and directing air traffic in South Korea are obviously upset because they issued a command to the South Korean pilots heading toward North Korea, and our officers would do nothing to stop them," General Park answered for Kwon. "They are being restrained before they can call for any American aircraft to scramble to try to stop them."

"They're hurting them, for God's sake!" Law protested. There were at least three South Korean soldiers around each of the Americans, who were struggling to free themselves.

"Do not worry, Madam Vice President," President Kwon said, reading Whiting's thoughts. "As you can see, none of my soldiers down there are armed with anything more than batons. We have no intention of hurting any of your people. They are only trying to do their jobs." A few scuffles broke out, but the Americans were quickly hustled out and replaced by Korean technicians. In a matter of minutes, the only Americans left were in the observation area.

A few moments later the Klaxon sounded again. This time they heard: "Jack Rabbit, Jack Rabbit, Jack Rabbit, this is Guardian on Guard. All aircraft evacuate P-518 immediately." The controller then read off a date-time group and a coded authenticator.

" 'Jack Rabbit' is the warning that a border violation has just occurred," General Park explained. " 'Guardian' is the call sign of the American Airborne Warning and Control System radar plane that monitors all air activity across the Korean peninsula. P-518 is the Tactical Zone, the area south of the DMZ where unidentified aircraft will be shot down without warning. The general officer aboard that aircraft is the fourth in command, behind the joint forces commander, the Korean tactical control director, and the American battle director. Since no warning of a border penetration was ever sent from this headquarters, it became Guardian's responsibility to issue the warning. Obviously, we cannot do anything to stop those onboard your radar plane. The cat, as you Americans say, is out of the bag."

Vice President Whiting watched in fascination. The computer screens now showed several tracks northbound across the DMZ, from the Yellow Sea all the way across the peninsula to the Sea of Japan. It was a coordinated launch of several dozen units, timed to perfection—they crossed either the DMZ or the coastline inbound to their targets at almost exactly the same instant. At the same time, several more tracks began moving northward from other South Korean bases.

"Mr. President, General Park, you must call a halt to

this right away," Admiral Allen said. "Sir, you cannot hope to stage this attack without a forceful and possibly disastrous retaliation from North Korea, China, or both. You cannot hope to cripple North Korea's armed forces enough to prevent a counterattack. At last analysis, the North has stationed half a million troops within sixty miles of the DMZ. Your Air Force can't possibly hope to stop them all."

"Admiral, it is not our intention to completely destroy the Communists' military forces," President Kwon said. "As you so correctly point out, that would be a costly and dangerous operation. General, please explain to the Vice President and the admiral."

General Park bowed to President Kwon, then turned to Whiting and Allen. "President Kwon rightfully stated that our intention should not be to reunite the peninsula and the Korean people by force, but to create the proper atmosphere, the proper conditions, for a revolution to take place in the North. The reason there has not been a people's revolt against the oppressive, brutal Communist dictatorship is that members of the military who belong to the party are rewarded with the basics of life—food, clothing, shelter, and security—for brutalizing and repressing their own people.

"The organizations responsible for this brutality and repression are the forty Spetznaz units, comprised of special operations battalions and Naval Infiltration Squadrons. These units were designed to operate inside South Korea, but the internal security and counterintelligence organs within the Korean Communist Party use them for internal security, counterespionage, and intelligence-gathering inside North Korea itself. They are brutal and bloodthirsty mongrels whose task it is to seek out and destroy the enemy using whatever means possible. They have created an atmosphere of fear inside North Korea that has stifled free thought and free expression for almost three generations."

General Park motioned to the large computer screens in the observation room, which were repeaters of the much larger presentation screens on the command center stage. "The active, reserve, and paramilitary forces of the Korean People's Army total about seven million, or about one-third of the entire population," he went on. "The army pervades every aspect of life inside North Korea. But of that massive number, only about one hundred thousand are party members or members of one of these elite terrorist units. Through our intelligence and infiltration methods, we have identified the top ten units and their locations—two naval infiltration groups, two special forces paratroop air wings, four Spetznaz battalions, and one terrorist infiltration training and operations battalion.

"In addition, we have targeted the headquarters and barracks of the Eighth and Ninth Special Corps. The Eighth Special Corps is President Kim Jong-il's personal protection unit, and the Ninth Special Corps is the unit designated to hold and defend the streets of Pyongyang against rioters, insurrection, and invasion. As I said, a total of one hundred thousand troops. They are in twelve general target areas—two naval bases, two air bases, five army bases, and within the capital of North Korea itself. We have no illusion that we can kill all of them, of course, but we think this will create the spark that can bring down one of the planet's last Communist dictatorships."

"What about the other six million nine hundred thousand fighters?" Vice President Whiting asked incredulously. "You dismiss them because they're not Communist Party members, but they're still trained to fight and they're indoctrinated in Communist ideology almost from birth. Are you just going to ignore them?

What about North Korea's weapons of mass destruction—their biological, chemical, and nuclear warheads? How can you plan such a limited attack as this and simply ignore the size and power of the forces that you *haven't* decided to attack?"

"Because I trust my intelligence officers and the defectors who reported their findings and observations to me," President Kwon said. "These patriots all told me the same thing, and it has been checked and cross-checked and triple-checked over many months: the North is desperate and is willing to do anything, even trigger World War Three in a nuclear holocaust, to break the cycle of poverty, starvation, and despair.

"From our sources, we estimated that ninety-five percent of the nation was suffering the effects of the corrupt, paranoid, power-mad regime. Ninety percent of the nation had not been paid in over three months, and seventy percent hadn't been paid in over a year. Sixty percent of the nation had no electricity, running water, fuel oil, or sanitary facilities for three or more days a week, every week of the year. Unemployment was at fifty percent. And forty percent of the population, *forty percent*, ate less than one thousand calories of food a day. Infant mortality is twenty percent in the countryside, ten percent in the cities.

"We knew war could not be far behind. War could do many things for the Communist government. It would give the people someone to hate other than their own government. It could give them a reason to fight, a reason to live, or at least a reason to leave the squalor. It could force the West to send aid, even if they were defeated. At the very least, it promised a quick end to their suffering. A bullet between the eyes, a bomb dropped from far above, a cruise missile launched from hundreds of miles away—even the millisecond flash of a nuclear explosion and the briefest sensation of the heat of the fireball. All would be preferable, less painful, than staying at home watching your children die of cold and starvation.

"And if the North struck first, Madam Vice President, our findings told us that we would suffer the loss of Seoul and more than five million people. And there would still exist the possibility of a thermonuclear exchange that could end our nation and even our race. But if *we* struck first, and struck quickly, we might have a chance of cutting off the serpent's head before its coils could reach out to us. With the internal security and enforcement apparatus of the party destroyed, perhaps the people could rise up and throw off their Communist slave masters once and for all."

Vice President Whiting shook her head. "You are living a pipe dream, Mr. President," she said, clearly upset. "You're risking your life, your people's lives and freedom, everything you've built and accomplished over the decades, for a fantasy, a fairy tale. The price of failure is almost too enormous to comprehend. You're also risking the lives of thousands of American servicemen stationed here who know nothing of this folly of yours. You're risking the peace and security of Asia, of the entire *planet*."

"No one knows better than I what we risk, Madam Vice President!" Kwon retorted angrily. "But I and my government could not sit idly by and wait for the Communists to send their chemical terror and armies and tanks across the frontier. China would certainly follow in support of her little puppet. I would rather fight on our terms than on the North's."

"That sounds like something North Korea would say to justify an invasion of South Korea!" Admiral Allen said sardonically.

"The difference, Admiral, is that we do not seek the death and destruction of the North—we only seek to trigger the inevitable revolution that we feel must occur in Communist Korea. We recognize the stakes are high, but such a task is so important to our future, our peace, our survival, that we dare even the safety and security of Asia to bring it about."

Kwon paused, looking hard at Whiting and Allen. "Frankly, madam, I am not sure whether our American allies would risk their own peace and freedom to save us. I think in order to avoid another nuclear confrontation, President Martindale would watch and wait until the North Korean forces were stretched too thin and the bulk of the Red Chinese Army was committed, and *then* decide whether or not to intervene. By then, my country would be ravaged. The entire peninsula, the whole Korean race, would be enslaved. We would again become the eternal battleground, a bone fought over by the Americans and the Chinese dogs of war."

General Park spoke in a low voice to the president in Korean, and Kwon turned to the monitors. Special Agent Law whispered to the Vice President, "Ma'am, I think we can get out of here if we want to, but with all that's going on . . ."

"This may be the safest place for us, after all," Vice President Whiting said. "I agree."

"But I wish we could contact Washington," said Admiral Allen.

"We'll do it right now," Law said firmly. She went over to the director's console and picked up a telephone. Someone responded in Korean. Law held the receiver up to President Kwon. "Tell the operator I want to be connected to the White House Communications Center immediately."

"*Mian hamnida.* I am sorry, Special Agent," Kwon said, "but I cannot allow any outside communications at this—"

Corrie Law raised her mini-Uzi, pointed it directly at

the President's face, and said, "Mr. President, you will never live to see whether or not your plan succeeds if you don't order this operator to put the Vice President of the United States through to the White House in Washington, D.C., right *now*. I will not allow the Vice President to be treated like an insignificant nobody."

Kwon was startled. He had never experienced a subordinate taking the initiative like this, especially without a command from a superior. But he nodded politely. "*Mullonijyo. Chamkanman kidaryo chuseyo. Of course. Please wait a moment.*" He took the receiver, gave a command in Korean, then handed the phone back to Vice President Whiting with a formal bow. "Please. But do not be long, madam. History will be made in the next few minutes."

It took only moments and a few coded authentication phrases, and Whiting's call was routed directly to the phone on the Oval Office desk. Courteously, President Kwon and General Park went over to the observation windows to allow her a modicum of privacy.

"Ellen, good to hear your voice," President Martindale said, his voice filled with relief. "I just got the call from Bob Plank about your coded message. Are you all right?"

"I'm fine, Mr. President," Whiting said. "I'm still in the Master Control and Reporting Center at Osan Air Base. I'm with Admiral Allen, General Park of the Korean Air Force, and President Kwon." She took a deep breath, then said, "Mr. President, President Kwon has just informed me that he has initiated an invasion of North Korea."

"*What?*"

"It's under way right now," Whiting went on. "President Kwon and General Park briefed me in detail. They have apparently infiltrated many North Korean command, control, and communications facilities to the point where they were able to shut down most of that country's early-warning, air defense, and command networks. His planes are crossing the border as we speak. All of the planes he was going to use in the Team Spirit exercise are going to be used against the North." Whiting's voice broke for a moment. "Mr. President—Kevin—this is . . . frightening. I'm afraid. The war is on and we don't know what's going to happen next."

"Ellen . . . Ellen, don't worry," Martindale said as calmly as he could. She knew what the President was just realizing: if the Chinese or North Koreans retaliated, that command center at Osan would probably be their primary target—and, faced with a massive invasion, it was very possible that either side could use chemical, biological, or nuclear weapons. China had certainly showed its willingness to use nuclear weapons just two short years ago. "I'm calling in the entire staff right now," the President said quickly. "We'll all be right here with you from now on."

"Do you want to talk with President Kwon or Admiral—"

"I don't want to talk with anyone or do anything else but be with you on the phone, right here, right now," Martindale told her. "Try to relax. Talk to me. What's going on in there?"

"Nothing . . . I mean, Jesus, Kwon and Park are watching the computer screens and chatting like a couple of guys watching a baseball game on TV. I can see dozens of lines moving north across the border. Lots of them heading toward Pyongyang, but most going after a base just north of Seoul. I . . . I can't believe how calm these little bastards are . . ." Ellen Whiting stopped, her eyes wide in surprise, then she bit down on her right index finger. "Oh God, Mr. President, did I just say what I thought I said?"

"Ellen, stop calling me 'Mr. President' for once,

okay?" Martindale said. "The name's Kevin, remember? And they sure as hell have given you a reason to call them some names, haven't they? I think you deserve to call them any name you goddamn feel like calling them right now."

"I . . . oh shit, oh shit . . ."

"Ellen, what is it?"

"I . . . dammit, my knees are knocking!" Whiting cried. She broke into laughter. "I can't believe this! I'm so scared, I'm shivering so much, my knees are knocking! I always thought that was a figure of speech or a cartoon thing. I guess your knees really can knock if you're frightened enough." She paused for a moment, then asked, "Are you going to leave Washington, Kevin?"

"I'll discuss that with Philip, Jerrod, and Admiral Balboa as soon as they get here."

"It might be a good idea . . ."

"I told you, I'm staying right here," Martindale said. He raised his voice so everyone else in the Oval Office could hear. "I'm giving a direct fucking order—I'm staying right here! End of discussion! Oh, good, Jerrod's here already . . . Jerrod, the staff meets right here, in this office. I'm not putting this phone down until I know the Vice President is safe . . . I don't care if we can transfer the call to Air Force One or the NAOC. I'm not putting it down." Whiting knew that NAOC, pronounced "kneock," was the National Airborne Operations Center, formerly known as the National Emergency Airborne Command Post, a heavily modified Boeing 747 that allowed the President to command and control American military forces all over the world—even launch ballistic missiles if necessary. In 1992 the NAOC had been placed on standby status at Offutt Air Force Base in Nebraska; but after the China nuclear conflict, another one was stationed on round-the-clock alert at Andrews Air Force Base, ready to evacuate the National Command Authority—the President, the secretary of defense, and other national defense officials—from Washington.

"Admiral, I want a company of marines on their way from Seoul or Inchon to retrieve the Vice President and get her out of Osan, and I want it *now*," Whiting heard the President order. "Do it with the ROK's cooperation, but you are authorized to use whatever means necessary to secure her and her party's safety. Is that understood?" Whiting heard the most enthusiastic "Yes, *sir*!" she had ever heard from Admiral George Balboa. "You still there, Ellen?"

"You're sending the marines in after me, Kevin?" she asked, managing to smile through the fear.

"Damn right I am."

"I think that would be very dangerous, given all that's going on . . ."

"It's their job, Ellen. Let them do it. I know a couple of jarheads who would gladly take on the North *and* South Koreans just for a chance to grab onto you, haul you over their shoulders, and whisk you off to freedom."

"Sounds very romantic."

"And I thought you hated military guys."

"I do. But I love heroes. Doesn't matter what they're wearing. Any uniform, any flag . . . or nothing at all."

"Hey, you're starting to sound like me," the President said. "Laughing and making crude remarks in the face of . . . of . . ."

"Imminent nuclear annihilation?" the Vice President finished the sentence for him. There was a long pause, then a heavy sigh "Yeah," she said, "I guess you *are* rubbing off on me a bit."

"It's about time," the President said.

"Mr. Presi—Kevin," Whiting said hesitantly. "I

should tell you how I feel about you. I want to tell you, I have always . . ." Then she stopped.

"Ellen? Always what?"

"Something's happening down in the command center," the Vice President said nervously. "A lot of excitement. Yelling, screaming . . . I can't tell what they're saying, what's happening . . . General Park, what's going on? General . . . ?" There was a long pause; then . . . "My God, *no*! Oh my God! Kevin! It's happened! Kevin, we're—"

And the line went dead.

OVER THE KOREAN PENINSULA
THAT SAME TIME

T he sleepy little coastal city of Kangnung, population 130,000, is the largest city and the main transportation hub on South Korea's east coast, and culturally one of the most vital and important places in all of South Korea. The city is the home of one national treasure, twelve lesser treasures, and hundreds of artifacts, ancient sites, homes, and properties, some dating back three thousand years. It is the home of one of the nine sects of Silla Buddhism and also of several famous Confucian scholars.

The site of one of Kangnung's three ancient Buddhist temples, Hansong-Sa, is only four kilometers from the city's Central Market and just outside Kangnung Airport, on the coast south of Anmok Beach. Although there is now a modern temple there, it was the site of a two-thousand-year-old temple from which two marble seated Buddha statues were taken, both of which are priceless national treasures. One statue is on display in the Kangnung Municipal Museum; the other is in the National Museum in Seoul.

As important as the national treasures are to all Koreans, even more important now were the military units at Kangnung Airport, located between Han-song-Sa temple and the Sea of Japan. In case of war with the North, it was the duty of the Fifth Air Division of the Republic of Korea Air Force to protect South Korea's rear flank, while most of the other air and ground forces would assist in the defense of the capital. Fifth Division had three air wings located at Kangnung: the Fifteenth Attack Wing, with almost a hundred American surplus A-37B Dragonfly light close-air sup-port fighters stationed there; the Twenty-first Attack Wing, with forty-eight British-made Hawk Mk60 light fighter-bombers; and the Seventeenth Fighter Wing, with American-made F-5E/F Talon fighters.

Located just thirty miles south of the DMZ, Kangnung had an important role in protecting Seoul from an attack from the rear and preventing any Com-munist forces from gaining a foothold in the Taebaek Mountains. Some of the bloodiest battlefields of the Korean War had been just northwest of Kangnung—Old Baldy, the Punchbowl, and Heartbreak Ridge, among others. The Koreans and their American allies created a massive air fighting force at Kangnung to as-sure complete domination in this vitally important northeast region.

All that was about to disappear.

Of one hundred and fifty-one operational nuclear-armed Nodong-1 and -2 ballistic missiles in North Ko-rea, only twelve launched that morning. The missiles had a maximum range of over twelve hundred nautical miles, but no missile flew farther than four hundred miles. All the missiles aimed at Seoul were intercepted by American Patriot PAC-3 antiballistic missile systems, as were the missiles aimed at the American air base at Kunsan. One warhead exploded just a few miles west of Inchon, causing massive damage to that vitally important port city.

One Nodong-1 missile missed its intended target by over two miles, but with a fifty-kiloton-yield warhead onboard, accuracy was not that important. The warhead exploded over the Central Market District of Kangnung, flattening everything within three miles and creating an immense fire storm that engulfed the entire vicinity as far south as Kwandong University and as far north as Kyongpo Lake. Everything above ground level at Kangnung Airport was either swept out to sea or exploded into a ball of flame, and its ashes blown out into the Sea of Japan.

The Nodong-1 missile fired from Unit Twenty near Sunan flew only one hundred and fifty miles, barely far enough to exhaust its first-stage fuel supply before ejecting its warhead. It, too, missed its intended target, in fact by several kilometers—but it hit the edge of the city of Suwon, twenty miles south of Seoul, destroying one of South Korea's largest industrial complexes, the immense Samsung Electric group in the southeast section of the city. The bulk of the blast missed the Republic of Korea Air Force base south of the city, but the blast's overpressure destroyed or damaged several other key companies and universities. The fifty-kiloton-yield nuclear warhead detonated twenty thousand feet in the air, digging a thirty-story-deep crater in the earth and instantly incinerating anything within three miles of ground zero. Almost fifteen thousand persons died in the fireball, most of them at work at the Samsung complex; another thirty thousand died in the fire storm and overpressure. Although air raid and attack sirens had been activated throughout South Korea, few had a chance to reach an underground shelter.

Although the blast was more than ten miles away, it felt like a direct hit to the occupants of the Master Control and Reporting Center at Osan Air Base, located south of Suwon. The entire structure shook and rolled as if in the grip of a magnitude-eight earthquake. The lights snapped off, replaced immediately by emergency battery-powered lights. Several of the large computer monitors down below the observation area shattered and imploded. Technicians leaped from their chairs and took cover under desks and tables as pieces of debris fell from the ceiling.

Vice President Whiting had never been in an earthquake before. It was chilling. The room vibrated back and forth, then rolled underneath her feet as if the floor were a mat of rubber floating on the ocean. The vibration lasted for fifteen or twenty seconds before and after the roll. Whiting was paralyzed with fear. Where could she go? What could she do? She was trapped in the grip of a force so powerful that she could not comprehend it. Her right ankle twisted under her body in the violent shaking, and she cried out.

Special Agent Corrie Law did the thinking for her. She pulled the Vice President under a desk, then blocked the open side with her body. But the observation room was solidly built, and little fell to the floor. The emergency lighting worked well. The large angled windows overlooking the master command room below wavered and buckled like soap bubbles, but they did not break and send glass shattering down.

In a minute or so, the shaking subsided. The air now smelled musty and very dry, as if filled with a thin misting of dust. Agent Law's face showed deep concern as she looked at the Vice President coughing. "Are you all right, ma'am?" she shouted.

"Yes, I'm fine," Whiting replied. She looked into

Law's worried eyes. "You're shouting, Corrie. Take it easy. Help me up."

"Sorry," said Law in a lower voice. Her strong, wiry arms pulled the Vice President to her feet.

"That Marine Corps training kicks in when something like this happens, eh?" Whiting asked with a wry smile.

"I guess so," Law replied sheepishly. "I was in an earthquake once, in Turkey. A whole building collapsed on top of us." She looked around. "This place looks spotless compared to that."

She and Whiting looked out over the battle staff and support staff operating areas. The place was in surprisingly good shape. The computers and consoles were dark, but they were surprised to see that the phones were still in use. As they watched, Korean technicians were busily rolling out huge mounted charts and large transparent greaseboards, setting up for monitoring the emergency the old-fashioned way, before computerized maps and real-time data feeds.

General Park came over to them. "Are you all right, Madam Vice President?" he asked. He looked unfazed himself, as if his command center got jolts like that every morning.

"We're fine," Whiting replied. "Where's President Kwon?"

"Down there, I am sure," Park replied, motioning toward the observation windows. Sure enough, they saw the president of the Republic of Korea, with two armed guards nearby, walking in front of the general staff positions, checking on them; it was clear he was exhorting them to find out what had happened. They saw the startled looks on the staff officers' faces as they realized their president was standing before them, and how quickly they scrambled back into their seats and picked up their telephones.

"I suggest we go downstairs, Madam Vice President. Communications are limited right now, and we will be able to hear the information as it comes in."

Officers and technicians had a second shock at the sight of the Vice President joining them in the battle staff area moments later. Seats were quickly found for them. Whiting had Admiral Allen on one side and President Kwon on the other, with Corrie Law behind her and one of the marine guards in front of her. General Park was crouched on the floor, wearing a headset and listening to his senior officers and controllers as they reported in to him. When the briefing concluded, he turned down the volume and stood up.

"Here is the information as we know right now, Mr. President, Madam Vice President," he began. "The Republic of Korea was attacked with perhaps as many as a dozen thermonuclear devices and several dozen chemical or biological warfare weapons, and several hundred shorter-range high-explosive missiles."

"My God," Whiting murmured. But when she turned to look at President Kwon . . . she actually saw him *smiling*!

"I must further report," Park went on, "that the Republic of Korea has suffered staggering losses. The city of Kangnung, a city of over one hundred thousand on the east coast of the peninsula, may have been completely destroyed. The city is the home of our largest air division guarding the capital from the east. The city of Suwon, just ten miles north of us, was hit by a single nuclear device. It was not a direct hit—the weapon exploded several miles to the east of the city, probably directly over the Samsung electronics manufacturing complex—but casualties are already estimated at over sixty thousand. Seoul was hit by three, possibly four, weapons dispersing unknown toxic substances. Inchon, Taejon, and Taegu were also hit by chemical or biological weapons. A single nuclear explosion was detected near Kunsan, thirty miles southwest of Taejon. Casualties are unknown at this time."

Vice President Whiting looked at President Kwon and could not believe her eyes—the smile on his face had given way to sheer delight. "Excuse me, Mr. President," she said. "I cannot understand what you're so . . . so happy about. Your crazed stunt led to an attack that may have killed hundreds of thousands of civilians!"

"Believe me, Madam Vice President, I am not celebrating," Kwon said. "But you must understand: the Communists had enough firepower on alert and ready to respond to kill *every living thing in South Korea ten times over*. If it is true and we were hit only with a few nuclear warheads out of possibly hundreds, or a few dozen chemical warheads out of literally *thousands,* it means our outreach program worked. The common man in the North, the conscripts, the everyday workingman and -woman, have decided to join us and throw off their Communist overlords. A few nuclear explosions, a few thousand martyred souls: this is a small price to pay when it could mean the end of Communist rule on the Korean peninsula and blessed *reunification*! A small price, indeed."

THE WHITE HOUSE SITUATION ROOM
THAT SAME TIME

We see it too, Mr. President," President Kevin Martindale said. He was on a four-way conference call with three other international leaders: Minister of National Defense Chi Haotian of the People's Republic of China, President Yevgeniy Maksimovich Primakov of the Russian Federation, and Prime Minister Kazumi Nagai of the Republic of Japan. All three world leaders called into the White House nearly simultaneously, and each call was taken immediately and merged without permission from any of them by the White House Communications Center.

"President Martindale, this is President Primakov," came a translation. "I must have assurances that this is not a prelude to a full-scale attack against North Korea! I demand it! Respond, please!"

"I am telling you, Mr. President, and all of you: the United States has no idea what's going on over Korea, and I promise you, we are in no way involved," Martindale said. In the brief time since the four-way call was established, this had to be the second or third time he had made that statement. With Martindale in the Situation Room were Secretary of Defense Arthur Chastain, National Security Adviser Philip Freeman, and Joint Chiefs Chairman Admiral George Balboa, along with backup aides and interpreters. They had all quickly moved to the Situation Room, an ordinary-looking room in the basement of the White House, when the call from Vice President Whiting was cut off.

"No American forces are involved, *none*!" Martindale insisted yet again. "We have radar surveillance planes over the peninsula and one carrier battle group in the Yellow Sea, but except for normal patrols, we have no aircraft whatsoever involved in this situation! I repeat, we have *none*!

"Listen very carefully, please, all of you: this situation appears to be an outbreak of hostilities between North and South Korea only. Our sources indicate that South Korean warplanes crossed the Demilitarized Zone first, and that North Korean rocket and artillery forces retaliated."

"Then you admit the South is the aggressor!" Chinese Defense Minister Chi exploded. "You admit that this hateful act was an attempt to destroy the Democratic People's Republic of Korea! You admit that this act of treachery is the fault of no one but your own allies, the South Koreans!"

"Mr. Minister, I admit nothing—I'm saying that our observations agree with all the others that have been reported, that it appears that South Korea started the conflict by crossing the Military Demarcation Line first," Martindale said.

"Our information also says that the South Korean air attacks used only nonnuclear air defense suppression weapons, not nuclear or bio-chem weapons," Prime Minister Nagai interjected. "North Korea has responded with nuclear, chemical, and biological weapons launched by medium-range ballistic missiles. Their response was clearly far out of proportion to the threat—"

"What did you expect—that the North Koreans would use flyswatters and harsh words to scare the South Koreans away?" Minister Chi retorted. "The South Korean aircraft overflew the capital with attack aircraft. The North's response was completely justified."

"And what will be China's reaction to this conflict?" President Primakov asked, his intense, rapid-fire tone muted by the translator's monotone. "Will China continue to bomb its neighbors, as you did two years ago? Will you now continue your moves against Taiwan and the Philippines?"

"And what of Japan, Mr. Minister?" Prime Minister Nagai asked. "Is this just a feint to cover an attack upon our homeland?"

"If provoked, yes, we will retaliate!" Minister Chi shouted in English. "If Russia or the United States tries to advance into North Korea or if any Chinese territory is threatened in any way, yes! Yes, we will fight with every weapon and every last man."

"Hold on! Everyone, *hold on*!" President Martindale shouted. "It's clear to me that none of us is involved in this conflict—"

"It is not so clear to us," Minister Chi interjected.

"I am telling you, the United States is not involved in this!" Martindale said sharply. "We are *not* involved. This fight is between North and South Korea. If any of us gets too trigger-happy, we're bound to touch off a world war."

"I find it hard to believe, President Martindale, that you have several thousand troops stationed in South Korea, plus several thousand more taking part in a large air combat exercise there, and you knew nothing about this sneak attack against North Korea," Chi Haotian said angrily. "Do you really expect us to believe that?"

"It's the truth, Mr. Minister," Martindale said. "American forces are in just as great danger as the civilians on both sides. Do you think I'd keep them in harm's way if I knew such an attack was going to take place? Don't you think I'd have at least launched my aircraft to give them a better chance to survive? You confirmed our own air defense radar observations: only South Korean planes are airborne and crossing the DMZ, not American planes. Few of my ground units are reporting to me now, but my airborne surveillance commander assures me that *no* American forces at all launched with the South Koreans. In fact, I have lost contact with my American commanders in South Korea—apparently, all the command centers are being manned only by Koreans now. All American commanders are off the air."

He took a deep breath, fought to calm his voice, and said evenly, "Listen very carefully, President Primakov,

Prime Minister Nagai, Minister Chi. The United States is not going to invade North Korea or anyone else. I promise you this. It is very important that we all remain calm, remain neutral, and not mobilize any of our forces in response to this conflict. This appears to me to be a Korean squabble. Let the Koreans handle it."

There was silence on the line for a very long time. Martindale was about to say something to make sure it was still open and clear when he heard President Primakov's voice and then the Russian translator: "What is the disposition of your strategic forces now, Mr. President?"

"American nuclear forces are on normal peacetime alert—that's DEFCON Four," Martindale replied. Actually, "normal" alert was DEFCON Five. But after the Chinese nuclear attacks against Taiwan—and the fact that no one officially knew who detonated the nuclear device under the aircraft carrier USS *Independence* in Yokosuka Harbor—the United States went back to DEFCON Four, which was the readiness state it had maintained during most of the Cold War.

A year later, however, in order to defuse the tense international situation, the United States unilaterally decided to remove all of its land-based intercontinental ballistic nuclear missiles from their silos and put them in storage, and also remove the nuclear weapons delivery capability from all its combat aircraft. This effectively equalized the number of nuclear warheads among the major powers. Martindale had received much criticism at home for the move, but it did serve to calm the fear that a new Cold War was emerging. "The only nuclear-capable forces we have on alert at this moment are our sea-launched ballistic missile submarines—no land-based missiles, no aircraft," President Martindale said. "Not even our stealth bombers. It's the same force structure we've maintained for the last two years. I'll tell you all again: the United States does not want war with anyone, of any kind, especially a nuclear war."

"Then you must tell President Kwon to recall his air forces from North Korea and cease all hostilities," Chinese Defense Minister Chi said. "The United States may not be directly involved, but such an attack could not have been possible without substantial assistance from the United States. It is therefore vital that the United States withdraws all such assistance and compels the South Koreans to withdraw their forces."

"I can make that request, Mr. Minister," Martindale said wearily, "but I'm telling you again, the United States is rendering no assistance to the South Koreans. None whatsoever. I've attempted to contact President Kwon but have been unsuccessful—no doubt communications have been disrupted by the North Korean nuclear detonations, and they'll surely be down for quite some time. But you can monitor the status of American forces around the world, and you can see for yourself that we have not changed the readiness of any of our forces and have not activated the Reserves. I'm asking all of you to do the same."

"Are you saying we should not defend ourselves?" Japanese Prime Minister Nagai asked angrily. "This we will never agree to, sir!"

"I'm not saying don't defend yourselves—just don't mobilize any counteroffensive or strategic units until all of us can analyze what's happened on the Korean peninsula," Martindale responded. "Don't move any troops in response to a situation that does not exist."

"And what of the American military forces in South Korea right now?" President Primakov asked. "You do not expect us to believe you will do nothing to protect them?"

Kevin Martindale took another deep breath, closed his eyes, let it out slowly, then said, "I promise all of you, I will not move one aircraft, not one vessel, not one soldier, not one weapon onto the Korean peninsula. The *Washington* carrier battle group will stay to help evacuate American personnel, including Vice President Whiting; they will launch aircraft and deploy their vessels for self-protection and humanitarian purposes only. I will do this as long as I detect no Chinese, Japanese, or Russian forces moving in any way toward the Korean peninsula. If I get evidence of any military movements, I'll respond likewise. But until that happens, I will not move any more forces into Korea."

"But what of the South Korean aircraft over North Korea?" Minister Chi retorted. "Will you not order their withdrawal?"

"Both countries, North and South Korea, have a responsibility to defend their homeland and pursue whatever military objectives they deem necessary," Martindale replied. "I will try to contact President Kwon and President Kim. But these two divided nations have been spoiling for a fight for almost fifty years now. I think it's about time we step aside and let the two of them duke it out."

"What kind of logic is this?" Prime Minister Nagai shouted. "What if the North continues to bombard the South with nuclear warheads? What if they decide to launch missiles against Japan? Or to begin an even bigger barrage against the South? Will you not strike back? Will you not support your allies in South Korea or Japan?"

"Our forces in the region will try to protect our allies as best we can, Mr. Prime Minister," Martindale responded. "It was your decision to remove all American military forces from your soil—we must now both deal with the consequences of that decision. But the only way to ensure that this conflict does not spread into a global thermonuclear war is if all outside countries stand aside, defend themselves, and let the battle in Korea go on. If the South is destroyed—well, they started the fight, and hopefully they can deal with the consequences."

Martindale did not even bring up what might happen if the North lost the fight—the idea that North Korea's three-to-one numerical advantage over the South would fail to protect them was inconceivable. South Korea's military was supposed to be defensive only in both size and composition—it was almost laughable to imagine the South capable of more than knocking out a few key bases or weapons sites, then withdrawing to its own borders. It would have to preserve its forces, reorganize, and await the North's counteroffensive, hoping the Americans would step in to back them up.

"You will not support your allies the South Koreans?" President Primakov asked incredulously. "If they beg and plead for your help in the face of a massive North Korean onslaught, will you not defend them?"

"I can't say what we'll do, Mr. President," Martindale replied. "But the South Koreans have engineered this conflict without consulting us. It is an act of aggression that we do not encourage, support, or condone. I want to preserve the peace and stability of Asia. If it is in our best interests to act, we'll act."

It was a flimsy response, wishy-washy, and Kevin Martindale knew it. But there was no way to answer Primakov's question without giving away more than he wanted to. He was trying not to provoke any of the superpowers while at the same time show that the United States still considered the region of vital American national interest. It was very possible that he failed to convince any of them of anything.

What was President Kwon Ki-chae thinking? Martindale wondered. Had he lost his mind, sending in a few fighter-bombers to destroy North Korea's million-man army? He had to know he would have to absorb some punishment—he could not be so stupid as to believe he could destroy all of the North's missile punch in one blitzkrieg air raid. If he was expecting the Americans to come to his aid no matter what, he was dead wrong to have assumed that.

"Brave but cautious words," Russian President and former KGB chief Yevgeniy Primakov said finally, through his translator. "You ask for peace but give us a veiled threat at the same time. You are willing to sacrifice a few thousand soldiers, hoping you can prevent several hundred thousand Chinese soldiers from sweeping down into the Korean peninsula to help the North."

"What are you saying, Mr. President?" Chinese Defense Minister Chi asked. "Are you saying that China is in any way supporting this war? We are not, sir! We have had no information whatsoever that the North was going to launch a nuclear attack, and we certainly did not provoke the South into sending in those fighter-bombers over Pyongyang! But if our comrades in North Korea request our assistance, we have an obligation to render any assistance we deem necessary."

"Then you condemn all of us to nuclear war!" Prime Minister Nagai shouted. "Such a response will surely require an equal response from the Americans, which will trigger a response from the Russians, which will trigger a bigger response from the Americans. We must all pledge to stay out of the fighting on the Korean peninsula. No one must interfere."

"This we cannot agree to," Minister Chi responded. "I will convey this conversation to my government, but I will advise President Jiang to support our comrades in North Korea and abide by our treaties of mutual cooperation, friendship, and defense. If the North asks for our assistance, I will recommend that we extend all necessary support, including full military support. We shall consider an attack on North Korea by the South as an attack on the People's Republic of China itself." And Minister Chi hung up.

"Insane. This is truly insane," came the voice of President Primakov's translator. "I am afraid Russia has no choice but to prepare to respond to the threat before us, Mr. President. We no longer have a treaty of mutual aid and cooperation with North Korea, but my government would not look favorably upon any superpower invasion of the North. A Chinese mobilization and ground counteroffensive into North Korea is no great concern to us. But if China commits its air or missile forces in a way that threatens Russian bases or nationals, or if the United States chooses to engage China on the Korean peninsula, we must respond in kind."

"And Japan would not look favorably upon any Russian mobilization of any kind," Prime Minister Nagai said hotly. "Our forces may be small and insignificant compared to all others, but we will fight to the last man to preserve our homeland from the forces that now ravage the Korean peninsula. With or without America's help, we will fight back."

"I implore all of you, hold your anger and your military forces in check until we can analyze the outcome of the fight between the two Koreas—" But it was too late. Primakov and Nagai had also terminated their calls.

President Martindale set down his receiver, then leaned back in his seat, mentally and emotionally exhausted. He had laid everything on the table, he thought. He promised to do nothing. But he received no reciprocal promises in return. Quite the opposite: Chi Haotian was virtually promising he'd send in the Red Army to help North Korea. Any such move would trigger a response in Russia, just as it did in 1950 when

North Korea invaded the South. What was next? he thought. And how soon before . . . ?

"Mr. President, something's happening," Secretary of Defense Arthur Chastain said. He was monitoring reports coming in from the Pentagon, which was receiving real-time radar and satellite data from American reconnaissance assets over Korea. "The border, the DMZ, it's being crossed. Massive movement south along all sectors."

"God," said Martindale. It was happening, he thought grimly. The North Koreans were invading. Soon the South would retaliate; the Chinese Red Army would surge southward . . .

CHAPTER FIVE

OVER SOUTHEASTERN NEVADA
THAT SAME TIME

Bullrider, this is Avalanche, outlaw at zero-three-zero bull's-eye, one hundred and twenty miles slowly descending from angels two-three-zero, speed three hundred and seventy knots, repeat, three-seven-zero. Right turn to zero-one-zero, take angels two-three to intercept."

The pilot of the lead U.S. Air Force F-15C Eagle air superiority fighter, from the 366th Wing at Mountain Home Air Force Base, Idaho, started a turn to the northeast and keyed his throttle-mounted mike button: "Roger, Avalanche. Bullrider's in the turn." He took a quick look out the right side of his canopy to be sure his wingman in another F-15 fighter was starting his rejoin.

Pretty damned strange, the lead F-15 pilot thought. The B-1B bomber crews must be playing it safe, or else they were getting soft. The Nellis range complex was open, and they were within the time allotted for the fighter intercept exercise, so this must be their target. But what was he doing just starting his descent to low altitude? Most bomber guys were already low, or at least screaming hell-bent for the ground whenever fighters were nearby. He was going slow too—way too slow.

These Guard guys from Reno were supposed to be the most successful, most outrageous bomber unit in the business. Their recent accident, the pilot surmised, must've softened them up a little. The 366th Wing was an Air Expeditionary Wing, with a mix of several different aircraft—F-16s, F-15s, F-15E bombers, KC-135R tankers, and B-1B bombers—all located at one base, ready to deploy and fight as a team. The fighter guys from Idaho knew bomber tactics, knew what a Bone could do. So far, these Guard guys from Nevada weren't showing them much.

"Hey, lead, what do you think?" the F-15 pilot's wingman radioed.

"I think we got a faker," the lead pilot responded immediately. They were thinking alike, the way a good hunter-killer team should. He had heard of Air National Guard guys decoying themselves by bringing their KC-135 aerial refueling tankers all the way to the range complex and having them fly the inbound strike routing, buying precious time for the bombers to sneak in low at very high speed to try to make it to their targets. "Avalanche, Bullrider. You got any low targets entering the range complex? We think we got a faker up high."

"Stand by, Bullrider," Avalanche, the controller aboard the E-3C AWACS (Airborne Warning and Control System) radar plane, replied. There was a long pause; then: "Bullrider, this is Avalanche, we're clean. Negative contact on any other bogeys at this time."

That wasn't definitive. A B-1 was hard to see when it was flying really low; visual contour at two hundred feet above the ground or lower would make it tough to detect at long range even for a skilled crew in an AWACS radar plane. This guy up high couldn't be a bomber, flying this high and this slow, so the real targets still had to be out there. But killing a tanker was worth a lot of points too, and a tanker in the hand was almost as good as two bombers in the bush. "Copy, Avalanche. We'll continue with this intercept."

He didn't need his radar to make the intercept, and the longer he kept his radar off, the closer he could get to his target without being detected. He knew the B-1B had a tail-warning radar system, called TWS, that would warn of any aircraft or missiles behind them, so as long as he stayed in front of the B-1 with his radar off, he could approach without being detected.

"Roger, Bullrider. Bogey's at your one o'clock, eighty miles low."

The lead F-15 pilot interrogated the unidentified aircraft, checking for any friendly IFF—identification friend or foe—signals, and found none. The rules of engagement, or ROE, for this mission profiled an area defense scenario, which meant that any aircraft not electronically identified using IFF or radio was to be considered hostile, even if many miles away from the defended area. Inside sixty miles—the approximate maximum range of a standoff weapon dropped from high altitude—he was authorized to "attack" any unidentified aircraft.

"Bullrider, lead, take the high CAP," the F-15 pilot said, directing his wingman to climb up to the "perch" so he could watch the entire area for more attackers. He knew that B-1 bombers always attack in packs, usually two or three bombers in trail offset a few miles or a few seconds so they cross the target area with at least ten seconds' spacing. "I'll make the first pass, climb up to the perch, and then you can take a shot. Keep an eye out for trailers."

"Two," the wingman acknowledged, starting a fast climb.

The bogey was increasing its rate of descent, but still not traveling anything near the speed of a B-1 bomber.

It *had* to be a decoy. "Avalanche, bogeydope," the lead F-15 pilot called.

" 'Clean,' Bullrider. Only bogey is at your one o'clock, sixty miles."

It didn't seem likely, but it could be that the Air National Guard B-1 guys were just taking it nice and easy. This was only the first day of their annual evaluation—they had another two weeks of this coming up. Maybe it was better to get the feel for live air-to-air combat the first day before . . .

"Bullrider, Bullrider, Avalanche has a new bogey, three-three-five degrees bull's-eye, range seven-zero miles, *low,* airspeed three hundred!"

There it was! the F-15 pilot said to himself. No wonder the AWACS guys couldn't find it—it was flying only three hundred knots, about half its normal speed. To reduce clutter on their radarscopes, some AWACS radar technicians "squelched" out targets flying below a certain speed. "I'll take that bogey, Avalanche!" the F-15 lead pilot radioed.

"Roger, Bullrider, left turn heading three-five-zero, bogey will be at your two o'clock, fifty miles." That was a close one—the B-1 almost got by him as they chased down the decoy up high. "Descend to angels ten, advise when you can maintain visual terrain clearance."

"I'm VMC, Avalanche." "VMC" meant that the F-15s were in "visual meteorological conditions"—they could visually see the ground. The AWACS controller could concentrate on setting up the intercept instead of keeping his fighters from hitting the ground. "Bullrider flight, rejoin on me."

"You want me to check out the high bogey, lead?" the second F-15 pilot asked.

"Negative. I need you to look for trailers." Because B-1s always fought in groups, the second and third aircraft were usually within ten miles of the leader. Killing a KC-135 tanker was too easy. Although they certainly got points for shooting down a valuable force multiplier like a tanker, they'd lose many more points if they allowed a bomber to sneak by and bomb a defended target.

"Roger."

"Twelve o'clock, forty miles," the AWACS controller reported. "Be advised, bogey is faded. Losing him in ground clutter. Come left twenty degrees to stay out of his TWS." But only a few vectors later, the AWACS plane was having trouble staying locked on. "Bullrider, bogey faded. Last solid contact twelve o'clock, twenty miles."

"Roger, Avalanche." He interrogated the target for an IFF signal—nothing. It was a bad guy, all right. High-speed bombers like the B-1 could elude even an AWACS radar plane the farther they got, so the lead pilot activated his APG-70 look-down, shoot-down radar and immediately locked it onto the newcomer. Got him! "I'm tied on radar, in high trail. Let's hook this sucker."

"Two!" the wingman crowed. Killing a B-1 bomber, especially with a short-range heat-seeking missile or with guns, was second only in excitement to killing a B-2 stealth bomber. B-52H Stratopig bombers, the few that were left, were such easy targets that they were left for the newbies, the new guys in the squadron, or killed with a BVR (beyond visual range) missile shot. Even chasing down and killing a cruise missile was considered poor sport these days.

Sure enough, the minute he locked in the low-flying plane with his radar, it sped up. Too late, chumps, the lead F-15 pilot thought.

Procedure for max kill points: maintain radar contact through at least two defensive maneuvers, close within twenty miles, shoot a radar-guided missile, maintain radar lock through one more defensive maneuver, close to within eight miles, shoot a heat-seeking missile, close to within two miles, make a cannon shot, then make and announce a visual ID within one mile. Piece of cake. Easy . . .

. . . Yeah, *too* easy! He was within twenty miles and had this guy locked up for almost thirty seconds, and he hadn't made one maneuver yet. His threat-warning receiver must've been screeching in his ears loud enough to deafen him! The lead F-15 pilot noticed the target had accelerated, but only to about four hundred knots—at least two to three hundred knots *slower* than he expected! What in hell was going on?

"Bullrider, this is Avalanche," the AWACS radar controller announced, "bogey number one has started a very rapid descent, heading down at thirty thousand feet per minute and accelerating to five hundred knots . . . he's descending below angels ten, now at six hundred knots. He's crossing over to your seven o'clock, forty miles. Suggest you break off your attack on bogey two and take vectors to bogey one."

Son of a bitch! the lead F-15 pilot swore into his oxygen mask. They did a double switch—they put the faker down low, and they put the real bomber up high. He *had* to go get the bomber before it got to terrain-following altitudes—the B-1 was difficult to chase and almost impossible to get a radar lock on once it tucked itself deep into the valleys at treetop level. But the tanker was less than fifteen miles away—an easy target and a lot of points. Losing a tanker in a two-week-long battle meant the B-1 squadron couldn't do a lot of their normal-length patrols.

"Billy, this is lead, you got me in sight?" the F-15 lead pilot asked.

"Rog."

"You get the guy down low. I'll clear off to the left and go get the bomber."

It would've made more sense for the guy on the perch to go after the bomber, but bagging a B-1 was a better prize, and he was the leader. "Roger, lead. I've got a visual on you. You're clear to the south."

"Lead's breaking left. Avalanche, this is Bullrider One, I'll take a vector to bogey one. Bullrider Two is going to nab bogey two."

"Roger, Bullrider." There was a touch of irritation in the AWACS controller's voice. It was a hazardous maneuver. His job was to bring aircraft together—preferably in a position where the good guy can kill the bad guy. It was not typically his job to *separate* aircraft. But he monitored the formation split, made sure the two F-15s were far enough away from each other as they maneuvered around to get pointed at their respective targets. At their combined speed, even twice the normal separation distance—ten miles each—gave them only *six seconds* to react to a collision situation.

The second F-15 pilot was a little miffed that he was given the "easy" kill, the tanker, but a kill was a kill. He'd get max points if he moved right in for a gun kill and didn't waste any missiles—he didn't even have to use his radar. As he pointed his fighter's nose down, he picked up speed and closed the distance quickly. Man, that tanker was low! Those crews must be sweating bullets, flying *below* ridgeline level like that!

Finally, at four miles' distance, he could see his quarry. Actually, he saw the tanker's shadow first—big, slow, and highlighted against the dry brown rocky hills occasionally broken up by dirty white snow, it was easy. "Avalanche, Bullrider Two tally-ho." The AIM-9M Sidewinder heat-seeking missile simulator he carried growled its lock-on warning. "Bullrider Two tracking heat."

"Copy, Bullrider Two, good heater."

"Rog. Withholding. Closing in for guns . . ."

"They took the bait," Patrick said. He was watching the profile of the attack on his threat profile display, which showed all of the "players" in the range. "They broke off from Two-Zero and they're going after the tanker."

"Both of them?" Rinc Seaver asked.

"Yep . . . stand by. No, one's going after Two-Zero, the other's going after the tanker."

"Aces, this is lead, looks like one's after you," Seaver radioed to Rebecca Furness on the interplane frequency.

"Roger. We're heading for mother earth. Looks like our tanker's had it, though," Rebecca responded.

"We can't let the tanker get nailed," Rinc Seaver said on interphone. "We won't lose Damage Expectancy points if he gets shot down, but . . ."

"But we lose a tanker," Patrick said. "They might not want to play with us anymore if we keep on sending them out to get shot down."

"Lock up that fighter air-to-air, Long Dong," Rinc said. "Put him in rendezvous mode." Patrick looked over at Rinc in surprise. Long reconfigured his attack radar to rendezvous mode, which was exactly like an F-16 fighter's radar's air intercept mode, and in a few seconds he had the F-15 Eagle locked up. The pilot's Horizontal Situation Display now showed a set of cross hairs—keep the cross hairs centered, and eventually they'd smack into the fighter.

"Steering is good, Rodeo. He's low and slow, closing in on our tanker."

"Not for long," Rinc said. He turned the bomber westward and cobbed the throttles to max afterburner.

"What's the plan, Seaver?" Patrick asked.

"No one chases one of our tankers, sir," Rinc Seaver said. He turned toward him, and Patrick could see his eyes dancing with excitement and evil. "No one messes with Aces High . . ."

It took only a few more moments. The tanker—a KC-135R Stratotanker, leaving a trail of black smoke several miles long as it struggled around the craggy hills—couldn't maneuver very well way down here. It was almost like closing in for an aerial refueling rendezvous—the pilot felt like calling "Stabilized precontact and ready," as if he was ready to move in and plug in for gas. Instead, he called, "Avalanche, Bullrider Two, visual contact on bogey two, a KC-135 Stratobladder, looks like California Air Reserves. Closing in for guns."

"Roger, Bullrider," the AWACS controller responded, "we copy your—" He broke off and shouted frantically, "Bullrider Two, Bullrider Two, pop-up bogey at your three o'clock low, low, low, range nine miles, airspeed eight-zero-zero, collision alert, collision alert!"

In a panic the pilot searched out the right side of his cockpit canopy. But before he could spot it, *it was right in front of him*—a B-1B Lancer bomber, wings swept all the way back, in what looked like a tight ninety-degree left bank. The F-15 pilot thought he could see the bomber pilots through their windshield, it was that close! For goddamn sure they were going to collide!

He thought about a quick snap-shot—just squeeze the trigger and hope to hit it—but survival came first. He hauled back on his control stick as hard as he could, then shoved in full afterburners. All he saw for a few seconds was the side of a mountain—and then his nearly blacked-out vision filled with blue sky. He kept the stick pulled back and his fighter's nose aimed for blue sky for several seconds, not wanting to release the back pressure until he was positive he was away from the ground and the mountains and all low-flying motherfucking planes. "Fighters were not meant for flying so damned close to the ground, not so close to the ground, not so close to the ground," he kept on muttering, like a mantra.

It was an illegal maneuver. It *had* to be. His range to the tanker was less than three miles, seconds before claiming a gun kill. Because this was the first day of the exercise, the ROE stated all opposing aircraft could close to no less than two miles, and closure rates were restricted to less than one thousand knots—no going nose-to-nose over the sound barrier. The F-15 pilot knew the rules, knew the bomber pukes busted the rules, knew he could get the AWACS radar controller to document the entire violation . . .

. . . but he didn't call "knock it off" and report the violation. Once he leveled off—at eighteen thousand feet, high enough that he *knew* he wouldn't hit any mountains—he had to laugh and, yes, tip his hat to the fucking bomber pukes. They saved their tanker and chased the United States' most advanced air superiority fighter right out of the damned playground. By the time he got himself turned around, reoriented, and pointed back toward the players, the KC-135 tanker decoy had exited the range complex and was on his way home.

He was never, *never* going to live this one down.

"Hey, lead, we got you drifting out to eleven miles," Rebecca Furness radioed to her wingman on the interplane frequency. "You defensive?"

"That's a big negative, Go-Fast," Rinc responded. "Just had to chase some fighter pukes out of our range.

Break. Pioneer One-Seven, this is Aces Two-One, tail's clear, you are clear to exit the range direct Hokum intersection. Squawk normal and contact Joshua Approach. See you in the patrol anchor. Thanks for your help. We owe you a night on the town."

"Pioneer Seventeen, roger," the pilot of the KC-135R tanker replied happily. "Thanks for the pick. We liked flying in the dirt with you guys. Go kick some butt. We're outta here."

"Thanks, Pioneer," Rinc radioed. "Break. Aces lead, you're clear down the chute. We'll keep your tail clear. You better drop some shacks, or don't bother comin' home. We're right behind you." On interphone, he said, "Okay, hogs: we keep our wingman's tail clear, we drop all zero-zeros, and we don't screw up. Keep it tight and lean forward. No mistakes."

Patrick had seen it all happen right before him—he thought he was going to die. He didn't know—didn't *want* to know—how close they came to that F-15 Eagle fighter. It was close enough to see the pilot's unit patches on his sleeve, see the collar of his flight suit turned up, see the kink in his oxygen hose as he looked out his big canopy and saw the big B-1 barreling down on him. Hell, it had to be close enough to hear that F-15 driver's asshole slam shut as he saw his windscreen fill up with 400,000 pounds of Bone cracking the speed of heat. Patrick knew it, because he thought he'd heard his *own* asshole do the same thing!

He would find out exactly how close later from the AWACS guys and the Nellis range controllers, since they had all the planes and the entire fifty thousand square miles of bombing ranges fully instrumented and could re-create every moment of a battle in exquisite computerized detail. When someone is that close to death or disaster, you can feel it coming at you—you don't need windows or radar or anything. In his eighteen-year career, Patrick had felt that feeling many, many, *many* times. They certainly busted the ROE big-time, and they probably came within seconds of creating one of the most spectacular midair collisions in the history of aviation. The tiniest of deviations—just a few seconds off, a few miles off, one extra turn, crossing east around a peak instead of west, a half-degree steeper dive or 1 percent more airspeed—could have had disastrous results.

"Center up, steering is good," John Long announced. His voice boomed over the quiet interphone channel like a gunshot in a tunnel. "Forty seconds to ACAL, sixty seconds to my fix."

"You see any brown streaks coming out that fighter's cockpit, sir?" Rinc asked Patrick, his voice light.

"SA-3 at two o'clock," the crew's defensive systems officer, Captain Oliver "Ollie" Warren, announced, checking his electronic warfare threat profile display. "Coming from the target area. I'm picking up high PRF and intermittent uplink signals, but not aimed at us—he must be trying to lock onto our wingman."

"Give 'em a shout, Ollie," Rinc said. "See if we can't divert their attention away from our wingman." Patrick shrugged—pretty good idea, although it would be giving away their position. Warren manually activated the L-band uplink jammer. At this range, the jammer would be only marginally effective, and it would immediately tell the enemy the range and bearing to the new threat. He shut it down after only a few seconds.

It worked. The "enemy" switched from the missile-guidance uplink to a wide-area search, trying to find the newcomer. It didn't last very long, ten seconds at the most, but that ten seconds could mean the difference between successfully dropping bombs and destroying the enemy, and getting shot down.

Seconds later Rinc and Patrick saw a brilliant sparkle

of white-yellow lights in the desert ahead on the horizon, spreading out in a long, wide oval pattern—the unmistakable look of a stick of detonating cluster bombs. At the same moment, the SA-3 search radar disappeared completely. "SA-3 down," Warren announced.

"Good shooting, guys!" Rinc crowed. Colonel Furness's crew obviously dropped its bombs close enough to the SA-3 site to score it as a "kill."

The crew heard *deedle deedle deedle* in their headphones, and Warren announced, "Fighter at twelve o'clock, fifteen miles, looks like he's heading down the chute after our wingman."

"Go-Fast, this is Rodeo, bandit on your tail!" Rinc radioed to their leader.

"We're on the rail, Rodeo," Rebecca in Aces Two-Zero responded. "We're lining up for the second release. Can't maneuver too much."

"You son of a bitch," Rinc swore. "We're going to fry his butt. Long Dong, we're going to racetrack around back and you can get your ACAL and a patch on the second pass. We're ten seconds ahead right now. If we do this right, we'll lose about thirty seconds time-over-target. We'll lose points, but not as many as we'd lose if our leader gets shot down."

"Go for it, pilot," Long said, but it was obvious he didn't think much of the plan.

Seaver didn't hesitate. He punched the throttles into max afterburner and turned sharply right to line up behind the lead F-15 fighter. "Lead, we're coming up behind you," he radioed to Furness. "Give me some S-turns so we can catch up. We'll get those Eagle pukes off your butt."

Meanwhile, Long switched radar modes on his APG-66 attack radar back to rendezvous mode and locked onto both the F-15 and their wingman in the other Bone. "Got them," he said. "Twelve-thirty, eight miles, fighter's at about a thousand feet AGL . . . range seven miles . . . six miles . . . five . . ."

"Tally-ho," Patrick shouted, pointing out the windscreen. Rinc followed his gloved hand and saw the fighter, highlighted against the blue sky.

"Gotcha!" Rinc said. They slid through the sound barrier and rapidly closed the distance. "Knock knock, motherfucker . . ."

"Bullrider flight, you're cleared to the perch," the lead F-15 pilot said on his interplane frequency.

"Roger, lead. I'm at your six, moving up. Got you in sight."

"What the hell happened, Billy? I didn't hear you call out a 'guns' on the tanker."

"I was three seconds from hosing the tanker and then the second B-1 popped out of nowhere and flew between me and the tanker," the wingman explained. "I lost sight of both of them and had to bug out before I hit a goddamn mountain."

Shit! Shit! Shit! the leader swore to himself. This morning was not going well at all. He was angry not only because his wingman failed to kill the tanker but because he couldn't catch up with the first B-1 before it bombed its first target. He couldn't see the B-1 down low, but he knew he'd been there—the sight of a bunch of cluster bombs detonating across the desert floor just a few miles in front of him was hard to miss. "Well, why didn't you call KIO or record a violation?"

"Because . . . oh, fuck it, just because," the wingman said. "I recorded a possible heater kill anyway. It was a gutsy move. They deserve the save."

"Like hell they do," the lead F-15 pilot shot back. "They deserve to get busted for doing a stunt like that."

But if the pilot on the scene didn't register a violation, there was no violation—even if the AWACS airborne radar controllers or range controllers saw it. No doubt the bomber crew would get a stern lecture on range safety from the commander, but if no one called a foul, there was no foul.

A bat-wing symbol appeared on the lead F-15's threat scope, but the pilot got no warning tone, indicating that he was being painted with friendly radar. He immediately dismissed the indication, thinking it was his wingman taking up his position on the perch again, covering his leader. "Avalanche, Bullrider One, moving into position on bandit one, record a heater track, now."

"Copy, Bullrider . . . Bullrider One, bandit at your six o'clock low, five miles, closing rapidly. Bullrider, can you delouse?" That was a request for the wingman to try to identify the newcomer.

Low? His wingman was *low*? That meant the target on his threat scope *wasn't his wingman*! Oh, *shit*! "Bullrider flight, you got that bogey? You see him?"

"Negative, lead!"

"Bogey one six o'clock, three miles . . . two miles, closing fast!"

"I got him, lead, I got him!" the wingman cried out. "He's right under you!"

Not for long. Just as the lead F-15 pilot rolled right a bit to get a better look underneath him, the B-1 bomber, in full afterburner, zoomed up directly in front of him. The pilot instinctively rolled hard left and pulled until he heard his stall warning horn, then rolled out. "Billy, you got him in sight? You got him?"

"Screw that, lead! I lost sight of you! I'm lost wingman! I'm blind! I'm level ten thousand!"

"Bullrider Two, collision alert, snap right forty degrees now!" the AWACS radar controller shouted. The lead F-15 pilot had rolled up and right into the path of his wingman on the high perch. The second F-15 took immediate evasive action. It was just in time—the two planes missed each other by less than two hundred feet, without either pilot seeing the other's plane.

The lead F-15 pilot mashed his mike button as he jerked his control stick over hard, waiting for the crunch of metal and the explosion he knew was going to happen. *"Knock it off, knock it off, knock it off!"* he shouted on his command channel. That was the signal to all aircraft to stop maneuvering, roll wings level, and assess the situation. He had lost complete situational awareness, and any maneuver he might make could cause an accident or death.

"I got you in sight, lead!" the second F-15 called, after he rolled out of his snap-turn. "I'm at your five o'clock, one mile. I'm climbing to eleven thousand."

The near-miss rattled the lead F-15 pilot so much he had to drop his oxygen mask to keep from hyperventilating. Damn, what in hell was wrong with those bomber pukes? They used their aircraft like missiles, not giving a damn about peacetime safety-of-flight. Two near-misses within just a few seconds of each other— that was too much!

"I'm going to nail those sons of bitches if it's the last thing I do!" the lead pilot shouted to himself as he snapped his oxygen mask back in place. No hot dog Guard bomber pukes are going to make any Eagle driver look like a putz!

At two hundred feet above the ground, Patrick felt safer now than he had for most of the flight in the Nellis range—he wasn't accustomed to flying so close to other aircraft while on a mission, let alone "enemy" aircraft. He noticed he had pulled his shoulder and lap belts so tight that they hurt, but he didn't even consider loosening them. Again, for the umpteenth time, he checked his ejection levers and ejection mode switches, mentally targeting the levers in case he had to go for them while they were upside down or pulling lots of Gs. This crew seemed hell-bent on making the worst happen.

Were they reckless? Maybe. Were they dangerous? Some might think so. But the question was—were they *effective*? Did they get the job done? So far, protecting their tanker and their wingman, the answer had to be yes. But at what price? When were these stunts going to finally catch up with them?

Rinc Seaver steered the bomber back around in a bootleg racetrack pattern, rolled back in over their lead-in point. Long got his altitude calibration, then took his initial fix and high-resolution patch of the target area. The bomb release—another Combined Effects Munitions cluster bomb attack, a few hundred meters beside where the other B-1 had dropped—was almost an anticlimax.

Were they effective at hitting their assigned targets? Definitely—but, again, at what price?

"I heard a 'knock it off' call, crew," Patrick announced on interphone. "Stand by. I'll be on the voice SATCOM. Everyone else toggle off." Patrick got an acknowledgment from the rest of the crew, then dialed up the secure voice satellite channel. "Firebird, this is Aces Two-One secure."

"This is Firebird," Dave Luger responded. They authenticated themselves once again; then: "Hey, Muck, we just got a call from Avalanche, the AWACS controlling your Red force in the range. They relayed a safety-of-flight violation regarding your crew. Claim you busted the ROE by flying too *close* to the fighters?"

"They call a KIO?"

"Affirmative."

"You get any radar data?"

"It's coming in now . . . Yep, it looks like your guys flew within a half mile of one of the F-15s. ROE says two miles on day one. Avalanche passed along more radar data that says you did it earlier too, but the Red force recorded no violation."

That was it, Patrick thought. A range safety violation was an instant bust on a predeployment exercise. If it was toward the end of a successful exercise, or if it was once at the beginning of an exercise, it might be forgiven—but not twice in one sortie. "Copy," he said. "Ask if Bullrider still wants to play."

"Stand by," Dave Luger responded. A moment later: "Message from Bullrider flight reads as follows: shit yes we'll play. Any ROE the Bones will comply with, they'll accept."

"Relay to Bullrider that the fight's on, level three ROE," Patrick said. "Anything else?"

"Yes, we're monitoring something on Air Combat Command's tactical comm network, an 'all stations' alert broadcast," Luger replied. "We're polling all our sources, but everyone seems to be shutting up and not answering the phones, just listening. We might hear it on CNN before we hear it from the DoD."

"Okay," Patrick said distractedly. They were fast approaching the second target complex. "I'll call you back after we leave the range."

"Copy. Sorry about the bust. Have fun. Firebird out."

THE WHITE HOUSE SITUATION ROOM
THAT SAME TIME

No, wait . . . sir, it's not an invasion," Secretary of Defense Chastain said in shock at the Pentagon reports he was hearing. "It isn't troops crossing the DMZ—*civilians* are. North Korean civilians. By the *thousands*. And there's no resistance from the South. All South Korean border posts are deserted. No response at all from North Korean border troops either. The DMZ is wide open and completely unmanned on either side. Hundreds of artillery emplacements, rocket launchers, tank traps, response routes, minefields—all deserted. On *both* sides."

"*What?*" Martindale exclaimed. "It must be some kind of mistake."

"I'll get confirmation, sir." But he stopped short. "Sir, I'm getting another report. This one's from the Korean Central News Agency—that's the official North Korean government bureau of propaganda. They're broadcasting that riots have broken out all over Pyongyang and that Government House and the presidential palace are under siege. They are calling for support from the Army to help put down the riots. And wait, more reports . . . They say that the central radio and TV broadcasting center is also under siege. They're broadcasting mobilization orders to dozens of active, reserve, and paramilitary units, including the two corps units set up to protect the capital."

"That's odd," said the President. "Why would the civil broadcasting system be used to issue response and assistance orders? Why not use the military networks?"

"And why haven't those units already responded to the South Korean attacks?" asked Philip Freeman, the national security adviser. "They must have seen those

South Korean jets coming almost as soon as they left their bases, and certainly long before they even crossed the DMZ. That was almost twenty minutes ago. What the hell's going on over there?"

Chastain put his hand up, listening intently; then he lowered the headset and stared at it blankly. "Arthur?" Freeman asked. "What's happened?"

"KCNA just went off the air," Chastain replied. "It reported that the government information bureau said the headquarters was being overrun by rioters and agitators, supported by deserting Regular Army soldiers. Then someone else came on a few minutes later and identified himself as a supporter of the new United Republic of Korea."

"The what?" Martindale asked. "Is that a nationalist faction? An opposition group?"

"I don't know," Chastain said. "Never heard of it before. But they claim to be the representatives of the new United Korea. They claim that President Kim Jong-il has evacuated the capital along with several members of the Korean Politburo and his cabinet. They say he's on his way to China to seek asylum."

"This . . . this is extraordinary," Martindale exclaimed. "I can't believe this is happening. North Korea is simply . . . *capitulating*? The borders and checkpoints just disappeared?"

"It's Germany all over again, sir," announced Director of Central Intelligence Robert Plank as he strode quickly into the Situation Room, carrying a stack of reports and photographs. "Sorry I'm late, sir, but I had to wait for all the latest downloads and field reports. It's true. Entire Regular Army, Reserves, and paramilitary units are deserting their commands and either marching on Pyongyang to join the rioters or moving south with their families and a few belongings. When they reach the Military Demarcation Line, they just keep right on going, because all of the South Korean checkpoints are wide open. Panmunjom, Kangseri, Kumhwa, Sehyonni, Sohwari—every one of the border towns has opened the barricades. All of the tank traps and artillery emplacements are still manned, but they're simply standing by in place—there's no attempt to stop, detain, search, or identify anyone. An entire army of spies could be crossing into the South, and nobody would know it. The minefields are being blown up in place—*by South Korean soldiers.* They're clearing a safe path for anyone from the North to cross over."

"What's the status of our bases?" the President asked.

"All secure and closed up tight," said Arthur Chastain. "However, the Korean-owned bases are wide open. They're being used as relocation and refugee centers. It's absolutely incredible. The South has simply opened its doors."

"That's right," said Plank. "Route 1, Route 3, Route 43, Route 5—all roads and highways that cross the MDL are open. No border inspections, no searches, no identity papers required. The South Korean government's already begun opening up relocation offices along the DMZ to assist North Koreans in finding relatives—it's clear they had it all planned. They're providing transportation away from the no-man's-lands around the border areas and are even changing North Korean won to South Korean currency! It's the most incredible thing I've seen since the fall of the Berlin Wall."

"I've got to talk to China," the President said. "It's urgent that I speak with President Jiang directly, right away."

"State is working on it," Chief of Staff Jerrod Hale called out in response.

The President shook his head in frustration. Jiang

Zemin rarely spoke to world leaders on the phone and never initiated calls. Martindale, too, preferred face-to-face talks, but this was a crisis, and this cultural stigma against using the telephone was maddening. "Bob, what are the Chinese doing?"

"Sir, I know it seems extraordinary—but I don't think they're doing anything," Plank replied. "All I have are the daily force status reports, but they all reported normal deployments and no unannounced troop or aircraft movements."

"But what can they hit us with? What kind of retaliation can we expect?"

"Sir, there's about a quarter of a million Chinese troops within one day's march of the North Korean border, and those troops can easily cross into South Korea and overrun the capital within days—we couldn't stop them if we wanted to without using nukes," Plank said. "We're trying to get a more precise status report now, but that could take a few hours. There are about a dozen rocket and artillery units that can launch an attack within moments, and another dozen with weapons that can easily reach into South Korea. The truth is, they can retaliate at any moment."

"If we launch our planes or mobilize any troops, we'll look like we're participating in what's happening," said Freeman. "And if we don't, they'll get slaughtered if China or North Korea attacks."

The President nodded. "We're sunk no matter what we do—unless everyone holds fast and stays away from the red button," he said. "I hope our words get to Jiang." He thought for a moment, then said, "Transmit an order to all our forces: everybody stand by. We watch and wait. No aircraft lift off—not reconnaissance, not intelligence, not support, and especially not attack planes."

"Mr. President," Freeman said earnestly, "I strongly

advise you take your command center airborne. That's the safest place for you, and you can still keep in close contact with all your forces globally."

"Will the Russians or the Chinese know if I depart Washington?"

"Yes . . . probably, after a time," Freeman said, after glancing at Plank and getting a nod. "But that doesn't matter. You should—"

"Then I'm staying," the President said resolutely. "Unless we actually see ICBMs appearing over the horizon, I'm staying. That goes for the senior leadership as well."

"Sir, you know that if the Russians launch an attack, all of our political and bureaucratic institutions will suffer greatly, even be wiped out," Jerrod Hale said. "Congress is still in session; the entire leadership is still in town . . ."

"I don't think the people will give a rat's ass if the political and bureaucratic institutions get wiped out, Jerrod," the President said wryly. "In fact, I think they'll see it as a sad but welcome relief." Then his tone grew serious. "But since you mention it, you'd better send a military aide over to the congressional leadership and let them know what's happening. I'll leave it up to them if they want to adjourn. But make sure they know I'm staying."

"But, sir," Hale protested, trying once more to convince his boss that it was not a safe move to stay, "the National Airborne Operations Center aircraft were designed and tasked to provide global communications in fluid emergency situations such as this. It is not a symbol of panic, desperation, aggression, or cowardice to use them."

"It is to me, Jerrod," the President answered. "Besides, I'm not going to run to the safety of the skies while the Vice President is in the middle of a nuclear fire storm. Now, since State hasn't been able to get through, you see if you can get President Jiang on the phone for me—and see to it that the congressional leadership is up to speed about what's going on."

As his chief of staff got on the telephone, President Martindale's eyes were on the banks of computer and TV monitors but not really watching them. CNN was showing a live broadcast from Seoul, which was little more than a cloud of black smoke on the horizon toward the site of a high-explosive rocket barrage and a chemical weapons attack. He had seen much worse. Then the focus shifted to the streets. They were filled with cars and people, but there was no sign of panic. In fact, it looked like the reverse. Surreal, that's what it was. There was a military attack under way, but it was as if the crowds realized something else was happening—something long awaited.

Just then Jerrod Hale, phone in hand, shouted, "Mr. President! It's the Vice President, calling from Osan!"

"Thank God," Martindale said. He snatched the telephone out of Hale's hand. "Ellen! Are you all right?"

"Yes, Mr. President, we're all right," Whiting replied. "We had a close call, but everyone inside the facility here survived. The fallout levels were low enough, so they decided to evacuate us."

"Good," he said. "We thought you didn't make it. Information is coming out very slowly, in bits. Where are you? We'll send someone to fly you out."

"I've got at least a couple of hundred marines within a stone's throw of me right now," Whiting said, her voice cheerful. "I feel very safe. They can evacuate me out in one of those tilt-rotor planes any minute, but I'm not ready to go back just yet."

"*What*? Why?"

"Mr. President, President Kwon is going to Pyongyang," Whiting said. "He's meeting with First Vice President Pak Chung-chu of North Korea, who apparently has been helping Kwon orchestrate this revolution for many months. Mr. President, the Communist government in Pyongyang, the entire Politburo, has fled the country, and the North Korean People's Army has disbanded. Kwon and Pak are going to announce the formation of a new democratic government, headquartered in Pyongyang. The peninsula has been reunited, Mr. President. *Korea is one.* And I would like to be there when they make the announcement."

Martindale sank into his chair. The reports Chastain had relayed were real. This was truly unbelievable. "Ellen . . . Ellen, how can you be sure it's safe for you?"

"I guess I can't, Kevin," Whiting replied. "But I feel I have to go. I'm going to take all the marines I can in the tilt-rotor, probably twenty or thirty. Kwon and Pak are taking an enormous risk, far greater than me." She paused. "Mr. President, this is an extraordinary opportunity for peace in Asia. It's up to us to seize it. The two leaders plan on meeting in three hours in Pyongyang. I want to be there. I want representatives from China, Russia, and Japan to be there too. If we do this, if all six of the participants in the Korean split appear at once when the peninsula wants to reunify, no one can argue that this is illegitimate. What do you say?"

"I'm worried about your safety, Ellen," Martindale answered. "But . . . of course. I'll call Beijing, Moscow, and Tokyo and try to arrange for some representatives, the highest-ranking ones I can find willing to go to Pyongyang so soon after the nuclear attacks. But make sure you listen to the marines. If they think it's unsafe, if they can't guarantee your safety, I want you out of there."

"Thank you, Mr. President. This is going to be wonderful. I can feel it."

"Maybe. But things are still explosive over there, Ellen. Remember, this revolution is still only hours old. Don't take any more chances. There's plenty of time for announcements and proclamations and photo ops when things are calmer."

He heard the line go dead abruptly. Another thrill of panic shot down Martindale's spine, and he held the phone to his ear for several long moments, hoping she would come back on the line.

Then he hung up. "She's going to Pyongyang," he said.

"What? *Pyongyang?*" Plank exclaimed. "The capital of North Korea? Why? Has she been captured? Is she all right?"

"She sounds all right," the President responded. "In fact, very much so. And apparently there is no North Korea anymore. The Politburo has fled the country, and the army has disbanded."

"There is no way we can verify that, sir!" Plank insisted. "Just because South Korean planes are freely flying over the North and they've opened the borders doesn't mean the North is safe for foreigners to travel, let alone the Vice President. It's too hazardous!"

"Sir, we wouldn't let the Vice President go to Disneyland without adequate preparation by an advance team," the chief of staff reminded the President. "We should at least try to postpone this. One day. Twelve hours. It'll give military intelligence a chance to look the place over first."

"I hear you," the President said, "and I agree one hundred percent. But events are moving too fast. President Kwon is on his way to Pyongyang right now, and he's going to stand right beside the vice president of North Korea and make the proclamation that will stun the world. We need to be part of it. Ellen accepts the risk, and I"—he swallowed hard—"and I accept the responsibility."

To Secretary of State Jeffrey Hartman, he said, "Jeff, Ellen says Kwon and Pak are requesting representatives of Russia, China, and Japan at the announcement. Make some calls and find out if they're interested."

The United Republic of Korea. United Korea. Despite a few apparently knee-jerk rocket launches, it really was virtually a bloodless birth: the people throwing off the shackles of communism that had left them ostracized by the rest of their country—and by the rest of the world. First independent Taiwan, now United Korea. What a way to start the new millennium!

But the wild card was still China. Would they stand aside and watch their Communist brothers vanish before their eyes? Would they launch the massive attack everyone had long feared they would?

"Jerrod."

"Sir?"

"Alert the media. Address to the nation in thirty minutes, from the Oval Office." He took a deep breath and said, "I'm going to announce my support of the United Republic of Korea."

OVER SOUTH-CENTRAL NEVADA
THAT SAME TIME

Aces, Two-Zero is defensive, triple-A at T3," Rebecca Furness, who was now dropping on their second target, said on the interplane frequency just as Patrick switched back to normal radio.

"What d'ya got, Go-Fast?" Rinc radioed.

"Big-time concentrations of triple-A north of T3," Rebecca said. "We had to scram west."

"Time for an airshow, boss," Rinc said on interplane. "Aces Two-Zero, how about airshow north plus three minutes, repeat, airshow north plus three."

"No way," Furness responded. "Just do the run and do the best you can with the threats. We'll be behind you to try again."

"Beck, they'll be expecting attacks from the same axis as before—we can't give it to them," Rinc said. "Airshow north plus three. That's plenty of room, and the range is ours."

There was a slight pause; then: "All right, Rinc. If you don't have a visual on us by three, scram east, I'll go west. Don't screw this up, Seaver!"

"Penetrate, decimate, dominate," Seaver said. "Kick ass, Beck!"

"Steering's good, Rodeo," Long said, after quickly entering several commands into his nav computer.

"What's the plan, guys?" Patrick asked. "What's an airshow?"

"You'll see, General," Rinc replied. "Just keep the bad guys off our butts, Ollie. Here we go." Seaver pushed the throttles into full military power, moved the wing sweep handle forward to thirty-six degrees, then started a steep climb and a fast turn toward the new destination coordinates.

Patrick had had the Nellis range crews set up a difficult nest of several antiaircraft artillery emplacements near the last planned gravity bomb target. He put so many ZSU-23s and dual 57-millimeter radar-guided guns near the target that even a B-1 going supersonic couldn't survive overflying the target. That was the purpose: to see if the crew would alter their tactics, and if so, what they would do next. Patrick could see that Rinc had offset them far to the east of their planned track, well away from the last target. They were passing twenty thousand feet and going higher.

"We're getting kinda high for some of the big threats out here, aren't we?" Patrick asked. If they stayed up this high for much longer, some of the long-range strategic surface-to-air missiles could "kill" them with ease, and at this speed and angle-of-attack, they couldn't maneuver very well. They were flying up high, obviously, to stay away from the triple-A threats that could kill them if they stayed low—but this was getting ridiculous. They were off course, off time, off altitude . . .

"SA-3 in search, twelve o'clock, forty-five miles," Ollie reported. "SA-10, three o'clock, fifty miles."

"We need to get the nose down, pilot," Patrick warned him. "We're naked up here. Airspeed's dropped below four hundred, AOA is eight. What's the plan?"

"Bandits twelve o'clock, forty miles and closing . . ."

"You got it, General," Rinc said happily—and then he pulled the wing sweep handle back to sixty-seven point five degrees, rolled the Bone *inverted,* and started a steep left diving turn, screaming for the ground.

"Mother of God!" Patrick shouted.

"Passing thirty for six," Long said calmly. Checklist pages and tiny bits of dirt and dust were floating around them. As they accelerated earthward, Patrick started to feel the pressure squeeze him into his seat as the G-forces built up. They had reversed their direction of flight and had rolled back upright, speeding toward the second target complex in the *opposite* direction they had planned—exactly opposite of the second B-1 on this bomb run!

"Hey, our track will put us nose-to-nose with our wingman," Patrick pointed out.

"We know that," Rinc answered. "He should be off our nose at sixteen DME, low." The crew kept the air-to-air TACAN system dialed in so they could tell exactly how far they were from each other. "Where are those threats, D?" he asked.

"SA-3 down, SA-10 four o'clock, search only . . . triple-A at twelve o'clock, fast-scan search. He's getting ready to range on us. We've got bandits now at six o'clock, thirty miles and closing fast, coming down the ramp at us."

"Wingman at fifteen . . . fourteen . . ." Patrick couldn't believe how fast the air-to-air DME was winding down.

"A little hot, Rodeo," Long said. "Give me a few seconds. Two should do it." Seaver responded by honking the Bone into two very steep, tight turns, one to the left and another to the right, to lose a little time without pulling off any power, still with the nose aimed earthward. "That should do it. Ten DME . . . passing ten for six . . . looking good . . . pop when ready, Rodeo!"

"Boards!" Rinc shouted. Patrick hit the OVERRIDE switch and deployed all four spoilers up into full speed-brake position. They all slammed forward against their shoulder straps as they quickly decelerated. As the speed decreased, Rinc swept the wings forward to fifty-four degrees to slow down even more.

"Triple-A locked on!" Warren shouted.

"Five DME!" Rinc announced over interphone. "Got them yet, General?"

"Raise the nose a little," Patrick replied, his head spinning. "A little more . . . contact, contact! Eleven-thirty, low!"

"Got 'em," Rinc said calmly. They were head-to-head with their wingman, the other B-1 bomber! Aces Two-One was screaming earthward from above while Rebecca Furness in the lead Bone was racing supersonic across the high desert. Their flight paths intersected directly over the second target complex.

"Bandit six o'clock, twenty miles!" Warren shouted. "Triple-A lock, *chaff, chaff!*" Then, just as suddenly: "Triple-A down! It's the fighter on our tail! They don't want to shoot at their own guy."

"Get your nose up a little, pilot," Long said. "Twenty TG to bomb release. We level at one thousand!"

But the call was too late. Out the cockpit window, they could see Aces Two-Zero laying down a string of five-hundred-pound bombs. Bright flashes of yellow light quickly made way for an immense cloud of smoke and exploding metal. The desert erupted and boiled as if it had suddenly turned to sand-colored lava.

The second B-1 passed within one mile of Furness's bomber, just three hundred feet underneath. Rinc was watching the first B-1 and was not paying attention to his altitude until the RADAR ALT LOW warning light and buzzer came on at eight hundred feet.

"Pull up!" Patrick shouted. Seaver pulled back on the control stick to level off, but not before the bomber careened through five hundred feet above ground—aimed right at the center of the detonation pattern. The crew felt a sharp jolt and a bouncing, pinging pebbly sound underneath the plane, like a car driving across a rough gravel road.

"Ten TG!" Patrick shouted. "We're too low! *Withhold!*"

Long ignored him. At that same moment, the bomb doors swung open, and Aces Two-One released their own Mk82 bomb load on their own target two complex. Again, the desert rippled and undulated as the bombs ripped apart the enemy vehicles set up below.

The B-1 was in a steep climb and escaped most of the effects of the Ballute-retarded bomb attack. The F-15 pilot chasing Aces Two-One was not quite as lucky. He stopped his descent and turned away as he saw the second B-1 bomber heading right for him, but he turned directly into the path of the first Bone's bomb fragmentation pattern.

"Avalanche, this is Bullrider One on GUARD," they heard on the GUARD emergency channel. "Bullrider One is declaring an emergency for a right engine fire and right wing structural damage."

"Roger, Bullrider One," the AWACS controller responded on GUARD. "All Bullrider and Aces playmates, knock it off, knock it off, knock it off. Bullrider One, you're radar contact, climb and maintain one six thousand, turn right heading one-five-three, vectors for the visual approach at Nellis, squawk normal. Bullrider Two, you are radar contact, squawk normal, say intentions."

"Bullrider Two will rejoin on Bullrider One for a formation visual approach to Nellis."

"Roger, Bullrider Two. Climb and maintain one five thousand, fly heading one-seven-zero, vectors for a rejoin, advise when holding hands with Bullrider One. Bullrider flight, push Red Five."

"Bullrider flight, Red Five, go."

"Two."

That was not the last word: the bomber crews heard a curt "Aces, Falcon five-oh-one," then the frequency was clear. No one in either bomber had to look up that "Falcon" code in their unofficial checklist pages—it was well known to most fliers. It decodes as "Kiss my ass."

"You can kiss *my* ass—at least we're not going home with a bent bird," Rinc retorted.

Patrick wasn't so sure—they were a couple of hundred feet low on their bomb release and could easily have fragged themselves with their own bombs.

"You've got steering to the anchor," Long said.

Rinc rejoined with Furness a few minutes later, and

they made their way to the refueling area, where Pioneer Seventeen, the tanker that had participated in their low-level penetration charade, was waiting for them. They topped off their tanks, the tanker departed safely, and the two bombers settled into their orbits to wait for targets of opportunity.

"So what do you think, General?" Rinc Seaver asked.

"I think I'd hate to see the underside of this plane after we land," Patrick replied.

There was a long, uncomfortable pause on interphone. Finally, Rinc said, "I think we were okay."

The first target-of-opportunity message, from the SATCOM text terminal, came in a few moments later, and Rebecca's crew broke off and took it, leaving Rinc's sortie in the holding pattern. Patrick got a call on the SATCOM secure voice channel several minutes later: "Go ahead, Amarillo. How did Aces do?"

"Shack—no problem," David Luger responded. "We heard about the F-15 getting fragged too. The commander of the 366th at Mountain Home wants some butts."

"He might get some."

"Roger that. Listen up, Muck. We got some shit happening in Korea."

"Korea? Did the North invade? I don't believe it! During Team Spirit?"

"No, it wasn't the North—it was the *South,*" Luger responded. "Do you believe it? *South Korea invaded North Korea.* Happened a little while ago. And get this: no massive invasion force. Apparently, the South has been spreading propaganda and stirring up shit in the North for months, maybe years. When the South started in, most of the North's defense network was already shut down. The civilians that aren't hotfooting it for the South are marching on the capital, getting ready to tear the place down. Looks like it's a South-assisted nonmilitary revolution in North Korea."

"Hol-ee *shit*," Patrick exclaimed. "I never would've expected that. I always thought of the North as this big monolithic Big Brother ultra-Marxist dictatorship. Who would have thought the South could ever pull off some-thing like that."

"I don't have all the details, but from what I've read, the North was going to implode under the weight of two million starving citizens anyway," Luger said. "But here's the real news, Muck: the North launched Nodongs and Scuds on the South. About a dozen ballis-tic missile attacks."

"Any special weapons?"

"I'm talking *only* about special weapons, Muck," Dave said somberly. "The Patriots got most of them, but a few fifty-KT nukes and a bunch of bio-chem war-heads made it through. The South didn't get hit as hard as everyone thought they might, but they got hit pretty good."

"Oh God," Patrick mumbled. He thought about the horrible loss of life, and he thought about the three rather small but dangerously significant nuclear con-flicts in the past five years, and what this world was transforming itself into as his young son was growing up . . .

. . . but what he really thought about was Lancelot, his B-1-based antiballistic missile weapon system. If Asia was teetering on the brink of a major conflict, pos-sibly a thermonuclear war, his air-launched antiballistic missile missiles might be the secret to defending Ameri-can interests in that region.

Was he thinking more and more like Brad Elliott these days? Was that how Brad corrupted his career and ultimately destroyed himself, consumed with develop-ing a response to a world crisis no matter what the cost? Patrick shook off those thoughts. Those were questions for another time, another place, perhaps with a therapist, with his wife, Wendy, and a glass of Banff-shire Balvenie in the hot tub. Right now, he had to put his plan into motion.

"Dave, I've got the first two Lancelot units lined up here," Patrick said. "I would like to talk with Earthmover ASAP." "Earthmover" was HAWC commander General Terrill Samson's call sign.

"You got it," Luger responded. "You going to terminate the pre-D now?"

Patrick thought for a moment, then replied, "Call out to Tonopah and tell the squadron to get ready to copy new deployment orders. In six hours, have them land at Groom Lake."

"What!" Luger exclaimed. "You want the squadron at *Dreamland*?"

"Amarillo, I know in my gut that Lancelot is going to get a green light," Patrick said. "From what the general told us, the 111th is going to get decertified and lose their bombers once word of this bust goes up the chain of command. Well, possession is four-fifths of ownership. I've got first dibs on the B-1Bs, and I'm taking them to Dreamland. You say we've got two kits ready to install and two more kits on the way—I'm going to install them, starting tonight. Clear out Foxtrot row for seven Bones, have the Support Squadron get some TLQs ready, and have Engineering stand by to start installing Lancelot."

"You got it, Muck," Dave Luger said happily. "Messages going out as we speak. I should get security clearance to recover planes within the hour. Hot damn! We're either going to get kicked in the ass or get us a bomb squadron tonight. Firebird out."

Patrick switched back to normal interphone and keyed his mike button: "D is back up, crew. SATCOM voice available again. Listen up, crew. We're going to divert to a different anchor. Colonel Long, I'll give you some coordinates to plug in."

"Is the pre-D over?" Rinc asked.

"For now," Patrick said. "I've got a reason for doing all this. If you show me something, I'll let you all in on it."

"I knew there was something else going down!" Rinc exclaimed. "I knew this was no ordinary pre-D. What are you planning, General?"

"Stand by," Patrick said. He recited a series of new navigation coordinates for Long, verified them carefully, then said, "Okay, crew, listen up. Pilot, first, notify Two-Zero that you want them to stay at this orbit point after they get done until we come back and get them. Call Los Angeles Center and get them their own Mode Three code."

"We going somewhere without our wingman, General?"

"Just tell them," Patrick ordered. Rinc did as he was told.

"Okay, General, the steering is good to a new orbit point."

"Roger." Patrick had Seaver engage the autopilot. Then he set special codes in the Mode One portion of the IFF and activated Mode Two and Mode Four beacon codes. "Pilot, once you reach the reference point, give me a racetrack pattern on a southerly heading at best endurance speed, two minute legs, left turns at half standard rate. If L.A. Center or Joshua Approach gives you a warning message telling you you're heading for a hot restricted area, I'll give you a PPR number, but my crew should've already coordinated our entry. They may assign you a new Mode Three code, probably with a 'zero-one' prefix; go ahead and set whatever they tell you."

"Entry? Entry into what?"

"We're entering R-4808 North."

"That's not approved, General," Long said. "That's off limits. *Way* off limits. We can lose our wings and go to jail for busting that airspace."

"Not today you won't," Patrick said. "Just do as I said, and hope that your ground crews set your Mode Two and Mode Four codes correctly or we'll all be in big trouble." The bomber immediately rolled into a turn—Patrick could feel the tension building.

"While we're navigating to the new orbit anchor, I'll explain what's going to happen," Patrick went on. "Here's the situation: the Bones are going to act like tactical attack aircraft. No more straight and level bombing. Every target is a target of opportunity. Got it?"

"Cool!" Rinc Seaver exclaimed.

"I'm willing to give it a try," Oliver Warren said. "It'll be like the old F-4 Wild Weasel days—cruise around until a threat pops up, then go in after it."

"Exactly," Patrick said.

"We don't have the equipment or the training for something like that, General," Long remarked.

"We're going to have to simulate it for now," Patrick said. "I want to go through the motions and see what potential problems we might have. Okay: This morning we're looking for ballistic missile launches. We can receive intelligence or reconnaissance data on the presence of mobile launchers in our area using radar planes like Joint STARS, and spot a missile launch using . . . other sensors, but today we have to spot the launches ourselves. Once you spot a launch, you need to cob the power and lead the missile's flight path."

"This sounds like total nonsense, General sir," John Long protested. "It's unrealistic . . ."

"It's totally unrealistic, Colonel," Patrick admitted, "but it's the best we can do with a stock B-1B."

"Does that mean there're Bones out there that aren't 'stock'?" Rinc asked. "We got Bones that are set up for this kind of thing?"

"You don't need to know that right now," Patrick said. "Just play along, and we'll see how you do. We'll be in the anchor in five minutes."

"What kind of threats are there in the area?" Oliver Warren asked.

"Good question—glad someone thought to ask," Patrick said. "Most mobile ballistic missile launchers are protected by short-range mobile antiaircraft systems. You'll get anything from triple-A to SA-4s to Rapiers to Hawks to Patriots—anything the bad guys might possibly have. Do whatever you think you need to do to get away from the threats. Any more questions?" There were none. The action started just a few moments later.

They received several warnings about entering restricted area R-4808, including one on the emergency GUARD frequency from Los Angeles Center and one from Avalanche, the Air Force AWACS radar plane that was helping the fighters hunt down the B-1s. After all the urgent warnings, Seaver and his crew—except for Patrick McLanahan—couldn't help but hold their breath as the miles-to-go indicator clicked down to zero. The radios got very quiet as Rinc started his holding pattern—it was as if no one at Los Angeles Center or any other civilian air traffic control agency wanted to talk to them anymore. The interphone got extremely quiet too. They, like the air traffic controllers, knew they were doing something profoundly special.

Patrick had been listening on the secure SATCOM channel. He clicked the interphone mike button: "Missile launch. Behind us, fifteen miles."

"I didn't see anything on the screen!" Ollie protested.

"You may see something, you may not," Patrick repeated. "Sometimes if there are bombers in the area close by, launch crews won't use the radar and just launch using forecasts or old data. It makes for a less accurate missile, but if you're launching nukes or biochem weapons, you don't have to be that accurate."

"Well, *hell*," Long protested. "What good is this goatfuck if it's *that* easy to pop one off? You put a Bone and a tanker crew in harm's way, and the bad guys can still launch? Why not just lay waste to the whole battle area and be done with it?"

"You flew in Desert Storm, Colonel," Patrick said. "The coalition forces *were* laying waste to Iraq—two thousand sorties a day—and the Iraqis were still launching Scuds. The answer is, it's not so easy to find these mobile launchers. Joint STARS can track every vehicle from a hundred miles away, unless it's hidden under an overpass or in someone's barn or in an underground bunker. But we still have to try to stop the missile launches."

"I guess you may need to have two planes in the orbit," Rinc offered. "That way, you got the whole horizon covered."

"I don't get it, General," Long pressed. "What good is it to wait for a missile launch? Sure, you take out the launcher, but the missile's still on its way. I don't—"

"I got one!" Warren suddenly called out. "No, it's gone . . ."

"Where, Ollie? Where did you see it?"

"Four o'clock, thirty miles."

Rinc immediately slammed the Bone into a tight right turn and rolled out after approximately 120 degrees. "You see anything on radar, Long Dong?"

"Stand by," Long responded. After a moment of tuning and searching: "I've got several hard targets between thirty and forty-five miles, between eleven and one o'clock."

"Try a patch on the largest ones first," Rinc suggested. "You might be able to patch on all of them—wait! I see smoke! Eleven-thirty position, range . . . shit, range . . . hell, use thirty miles! I could use a laser range finder here—it's tough estimating distance."

"Got it," Long said. "Three targets right around in that same area, within a few miles of each other."

"Target all of them!" Rinc said. "Load all the targets. We make one pass with JDAM."

"Sure would be a waste of a lot of bombs," Patrick interjected, trying to make them think like a Lancelot attack crew.

"Then we try to see a launch from one of them and target that one," Rinc said. "If we can't get a bead on the right one, we'll take 'em all out."

"Sound good to you, Colonel?" Patrick asked.

"Affirmative," Long said. "It's the best we got until someone gives us a sensor made for this kind of mission." Long quickly had the Offensive Radar System compute the GPS satellite-derived coordinates of the three objects on his radar screen, then fed the data into the Joint Direct Attack Munitions navigation computers. The bombing computers calculated the release zone for each target, computed a release track based on the time the internal bomb bay rotary launcher moved a new weapon into drop position, then fed the navigation information to the Bone's autopilot.

"Steering is good to the release track," he said a few moments later. "Stand by for weapon release in ninety seconds. Give me point nine Mach, pilot."

Just as Rinc began pushing the throttles forward, Warren shouted, "Hey, I've got a search radar up . . .

and it's staying up too. Ten degrees right, twenty-five miles."

"Drop on all three targets," Rinc said. "We have no way of knowing which . . ." Suddenly, he pointed out the window and shouted, "Look! There's a rocket lifting off, right in front of us! I can see it! Holy shit, I've never seen a rocket launch before."

"Pilot, I want max afterburners *now*!" Patrick shouted. "I want you to aim the nose right at that missile until you can't hold it any longer!"

"What? You want what?"

"I said, max AB *now,* and keep us pointed right at that rocket for as long as you can! *Go!*"

Rinc shoved the throttles all the way to the stops and swept the wings back to full. The Bone leaped forward like a meteor. The rapid acceleration and gradual but unrelenting pressure of increasing G-forces pressing Patrick into his seat felt great, like the power and exhilaration of a race car or speedboat. Rinc kept on raising the nose, and the G-forces kept right on coming. It was easy to think he was an astronaut, riding a column of fire into space.

But unlike a spaceship, the Bone couldn't keep on raising its nose and accelerating at the same time. Patrick had started a timer when Rinc began the maneuver, and after only twenty seconds and twenty degrees above the horizon, the speed was already dropping off. In full blower, they might have to hit a tanker if they kept this up much longer. But about then, Rinc said, "Hey! The rocket is nosing over—it's starting to descend."

"That was just a test rocket—it burned out just to make sure it didn't fly outside the range," Patrick said. "Good job, Major."

"What do you mean, good job?" Seaver asked as he

leveled off and pulled the throttles to normal power settings. "What did I do?"

"Later," Patrick said. "Okay, crew, let's go back and get those launchers back there."

"What? Now you want us to bomb those targets? Why didn't we do that be—" But Rinc stopped his protests as the lightbulb finally popped on in his brain, and he turned back to the first target. At 32,000 feet, the altitude he had climbed to when he stopped the chase on the test rocket, the JDAM satellite-guided bombs could glide over fifteen miles. As fast as the rotary launcher could spit them out, the JDAMs dropped into space.

A few minutes later, after clearing off to the voice SATCOM channel, Patrick reported, "Good work, everyone. Three good hits, all within thirty feet, which is pretty good for JDAM. One bomb hit within ten feet—a shack. Only one was the launcher, but the other three were simulated maintenance and crew vehicles—legitimate targets in anybody's book. Let's head back to the orbit area."

"Okay, General, what was that climb for?" Rinc asked as he started a turn back for the patrol anchor. "We gonna chase rockets now?"

"Just wanted to distract you a little."

"If I can speak freely, General sir—bullshit," he said. "You don't just want to go after launchers—you want to go after missiles too! Tell us, General—do we have a weapon that can take down a ballistic missile? You got a weapon you can put on a Bone that'll take down a ballistic missile?"

"No comment."

"So you *don't* work for the Air Force chief of staff, do you, sir?" Long asked. "You work for some R and D unit—maybe even for the supersecret squirrels down there at Dreamland, huh?"

"Time out, all of you. That's the last we talk about any of this," Patrick warned. "You say a word about this to anyone outside this airframe, and your life will turn into an endless maze of courtrooms, lawyers, investigators, and maximum security cells. Do you all understand?"

"Fine, fine, General," Rinc said. "Now tell us: What do you have in mind? What's the mod? Is this what Block G is going to do? You gotta tell—"

"Hey!" Ollie shouted as the crew heard a slow-paced *deedle deedle deedle* tone on interphone. He had to remember to key the mike switch in his excitement: "SA-4 up." The SA-4 "Ganef" is a mobile high-altitude SAM, an older system, but still deadly to any aircraft flying higher than five or six hundred feet. "Better get our asses down, boys!"

"Not quite yet," Patrick said. "Max range of an SA-4 is fifty miles, but lethal range is about twenty miles, so we should be safe—they'll wait until we get well within lethal range. They can see us up here, but they won't attack yet. Let's make the SA-4 our next target. Ollie, keep on feeding us position data."

"Okay," Warren said. "Rodeo, right ninety degrees, target at thirty miles." Rinc made a tight turn and rolled out precisely on heading.

"Right five degrees, twenty-nine miles . . . okay, dead ahead, twenty-eight miles."

"Stand by." Long moved his cursor control out the proper amount, then adjusted the gain and brightness controls to tune out the terrain features on the radarscope. He then moved his cross hairs onto the largest radar return still on the radar image. "I'm going to take a patch. Left fifty, pilot," he ordered. Rinc made the turn. With the target offset the proper amount, Long was able to take a high-resolution "patch" of it, then examine the magnified image. "There it is. Pretty good look at an SA-4 Ganef SAM."

"Cool!" Warren exclaimed, straining over to look. It didn't actually look like much—just a group of boxes—but on one box, the upraised missiles could clearly be seen. "Hey, that's pretty neat."

"I've got the coordinates loaded . . . bombing computers are programming JDAM . . . programming complete," Long announced. "Okay, pilot, steering is good to the release point. Give me Mach point nine, right turn to the release point, stand by for countermeasures and evasive action."

No sooner had Rinc shoved in the throttles to full military power and finished the turn than the threat-warning receiver issued another alert tone, this one a faster-paced *deedledeedledeedle*. "Missile warning," Warren called out. "Pilot, stand by for maneuvers . . ." Then they heard another warning tone, and Warren watched as the left chaff dispenser counter clicked. "*Missile launch! Break right!*"

Seaver reacted instantly, yanking the control stick hard right and pulling, waiting until their speed had slowed to cornering velocity, then rolling out and shoving in full afterburner again to regain their speed.

"Should we go low?" Rinc shouted on interphone.

"Uplink down . . . height finder down . . . SA-4 back in search," Warren said.

"If we descend, we'll have to fly closer to the target," Long said. "Stay up here. Center up, steering is good. Twenty seconds to release. If we get another launch, pilot, we have to stay wings-level until bomb's away. Don't turn until I tell you. Fifteen sec—"

Another warning tone. "Missile alert! Height finder up!" Warren shouted.

"Hold heading! Ten . . . doors coming open." The rumble of the doors was not as loud as before, since with a JDAM bomb release from the rotary launcher, the bomb doors needed to open only halfway.

Another warning tone. "Missile launch!" Warren shouted, reading the blinking alert message on his multifunction display. "Chaff! Chaff!"

"Hold heading!" Long shouted. Ollie swore and hit the CHAFF EJECT button as fast as he could. Chaff bundles shot out of the ejectors atop the forward part of the fuselage, creating a larger cloud of radar-decoying metal slivers that ballooned the radar cross section of the B-1 several hundred times. "Bomb away! Doors closed! *Pilot, scram left!* Clear to descend!"

Rinc immediately started a hard turn and hit the TERFLW button on his autopilot control—but he didn't wait for the computer to point the nose earthward, he rolled the B-1 nearly inverted. The terrain-following fail-safe fly-up system immediately pulled the B-1's nose downward, and the Bone plummeted to earth.

Seaver jammed the throttles to idle and popped the spoilers to try to slow down while descending at the same time. He kept the bomber nearly inverted until the nose was over forty degrees below the horizon, then pulled the pitch interrupt trigger to temporarily disconnect the autopilot. But when he tried to roll upright, nothing happened. He shook the stick, pulled it in every direction—the nose stayed down, airspeed kept on decreasing, and the earth was rushing up to meet them in a hurry.

"Five thousand to level, pilot," Patrick warned. "Check your attitude."

Rinc pulled the pitch interrupt trigger all the way to disconnect the autopilot, then tried the controls again. Nothing. He shoved in full military power and tried to roll wings-level—nothing. He swept the wings forward right to the airspeed limit "barber pole"—still nothing. No stick control at all.

"Four thousand!" Patrick shouted. "Pilot, *roll out*!"

"Can't!" Rinc said. "I got no roll response!"

"Three thousand!"

Patrick tried his own control stick—still no response. "We're mushing . . . no response . . . we're in a full stall, dammit . . . we got the nose down and mil power and we're in a full damned stall . . . What in hell's happened?"

"Two thousand!" Long shouted. "Seaver, you motherfucker, you got it? *You got it?*"

Rinc reached over with his left hand and hit the PRE-PARE TO EJECT switch. A yellow warning light illuminated over every crew station.

"Hey, what the hell?" Ollie asked. *"Rodeo?"*

"One thousand feet!"

Patrick frantically scanned the instrument panel, then reached down, not to his ejection handles, but to the center console, and flipped the four SPOILER OVERRIDE switches back to NORMAL. The airspeed immediately began to build. Seaver shoved the stick to the right, and the bomber responded. Barely five hundred feet above the ground, the B-1 bomber rolled upright, easily nosed skyward, and started a rapid climb. The abrupt pull-up from the steep dive squished them all into their seats, but the Bone settled into a fast two-thousand-foot-per-minute climb.

"Hol-ee shit!" Warren exclaimed. "What happened? Did we stall? Did we lose an engine?"

Rinc looked at Patrick. In order to start a rapid descent with the wings swept back, he had had to raise the spoilers—and to do that with the wings swept back, he had to override the flight control computers. But when he raised all four spoilers after rolling nearly inverted, he didn't have the flight control authority or the airspeed to roll upright again.

"My fault," Rinc said. Patrick shut off the PREPARE

TO EJECT light. "I had switches out of position for TERFLW. I fucked up. The general found my spoiler switches out of position. He saved our asses."

"Good going, sir," Ollie said.

"Everybody relax," Patrick said. "Climb back to the new patrol anchor. I'm clearing off to SATCOM. Everyone else toggle off." He switched his interphone panel, then keyed the mike: "Firebird, this is Two-One, requesting scores." No conversation this time: Patrick copied down a string of numbers and letters, cleared off SATCOM, then used a decoder document to decode the message.

"TOSS bomb score on the SA-4 site, guys: two-nine-five degrees, sixty-seven feet. Not too shabby. With a two-thousand-pound bomb, I'd call that a kill." No one celebrated this time—they were still too stunned by the near-crash. "Now for the bad news: first SA-4 missed by three hundred eighty feet. We might have survived that one. Second SA-4 . . ."

"Second?"

"SA-4s always fire in salvos of two, like a Patriot system," Patrick said, "and each SA-4 battery has three launchers. Second SA-4 estimated miss distance was only one hundred twenty feet. With a two-to-three-hundred-pound warhead, I think we would've taken a major hit."

"Well, it's bullshit going after something like an SA-4 with a JDAM," Ollie said. "We still gotta fly within its lethal range, even if we drop from high altitude—which exposes us even more."

"Damn right," Rinc said. "Give us a HARM or a Maverick or SLAM, and we can take it out without getting shot down."

"Let's wrap this up, folks—I think we've had enough for the day," Patrick said. "Let's head back to the first patrol anchor and pick up our wingman. Then I'll give you vectors for our new destination."

"New destination?"

"We're not going to Tonopah."

"We're not? You get something on the SATCOM? Are we going back to Reno?"

"I did get some news on SATCOM, and I decided to change our itinerary," Patrick said. "Get Two-Zero tied on radar."

"What's the story, General? Where are we going?"

"Somewhere over the rainbow, boys and girls," Patrick said. "Somewhere over the rainbow. I just hope we don't run into a wicked witch after we get there."

The rejoin with Aces Two-Zero went off without a hitch, and soon both bombers were in close fingertip formation, visually inspecting each other for any signs of damage or hanging ordnance after their live releases. Each plane did a turn over and around the other, checking all possible sides. "You look clean, lead," reported the copilot aboard Two-Zero, Annie "Heels" Dewey, on the secure HAVE QUICK interplane frequency. "Hey, where were you guys?"

"We can tell you—but then we'd have to kill you," Rinc said, but there was no humor in his voice.

"Put a cork in it, Rodeo," Furness said.

"Crew, I'm clearing off to SATCOM voice," Patrick said. "Make sure you're toggled off." Patrick switched over to the secure satellite communications channel and reauthenticated with Dave Luger. "How are we coming, partner?"

"We're ready and waiting, boss," Dave replied. "Foxtrot row is ready. We've diverted Aces Three-Zero and Aces Three-One, and they'll be arriving in your patrol anchor shortly. You can come in as a four-ship. We might have problems with the three planes that were supposed to deploy to Tonopah, however."

"Problems?"

"Muck, half the world is hopping mad at you right now," Luger said. "Air Combat Command has been screaming at the Nevada Air Guard and at us for the last hour, asking if your guys and you have gone off your collective rockers. They're pissed about the ROE violations, and they're ready and anxious to prosecute all of you for dropping live ordnance over R-4808 without prior coordination. They've issued orders to the three planes still in Reno to cease all operations. The Nevada adjutant general isn't arguing with ACC.

"I tried to explain that Genesis was driving this exercise," Dave said, using HAWC's unclassified call sign, "but I don't have nearly enough juice to put out this fire. General Samson wants to meet with the chief of staff and/or the CJSC, but with this Korea thing exploding, no one's available to take a meeting."

"Has General Samson talked with General Bretoff?"

"Affirmative," Dave said. "Bretoff's a nice guy, but this squabble is way over his head, and he's swinging whichever way the wind's blowing. I think if General Samson will run interference, Bretoff will run with the ball and let us play. I think this was just plain bad timing, Muck—everyone would be a lot less tweaked if the Korea thing hadn't erupted."

"Gotcha," Patrick said. "I'm not really concerned about ACC right now—what I want is those planes."

"Bottom line: I think all you'll get are the planes that are airborne right now, my friend," Dave said. "Might be better to leave it at that. We only have kits and weapons for two birds anyway, and funds for only two more. Get the four on the ground at Dreamland, and only the SECAF or higher can dislodge them. CSAF is already onboard, if your boys haven't pissed him off too much."

"We'll see," Patrick said. "Thanks, Dave. See you on

the ground shortly." He switched back to interphone. "Co's back up, crew. I'm going to interplane freq." He switched to the air-to-air frequency: "Aces Two-Zero, check."

"We're up," replied Rebecca Furness in the other B-1 in the patrol orbit.

"Aces Three-Zero flight, check."

The transmission was a little scratchy, but they heard, "Aces Three-Zero flight of two is up. Hiya, hogs."

"Three-Zero?" Furness remarked. "What's going on, sir?"

"You'll see." On the interplane frequency, he said, "Three-Zero flight, Two-Zero flight is in fingertip in the anchor at one seven thousand block one eight thousand. I want you in the block one-niner to two-zero." Both flights verified their positions on air-to-air TACAN and radar, then coordinated the rejoin with Los Angeles Center. Once both formations were within three miles of each other, McLanahan had Furness declare MARSA—"military assumes responsibility for separation of aircraft"—with the other formation. The civilian controllers seemed very relieved to relinquish responsibility for this strange and unusual gaggle of military aircraft.

"Hey, you guys hear what's happened?" the pilot in Aces Three-Zero said on the secure interplane frequency after they were safely in the patrol orbit. "War has started in Korea. They expect the balloon to go up any second."

"I think the balloon has already gone up—right on top of *us*," the pilot of Aces Three-One chimed in. "We've been getting messages from the command post and SATCOM messages telling us to put down back in Reno. They say our whole unit's been *violated*. What's the story, boss?"

"I'm going to let the general explain," Furness said, "because I don't fucking understand it one bit."

"Okay, listen up, all of you," Patrick said on interplane. "This is Major Seaver's copilot. A situation has developed related to the Korea crisis, and using my own discretion under the authority of the chief of staff of the Air Force, I have ordered all of the 111th's aircraft and deployable aircrews to another location. We're on our way there right now. It's imperative that you follow my directions exactly, or you'll be shot down. Do you understand?"

"What's going down, Go-Fast?" asked Pogo Lassky in Aces Three-One. "Is this for real? What does he mean, shot down?"

"Shut up and listen, all of you," Furness said. "I don't know what's happening, but the general is in charge. Be quiet, pay attention, and do like the man says."

"How's your fuel level, number one?" Lassky asked.

"I'm not under duress, Pogo," Furness answered immediately. Lassky's question was a code phrase, asking in as natural a manner as possible if there was a hijacker or any trouble onboard. "This is for real. We'll be on the ground shortly, and then he'll explain everything. Now listen good."

"Hey, are you a terrorist or something?" John Long asked. "Is this some twisted plot to steal our planes and bomb Canada or something?"

"It's a twisted plot, all right," Patrick said with a smile in his voice. "And yes, I am stealing the planes—sort of."

"Is this part of the pre-D?" someone else asked. "Is this part of the exercise? Some kind of loyalty or anti-terrorist test?"

"No, this is not part of the pre-D, and no, it's not a test of your loyalty," Patrick replied. "You can refuse to participate in what I'm planning on doing. I will not order anyone to follow my directions. You can fly back to Reno. I'll even invalidate the flying portion of the pre-D."

"Say *what*?" Furness asked incredulously. "You'll what?"

"The squadron did almost perfectly in the generation and predeployment," Patrick said. "You didn't do so well in the flying part. I've already received hate mail from Air Combat Command, the Guard Bureau, and several wing commanders, and I'm sure there are more waiting to chew some butt. But I'm willing to tell ACC, the National Guard Bureau, and the chief of staff of the Air Force that I unfairly influenced the flying portion to make it more difficult than the regs allowed. You keep all your Probability to Launch and Survive points, and you do the flying part some other time with some other evaluator."

"Why invalidate the flying portion of the pre-D?" the pilot aboard Aces Three-One asked. "What happened? How did we do?"

"I don't know," Patrick said. "I haven't tallied the reports yet. I'll debrief you all later."

"If we were doing okay, I think you'd tell us, sir," another crew member said. "Why don't you tell us the truth? We're big boys."

"Any objections, Colonel Furness?" Patrick asked on interplane. There was no response—Patrick decided Furness knew exactly what was coming and was afraid to countermand a full report in front of the troops. "Very well. All in all, the squadron did very well—I'd rate you an 'excellent' overall, in fact. Almost perfect in Probability to Launch and Survive points. Almost perfect . . . right up until Major Seaver taxied out of the parking area. After that, it all went downhill."

"*What* . . . ?"

"One documented ROE violation, three observed range safety violations, one observed weapons safety violation, one possible safety-of-flight violation," Patrick said. "That gives Two-One's sortie a zero Damage Expectancy score, which takes you down to eighty-six percent even if everyone else was *absolutely* perfect. You need an eighty percent to pass. If Two-Zero gets charged with a range safety violation for participating in that 'airshow' stunt with Seaver, they'll get a zero DE score too. Two noneffective sorties out of seven is an automatic fail."

"Stand by!" Rinc Seaver thundered. "What the hell do you mean, we failed? What right do you have to tell *my* fliers something like that? Who the hell do you think you are, McLanahan?"

"That's 'General' or 'sir' to you, Colonel!" Patrick snapped. "And don't give me this innocence routine. You all knew what the ROEs are for this ride, and you deliberately broke them—not once, but *three times*: twice with the fighters and once with your own wingman! And you know damn well that you were two hundred and twenty feet low on that last bomb release—you could've killed us all. I've got verified radar data from the AWACS plane. We haven't even *landed* yet, and I've already received safety-of-flight complaints! You just don't push the envelope or bend the rules, Seaver—you disregard them. You're *unsafe*."

"So if I'm such a hazard and a risk, why did you have us do all that other crazy shit over R-4808?" Rinc asked. "You want us for something, don't you?"

"Right now I want your planes," McLanahan said. "I'll decide if and which crews I want for them later."

"And what if we decide not to go along with this cockamamy scheme of yours?" Rebecca Furness interjected. "Why in hell should we do all this and risk getting busted and maybe even handing our planes over to a terrorist or some wacko? We don't know jack shit about you or what's going on. Why should we trust you?"

"The answer is, you shouldn't if you don't want to," Patrick replied. "Anyone who wants to can depart the anchor, get a clearance and a squawk from L.A. Center, and take your plane back to Reno. I'll invalidate the flying phase of the pre-D exercise, and I'll make sure you get full recognition for your outstanding job during the generation and deployment.

"I don't know what will happen if you return to Reno, guys," Patrick went on. "If you're lucky, Major Seaver and maybe Colonel Furness will get fired or reassigned, and you'll get to do your pre-D all over again after a six-month probationary period. But odds are, you'll get decertified. The Nevada Air National Guard will lose its Bones, and it'll take every ounce of juice from your congressional delegations and state lobbyists to get a military flying unit back into the state of Nevada, let alone to Reno."

"So what happens if we go with you, General?" Furness asked.

"Maybe the same thing," Patrick admitted. "The Air Force and the Pentagon can nix my entire plan. Then *I* get canned along with you and Seaver.

"But if the Pentagon signs off on my plan, by wintertime we'll be flying the most high-tech warplanes on the face of the earth," Patrick continued. "You'll be placed on extended active duty for training in a new class of warplane. You'll train a new generation of bomber crews with a mission unlike anything the world has ever seen before."

"Well, shit, General," Seaver said sarcastically. "When you put it that way, what's the big deal?"

"This is the big deal," Patrick said. "My program is 'black' right now. That means it's so classified that everything and anything that comes near it is sucked into a bottomless, agonizing pit of security rules that at best will drive you nuts.

"If you all agree to this, your lives will change forever. Your personal and professional lives, and the lives of your family, friends, and acquaintances, will be under intense scrutiny for decades. You will be giving up most of your personal freedoms and liberties by agreeing to do this. I know many of you joined the Air Guard to escape the life of an active-duty career military officer—well, if you agree to do this, life in the active-duty force will seem like a vacation in Hawaii compared to what you'll be subjected to. You'll be jerked around as soon as you get on final approach to our destination—I shit you not."

Patrick waited for several moments; then: "According to my watch, we've got twenty minutes of fuel left before we need to head back to Reno. That's how long you've got to think about my offer. Ask any questions, talk it over with your crews or with the colonel. Then give me an answer. Once we get back to Reno, the decision will be made for you."

"We don't need to talk about it," Furness radioed. "I'm still the commander of Aces High, and I make the decisions."

"Not this time, Colonel," Patrick said. "This decision affects each aviator personally. It's not a squadron decision."

"They're in my planes—it's *my* decision, General."

"I said, no it's not, Colonel," Patrick snapped. "Each man and woman makes this decision on their own."

"You don't know shit about command, do you, General?" Furness said. "Listen up, hogs. The general's right on one count: we blew it today. We all know the rules of engagement exist so the fighter pukes can have a chance of bagging us. We all know they're bullshit.

But we get paid to follow the rules, and we broke them because protecting our guys and doing the job means more than following some desk jockey's safety rules. The pud-pounders have been looking for an excuse to shut down Aces High, and it looks like we gave them an excuse this morning. Fuck it. Our mission was BOTOTCHA, not playing by some stinking nice-nice rules. We put bombs on target and came out alive. We did our job."

"I don't know what game the general's playing," Rinc Seaver broke in, "but I got a peek at his super-secret project. It looks pretty cosmic, and it looks like it's exactly up our alley. If we go back to Reno, we'll probably be sucking wind. If we stay together and keep pushing forward, we might get a chance to do some pretty cool shit. We're going for it. Everyone copy?"

"Two."

"Three."

"Four."

"Colonel Furness is not being entirely straight with you guys," Patrick said. "I don't know what will happen to your unit if you return. Like I said, my guess is that the two pilots involved in the 'airshow' incident will be forced to retire or reassigned. Your unit will probably continue on . . ."

"And I don't think the general's been entirely straight with us either," said Seaver. "The general has a hidden agenda: he wants our planes more than he wants us. We've been ordered back to Reno. If we land someplace else, we've violated a direct lawful order. We could all get shit-canned on the spot. But the general will end up with our planes, which is probably all he's wanted ever since he showed up in town. Tell me I'm wrong, General McLanahan."

"You're wrong," Patrick said. "My underlying agenda involves finding the best crews and the best planes for a new attack mission. I think you're it. But my primary reason for coming to Reno was to conduct your predeployment inspection. Your showboating and the conflict in Korea has just sped up my timetable. It's your hotdogging that's put this unit in jeopardy, Major, not my agenda."

"Thanks for the clarification, General—I think it agrees with what I just said," Furness said. "We'll leave it up to the crewdogs. Okay, hogs. Talk among yourselves, then report back and tell me if you're in with me or out. If you want out, fine. No hard feelings."

"Two's in," Rinc said immediately.

"Three's in."

"Four's in."

"That good enough for you, General?" Furness asked, a sharp edge to her voice.

"I guess it'll have to be," Patrick said. "Welcome aboard, guys and gals. Welcome to hell. Listen up carefully:

"We're going to break out of this anchor and shoot an ILS approach at an undisclosed and uncharted military airfield. I have no doubt you'll figure out which one I'm talking about shortly. As you might guess, security there is extraordinarily tight. Overflying the base is not allowed at any time no matter what the circumstances. We need to do this precisely so the security forces on the ground don't encounter any surprises, because they have only one response to surprise aircraft overflying their location—they'll destroy it. Plain and simple. They've done it before and they'll do it again. Any aircraft, any person aboard—dead, if they don't follow procedures. We are expected, so we're not a total surprise for them, but this hasn't been coordinated in advance, so all the security forces will be high-strung.

"Once we break out of this anchor, I want everyone three miles in trail and stacked up five hundred feet, *and nowhere else,* unless I give other instructions. It's VMC today, clear and a million, so we shouldn't have any formation problems. But if you lose contact with the aircraft in front of you once we enter the area, you must stay on the assigned heading and altitude—don't make any turns unless directed by the security controller, and don't do the normal lost-wingman procedures."

"What area is he talking about, Rodeo?" Rebecca asked.

"I'm talking about the area we're about to fly into," Patrick replied. "You'll find out soon enough. Remember what I said—you follow the controller's instructions exactly, or they'll blow you out of the sky. These guys are ultraserious.

"Once we're lined up and on the approach, you'll set one hundred ten point eight in the ILS and set an inbound course that I'll give to you later," Patrick went on. "That'll be your approach for landing. It'll be a four-degree glideslope. *Four degrees.* That's way steeper than normal, so watch your power and sink rate—we'll start up high and go down fast. Once you're established on the localizer and glideslope, you have to stay on it. If you need to go around or deviate for any reason, or if your ILS goes tits-up, you have to announce what you will do and get approval. If you say something and then do something else, or if you don't announce it first, you'll get shot down.

"Important: do not raise your landing gear if you need to miss the approach. Flying anywhere near this base in a configuration that looks like you may be able to drop a bomb will be considered a hostile act. If you lose more than two engines and you can't do a go-around with your gear down, crash-land on the dry lake bed. Bottom line: don't make any sudden moves.

The troops defending our destination have real itchy trigger fingers.

"Couple more important things: Os, *do not activate the attack radar* once you're inside the area. In fact, everyone, shut 'em down right now and leave them off—not in 'standby,' in 'off.' If you radiate, they'll think you're on a bomb run and blow your shit away. We maintain distance on the approach by air-to-air DME, *not radar*. DSOs, same with the ECM gear. If you turn on anything, accidentally jam a radio or radar, drop a flare or chaff bundle, or do anything to make it look like you're hostile, they'll shoot with everything they got, immediately and with no warning. Shut 'em down now. All the way off. Questions or comments." This time there were none. "Report to me when you've shut down the ORS and ECM gear."

"Two."

"Three."

"Four."

"Good. Make sure your weapons are safe and locked, but if you can't get a good safe and lock, don't worry about it.

"Now, when we arrive at the base, you'll be directed where to taxi. They will leave no doubt where you should go. It's hard to see the taxiways, so follow the leader carefully. Stay as close to the plane in front of you as you safely can. Do your before-engine shutdown checklists while taxiing—you'll have lots of time to do it. I'll guide you through the things I want you to do. Don't acknowledge any transmissions unless it's an emergency or unless you really get confused, and I'll warn you now, try not to get confused while you're down there."

"Too late, General," said one crew member Patrick couldn't identify. "I'm confused already."

"We'll be directed straight into hangars," Patrick

said, ignoring the flippancy. "Taxi directly inside. Maintain taxi speed—don't creep into the hangar. The door in front of you will be partially closed. Shut down the engines as soon as you stop. The hangar doors will be closing behind you, so don't run engines up or scavenge oil or anything like that. Don't worry about the weapons, the bomb doors, INS alignments, preserving the maintenance data or the bomb-nav computer data, or anything else but shutting your gear off. Open the entry hatch as soon as the plane stops. Security guards will be up to escort you out. Step on out, follow the guards, and do what they tell you. Any questions?"

"Sounds like you've been watching a lot of *X-Files* lately," someone quipped.

The formation spent nearly another hour in the anchor while Patrick got on the secure voice SATCOM and coordinated their arrival. Now they had barely enough fuel to make it to Nellis Air Force Base with legal fuel reserves, and that base was only sixty miles away. They couldn't legally land back at Reno even if they wanted to without an emergency air refueling. They were indeed committed to their decision.

If any air traffic control agencies were surprised about their flying into the world's most restricted airspace, they kept their comments to themselves. But they heard the same warnings from all the civil controllers several times; one controller violated Furness and ordered her to contact Los Angeles Air Route Traffic Control Center upon landing, even giving her the telephone number. Furness replied with a curt "We don't need no stinkin' vectors, Center," and ignored all other directives.

The approach was completely routine, if flying into a hornet's nest could be considered routine. If they still had their electronic countermeasures gear on, their threat-warning receivers would be alive with surface-to-air missile tracking radars and height finders, including Hawk and Patriot antiaircraft systems. As they got closer, Furness and Seaver could see several missile emplacements. The Patriot launchers weren't pointed directly at them—they didn't need to be—but the I-Hawk and British-built Rapier missile batteries tracked them all the way. It was like looking right down the barrels of a triple-barreled shotgun. They were aimed at an immense dry lake bed, with hard-baked sand stretching as far as they could see. Majestic multicolored mountains ringed the valley, some still with snow at the highest peaks.

The scenery was magnificent—and they would have enjoyed it more if they weren't so afraid of messing up and getting shot down by their fellow Americans.

As they followed the glideslope down and got closer to touchdown, more and more details became obvious. The runway emerged from the dry lake like a mirage. Several vehicles were parked on the dry lake—a disconcerting mixture of fire trucks and Avenger mobile antiaircraft weapon systems, as if their soon-to-be hosts were eager to both hurt them and help them.

At one point in the approach, Patrick said, "We've got traffic at our three o'clock, boys." Rinc leaned forward in his seat and saw an F-22 Raptor fighter just off the right wingtip. He knew that the F-22 with its thrust-vectoring nozzles could turn and shoot its 20-millimeter cannon right from where it was, without having to maneuver or line up behind the Bone. He saw no missiles, but he remembered that the F-22 carried its missiles internally. He strained a look in his rearview mirror and saw another F-22 fighter sitting off the third Bone's wingtip. It was very impressive to get such a welcome, but it was even more impressive when you considered that the F-22 was in production only and wasn't scheduled to become operational for almost five years. This place had *four* of them, manned, fueled, and presumably armed, available for a simple escort mission.

The runway felt concrete-hard but sandy as Rinc touched down. He stayed off the brakes completely until he saw several armored vehicles arrayed before him nine thousand feet down the runway, blocking it and showing him where to turn off. Patrick had the after-landing and before-shutdown checklists ready to go. Security vehicles, all with roof-mounted machine guns—some with grenade launchers or antiarmor missile launchers at the ready—lined the taxiways. Yep, there was no doubt where they were supposed to go—just taxi in between all the security vehicles with the guns pointed at them.

They were taxiing right at the Bone's twenty-knot taxi speed limit, but it seemed much faster because of the lack of any outside references—it was as if they were in a dune buggy speeding across the desert. "Bitchin' place you got here, General," Rinc said. "Lots of room to stretch out. Good hunting and fishing?"

"You may find out, Major," Patrick said.

"So this is Groom Lake, right?" Rinc asked. "The supersecret military base. Looks pretty ordinary to me. I've seen the four-meter Spot recon photos in the mission planning software too—it looks like Plant 42 at Palmdale. How many folks do you think are taking our pictures from those hills right now?"

"None," Patrick said. "Our security guys rounded up all the trespassers before we came in. The closest UFO watcher was eight miles away, and we got him. We let them come close to the base once in a while so we can learn their ingress routes, which makes it easier to find them and shut them down when we need to. There were a few satellite overflights we had to avoid too—one Russian, one Chinese."

"Somebody had to have seen us, General," Rinc

said. "How can you hide four Bones making a straight-in approach to nowhere?"

"If we were worried about just being seen, Colonel, we would've had a tanker come up and refuel us, then land at night," Patrick replied. "We fly all sorts of airplanes in and out of here every day. The spies and looky-loos aren't interested in the old Bones—they're interested in what new planes we got here. But the real research these days isn't on new platforms—it's on new expendables, like missiles and bombs."

"I thought Eglin tests that stuff." Eglin Air Force Base, near Fort Walton Beach, Florida, was the home of the Air Force Research Laboratory's Munitions Directorate, the headquarters of most weapons development in the Air Force.

"We get everything here, from airframes to avionics to software to bullets," Patrick said. "We test it all before it goes to places like Eglin or Edwards or Langley, before they write the tech orders or train the instructors or technicians. We test it—and then, after it's fielded, we try to make it better. That's what we're going to do with you." Patrick pointed out ahead. "There's your parking spots. You're on the far left. Keep your speed up and zip right in." On interphone, Patrick said, "Hold on, crew. We're going to make a hard stop."

In the distance they saw a row of ten large sand-colored hangars, all by themselves seemingly in the middle of nowhere. The security vehicles positioned themselves to herd the Bones into individual hangars. They kept up a fast pace, so when Rinc did taxi inside his hangar, the stop was dramatic. Most of the switches were already positioned, and they didn't need the auxiliary power unit, so it was quick and simple to shut down the engines.

Moments after shutdown, after the entry hatch was motored open, Patrick called out, "Just shut off the battery and leave everything. Step on out." Seaver, Warren, and Long did as he said. They were surprised to see a young black officer in desert camouflage with a flashlight, a submachine gun attached to a harness on his chest, and a big .45-caliber automatic pistol holster on his hip, standing at the bottom of the boarding ladder waiting for them to come down. "Afternoon, sir," he said, flashing them a smile. "Welcome to Elliott."

The high-powered air-conditioning system inside the hangar was already working to pull the last bit of exhaust and heat from the structure. Security guards were searching McLanahan, and they quickly set to work searching Furness, Seaver, and the others. The guards then asked them to take an arm out of their flight suit sleeves and uncover a shoulder. Using a pneumatic hypodermic, the black security officer shot something into their shoulders, then clipped vinyl-covered bracelets onto their wrists. "What the hell are you doing?" Furness asked. "Is that an anthrax vaccine or something?"

"Wiring you folks for sound," said the officer cheerfully. "Welcome to the club."

"This is Lieutenant Colonel Hal Briggs, my security chief," Patrick said. "Hal, meet . . ."

"Lieutenant Colonel Rebecca Furness, Nevada Air National Guard. Nice to meet you." Briggs shook hands with Furness, then introduced himself to Dewey and Seaver. Furness studied the gun he wore on his chest harness. It was an MP5K, or "Kurz" (short) model, a very small, close-range submachine gun, so small that it was originally intended to replace an aviator's personal survival weapon. The submachine gun, with one 15-round magazine already locked in place, was attached to the harness with a quick-release strap, which kept it ready for action while keeping the hands free. Parachute cord connected the folding stock with the harness, so as soon as Briggs drew and elevated the gun to firing position, the stock would unfold and he'd be ready to fire. "I know all of you—probably in disgusting detail."

"Hal was in charge of the security evaluation at the 111th," Patrick explained. "He likes doing his homework. Explain what the microtransceivers do, Hal."

"You've just been injected with a subcutaneous microtransceiver, and those wristbands are the power source and antenna," Briggs explained. "The devices do a number of things. Basically, they're like a dog's electronic ID tag. The microchip has coded information on you. The bracelet is the power source and transceiver—the microchip is inert without it. We can monitor your location, track you, talk with you, give you directions, monitor body functions, and a number of other things."

"Who the hell said I wanted you to shoot a microchip into my arm?" Furness asked.

"You did—'Commander,' " Patrick said. "I told you the level of intrusion into your life here is intense, and you didn't believe me. Well, now your body and your men's bodies are wired for sound, and someone will be listening and monitoring you—for the rest of your lives." He glanced at Rinc Seaver and added, "Think about that the next time you're alone with someone special. Big Brother is not just watching—he's listening and tracking you too."

Seaver smiled. "Cool," he said, rubbing his shoulder. He couldn't see or feel the microchip.

Furness looked ready to explode. "You're shitting me!"

"Attention in the area!" someone called out. The guards remained at port arms, but everyone else snapped to attention.

"As you were," another voice boomed. Furness turned and saw an immense black three-star general in a flight suit, garrison cap, and spit-shined flying boots stride over to the group. McLanahan and Briggs saluted as he walked over to them. "Nice to have you back, General," he said to McLanahan. "It should make it a little easier to keep you under some kind of restraint, I hope."

"Nice to be home, sir," Patrick said with a sly smile. "Sir, may I present Lieutenant Colonel Rebecca Furness, commander of the 111th Bomb Squadron, Nevada Air National Guard. Colonel Furness, this is Lieutenant General Terrill Samson, commander of the High Technology Aerospace Weapons Center, Elliott Air Force Base, Groom Lake."

Samson returned Furness's salute, then they shook hands. "I hear good things about you, Colonel," Samson said cheerfully. "I look forward to seeing some good stuff from you. Welcome."

"Thank you, sir."

Samson was introduced to Rinc Seaver. "Major," Samson said coolly. Seaver tried to match him stare for stare, but quickly wilted under the sheer physical presence of the big man.

Samson turned his attention back to McLanahan, for which Seaver was grateful. "Patrick, I know I signed off on the concept, but I didn't expect you to hijack four Nevada Air National Guard B-1 bombers and their crews," Samson said. "We've got some phone calls to make. Ladies and gentlemen, I'm going to leave you all in the hands of Colonel Briggs, who will escort you to your quarters. But I have a few things to say first:

"I know General McLanahan has probably told you this already, but I'm going to reiterate it for you: you are now part of our nation's most top-secret weapons research facility. What you do here will decide the shape of the United States Air Force and the American military for the next twenty to fifty years. Our team members here understand and respect the awesome responsibility we place upon them, and they protect the technology and information here as closely as their own lives.

"Nonetheless, we don't rely on that—if we want to keep an eye on you, we do it, however and whenever we want. That's the price you pay for agreeing to be part of what goes on in this place. You will find your work here enjoyable and stimulating—many say eye-popping.

"However," and he paused and looked them all in the eye before continuing, "you will find your life here *sucks*. If you thought the worst assignment in the Air Force was in the Aleutians or Greenland, think again. And if you thought you've already encountered the worst, most hard-assed commander to work for, think again. *I* am that man."

Samson walked up to Rinc Seaver and looked him straight in the eye as he addressed them all. "I've received reports about this unit, about your activities in and out of the cockpit, about your performance—and about your attitude," he said in a cavern-deep voice. "You're supposed to be the best of the best. But that doesn't matter anymore. Your past successes don't matter anymore. This base is filled with the best of the best, the top one-half of one percent of this nation's engineers, scientists, technicians, and aviators. We fly jets and operate weapon systems that will make history in future conflicts. You'll have a chance to prove yourselves, I guarantee that. But I don't let anyone come near my new weapon systems unless they prove to me that they can work as a team. Your trial starts now. Questions?"

"I have one request, General," Rinc Seaver said.

"Major?"

"We're going to need a hand receipt for those planes, sir," Rinc said.

Samson's eyes flashed in anger—but then he smiled, an evil crocodile smile. "Sure, Major," he said. "Got a pencil?" Before Furness could react, Samson grabbed Seaver by the left shoulder of his flight suit, grasped the left sleeve near the pencil pocket, and ripped the sleeve clean off in one quick, fluid motion, making it look as effortless as tearing a sheet of paper. Rinc did not react; it was as if he had expected the big man to do it.

Samson reached down to the shards of Nomex and retrieved a black grease pencil. "I guess this will have to do," he said. "Now I need something to write on." He grabbed the top of Seaver's flight suit and ripped it open with a quick snap. Pieces of zipper and fire-retardant fabric went flying in all directions. On Seaver's white T-shirt, he wrote, "Four (4) each B-1B Lancer bombers," then signed his name and dated it. Rinc stood at attention, eyes caged, fixed straight ahead the entire time.

"There's your hand receipt, smart-ass," Terrill Samson said, sliding the grease pencil behind Seaver's right ear. "Anything else I've overlooked, Major?"

"No, *sir*," Rinc replied.

"Good. Thank you for the reminder. I hate to leave the paperwork until the last minute. Colonel Briggs."

"Sir!"

"Get this paper-pushing clown and these other crewdogs out of my sight. And get Major Seaver a new flight suit—he's out of uniform."

"Yes, *sir*," Briggs said, not trying to hide his smile. "If you'll follow me, folks." Furness saluted Samson, received a salute in return, and walked away with Briggs. Seaver did not even attempt to pick up the tattered pieces of his flight suit.

Patrick watched his boss's face as the guardsmen

were escorted to a waiting van to take them to their quarters. Samson was scowling, but there was a hint of a smile on his lips. "You enjoyed that, didn't you, sir?"

"What I would've enjoyed more is kicking him in his fucking ass," Samson said. The thought of doing that made him grin. "But unfortunately, he's on the right track. Those planes aren't ours yet—they belong to the state of Nevada. We can't touch them without their permission."

"I don't think that'll be a problem, sir," Patrick said. "But if Air Combat Command wants those planes for spare parts, or if Nevada wanted to sell them to another Guard unit, I may have set you up for a food fight with them."

"If you get me written authorization to modify those planes, Patrick, I'll deal with ACC," Samson said. "Even if the Air Force decertifies the unit, the planes still technically belong to Nevada, and they're free to loan them out to anyone with Class One resource facilities—including us." He turned to Patrick and said warmly, "But you knew all this, didn't you? That's why you brought them here. You knew that once they were in our hot little hands, it would take a papal edict to dislodge them from here. And if Nevada gives us the go-ahead—sweetened with some money for upkeep and personnel, no doubt—there's not a thing anyone can do about it."

"Even though we may have possession now, sir," Patrick said, "we can't hold on to them forever. We need to water some eyes. As soon as I get permission from the governor to play with his planes, I'd like permission to start installing the Lancelot kits in two planes."

"Approved," Samson said. "You have permission to get the other two ready for modification as well. How long before we can test-fly the first two birds?"

"Two months—three at the outside."

"Make it no more than two, and you might have a chance," Samson said. "Even better, if we can deploy two bombers as part of an air task force participating in this Korea conflict or revolution or whatever is happening, we might get approval to convert the entire unit—maybe even get funding for an entire wing. But you gotta dazzle them, Patrick. Hit 'em between the eyes with all the magic you can."

"I'll get on it right now, sir," Patrick said. "Sorry you have to go nose-to-nose with Air Combat Command. I suppose we could've done this another way—requested use of the planes through official channels. The Pentagon is going to think we've all flipped our lids."

"It's the spirit of Brad Elliott, Patrick," Terrill Samson said. "It's funny—a lot of the brass, in and out of uniform, understand that already. I don't have to tell them. Carry on."

OVER THE YELLOW SEA
THAT SAME TIME

The American E-3C Airborne Warning and Control System radar plane, call sign "Guardian," had been on patrol now for six hours. It had topped off tanks just a few minutes earlier. Since no more tankers were available, this was going to be its last patrol—four more hours on station, then a couple of hours' flying time to Kadena Air Base on Okinawa, with enough fuel for two hours' reserves over the high fix. Normally, it would be on station for eight hours, refuel at Kunsan Air Base in South Korea, then go on another eight-hour patrol until relieved. But needless to say, no one was landing in South Korea for a while.

Unfortunately, because of the start of hostilities and orders from Washington, no one would be launching from any bases in South Korea or Japan. That meant no fighter protection. There was no sign of North Korean air activity at all, but the big modified Boeing 707 with the thirty-foot rotodome mounted on tall legs near the tail was a sitting duck, especially in daytime.

But there was another reason for the E-3C to be on station: this was a unique opportunity to see what it was like to operate AWACS in a nuclear environment. This was the first time an E-3 was airborne while a thermonuclear attack was under way, and engineers and crews wanted to see what it was like to use the powerful APY-1C radar in the vicinity of nuclear detonations. Of course, all this had been simulated by computers and in electromagnetic research laboratories at Kirtland Air Force Base in New Mexico, but now it could be done for real.

The experiment was working very well—so well, in fact, that the radar operators aboard Guardian spotted the flight of aircraft lifting off from Sohung Air Base in North Korea, about thirty miles southeast of Pyongyang, from well over 150 miles away.

The radar operator detected the airborne targets and assigned a "U" with a diamond symbol to the contact, meaning "unidentified, considered hostile." "Radar has bandits in sector three, heading one-niner-zero, climbing through angels eleven, speed four-twenty," he announced on ship-wide interphone.

"Sector three roger," the sector intercept officer responded. "I've got negative modes and codes. ESM, stand by for identification. Attention crew, sector three has three, repeat three, bandits on an intercept course. Stand by for tactical action. Charlie?"

"Charlie's up and I've got the contacts," responded the senior controller, call sign "Charlie." "We don't need ESM—let's classify as hostile fighters. Crew, stand by for evasive maneuvers. Radar, engineering, shut the rotor down. Crew, we're going dark. Pilot, Charlie, right turn heading one-two-zero, let's head for the deck." The radar crew and the engineering technicians shut down the powerful APY-1 radar and all other electrical emissions while the pilots started a steep turn and a rapid descent to try to get away from the inbound fighters.

"Crew, this is Echo, I've got contact on our bandits," the electronic support measures officer, or ESM, call sign "Echo," reported. ESM was a passive backup and augmentation system that allowed AWACS not only to detect aircraft and ships but to identify them by their electronic emissions. In addition, when the active radar was shut down as it was right now, ESM allowed the crew to continue tracking targets by their electronic signatures. It wasn't a perfect system—if the enemy fighter wasn't transmitting any signals, AWACS would be completely blind. "I've got a Slot Back One radar. Looks like North Korean MiG-29s, range eighty miles and closing fast." North Korea operated only two squadrons, fewer than thirty, of MiG-29 Fulcrum fighters, made in the Soviet Union, but they were some of the world's most capable and deadly fighters. Typical air defense load was two R-27 radar-guided missiles, four R-60 heat-seeking missiles, and 150 rounds in its big 30-millimeter cannon.

The senior controller got on the emergency GUARD channel: "Mayday mayday mayday, this is Guardian three-oh-one, sixty-five miles southwest of Seoul VOR, we are under attack by North Korean hostile aircraft. Requesting any assistance. Please respond."

But he knew it was no use using the radios. The

nuclear blast that destroyed Suwon sent a wave of highly charged energy, called the electromagnetic pulse, or EMP, many miles in all directions, turning the atmosphere into a mass of random electrical sparks. Even if anyone was listening, all they would hear was static. The EMP at the time of the blast itself was powerful enough to fry electronic devices many miles away. The effects of an EMP on the atmosphere could last for many hours, even days.

"Six o'clock, sixty miles," the ESM officer reported. "He'll come within max Alamo range in less than two minutes." The Russian-made R-27, code-named "Alamo," had a maximum range of about forty miles. The senior controller knew that was probably their countdown to die—because there were no friendly aircraft up in the vicinity right now. In an effort not to appear too hostile or offensive, all American aircraft that survived North Korea's initial ballistic missile attack were grounded. The South Korean Air Force was being used to attack a few targets inside North Korea, relying on ground-based air defense to protect the cities from air attack.

So there was no one up protecting Guardian from air attack.

But they still had a chance. They were less than one hundred miles from the coastline, heading toward Kunsan Air Base. That base was fully operational, and it was armed with Patriot surface-to-air missiles, with a maximum range of sixty miles. It was a footrace now to see if they could get inside the Patriot's protective umbrella before the North Korean MiGs caught up to them.

"Crew, this is Echo, I've got hostile ESM contact at eleven o'clock, fifty miles. Another Slot Back radar—looks like more MiG-29s over South Korea." Their worst fear had come true: the North Koreans had begun their counterattack and had already penetrated deep inside South Korea, all the way to the southern part of the peninsula. The North Korean MiG-29s would clear the skies of enemy fighters well enough to allow the North's large but older and less capable fleet of fighter-bombers to sweep across the South and finish off what their ballistic missile barrage failed to do.

"Let's get this beast down on the deck *now,* pilot!" the senior controller shouted on interphone. The E-3C AWACS radar plane had a suite of electronic jammers and decoys, but in daytime in good weather, enemy fighters didn't need electronic sensors to kill a big E-3. Even North Korea's lowest-tech fighter in the hands of young, inexperienced pilots could do it with ease. A MiG-29, with its outstanding maneuverability and close-range kill capability, could move in and kill an AWACS without even altering its flight path.

"Bandit at eleven o'clock, forty miles . . . bandits at six o'clock, forty-five miles . . . eleven o'clock, thirty miles . . . six o'clock, thirty miles . . . stand by for evasive maneuvers, crew . . . eleven o'clock, twenty miles . . . six o'clock, twenty miles . . . bandit at twelve o'clock, *missile launch, missile launch, pilot break left*!" As the pilot started a steep, swift turn, the ESM officer pressed a button, ejecting clouds of radar-decoying chaff into the sky.

It was a desperation move, nothing more. A big E-3C AWACS plane couldn't do a break or any other maneuver fast enough to defeat an air-to-air missile. But it might be enough to break a radar lock long enough for the enemy missiles to lose track, long enough for someone from Kunsan or Taegu to help. It was their only hope . . .

"Bandit six o'clock, fifteen miles, locked on, *missile launch, missile launch*!" the ESM officer shouted. Both MiG-29s were firing . . . both were locked on . . .

Then, suddenly, the North Korean MiG-29 behind them disappeared, followed seconds later by the MiG ahead of them. "Pilot, roll out!" the ESM officer said. He punched out more chaff as the pilot started to level off. "Crew, Echo, I have negative contact on both bandits. Stand by for evasive maneuvers." The only possible explanation: both North Korean fighters had moved within IRSTS, or infrared search and track system, heat-seeking sensor range. With IRSTS, a MiG-29 didn't need radar to find and track a target. Now their only indication of an attack would be the AWACS' tail-warning system, which used heat-seeking sensors to detect fighters and the flare of a missile's motor to detect a missile launch.

"Contact!" the pilot called. "I've got bandits at twelve o'clock high!"

"Go nose-to-nose, pilot!" the ESM officer shouted. "Stand by for defensive maneuvers!"

"It's moving in on us!" the pilot yelled. "It's closing in . . . Shit, it's got us, it's got us dead in its sights, twelve o'clock, three miles . . ." Then the pilot stopped. Nothing.

"Pilot, where is he?" the ESM officer asked. "Where did he go? Can you see him?"

"He's . . . he's off our left side, range . . . range about *one mile,*" the pilot said. "Holy shit, it's a *Japanese fighter*! I see a red rising sun on its tail! It's a Japanese MiG-29 fighter! Damn, they must've killed those North Korean MiGs chasing us!"

It was an unbelievable and very welcome sight. Two Japanese Self-Defense Force fighters, on patrol over the Sea of Japan, had raced across the Korean peninsula, risking attack by South Korean air defenses, to rescue the AWACS plane. The Japanese government, in retaliation for increased American presence and influence in Asia over the past few years, had spurned American military hardware and purchased large numbers of Russian weapons, including the modern and powerful MiG-29SMT, the Western-modernized version of Russia's most advanced fighter-bomber. The Japanese could buy three times as many MiG-29s as American F-15s, F-16s, or F/A-18s, and get a plane that was every bit as capable as its Western competitors.

"I'll be damned," the pilot murmured on interphone. He waved at the Japanese fighters and watched as they wagged their wings in response and peeled off. "They saved our asses big-time. I'll never bad-mouth the little buggers again."

SEOUL, SOUTH KOREA
LATER THAT DAY

The anthem of the Republic of Korea played in the background as the lights came up. The first thing seen was a strange new banner—one that combined the flags of the Democratic People's Republic of Korea and the Republic of Korea.

There were two dark blue bars, at the top and bottom of the banner, representing the sky and the strength of the earth. The white middle section symbolized the united land. The circle in the center, the *t'aeguk*, represented yin-yang, the power of opposites. Its red "yang" upper half, or positive side, represented life, goodness, and fire; the lower "yin" blue half, or negative side, represented evil, death, darkness, and cold. The two segments were entwined, meaning that they could never be separated. Surrounding the center circle were the four broken-bar trigrams, taken from ancient Taoist and Confucian thought, representing virtuous ideals important to a long and happy life.

On either side of the new banner were four other flags: those of the United States, the Russian Federation, the People's Republic of China, and the Republic of Japan.

As the anthem played, two men walked to lecterns set up before the flag, bowed deeply to each other, and shook hands warmly. At that moment, three men and one woman walked out and took their places in front of their respective flags: Vice President Ellen Christine Whiting from the United States; Deputy Foreign Minister for Far East Affairs Dmitriy Antonovich Aksenenko of the Russian Federation; Minister of Foreign Affairs Ota Amari of Japan; and the assistant deputy secretary for cultural affairs of the Chinese embassy in Pyongyang, Xu Zhengsheng. All stood at attention behind the lecterns until the anthem finished.

On a signal from a stage director, Kwon Ki-chae, president of South Korea, bowed to the others, then bowed to the camera, and said: "My fellow Koreans, it is with great sorrow and also great happiness that I address you today. I am pleased to speak to you from the Hall of the People at the Korean Workers' Party headquarters in Pyongyang, the capital of the Democratic People's Republic of Korea.

"This morning, in a show of solidarity, unity, trust, and hope, the people of North Korea marched on the capital here in Pyongyang, demanding an end to the repressive dictatorship of Kim Jong-il. Members of the First Army of the Korean People's Army supported the North Korean patriots and either laid down their arms or joined in this historic, peaceful display of the voice and will of the community. Hundreds of thousands of soldiers from all over the North joined the patriots and left their barracks to support this action. As a result, the dictator Kim, all of the members of the

Communist Party Politburo, and most of his cabinet members fled the wrath of the citizens.

"In the spirit of cooperation, peace, and divine reunification, the government of the Republic of Korea assisted this people's revolution by sending in fighter-bombers to attack the Korean People's Army internal 'black operations' units, the Spetznaz, who are responsible for crushing free speech and human rights in the North. They also attacked and destroyed many of the North's weapons of mass destruction. Unfortunately, we could not stop all of them in time. Several missile volleys were launched into the South, killing thousands and injuring several hundred thousand. We pray for the souls of the dead and offer our condolences and our hands to the survivors.

"But at the same moment as Communist rockets were hitting the South, we were opening up our arms of friendship and reunification to our family in the North. I am pleased to announce that the Military Demarcation Line, the unholy gash that has torn our people apart for over half a century, is no more. The checkpoints, minefields, border crossings, observation towers, and no-man's-land separating our two countries no longer exist. Thousands of citizens of the North have crossed the frontier to reunite with long-lost family members. Korea is no longer divided. Korea is one. Mr. Vice President?"

Pak Chung-chu bowed to President Kwon, bowed to the other guests, then bowed to the camera. "Thank you, Mr. President. My fellow Koreans, I am Pak Chung-chu, first vice president of the former government of the Democratic People's Republic of Korea. It is my great honor to announce to the Korean people and to the world the formation of the United Republic of Korea. My first official act will be this." He withdrew a red Korean Workers' Party identification booklet from his jacket pocket and ripped it into pieces. "Before the gods, before my ancestors, and before you, my fellow Koreans, I am completely and absolutely rejecting and condemning the Korean Workers' Party and the Communist Party of Korea for the Reunification of the Fatherland. The party was unfaithful and betrayed its people. I hope all true and loyal Koreans will join me in doing the same."

Head held high, Pak went on: "The capital of our new constitutional, democratic republic will be Seoul, which is and always has been the spiritual and historic center of our nation and our people. Pyongyang will be rebuilt and modernized, and will soon become the model for a new and revitalized Korea, a shining example of the spirit and dedication of the Korean race. The people of Korea are hereby free to travel about our great land as they choose. I know the rest of your brothers and sisters welcome you.

"Together, Comrade Kwon Ki-chae and I will oversee the technical details of reunifying our country. Our primary concern is for the well-being of millions of our citizens of the North, who under the repressive Communist regime have been suffering from malnutrition, poor health care, homelessness, and poverty. We are here to assure all our people that help is on the way. We urge you to place your trust in your brothers and sisters of the South. This is the day we have long prayed for, and we must learn that our enemies were our warring governments, not the people. The help that may arrive at your village may be soldiers from the South. They are coming to help you in any way necessary, not to hurt you."

Pak Chung-chu bowed to Kwon once again. Kwon bowed in return, then spoke: "Thank you, Comrade Pak. I echo those words most sincerely to our fellow Koreans in the South. The peninsula is whole and one again; travel is free and open to all Koreans without restriction or identity papers. Please welcome all who come to you for help, employment, or assistance, regardless of the regime under which they lived before this date. True peaceful unification is possible only if it exists in your heart. Do not allow mistrust and fear to ruin this long-awaited, blessed moment in history.

"Comrade Pak and I will share in presiding over this transition period of our new government until such time as new elections can be called. Voting rights will be extended to all Koreans over the age of seventeen—one man, one vote. Other details of the peaceful transition to one national system of government, finance, and law will be announced as soon as possible. Our task is to make this transition as smoothly, as equitably, and as peacefully as possible. Our land is rich, strong, and generous, and it is our task to see that all our people share in its blessing together. It will be a difficult task, but one which must take place. The world is watching. For the sake of our heritage and our children's future, we must not fail."

Kwon motioned to the world leaders beside him and went on: "As our country undertakes this day to reunify and rebuild, we look upon the governments around the world, and especially those who are represented by our distinguished guests beside me here today, to bless, support, protect, and defend the Korean people as they come together in the spirit of peace and harmony. Comrade Pak and I pledge to help forge a good, strong, law-abiding neighbor for you all. We desire only peace and prosperity for everyone. Thank you for being with us to share this blessed event.

"I would like to invite all of you to say a few words to the people of Korea and to the rest of the world. Madam Ellen Whiting, Vice President of the United States of America, if you please." Kwon motioned to

Vice President Whiting and bowed. She bowed in return and stepped forward to the microphone.

But before she could speak, Kwon returned to the microphone and said, "A thousand apologies, Madam Vice President. There is one more important announcement I wish to make before Vice President Whiting speaks:

"In the interest of peace and universal trust, Comrade Pak and I wish to declare that all foreign military forces will be asked to leave the Korean peninsula as soon as possible. This includes the Chinese Twentieth and Forty-second Group Forces, all Russian advisers and training posts, and the joint Korean and American Combined Forces Command."

Vice President Whiting could feel the sting in her ears and fought to maintain her composure as Kwon went on: "We welcome the presence and assistance of the United Nations Commission on Reunification and Disarmament of Korea, and we look to them for support and guidance. But we respectfully request the dismantling and removal of the United Nations Military Command and the United Nations Demilitarized Zone Monitoring Agency. For the first time in almost a century, Korea now belongs to the Korean people. We hope the world as well as the parties involved support and respect this decision and help us to take our rightful place in the world community by diminishing the risk of our land becoming again a bloody battleground."

Vice President Whiting kept her face impassive as Kwon Ki-chae said with a broad smile, "And now, may I present Madam Ellen Whiting, Vice President of the United States." But she was in shock. Neither Kwon nor Pak had said anything about removing the United States military forces from Korea! Yet it was urgent that she pull herself together and say something coherent.

The presence of the foreign leaders there at the televised announcement ceremony was a setup, and they all knew it now. By standing there in front of the new United Republic of Korea flag, the foreign leaders were tacitly agreeing to all that was being said—including the removal of their military forces. The Chinese representative, Xu, was a minor functionary from the Chinese embassy in Pyongyang—he didn't grasp what had been said. He was there simply because he was the nearest and least influential Chinese government official who would dare enter Korea.

But the other representatives knew what was happening. In the spirit of peace and in the hope of a cessation of further nuclear exchange, they had been cleverly duped into coming here and giving their blessing to the biggest coup of the young millennium. Vice President Whiting would never have entertained the idea of American peacekeeping forces leaving the Korean peninsula until the United States was sure the new Korean government was established, secure, and safe from internal or external intrigue or attack. Now, by her very presence, she was agreeing to precisely that. So were the Chinese, Japanese, and Russian governments.

In the blink of an eye, the American presence in Korea was over.

NEAR KUJANG, PYONGAN PUKDO PROVINCE,
UNITED REPUBLIC OF KOREA
(FORMERLY NORTH KOREA)
A SHORT TIME LATER

There is your proof," Captain Kong Hwan-li said bitterly as he shut off the short-wave radio. "A propaganda ploy, combined with an aerial attack. Every uneducated pig in the army fell for it. It disgusts me."

Kong was pacing in front of a small campfire, surrounded by several other Korean People's Army officers. He had kept his voice low and the group remained silent, fearing that their voices might carry in the stillness of the countryside; the fire was small to avoid attracting attention.

A few moments later a guard escorted another soldier to the campfire. He stepped before Captain Kong and saluted. "Sir, my name is Master Sergeant Kim Yong-ku, noncommissioned officer in charge, Unit Six, Forty-fifth Regiment, Sixth Battalion. I am reporting to you as ordered by my commanding officer, Lieutenant Choi Yeon-sam."

"Where is the lieutenant?" Kong asked.

"Sir, he was captured, tortured, and left to die by a roving band of deserters on his way to this meeting," Kim replied. "He was attacked about a kilometer from where our unit is in hiding. Security forces from Unit Six responded to his cries for help, but we were not in time. But before he died, the lieutenant told me about this meeting and how important it was for someone from our unit to attend. He said it was the only way our country had to reconstitute our strategic forces in order to drive the invaders out."

Captain Kong drew his sidearm and aimed it at the sergeant. "How do we know you are not one of the deserters?" he asked. "How do we know you didn't torture the information out of Choi and come here to us, hoping to lead the capitalists or their American overlords to us?"

Kim bristled angrily, then stiffened his back almost to attention. "I may not be an officer, sir, but I am a loyal and faithful soldier and servant of the fatherland and of our Beloved Leader," he said. "I did not flee to China when the deserters and traitors left my unit—I stood at my post and did my solemn duty. When marauders and thieves attacked our unit, I fought them off. When my commander was killed, I avenged his death. If you still believe I am a traitor to the fatherland, I give you permission to end my life. I do not deserve to live if I cannot serve the fatherland or the People's Army."

Kong lowered his sidearm. He had noticed that the sergeant still wore his People's Army uniform. That said a lot, especially now. Anyone in an Army uniform was being shot at on sight. Most important was the news that word of the meeting had managed to reach the commanding officer of Unit Six. The unit's expertise was vital to Kong's plans. He holstered his weapon. "We welcome you," he said. "We will ask you to prove your worth, and if you are really a traitor to the fatherland, may your ancestors curse your name forever. You are now Lieutenant Kim Yong-ku, commanding officer of Unit Six. How many men in your unit?"

"Five, sir," Kim responded. "Three launch technicians, my maintenance supervisor, and one locomotive engineer."

"Barely enough to do the job," Kong said. "But we will do it, no matter how many traitors there are around us." To the assembled group, he said, "Loyal soldiers of the fatherland, I will not try to minimize our situation—it is very grim. Unit Six represents the last and possibly the only ballistic missile assets still operational in the People's Army—two Nodong-1 units, two Scud-B units, and one Scud-C unit. I have tried to contact the rest of the command, and you are the only ones who have responded.

"But there is good news, comrades: I have been in contact with our government-in-exile in Beijing," Captain Kong went on. "Efforts are under way to reconstitute the government as we speak. We have been instructed to use every means at our disposal to transport our weapons as far north as possible, to Chagang Do province. If we are successful, we can expect support from the People's Liberation Army." That bit of news led to a round of muted cheers. "We shall be the trailblazers, the first to establish a home for loyal Communist supporters in the fertile Tongno River plains. Our comrades in the People's Republic of China will help us recapture and hold Chagang Do province. We will make it an autonomous entity within the new Korea. It will be a haven for all those who seek to restore the world socialist dream illegally taken from us.

"As you all know, Chagang Do province was the heart of our nation's modern weapons development program, including the weapons that are now in our charge," Kong went on. "It was doubtless a major target for attack or occupation by capitalist forces. Traveling to Chagang Do will not be easy. We cannot rely on the People's Liberation Army to protect us until we are close to our objective. We must therefore do everything in our power to get as close to Kanggye as possible and hope that our friends the Chinese will intervene if we are intercepted.

"To accomplish this goal, I have received authorization to create a diversion by staging our own attack on designated targets within South Korea. Our presence will certainly become known, so we shall attack the military targets most likely to participate in a search for us. The best way to assure that our attacks will have the greatest chance of success is to coordinate our launches. I have devised a plan, approved by the Ministry of Defense and the Politburo-in-exile, to disperse our forces and proceed to presurveyed launch points. Based on distance to target, we shall compute a launch time and date and proceed with a simultaneous launch. Five missiles reentering from different directions will have a better chance of penetrating any capitalist defenses than one. I have set up the first coordinated launch in three days. The units with reloads will then relocate to a new launch point and launch again."

Kong handed out sheets with a list of geographic coordinates, elevations, nearby landmarks, surveyor's distance and bearing coordinates, and celestial data needed to help align the missiles' gyros. "Here are the planned and alternate launch points I've selected for your units," he explained. "Some may be unfamiliar to you. I have rejected several of our normal launch points because I suspect some are known to the capitalists or have been compromised by deserters. It will be up to you to locate the new launch points. Use your GPS receivers to work yourself down as close as you can to the presurveyed point, locate the landmarks, then cross-check with the surveyor's coordinates.

"It will be up to each unit to find a hiding place," Kong went on. "Do your best to find and secure a good location. On the date listed on your handouts, move to the launch point, do a coarse celestial heading alignment, store it, then stand by. At the time listed, power up, elevate your weapon, do a fine alignment, then launch. Remember to retreat back to your hiding place immediately after launch—do not wait to reload. Even better, try to retreat several miles to the north. Then proceed with reload procedures.

"Each of us has at least one reload. Unit Twelve has two Scud-B reloads; my Unit Fourteen, which is a Nodong-1 unit, has two reloads as well. After you secure your units, we will try to meet at this location three days after the first launch, or at one of the other rendezvous locations listed on your sheet in four days; we will contact you with instructions. We will then proceed to secondary launch points inside Kangyang Do province. Depending on the success of our first launch, we may decide to try to split up the reloads, or we might try to get more reloads from one of our bases.

"Most important, comrades, is this: survival," Kong said. "We represent the last and only hope for the restoration of our nation. We are possibly the only weapon left that can stop the capitalists from destroying us. Guard your weapons with care. Do whatever is necessary to preserve your forces and carry out your assigned mission. If one of you is down, destroy or cache any remaining weapons, destroy all classified documents, then rendezvous with another unit to assist them. Remember: your mission is not complete until you receive verified, competent orders from myself or from headquarters telling you otherwise."

Kong looked at the men assembled around the campfire. He saw that his message had stirred them, but he also saw the fear in their eyes. Their nation was imploding, coming apart at the seams. They had all heard the muted whine of enemy planes overhead, wondered when the cluster bombs or nuclear detonation would hit, whether the end had come. They had a long march ahead of them, at least five hundred kilometers. Under normal conditions, such a march would take less than a week. Under current conditions, it could take months.

It was not just the South Korean warplanes, or the threat of an American nuclear-loaded cruise missile that posed the greatest risk—it was the threat from one of their own, their comrades-in-arms. They were more likely to be killed by a bullet from a North Korean rifle than an American bomb. The man they shared a meal or a laugh with yesterday, someone they had known or trained with for years, might be the man who would put a bullet through their head tonight.

"This is the time to be strong, all of you," Kong Hwan-li said as forcefully as he could. "We have trained for this our entire lives. The skills and knowledge given to us by the party and the fatherland are not just a means of livelihood—they are a solemn duty, a terrible and important responsibility.

"We have always said in our command that we are the point of the spear. It has never been more true than now. We may be the last hope of the fatherland. The Democratic People's Republic of Korea lives, but it needs our spirit to nourish it if there is any hope for survival against the imperialists. You are not alone out here. Your lives and your actions will set the course of history. Your ancestors will be the witnesses, your descendants the judge. Do not disappoint them."

HEADQUARTERS, HIGH TECHNOLOGY AEROSPACE
WEAPONS CENTER,
ELLIOTT AIR FORCE BASE, GROOM LAKE, NEVADA
THAT EVENING

G eneral Samson here and secure."

"Earthmover, Jester here," Air Force Chief of Staff General Victor Hayes responded.

"Thank you for returning my call, sir," said Terrill Samson, commander of Dreamland. "I know it's late. Did you get my proposal outline, timetables, and budget proposals, sir?"

"I'm not returning your call, Earthmover," Hayes said somberly. "I need to find out what in the hell you're up to out there."

"Please be a little more specific, sir."

"McLanahan. The Nevada Air National Guard B-1s. Dreamland. Balboa is getting it in Surround Sound from the Navy, from the Air Force, and from the National Guard Bureau about General McLanahan's project, and now he's pissing on my desk," Hayes said. "First, you guys set off that plasma-yield thing without telling the Navy. Bad. That went straight to Balboa. We cooled things down with him and the Navy, but he's got a burr under his saddle. He hears about B-1s and Dreamland and McLanahan and Samson and immediately gets a bad butt-rash.

"Next, a wing commander in Idaho claims a couple B-1 bombers almost rammed his jets *deliberately*. That was a Class One incident, Earthmover, a near-miss observed by both military and civilian radar facilities on the ground and in the sky. They had no choice. The reports went straight to Balboa's desk and got cc'ed to the SECDEF. More bad press.

"But that's not the best part, Earthmover," Hayes went on, his anger growing in intensity. "As part of the Class One incident investigation begun by the secretary of the Air Force's safety office, we start looking for the planes. We can't find them. Someone pushes the panic button and the word goes out right up to the Pentagon and on to 1600 Pennsylvania that *four* B-1 bombers with weapons aboard are *missing*. Shades of the A-10 suicide. Shades of the F-117 hijacks in California. National Guard, FBI, CIA, DIA, FAA, every alphabet noodle in the damned soup can is mobilized.

"So where do we find them? Where are they? *In your sandbox*, Earthmover! You got 'em! And no one can touch them! Now everyone is howling at me, at Balboa, at the SECDEF. Everyone wants some butts, Terrill! And I look like the biggest dipshit in the universe because I authorized all this and I didn't know what the hell was going on! Hell, everyone was saying those B-1s were hijacked by North Korean terrorists in retaliation for the South taking over their country, and that seemed like the best possible scenario! Now, what in the hell is going on out there?"

"Sir, we're moving ahead with Coronet Tiger and deployment of Lancelot," Samson said. "General McLanahan has been working closely with the Air National Guard unit from Reno, and he's determined that they're best suited for Coronet Tiger. When the Korea incident occurred, and since we had operational control of the Nevada B-1s, I decided we should implement the plan ahead of schedule. Since General McLanahan already had the bombers near our base, I authorized him to bring them on in to begin the conversion process, as previously planned."

"The 'best suited'? Are you crazy, Terrill? They almost rammed two F-15 fighters—not once, but *twice*. Then they almost rammed each other! They're nuts! They're crazy! And so are you and McLanahan if you think you're going to use them!" He paused, and Samson could hear swearing on the other end of the phone. "Terrill, you can't tell me that you knew and approved of all this. I know you too well. You're not like Brad Elliott. You would have come to me first. McLanahan did all this, didn't he?"

"I tried to contact you earlier, sir, but with the Korea thing erupting, the networks were a jumble," Samson lied. "And General McLanahan has a lot of initiative, and I give him a lot of authority and responsibility around here, but he doesn't do anything unless I give him approval. The B-1s' arrival was coordinated well in advance . . ."

"Don't bullshit me, Earthmover," Hayes interjected. He paused again, then went on: "Don't touch those bombers until I tell you to, Terrill. Don't even gas them up. Discontinue all test flights and weapons trials. You, McLanahan, and the Nevada Air Guard crews will probably face disciplinary action for what you've done today. I can't help that. Coronet Tiger and the Lancelot project might be all that keeps you two off the unemployment lines—or out of Leavenworth."

"Sir, with all that's going on in Korea right now, General McLanahan and I feel our program might be the best option if China starts—"

"You obviously didn't hear what I said, General Samson," Hayes cut in angrily. "Cut the Air National Guard guys back to their unit and stand down, *now*, or drop your stars in the mailbox on your way out of town."

ELLIOTT AIR FORCE BASE, GROOM LAKE, NEVADA
THE NEXT MORNING

As before, the only item on the news when the members of the 111th Bomb Squadron woke up the next morning was events in Korea. They hardly noticed what they had for breakfast or how long the coffee had been standing—every one of them was glued to the TV sets, which as in their own unit were tuned to CNN.

The news of the creation of the independent United Republic of Korea rippled around the world faster than a meteor, and as the sun rose on various parts of the globe, world leaders one by one endorsed and welcomed it. Even close North Korean allies, such as Russia, Iraq, Iran, and Libya, seemed to at least accede that the people might be better off. Revolutionary ideas, they said, might be better spread throughout a united, independent Korea rather than a divided peninsula with lots of foreign troops stationed on either side.

The People's Republic of China was the one glaring holdout. The president of the former Democratic People's Republic of Korea, Kim Jong-il, had set up a government-in-exile in Beijing, and Chinese President Jiang Zemin had warmly welcomed him. China had not committed any troops when South Korean planes started flying over North Korea—in fact, China had not even mobilized troops. But despite the televised appearance of a Chinese government functionary at the announcement, no one believed China would support a united, independent Korea that was not Communist, and they did not.

The world was holding its breath, afraid to move too fast or even blink for fear of touching off a global thermonuclear exchange. But it really did appear as if this was going to work: a Korea that was one nation again for the first time in nearly fifty years, and free from foreign troops on its soil for the first time in almost one hundred years.

Breakfast was served in the bottom-floor dayroom of the dormitory in which the 111th Aces High men and women were billeted. It resembled a standard Air Force base's transient lodging facility—except for the security. Like every building they could see, it was surrounded by tall barbed-wire fences and ringed by security cameras. They decided it was very much like being in prison.

Breakfast was "continental"—rolls, toast, cold cereal, juices, and coffee, wheeled in a tall stainless-steel warming cart, along with the Las Vegas newspaper and *USA Today*. Like the TV, the papers focused on the Korea situation.

Except for occasional comments about a TV or

newspaper item, there was almost no talk. Then John Long and Rinc Seaver reached for the copy of *USA Today* at the same time. "You've got it, Long Dong," Rinc said.

"No. Go ahead."

"I can wait."

"Jesus Christ, Seaver, you irritate the hell out of me every time I talk to you," Long snapped. "Take the damn paper, I said."

"Is that an order, *sir*?"

"Hey, how about I order you to shut your fucking mouth, asshole?"

"What is it with you, Colonel?" Rinc asked angrily. "You can't give me one goddamn break. I do a good job for you, I bust my nuts to be the best, and all I get is grief."

"Everyone gets what they deserve, Seaver," John Long said. "Maybe you get grief because you deserve it. Maybe you just rub most folks the wrong way. That's why everyone hates your fucking guts."

"No one asked you, Long."

"Hey, Major Jerkoff, you watch who you're talking to!" Long retorted. "Act like an aviator instead of teacher's ass-kissing pet . . ."

"I got an ass for you to kiss, Long, right here."

"Maybe you ought to be kissing a little less butt with your buddy the general and concentrate on doing your job," Long said. "You almost killed us yesterday on the range. I'm surprised you didn't punch out again, Seaver."

The other members of Aces High were startled; this was the first they had heard of the incident. "The general probably had to fight to keep your hands off the handles."

"You're the ass-kisser, Long," Seaver said. "You got

your nose so far up Furness's ass that she needs to fart for you to breathe."

Long lunged at Seaver in a rage so violent that it stunned. Long got in one good shot at Seaver's face and drew blood from a cut on the lip before Seaver fought him off.

"Knock it off!" Furness shouted. Someone tried to grab Long's arms from behind, but he shrugged them off and went at Seaver again. This time it was Furness who got in his way. "I said knock it off, John!" she shouted again.

"I'm gonna kick that asshole's butt but good!" Long yelled. "He damned near kills his crew again, and he has the nerve to mouth off at you and me?"

"Room, ten-*hut*!" someone called out. Everyone automatically snapped to attention as Patrick McLanahan and Hal Briggs entered the dayroom.

Patrick looked at Seaver's cut lip, then at Long, and finally at Furness. "What the hell is going on in here, Colonel?" he asked.

"Hangar flying, sir," Furness replied.

"Don't shit around with me, Colonel!" Patrick snapped. "I'm asking you again, *what the hell is going on in here?*"

"We are having a critique of our first day on the ranges, sir," Furness replied. "Our discussions sometimes get a little heated."

"How did the major's lip get cut?"

"I cut myself shaving, sir," Rinc replied.

"Is that right?" Patrick walked over to Seaver and looked him in the face. Seaver kept his eyes straight ahead. "It looks to me like you got hit, Major Seaver. Colonel Briggs?"

Hal Briggs grabbed John Long's right hand and lifted it up so everyone could see. Long tried to snatch it away but found Briggs's grip as strong as steel. There was a gash on his right middle knuckle. "Looks to me like Colonel Long hit him with his right fist, sir," said Briggs.

"Did he hit you, Major?" Patrick asked.

"No, sir."

"Don't lie to me, Major!" Patrick shouted. "There are reasons for every argument, and even reasons for someone to take a swing at another officer. I can understand such actions. I can even excuse them if they're provoked, or if there's good cause and the man is genuinely sorry and willing to repent. *But I will not tolerate lying for any reason.* A liar is someone of imperfect and questionable character. A liar is not fit to fly in my planes. A liar is not fit to wear a uniform or command a fighting unit. A liar is not fit to walk upon the same ground that true American heroes have walked on. I will turn in my stars and wings before I allow a liar to remain one second longer on this base and tarnish the honor and memory of the great men and women who have stood here and given their lives for this country."

Patrick stood face-to-face with Rinc Seaver. "Now, which are you, Major? Are you going to lie to my face? Are you going to show me you have no character? Or are you going to tell me the truth and let us deal with this incident like officers?"

"I will tell you the truth, sir," Seaver responded.

"That's all I ask, Major," Patrick said, much more gently. "After all, it does look like you were the wronged one. The truth never hurts the innocent. Now, what happened? Is my chief of security's observation wrong? Did Colonel Long strike you?"

"I cut myself shaving, sir," Seaver said.

"What are you, Major, some kind of idiot?" Patrick asked angrily. "Where do you think you are, back in your high school gym locker room in Galena having an argument with your school pals about who's going to ask Polly Sue to the prom? Remind him, Colonel Briggs."

"This is Dreamland, Major," Hal Briggs snapped. "Everything and everyone within one hundred miles of where you're standing is wired for sound and video and recorded twenty-four hours a day every day of the year. *You* are wired for sound. These walls are wired for sound and video. You can't jerk off under the covers of your rack without us knowing about it, Major!"

"All we have to do is pull the tapes of your little 'hangar flying session' and we'll know the truth," Patrick went on. "Now, I'm going to ask you once more, and you better tell the truth or I will destroy what's left of your military and civilian aviation career: did Colonel Long strike you?"

"Sir . . . ," Rinc said. He swallowed hard. "I cut myself shaving, sir."

Patrick McLanahan glared at Seaver, clenched his jaw as if he was going to continue the tirade—then nodded. "Very well, Major," he said. "If that's what you say, then you live with it." He turned away to wipe off the smile that had started in spite of himself, then addressed Furness. "Anything to say, Colonel?" he asked.

"No, sir."

"Good." He straightened up and faced the squadron members, still standing at attention. "Get your gear packed," Patrick said. "You're leaving."

"Leaving?" Furness said in astonishment. "Why? What's going on?"

"There's no mission, no program," Patrick told them. He forced himself to look the squadron members in the eye and found it very difficult. "Seems ACC disapproved of my methods to recruit fliers and airframes for my project. We're shut down. Get your gear together and stand by to depart."

There was a long, stunned silence. Patrick turned for

the door, but Furness's words stopped him. "What about . . . us, sir?"

He faced the members of Aces High and said, "You've been decertified by Air Combat Command as not mission-effective, based on the results of yesterday's range activity. You are therefore unqualified to be federalized and ineligible to be tasked for any missions in support of the active-duty force. The state of Nevada is thereby ineligible to receive any federal funds to support further flying activity. Therefore, the squadron has been stood down as of today by order of the Nevada adjutant general and the governor.

"Since you were Nevada's only Air National Guard organization, and the state has not been offered any other flying missions by the Air Force, there is no reason to keep you on the state payroll any longer. You have all therefore been placed in inactive mobilization augmentee status until you can be reassigned, transferred, or dismissed from state service. That is all."

"That's horseshit, sir!" Seaver cried. "They can't do that to us! *You* can't do this to us!"

"I'm not doing a thing, Major," Patrick said, trying to keep his voice under control. "Air Combat Command looked at the radar data from your mission and busted you for range safety. It's simple. You knew the ROE, and you broke them. Everything that happened afterward is a result of what you did on the range. You're decertified. Pack your bags and prepare to depart the fix."

"What happens to our planes, General?" Rebecca asked. "Or is that classified super-top-secret too? You always wanted our planes—now you've got them."

"The planes don't belong to me—they belong to the state of Nevada," Patrick said. "As soon as they decide what to do with them, we'll ferry them out. But I can almost guarantee they won't be going back to Reno, and I can definitely guarantee that they won't be flown by the 111th Bomb Squadron."

"General McLanahan, we're asking you to reconsider," Rinc Seaver interjected.

"Not possible. Not being considered."

"You know as well as I do that no one else in the world can fly the Bone like we can," Rinc said. "Yes, we got busted for range safety violations, but we beat two F-15 Eagles and every SAM and triple-A site you threw at us and we hit every assigned target. The only way we could do that was to bust ACC's ROE. Tell me, sir: Does Dreamland even *have* a ROE for their ranges? Is there any such thing as Level One, Level Two, or even a Level Three ROE? Or are you allowed to fly however possible in order to get the mission accomplished?"

Patrick said tersely, "All good points, Major. Except for one problem: no one gave you permission to invent your own ROE in Air Combat Command's ranges during their evaluation. You knew the rules of engagement, and you broke them. If you showed me your skills and accuracy while following the ROE, we could've taken it one step further—we could've taken it into *my* ranges, where you could've rocked and rolled your asses off. But you didn't do that. You busted. You're out."

"But, sir . . ."

"End of discussion!" Patrick snapped. "Be ready to depart in twenty minutes. That is all." Patrick stormed out of the building, followed closely by Hal Briggs. The security guard outside the gate barely got it open in time to avert the general's wrath.

"I'll drive," Patrick said to Hal as they reached his staff Humvee.

"Oh shit, you must be really pissed," Briggs said. He got his seat belt on just as Patrick roared off. He pulled out his secure cell phone. "Those Guard guys, they got some nerve talkin' to you that way," he said.

"They can talk all they goddamned want," Patrick snapped. "They're out of here. They learned the hard way that there's a time for the crazy shit and a time to follow the proper procedure. They've flaunted the rules for years. It cost them a bomber and three crew members, and they *still* fly like they're insane. They deserve to get shit-canned."

"Absolutely, sir," Hal said. He started speed-dialing a number. "They sure are nutzo. Totally unpredictable. They fly like they've got nothing to lose. They're not afraid to do whatever is necessary to get away from the bad guys and kill the target." He stopped, listened, then said into the phone, "Yes, sir. General McLanahan calling secure from Elliott Air Force Base . . . Yes, sir, please stand by." And he handed the phone to Patrick.

"Secretary Chastain?" Patrick asked him.

"No."

"C'mon, Hal. You're getting slow. I thought you could anticipate my every—"

"It's the White House," Hal interjected. "General Freeman, national security adviser. He wants to meet with you. In Washington. Right away."

Patrick looked at Briggs's broad, shit-eating grin. "That'll do, Hal. That'll do," he said, and took the call.

They drove back out to Foxtrot row, where the Nevada Air National Guard B-1 bombers were stored. General Terrill Samson and Lieutenant Colonel David Luger, along with the adjutant general of the state of Nevada, Adam Bretoff, and the governor of Nevada, Kenneth Gunnison, were waiting for them. They had just come down from the first modified EB-1C Megafortress bomber, and Bretoff's stunned expression was still fresh on his face.

"General Bretoff, Governor Gunnison, may I present General McLanahan, my deputy and chief of operations," Samson said. "He's in charge of the Coronet Tiger program."

"I feel like we've already met, General," Bretoff said as he shook hands. He was a short, rather round man, but the devices on his uniform, both Regular Army and Nevada National Guard, attested to a long and distinguished military career. Gunnison was tall and silver-haired. He looked like a rancher or an old-time oil wildcatter; his steel-blue eyes promised no nonsense and warned that he would take no bull from anyone.

"Nice to finally meet you in person, sir," Patrick said. "Sir, I realize you may think this is dirty pool, but it was the best way I could think of to convince you to agree to our plan."

"I don't understand half of what I've just seen," Governor Gunnison admitted, "but I've never seen old Adam here so bug-eyed before, so it's gotta be good stuff."

"It's the only one like it in the world, sir," Patrick said. "We want to build an entire squadron of them, and we want to base them in Nevada. We need your support to do it."

Gunnison looked the Megafortress over again, then rubbed his chin. "You know, son, I'm all for supporting our military and all that shit," he said. "But we need to talk about the bottom line. Nevada doesn't have a lot of money to invest in military planes, especially planes that the state can't use for disaster relief or quick logistics, like we did the C-130s we had in Reno. This is all Cold War stuff to me."

"We're talking about basing at least eight and as many as twenty B-1 bombers in your state," Patrick said. "Making improvements, hiring workers. The infrastructure construction and improvements would all be at federal expense. We give you the tools, pay to fix up your installations and surrounding infrastructure to our standards, and pay for training and upkeep. The state pays a small salary to keep highly trained guardsmen and their families in the state; but when they are federalized, which we think with our mission will be quite often, they're on our dime, not yours."

"I've seen the budget figures and mission projections, sir," Bretoff said. "Quite impressive. A one-of-a-kind mission, high-profile and very exclusive."

"Where are you thinking of basing this unit?" Gunnison asked.

"They would be here until the unit stands up," Terrill Samson said. "But we were thinking northern Nevada again, though perhaps not Reno. The old training base near Battle Mountain is a good possibility. Plenty of land, good neighbors, the old runway in pretty good shape for our planes. We know you want to send a little more industry and opportunity into the northern part of your state. We can help."

That sold it for the governor. Any talk of bringing growth to sparsely settled north-central and northeastern Nevada was music to his ears. "I think we might be able to talk business, General," Gunnison said. "What do you need from me?"

"We need you to assert your rights to these planes, that's all," Patrick said. "Your flight crews were involved in some . . . well, some aggressive flying tactics yesterday. The Pentagon wants to slap the crews down and confiscate these planes. You can't let them do it, sir."

"I've slammed my door in Washington's face before, gents. We Nevadans enjoy doing that sort of thing."

"They'll threaten you with everything in the book," Samson warned the governor. "Lawsuits, obstruction of justice, investigations, bad press, political pressure, threats to cut off federal funding . . ."

Gunnison took this in stride too.

"We're not too concerned about that either," Patrick said. "Frankly, sir, we're worried about when the Pentagon gets to the money phase."

"Oh?"

"Your planes here are worth a lot," Patrick admitted. "The Pentagon will start with small numbers—fifty million. But they're worth two, maybe three hundred million in spare parts."

"Holy shit," the governor exclaimed. "All that for these four little ol' planes?"

"I'm talking three hundred million *each,* sir." They saw him gulp in surprise. "I know, it's a lot of money. But we're asking you to say no. We don't have a billion-dollar budget, but we're offering to set up a flying unit like no other in the world. Only Nevada will have it. In fact, it may be worth more than a billion dollars to Nevada, but only in ways that can't be shown on a balance sheet."

"Who knows?" Samson added with a mischievous smile. "Maybe someday they'll rename the base after the governor who took a chance and started it all."

Gunnison hesitated—but only for a split second. He held out a hand, and Samson shook it warmly. "You got yourself an air force," he told them. "Any chance I get to thumb my nose and bare my hairy cheeks at Washington I'll take—they fuck with Nevada too much as it is already. You can do whatever fancy shit you want to 'em—the more the merrier. Battle Mountain is a pretty good name for the base—maybe name one of these monsters after the wife, paint one of those sexy nose art portraits on there." He paused, then asked, "You're going to fly these things over there in Korea, aren't you? Protect Korea from being fucked by the Chinese again?"

"I'm afraid we can't talk about any possible missions we might be involved in, sir," Patrick said.

"Good answer, son," Gunnison said, smiling. "I was in the first Korean War, and when I left I felt we still had a job to do. 'Battle Born' is our state motto, you know. Maybe now, with a few of these Battle Born beasts over there, you can finish the job me and my buddies set out to do back in '52. Get to work, and give me a ride in her when you get done kicking some ass over there in Korea."

CHAPTER SIX

NEAR NAMPO, PYONGYANG PROVINCE,
UNITED REPUBLIC OF KOREA
(FORMERLY NORTH KOREA)
SEVERAL WEEKS LATER

It was the most astounding sight imaginable: long lines of Chinese troops and vehicles marching to the Nampo docks, and hundreds of Korean citizens—residents of both the old North and South Korea—jeering and shouting at them. There were occasional former North Korean soldiers, mostly officers, in the march, and they had to dodge an occasional piece of fruit aimed in their direction. United Republic of Korea soldiers—again, from both North and South, genuinely united—stationed themselves between the demonstrators and the departing troops, keeping the citizens out of the road itself, but the crowds were orderly and the soldiers made no effort to stop their shouts and jeers.

And yes, there was even fruit to throw. When the former North Korean warehouses were opened up, citizens found tens of thousands of tons of food, fuel, clothing, and other supplies cached away all over the country, kept for party members, bureaucrats, and Chinese troops, or rifled by smugglers and black marketers. The black marketing was under control now—UROK troops dealt severely with the crooks—and for the first time in ages, fresh produce was reaching ordinary citizens.

The naval base at Nampo was one of the largest ports on Korea's east coast, and North Korea's largest naval facility. It was also the home of the People's Republic of China's Korean flotilla, a small fleet of surface and subsurface vessels based in North Korea to help train their client state's large- and medium-ship fleet. China had had over twenty thousand personnel and forty ships permanently based at Nampo, plus several dozen other vessels that visited the port monthly while on maneuvers in the Bo Hai and Yellow Seas.

Today, however, the base represented the beginning of the end of Chinese occupation of the Korean peninsula. The last of the Chinese troops and their heavy equipment, that which could not be sent by rail or along the highways north to China, were preparing to leave the country. Twenty heavy roll-on, roll-off container ships were waiting at the docks to take the last of China's war machine out of Nampo.

Korean troops lined the way, watching the procession. The departure was going smoothly until two American-made Humvees veered into the street and set up a blockade in front of a large green tractor-trailer rig. The Chinese officer in charge of the heavy equipment motorcade, who was riding in a general-purpose transport ahead of the rig, called an instant halt to the march and ordered his security troops to prepare to repel attackers.

At the sight of the Humvees, and the large, strange antennas atop them, the officer knew that what he had feared most had just happened. He got out of his vehicle and stormed toward the Humvees blocking the path of his trucks, his face looking appropriately outraged, annoyed, and murderous. He was encouraged to note that his own security forces clearly outnumbered the Korean troops lining the street. If there was going to be a fight, he would win it easily.

"What is the meaning of this?" the officer shouted. He had been assigned to Pyongyang for many years, and his Korean was fluent. "I demand to know why my trucks are being detained. Move your vehicles immediately or I will order my men to remove them for you!"

A Korean officer stepped out of one of the Humvees, approached the Chinese officer, bowed politely, and saluted. The Chinese officer noted the new United Republic of Korea flag hastily sewn onto the jacket, and sneered.

"Please forgive me, sir," the Korean officer said, bowing again. The Chinese officer knew that Koreans seldom literally mean what they say—they might apologize a thousand times over, yet never mean it. Such was certainly the case now. "But we must search this vehicle for contraband weapons," the Korean said. "I promise it will not take very long."

"You will do no such thing!" the Chinese officer retorted. He withdrew a folded legal document with the seal of the new United Republic of Korea and the seal of the People's Republic of China on its cover. "Under the terms of the agreement between our nations, we are permitted to pass without hindrance during this withdrawal period. Step aside!"

"You are permitted undisturbed movement of personnel and equipment as long as you do not possess contraband items," said the Korean officer. "We have reason to believe that you are carrying illegal special weapons." He motioned to the large antennas on his trucks. "Those are radiation detectors, sir. It is our opinion that you are carrying at least two and possibly more nuclear warheads in those trucks. You must allow us to inspect your trucks before you may pass."

"We will not!" the Chinese officer shouted. "You are not entitled to inspect our cargo. We are carrying only official records, personal items, and office equipment.

All of it is the property of the People's Republic of China. These trucks contain the remains of Chinese soldiers and family members who wish to be reinterred in their homeland. Disturbing their caskets would be sacrilege, punishable by the shame and humiliation of your ancestors. Now step aside, sir. This is your last warning." He shouted an order to his troops, who promptly knelt and raised their weapons to port arms, ready to open fire. "Your men are far outnumbered, sir. Now stand back and let us pass, or there will be bloodshed."

"We will not stand aside, sir," the Korean replied. "We do not want a fight, but we will respond with force if necessary. If you have contraband weapons in that vehicle, they will be confiscated, and the rest of your men and equipment may board the ships. Do not force us to fight."

"Then move your vehicles. Let us pass without any more delay, and there will be no fighting," the Chinese said. He turned again to his men. "You men, move those vehicles! Do it peaceably, but use force if—"

Suddenly, there was a *swooosh* and just a hint of a streak of smoke through the sky, and seconds later the Chinese officer's vehicle was hit. A cylindrical missile, perhaps three feet long and six inches in diameter, spun through the air like a stick tossed into the air, then bounced and skittered across the ground, with smoke belching from the blunt aft end. It did not explode, but it knocked the vehicle sideways so hard it almost sent it off the road. The Chinese troops scattered; some took cover, but remarkably, no one opened fire. The demonstrators also scattered, moving a safe distance away, but not so frightened as to leave the scene.

The missile was silver-colored, with short, straight fins protruding from its midbody and aft end. The nose was blunt. A thick tangle of thin wire, like monofilament fishing line, trailed behind it. The Korean officer went over to the missile and kicked it with the toe of his boot, then lifted up the wire so the Chinese officer could see. "This, sir, is a TOW missile round," he said. "Wire-guided, range of approximately four kilometers, with a four-kilogram high-explosive impact warhead. This is only a dummy round, of course. But I promise you, sir, all of the rest of the rounds we fire will be live ones. We have over a dozen gunners scattered nearby, and two helicopter gunships with more TOWs and Hellfire missiles ready to respond. Many of us will die if fighting starts, but many more of you will die too. We will then proceed to sink your transport ships and kill every last one of your soldiers onboard."

"We were promised that there would be no interference or coercion during our withdrawal!" the Chinese officer shouted, his voice quivering in fear. "We were promised no demonstration of force, no military presence, no intimidation . . ."

"And we were promised that all nuclear, chemical, and biological weapons would remain in place for proper disposal," the Korean officer retorted. "My men have detected nuclear weapons in that vehicle. We will now search it and confiscate any contraband weapons, or we will kill every last one of your men and destroy all of your ships and vehicles. You may choose, sir. Choose wisely."

"You would dare to disturb the eternal sleep of the honorable dead?" the Chinese officer asked. "Have you no conscience? Have you no shame?"

"If I am wrong, sir, then I will publicly and personally apologize to the families of those whom I have disturbed," the Korean officer replied. "I will accept the shame of my nation. But I will search these vehicles. *Now*. Will you please step aside, sir?" The Chinese officer shook his head, then ordered his men to back away from the trucks.

Sure enough, the semi was filled with six large wooden boxes, sealed with steel straps. The boxes bore the inscription of death, plus information on the deceased's family and town of origin. Some were draped with regimental flags, the symbol of a dead soldier; one was draped with a Chinese flag, signifying the remains of a high government official. The inscription said the remains were that of the senior military attaché assigned to Nampo, the third-highest-ranking member of the Chinese bureau in Nampo.

"This one," the Korean officer said to his men. "Open it."

"How dare you!" the Chinese officer shouted. "Do you realize that that contains the blessed remains of Vice-Marshal Cho Jong-sang himself? He was a former commander in the People's Army, next in line for chief of the general staff, and one of the highest-ranking Chinese diplomats in North Korea."

"I said, open it!"

"Why don't you open another one, if you charge there is more than one contraband weapon in the truck?" the Chinese officer asked. "Do not desecrate the vice-marshal's name by disturbing his coffin!" But the Korean officer refused to yield. Four of his soldiers removed the steel bands and opened the wooden crate, revealing a magnificent mahogany coffin inside. The locks had to be drilled out, which took some time, but the casket was finally opened . . .

. . . and indeed, there lay the withered body of the vice-marshal, in full military uniform.

"You bastard!" the Chinese officer spat, unleashing a tirade of invective as the coffin was sealed shut again. The Korean officer stood unmoving at its head, bowed deeply at the waist, and suffered the onslaught in silence. Then, before the crate was lifted back into the truck, he apologized, saying, "I am most deeply sorry for my mistake," turned to his soldiers, and pointed. "That one next."

"What?" the Chinese officer shouted in disbelief. "You are going to open *another* one? How dare you? You will be imprisoned for this, I promise you! You will not see the light of day for fifty years!" He positioned himself directly in front of the Korean officer, going face-to-face with him. "This will cause an international incident of the worst kind if you do not stop immediately! You—"

"Step aside, please, sir."

"I will not! You have delayed us long enough! I will order my men to keep your men away from these trucks until I can contact my embassy. Stop immediately, or I will . . ."

But he stopped as the four soldiers tried to lift the wooden crate—and it would not budge. With their flashlight, they could see that this crate and a couple of others, most of them located in the front area of the truck, were fitted with special hardware so they could be moved by forklift. They also found roller pallets that could help move the heavy crates.

"How interesting," said the Korean officer. "The vice-marshal's remains can be easily lifted by four men, while this one cannot be moved even a centimeter. This is rather unusual, don't you think, sir?"

The Chinese officer swore under his breath. "You have no idea of the havoc it will cause if these crates are not delivered to China. My country is willing to go to war over these devices! Do you understand? What you are doing is tempting war between our countries. Do you want that for your brand-new little nation? Do you want to celebrate your first few weeks of existence with a Chinese invasion? *Do you?*" The Korean officer was unmoved. The Chinese officer wiped beads of sweat from his forehead. "They will execute me if I do not return with them," he whispered. "I will be killed the minute I set foot on Chinese soil."

"Then do not return," said the Korean. "Remain here in United Korea. You will be welcome."

"That would save my life, I suppose," the Chinese said, "but it would not preserve my honor or the honor of my family, would it?" He looked at the Korean officer's field jacket and recognized the outlines of some of the patches and insignia that had been stripped from it. They fitted a North Korean People's Army unit. This man had been a *North Korean officer*! "Tell me, sir," he asked, "what preserves *your* honor? You not only turn your back on your oath and your country, but you do not even procure another jacket to wear. You dishonor your country of birth by sewing this abomination on the jacket that kept you warm and protected."

"The flag I served under, the bureaucrats and government officials that I pledged to support and defend, starved my family and me for months," the Korean officer answered bitterly. "Last year it cost the life of my youngest son. Every family I know, military or not, was hurt by what the Communist government was doing. When the opportunity came to bring the government down, I took it. I invoked the name of my dead son for strength. His strength supports me still. Now my family is being cared for—and now I would give my life for the new nation that saved them from certain death.

"Now step aside. Order your men to leave the contraband weapons right where they are and board your ships, and you may depart in peace. Otherwise, I will order all these vehicles and your ships destroyed. I will be happy to join my son in eternity. I am ready to die. Are you?"

About an hour later the march toward the transport

ships resumed. It took several more hours to load the ships; then the last of the Chinese Army members boarded and the vessels unleashed thick clouds of smoke as their engines pushed them away from the Korean shore. Korean helicopters flitted overhead to escort them clear of their territorial waters.

Left behind on the wharf, to the stunned amazement of the onlookers, were thirty-seven gray steel coffins, off-loaded from the trucks. Each coffin was about six feet long, three feet square, and weighed well over eight hundred pounds . . . and each contained a thermonuclear warhead for a short-range Scud missile. Some were smaller North Korean–made ABD warheads, with approximately a ten-kiloton nuclear yield; a few were Chinese-made OKD warheads with anywhere from a forty- to a three-hundred-fifty-kiloton yield.

Once word spread about what was inside those coffins, the demonstrators who had thronged the roadsides quickly left the military port at Nampo. They never wanted to set foot there again.

THE WHITE HOUSE, WASHINGTON, D.C.
THE NEXT MORNING

hank you for taking my call, Mr. President," said Kevin Martindale, speaking on the secure videophone hookup. Out of view of the videophone camera, chief of staff and senior adviser Jerrod Hale scowled at the President's courteous words. No President of the United States of America, he said in silent admonishment, should ever have to suck up to a foreign leader, however grave the situation. Vice President Whiting and National Security Adviser Freeman were also in the Oval Office, and out of camera view.

"I am pleased to take your call and I place myself at your complete disposal, sir," responded United Republic of Korea President Kwon Ki-chae. The man looked more cheerful than Martindale ever remembered seeing him. Well, why shouldn't he? His grand, daring scheme to reunite the Korean peninsula had worked unbelievably well.

"Mr. President, I have just received a briefing from my staff," Martindale began. "We heard the news of the stockpile of nuclear warheads confiscated at Nampo. Congratulations, sir, for taking control of those devices without bloodshed. Any one of us here would have guessed that the Chinese would have fought to the death before relinquishing them."

"I thank you for your kind words, Mr. President," Kwon said. "We thank the gods of chance and of reason that bloodshed was avoided. But when you have nothing to lose except your freedom, acts of desperation are your only alternative. Unfortunately, my military analysts tell me that it is possible we only succeeded in confiscating a fraction of the warheads stored in Nampo and the First Army region. We fear many more were already smuggled out in the opening days of the transition."

"I agree, Mr. President," Martindale said. He paused for a moment, then went on: "Mr. President, the confiscated warheads are the reason for my call. My analysts tell me you have uncovered over sixty such weapons caches throughout North Korea in the past few days— and these are only weapons stores that *you did not know about* before the transition."

"That is true, Mr. President," Kwon acknowledged. "Your intelligence information is quite accurate. We have unearthed"—he paused, checking his notes— "sixty-three weapons caches. It is also true that we did not know about these hidden weapons before the transition. Most appear to be weapons in maintenance status that Communist loyalists tried to hide. Thankfully, those who believe in peaceful reunification reported their existence and led our teams to them."

"We do not have an accurate guess as to how many warheads or devices that represents," President Martindale went on, "but if each cache was only half the size of yesterday's Nampo discovery, that is over six hundred weapons of mass destruction discovered."

"It is indeed shocking," Kwon said, choosing not to confirm or deny Martindale's estimate. "To think that all these years the Communists denied they stockpiled such weapons. We are indeed fortunate that the Communists never had a chance to employ them against us. It would have decimated our country ten times over."

"The entire world is grateful for your courage, wisdom, and strength through this incredible ordeal, Mr. President," Martindale said. He looked at Hale's scowl and nodded, this time acknowledging that his civility might be a touch excessive. "Those weapons represented a substantial threat not just to Korea directly, but to the entire world. We believe, and I'm sure you'll verify, that the Communists were selling those warheads, along with the delivery vehicles, around the world for hard currency. Their balance of payments certainly bears this out." Kwon said nothing.

"Mr. President, I've spoken with representatives of the Chinese government," Martindale went on. "They're worried about what you intend to do with those warheads. The stockpiles must be enormous— while North Korea's chemical and biological warfare capability was well documented, we now realize that their nuclear capability was equal to or even greater than what we ever anticipated."

Still, Kwon said nothing. He stared directly at the

camera, hands folded, a slight benign smile on his face, as if waiting for the punch line to a joke.

"President Kwon? Can you hear me, sir?"

"Of course, Mr. President," Kwon responded.

"I ask you, sir—what do you intend to do with the special weapons you have?"

At the Blue House in Seoul, United Republic of Korea, President Kwon sat with his national security advisers, all out of videoconference camera range: Defense Minister Kim Kun-mo, a retired Army general; Prime Minister Lee Kyong-sik; Foreign Affairs Minister Kang No-myong; Director for National Security Planning Lee Ung-pae; and Chief of the General Staff General An Ki-sok. Kwon looked at each of them, searching for some indication of what he should say to the President of the United States. Finally, he said, "Please forgive me, Mr. President. I must confer with my aides," and put the videoconference call to Washington on hold without waiting for a response.

"So," he said to his advisers. "The question has been asked, as we feared it would be. Your thoughts, please?"

"Do the Americans *deserve* an answer?" General Kim asked angrily. "They sound to me as though they are accusing us of some duplicity. How dare they?"

"In case you have forgotten, General, the United States protected South Korea for two generations," President Kwon retorted. "They spilled the blood of their children on our soil less than ten years after fighting a terrible world war that eventually defeated our Japanese oppressors. They risked nuclear devastation to keep South Korea free and democratic. I think they deserve to know."

"Sir, it is as you have said in the past: they did this in

their own self-interest. The Americans, like the Chinese and Russians in the North, used Korea as a way to intimidate their superpower enemies, not to protect us," Kim replied. "You know as well as I that Washington would have never agreed to your plan to reunite the peninsula. We were forced to do it on our own because of American intransigence. And now they want to take our hard-won weapons away? I say no!"

President Kwon was accustomed to his defense minister's strident tone, although it troubled him. He looked around the conference table. "Your opinions, gentlemen?"

"I disagree with Minister Kim, sir," Foreign Minister Kang said rather nervously. "Retaining those weapons will only harm our relations overseas. We will be seen as a nuclear wild card, like Israel or Iran. That will not be good for our cause."

"I agree with Minister Kim," General An said. No surprise there, Kwon thought. Although in this room he was considered an equal in rank and status, An needed Kim's endorsement to move up the ladder and become the next minister of defense when the general retired, so he usually sided with Kim on policy questions. "We should deal with China and the rest of the world from a position of strength, not weakness. Although I agree that the United States has been a trusted friend and ally to us, they do not have the right to dictate terms to us."

"I am sorry to put the monkey on your back, sir," Prime Minister Lee said with a wry smile, "but I disagree with Kim. We should not keep any weapons of mass destruction. I do not think we have anything to fear from China *unless* we keep those weapons."

General Kim could sense that the tide was turning away from him, so he said, "I certainly see their point, sir. Maintaining a nuclear weapons deterrent will undoubtedly cast our new nation in a different and disturbing light. But I truly feel it is our best and perhaps our only deterrent to Chinese aggression.

"Consider this, sir: We use those weapons not as devices for mass destruction, but as bargaining chips. We force China to agree to stop harboring Kim Jong-il or supporting his government-in-exile in exchange for removing those weapons. Or we remove the weapons in exchange for a disarming of our border with China—an equal number of troops within three hundred kilometers of the border on both sides. Or both. But we should not even hint that we are willing simply to hand over the weapons to anyone, not even the United States."

"I think that is a very good tactic to pursue," Prime Minister Lee said quickly, thankful that an option presented itself that would avoid directly opposing the powerful retired general.

President Kwon thought for a moment, then nodded. "Thank you, gentlemen, for your thoughts. You are all indeed true patriots." He pushed the HOLD button on his phone and resumed his videoconference call with the President of the United States.

"What is it that concerns you, President Martindale?" Kwon asked when his image reappeared on the videophone screen. "What is it that concerns President Jiang?"

"What concerns *us*?" The President stared at Kwon in surprise. "President Kwon, it is well known that the People's Republic of China views the existence of weapons of mass destruction at or even near its borders as a threat to its national security and sovereignty. The United States and the former Republic of Korea have honored China's concern and have not stationed any nuclear, chemical, or biological weapons on the Korean peninsula for over twenty years. If you keep these confiscated weapons, China will certainly view it as a threat."

"President Martindale," Kwon said, "it is incongruous in the extreme to let such a notion concern you."

"What? Why do you say that?"

"In the light of our recent discoveries, sir, it is apparent that weapons of mass destruction have been placed on Korean soil for many years," Kwon said. "The world knew about North Korea's chemical and biological weapons, and now we see that a great many thermonuclear weapons were based here too. Why then should we be concerned if China is upset that we now possess the very weapons that they in all likelihood placed on Korean soil in the first place?"

"The difference is, sir, that North Korea and most certainly China jointly controlled those weapons, and now they don't," Martindale said. "I understand what you are saying, Mr. President. But the cold hard fact is that China is upset that you are capturing these weapons and have not declared your intention as to their disposition. China has thankfully stayed out of this incident because they recognized, as did the world, that this was an internal struggle. When the pro-democracy forces won and it was apparent that the former North Korean citizens were being welcomed and integrated into the new United Korea, China was careful not to interfere and cooperated in a timely manner with a complete military troop withdrawal."

"We have done all that we promised," Kwon said. "We are one people. Nothing can deny that."

"President Kwon, I am not sure you understand. If China thinks it a possibility that you might point those nuclear, chemical, or biological weapons at *them,* they may not be so cooperative," Martindale warned the Korean president. "In fact, they might get downright upset. They have almost a quarter of a million troops sitting on your northern border right now, and another quarter million within seven days' march.

"You must declare your intentions, sir. My recommendation to you is to agree to turn over all those confiscated special weapons to the United Nations Nuclear Disarmament Agency. The United States will pay all costs of transporting, dismantling, incineration, disposal, or secure storage of the weapons. We can announce the action at a joint news conference, and this time I'll be sure that President Jiang of China himself is there to endorse and support it. You can declare the Korean peninsula a certified weapons-of-mass-destruction-free zone and challenge China to turn Asia into a WMD-free continent."

Kwon Ki-chae sat back in his chair, a move that startled Martindale and Hale. It was an extraordinarily casual gesture in a man who was normally extremely conscious of appearances. "I very much appreciate your concern and thoughts on this subject, Mr. President," he said. "I am of course in full agreement with your sentiments. A WMD-free Asia would be in the best interests of everyone in the world."

Martindale smiled, although a knot was forming in his stomach. He was afraid Kwon was about to let the other shoe drop.

"However, I think it would be best if we kept these weapons for the time being," he said, sitting up straight again, his tone and mannerisms now grave. "We believe it would be a more persuasive show of sincerity and unanimity if President Jiang joined me in turning over all of his weapons of mass destruction to the United Nations."

"Are you . . . serious?" Martindale blurted out. "Are you saying you will not turn over any warheads unless *China* agrees to turn over its warheads at the same time? Mr. President, do you seriously believe that's ever going to happen?"

"Apparently you do not believe it," Kwon replied. "But why is this so hard to believe, sir? Where is the threat? Certainly not from the United States, correct? Russia has not the capacity for war, and certainly not against a powerful neighbor. Let us all agree to lay down our weapons together in a total show of a lasting commitment for peace. What a glorious way to begin the new millennium."

"Mr. President . . ." Kevin Martindale forced himself to control his rising anger and frustration. "Mr. President, please reconsider. The threat potentially facing Korea is very, very serious. If China perceives you as a threat, they may launch a preemptive attack against Seoul and against all of your military installations, North and South. The death and destruction could be enormous. China has certainly shown in recent years that it will react harshly and quickly to any threat to its security and regional hegemony. I believe you have an opportunity to be a world leader in the pursuit of peace and global nuclear disarmament. Please reconsider your position."

"I will attempt to state United Republic of Korea's position as plainly as I can," Kwon said sternly, leaning toward the camera. "Our republic faced imminent destruction for almost fifty years. We endured two generations of schizophrenia and paranoia, brothers torn apart by a world that saw Korea as nothing more than spoils of war to be divided up like bits of clothing and equipment taken from the bodies of the dead on the battlefield.

"For decades, both North and South were forced to accept foreign powers on our soil. We were led to believe these powers were there to protect us from ourselves. We now know that they were really there to provide a forward presence for themselves, to act as a deterrent in their own selfish interests. Neither China, the United States, nor Russia cared about the Korean people. All you cared about was the military and geo-political advantages that stationing troops on our soil, near your potential adversaries, could provide. You were protecting no one else but yourselves. *No more.*

"I will introduce an emergency bill in our new legis-lature, authorizing the Korean military to keep and control all military weapons and devices, including weapons of mass destruction," Kwon said. "It will authorize the establishment of a positive control sys-tem, supervised by the president and the minister of defense. It will authorize training, maintenance, and de-ployment of all types of weapons now on Korean soil. And it will authorize that these weapons be deployed against whatever power threatens the peace, security, and sovereignty of United Korea."

Kwon waited to let his words sink in, then went on: "With all due respect, Mr. Martindale, I was not able to believe you when you showed concern for Korea and expressed your hope that we would help contribute to world peace by turning over our weapons of mass de-struction. You hoped we would do so because you asked us to. You hope that we will do so now because then you can save face before the Chinese government. Although we no longer look to the United States for our protection, the Chinese still believe we look to you for guidance and support—they believe we are still Ameri-can puppets. You were hoping this was true. It is not.

"The weapons we have confiscated will stay in Korea until such time as we feel they are not necessary to se-cure our citizens, our borders, our government, and our way of life. I sincerely hope all such weapons can be destroyed around the world. But we must do it together. Until then, we will look to ourselves for our security."

"President Kwon, I think you're making a big mistake," President Martindale said. "China . . . no, the *world* will react negatively to the news that Korea has decided to keep perhaps several hundred WMDs. You will undo all the great things you have accomplished in the past several weeks."

"Was France ostracized and in danger of attack from Russia or the United States because it broke away from NATO and decided to control the fate of its own nuclear weapons?" Kwon asked. "Did the United States dismantle its nuclear arsenal because the Soviet Union was upset about you aiming ten thousand nuclear warheads at its cities? We will not willingly surrender any weapon in the hope that belligerent nations will follow suit and lay down their weapons too. That is a typical American folly that Korea will not repeat.

"I hope you are wrong, Mr. Martindale," Kwon went on. "I hope China sees us as a stabilizing influence in Asia and not a destabilizing one. But it does not matter *what* they think. Korea will use all the resources available to it to defend its borders, its government, and its people. If it means war with China—well, many have said such a war was inevitable, that two such ideologically opposed nations can never coexist or even peacefully share a border. China has dominated Korea in the past, and if history shows us anything, it is that it may happen again. But this time we are united. Any who wish to attack or invade will find a stronger, more determined Korea standing in their way."

"President Kwon, please, let me meet with you as soon as possible," President Martindale said. "In Tokyo, in Singapore, in Manila, in Paris—anywhere you wish. We must sit down face-to-face and talk more."

"I am very sorry, Mr. Martindale," Kwon said, "but

I have a fledgling country to run—and a military to organize. If China is indeed a threat to us, as you say, we must prepare. Good day to you, sir." And the video-conference connection went dead.

Martindale was exhausted, physically and emotionally, when he dropped the receiver back on its cradle. He shook his head and massaged his aching temples. "You were right, Ellen," he told the others in the Oval Office. "They aren't going to give up the weapons. He sees them as his best opportunity to hold off another invasion by China. Kwon must be crazy to think he can stop China."

"Kwon is not crazy, not by a long shot," Vice President Whiting said seriously. "He is like a grand chess master, which in reality I believe he is: he can see six moves ahead, and he is dogged in his determination. He has infinite patience and a simple, clear, concise set of objectives—the creation of a united Korean nation. If keeping hundreds of WMDs will help him achieve that, he'll do it."

"I can certainly see his point," General Freeman said. "He knows that China can march right in and take Korea at any time if they choose to do so. Having a WMD arsenal, with missiles powerful enough to hold Beijing itself at risk, is the only way they can hope to deter China."

"But if China was going to invade, they could have done it a long time ago."

"Not with American troops stationed there," Freeman pointed out. "We were only a trip-wire force there, true, but it was an *effective* trip wire. Our little forty-thousand-troop force successfully held hundreds of thousands of Chinese soldiers at bay for forty years— backed up by our nuclear deterrent, of course. The only time we ever felt threatened by the Chinese is when we started to draw down our strategic forces to the point where China believed it could withstand an American retaliation. They took a shot at subduing Taiwan, and only by stepping in with substantial firepower did they back off."

"And now, with Korea?"

"It's déjà vu all over again—except China might have the public opinion advantage in this one," Freeman replied. "You are absolutely correct, sir—if Korea keeps those weapons, they'll be perceived as the antagonizers, perhaps even as the aggressors. It is as if Cuba suddenly acquired a tremendous nuclear, chemical, and biological weapons arsenal and then dared us to ignore the fact—the world would condemn Cuba. China can claim it is a destabilizing event. The world will not only be horrified to learn that North Korea had a nuclear arsenal greater than most any other non-superpower nation on earth, but that now United Korea has those weapons. China *must* respond to this development."

"How?"

"They might increase the number of troops on the border and in the region, increase the throw weight of missiles and artillery aimed at Korea—all peaceful, all on their side of the line, and all fully justifiable," Freeman went on. "This could continue for months, even years. The world could be on the razor's edge for an indefinite period of time, even with continuous and strenuous negotiations going on. But worse: if something happens—an accident, an error, a skirmish—all hell could break loose in the blink of an eye. We destroyed China's intercontinental ballistic missile fleet in 1997 during the Taiwan conflict, but we didn't put much of a dent in their medium- or short-range ballistic missile arsenal. Most of it is intact, and it's potent."

"And Korea no longer has all of the Patriot antiaircraft and antimissile systems it had just one month ago," Ellen Whiting pointed out. "We took most of those systems home with us when our troops left, didn't we?"

"Yes. Less than a third of the thirty Patriot batteries are still there," Freeman said. "Each battery has three launchers, one radar, and six reload canisters. That's about forty shots against aircraft—Patriots always fire in two-round salvos—and less than twenty shots against tactical ballistic missiles. This means one attack could deplete their antiaircraft and antimissile capabilities. Plus, Kwon has to face the idea of dispersing those ten batteries throughout the entire peninsula, not just the South. Thirty batteries located in South Korea protected the nation very well against just about any airborne threat—but ten batteries spread out over the entire peninsula will be stretching it pretty thin."

"And what do we do if Kwon wants to buy more Patriots?" Vice President Whiting asked. "What do we tell him? Or what if he goes to Russia, or Israel, or Great Britain, looking for air defense equipment?"

"Let's not get too far ahead of ourselves here," the President said, holding up a hand. "One crisis at a time, please." He thought for a moment, then said, "Okay. What do we have in the region right now? Anything at all we can add to increase the deterrent factor?"

"All of our assets are afloat," Philip Freeman replied. "The *America* and the *Eisenhower* carrier battle groups are in the area. The *America* is in the Yellow Sea, helping move our remaining troops out of Korea; it was to have been decommissioned two years ago, but with the destruction of *Indy,* it's still in service. The *Eisenhower* is in the Sea of Japan, standing by to help, trying to monitor the situation, and providing some cover for Japan. Not that Japan needs it—they've been flying regular MiG-29 patrols right up to the Korea-China-Russia frontier, with Korea's blessing. We have two other carriers, *Roosevelt* and *Vinson,* en route to the area."

"That's it? No other forces near Korea?"

"Sir, that's *one-third* of our carrier fleet," Freeman acknowledged somberly. "And they all must operate with minimal forward-basing capability. Seventh Fleet was forced to move from Yokosuka to Pearl Harbor because of the *Independence* disaster, and all attack-capable military units were removed from Japan following the nuclear attack on the *Independence*. We have a few assets at Yokota and Misawa, all air defense and transport units. It took two years of hard negotiating to keep our bases on Okinawa. The units on Okinawa are there to maintain air base operations and provide fleet support only—we are prohibited from basing or staging any attack forces from there. Anderson Air Base on Guam is still uninhabitable; Agana Naval Base on Guam is just coming back up after being heavily damaged in the Chinese attack. The nearest American military base is Elmendorf Air Force Base." When the President looked up at Freeman with a quizzical expression, he added, "In Anchorage, Alaska."

"Anchorage!" the President exclaimed. "The closest military base we have to Korea is in *Alaska?"*

"The former Adak Naval Air Station in the Aleutian Island chain is thirteen hundred miles closer, but it is completely uninhabited except by caretakers—the Navy left in 1998," Freeman said. "First-class airfield, first-class dock facilities, first-class communications facilities, enough housing and infrastructure for almost ten thousand folks—just uninhabited for two years. It's a three-hour plane ride from Anchorage, if the weather is good." He gave the President a wry smile. "The Navy got along well with the neighbors—the nearest civilian community of any size is over one hundred miles away."

"My God," the President muttered. "No nearby military facilities. What're the next closest bases?"

"About equidistant between Anchorage and Honolulu," Freeman said. "Over four thousand miles away—eight hours by jet."

"God," the President muttered again. "Philip, I need a contingency plan to deal with this, right away. If China attacks United Korea, what are we going to do about it? What will our response be? We also need to have sufficient forces in place to protect Japan, even if they don't want us based on their soil. My thoughts are this: we place enough deterrent forces in the region to show China that we are ready to respond. At least three carrier battle groups, plus a bomber force on alert in Alaska, loaded with enough firepower to blunt a Chinese ground invasion. Philip, I need you to draw up something like that as soon as possible."

Philip Freeman walked over to his briefcase and withdrew three copies of a thick manuscript. "Fast enough for you, sir?" he quipped, handing a copy to Vice President Whiting as well. The manuscript was entitled "United Republic of Korea Show of Force Ops Plan."

"You've been busy these past few days, Philip," the President said approvingly. "Very good. Give it to me in a nutshell."

"You've given it to me already, sir," Freeman responded. "Priority number one: increase our presence in northeast Asia without the use of foreign forward-operating bases. Priority number two: deter aggression by China or Russia against the UROK or Japan. Priority number three: be able to stop or blunt a land invasion by either China or Russia into the UROK with rapid, sustained, massive firepower.

"This document was written by Brigadier General Patrick McLanahan of the High Technology Aerospace

Weapons Center. It's biased, of course—McLanahan and his team develop air weapons, mostly Air Force—but he has a workable plan that I'd like to present to you for consideration. He relies on some naval assets and some assets of other services, but mostly he relies on experimental assets being developed by him and his team at Elliott Air Force Base."

"Why am I not surprised?" the President asked sarcastically. He inwardly winced when he heard the name "Elliott," as in "Brad Elliott"—as he feared, that three-star bastard was still haunting him, tormenting the White House from beyond the grave.

"Response number one: increase surface combat tasking in the region," Freeman went on. "The first choice would be carriers, and we'll have to start with the ones we have in the region, but McLanahan outlines a different proposal in his plan. Response number two: increase commitment of long-range air combat forces to the Asia theater. Response number three . . ." He hesitated, then said, "Commitment to use special weapons in the NEA theater."

"Special weapons? You mean, *nuclear weapons*?" Ellen Whiting exclaimed.

"It's the only viable alternative, ma'am," Freeman said. "We have less than one hundred active long-range bombers and less than three hundred medium bombers in the Air Force, and with three carrier battle groups we add only another eighty Navy medium bombers and perhaps a thousand cruise missiles. Even if we could surge these aircraft to two sorties a day and limit attrition to one percent, we won't have nearly enough assets to even put a dent in a massive Chinese ground and armored invasion. And we have to consider the real possibility that China will switch to weapons of mass destruction itself when American forces respond. Therefore, I believe we need to make the commitment right up front to deploy and use tactical nuclear, subatomic-yield, or plasma-yield weapons."

The President and the Vice President were too stunned to react, so Freeman went on: "There are other concerns as well. This will put a tremendous strain on our other world commitments, since every few months at least one additional carrier needs to be rotated in—that's more than one-third of our carrier fleet committed to northeast Asia. This will leave important parts of the world, such as the Atlantic Ocean and the Mediterranean Sea, without a carrier battle group for long periods of time. If a crisis erupts in the Balkans, the Aegean, the Baltic, or the eastern Med, we couldn't respond rapidly. We would have to commit large portions of our air forces to the Pacific theater—bombers, tankers, and support aircraft—and since we're talking about the northern Pacific, that means deploying those forces north, to Alaska . . ."

"Aha—the mention of Adak and Elmendorf wasn't a fluke, eh, Philip?" the Vice President said as she flipped through the report.

"No, ma'am," Freeman replied. "As soon as we lost the use of our bases in Japan, the Pentagon started looking for other alternatives—and that meant Alaska. Now, with the loss of Korean bases as well, Adak's importance has skyrocketed. We have proposals awaiting authorization to dump a billion dollars into Adak in the next five years and base as many as thirty support aircraft there year-round."

"Looks to me like you'd better get that proposal into the congressional paper mill right away," the President said. "I'll bet you have an emergency spending plan drafted up as well?"

"One hundred million dollars over the next two years," Freeman answered. "We can have the Pentagon tack it onto some other spending authorization bill and have it back on your desk for signature in a few days. It won't exactly be a plum base of assignment, but we operated aircraft out of there for decades before."

"Do it," the President said. "Good work. But I'm still bothered about those carriers, Philip. China will start howling at us if we put three carriers around the Korean peninsula. Besides, the carriers are too attack-heavy. How about just a few ships—a little less intrusive, a little more defense-oriented?"

"Section Three," Freeman said. The President and Vice President smiled and flipped the pages in their documents. "I had another little talk with General McLanahan just a few days ago, and he sent me a draft of a proposal that has been circulating around for years which we appended to his plan. He says we can effectively increase our forward presence around Korea by a factor of between two and five, using assets we already have. He says with a budget, he can set up a missile defense screen *over the entire Korean peninsula* without one ground-based system at all."

"What?" the President exclaimed. "How in the hell is that possible?"

"I can get him in here in a matter of minutes and he can explain it all to you," General Freeman said. "He just happens to be on his way to Washington."

"Just happens to be?" the President said. "Good. Let's get him in here and do it." He skimmed through the document, shaking his head in amazement. "Unbelievable. Simply unbelievable. How come we didn't implement this plan before?"

"General McLanahan won't say so, but we both suspect it was because of General Elliott. You remember how fond he was of the Navy." Sarcasm dripped from every word.

The President shook his head, reminded that interservice rivalry and mistrust had set fine military plans like these back so many years. "Christ, if he was still alive, with George Balboa still at the Pentagon, we'd be lucky to stop the fighting in our own *hallways,* let alone in Asia."

"You mentioned a couple of things I'm not too familiar with, General—subatomic-yield and plasma-yield weapons," Vice President Whiting said. "What are those?"

"Section Five, ma'am," Freeman said. "That was drawn up by General Elliott's successor, General Terrill Samson, the commander of the High Technology Aerospace Weapons Center, along with General McLanahan. He recently made this presentation before a Senate subcommittee. They have devised a way of using the next generation of powerful weapons for use in both attack and air defense applications.

"Subatomic-yield weapons are weapons such as neutron bombs that kill with high doses of radiation but cause little blast effect. They are unpopular, politically and otherwise, for obvious reasons; they can kill humans—sometimes with excruciating pain over many months—but leave buildings and weapons largely undamaged."

"Never heard of a weapon that *was* popular," the President said. "What about that other thing, the plasma-yield weapons?"

"Plasma-yield weapons are just making it out of the testing facilities and into field testing," Freeman went on. "They kill and destroy with much greater effectiveness than any other kind of weapon ever devised. They use a small nuclear explosion to generate tremendous amounts of plasma energy—heat so intense that it instantly vaporizes anything it touches. The effect is devastating—targets don't just blow up, they *vanish.*"

"What do you mean, vanish? Like a space ray or something? Like a *Star Trek* phaser beam?"

"Exactly," Freeman said. "Matter is turned into plasma energy, which cannot be sensed by humans—the target vanishes."

"Talk about politically unpopular!"

"The weapon has many advantages and many disadvantages," Freeman went on. "It works poorly in the atmosphere. It is horrendously expensive. But a plasma-yield detonation causes no blast effects—no overpressure, no heat, not even much noise, and the size of the blast can be electronically limited and controlled to a great extent. Both weapons are in short supply, but they represent a way to respond to greater threats without resorting to full-yield nuclear weapons."

The Vice President shook her head. "I'm not sure I like where this discussion is going, Mr. President," she said. "We're planning on deploying nuclear weapons again? And these Buck Rogers weapons sound like political suicide—the spies and saboteurs will be fighting with the protesters for access to the labs and bases where we keep these things. Isn't there any other alternative?"

"Yes, there is. It's called peace," the President said. "As long as everyone involved agrees to stay calm and not overreact to a situation, we might be able to get through this without having to resort to special weapons. I hope—we all hope—for this best resolution. But we need to plan for the worst." He looked at Freeman and nodded. "Let's get Defense and the boys from Dreamland in here, Philip. We need to get something set up right away, before somebody goes and does something stupid."

MASTER CONTROL AND REPORTING CENTER,
OSAN, UNITED REPUBLIC OF KOREA
(FORMERLY SOUTH KOREA)
THAT SAME TIME

The very first indication of danger was a tiny yellow flashing light that could have been missed in the huge array of other lights and indicators on the panel. But the controllers on duty—all Korean now, with no Americans at all—were attentive, and one of them noticed the indicator immediately, as if expecting it.

One press of a button, and the computer display at the controller's station changed to a pictorial depiction of the detection, plus radar data on the new track. It took only seconds for the controller to study the data and determine what it was. He hit a yellow ATTENTION button, which flashed a warning at all controllers' stations and connected his mike to them. "All stations, all stations, sector seven reports many inbound radar tracks, southbound courses, altitude and speed increasing. Verification protocols in progress, all stations stand by."

The next step took only seconds as well; a second radar array was tasked to cross-check the first radar's information. Once the two systems verified each other's information, identification was positive. The controller hit a red WARNING button, which illuminated red flashing lights throughout the entire complex and put the controller's microphone on Hot Call, which overrode all other communications in the MCRC. "All stations, all stations, missile warning, missile warning in sector seven. Multiple inbound tracks verified and confirmed. All stations, go to threat condition red." At the same moment, his track data was displayed up on one of the electronic screens in the front of the command center so the other controllers and on-duty commanders could study it.

"Projected targets?" asked the commander, UROK Air Force Chief of Staff Lieutenant General Park Yom. He had been on duty at the Osan MCRC ever since the visit by the American Vice President, when the attacks on North Korea and the transition to reunification began. He had not seen the light of day since that fateful morning. But he didn't care. The citizens were celebrating above, but Korea was still in danger.

"One . . . no, two tracks on Seoul," the controller said. "Possibly one of those targeting Inchon. One track on Kunsan, one on Pusan. One track . . . sir, one track heading out over the Sea of Japan, target Japan."

"Payback for Japan's assistance in the revolution, no doubt," General Park said. "Do we have an origin yet? Do we know where these missiles came from?"

"Very confusing tracks, sir," the controller responded. "The track aimed at Seoul is a very low-altitude ballistic profile. Same for the one aimed at Inchon."

"Are you saying that they came from somewhere on the Korean peninsula?"

"Affirmative, sir. We are processing a possible launch point now."

"It should have been computed by now. Get on it." The secure phone rang at Park's station. "General Park."

"This is the president, General," Kwon Ki-chae said. "What is happening? The air raid sirens have gone off." Air raid and poison gas sirens were as much a part of life in Korea as *kimchee* and *hanbok*.

"Have you taken cover, sir?"

"Yes. I'm crowded into the subway terminal at Seoul National University, along with about five thousand others," Kwon replied. "I may die of asphyxiation or be trampled before I die of an attack. What is happening?"

"We show two inbound on the capital," Park said. "Kunsan and Pusan are also targeted. In addition, one missile is headed for Japan."

"Oh, no," Kwon said. He was silent for a moment, then said, "It appears they are still aiming for military targets, does it not?"

"Yes, sir. Except for Pusan."

"Where did the missiles come from? I want the origins bombarded immediately."

"The origin of at least some of the missiles appear to be inside the peninsula," Park said. "We suspect Communist mobile missiles. Stand by . . . Sir, we have indications of successful intercepts over Seoul . . . Sir, we have reports of one Vx toxin warhead impact on the outskirts of Kunsan."

"Any casualty reports?"

"No, sir," Park replied. "Not yet. But the industrial facilities would most likely be on the graveyard shift. Perhaps a few thousand casualties, maybe less if the population made it to shelters in time. And as you know, most of our population—North and South—is well trained in the use of gas masks and chemical exposure suits. However, there were a great many refugees being housed at the military facilities there, and we do not know whether they were similarly equipped."

"Where are those missiles coming from, dammit?"

"We have points of origin on the missile aimed at Japan, sir," Park said, reading from one of his computer monitors. "The launch point is in southern Yanggang Do province, near Toandonggu. Since it is probably a rail-mobile missile, we will concentrate our search along the rail lines."

"No chance that missile came from China?"

"Unlikely, sir. Same for the others. Their trajectory

is too low for such short range . . . One moment, sir . . . Sir, we are receiving reports of a chemical weapons detonation three kilometers northeast of Tonghae. Estimate a Vx nerve gas attack."

"*Poison gas?*" Kwon gasped. "It cannot be! Against *Pusan?* Where are the winds blowing?"

"From the north, sir . . . Sir, the release may have hit well east of the Kyejwan Mountains," Park went on, trying not to distract himself with the enormity of the death and destruction in one of his country's most beautiful cities. "The mountains may have protected Pusan from serious damage." Most of Pusan was located inside a mountainous bowl—the name "Pusan" means "cauldron"—and it was possible that the mountains, some rising as high as three thousand feet, might have diverted the deadly nerve toxins. But if they blew in and settled past the mountains, they would be trapped inside the bowl and their effects would linger.

"Casualty estimates there?" But the president already knew the answer. Pusan had a population of about four million; the Tonghae district, about a quarter of a million.

Kwon Ki-chae felt the fury rise in his throat. It was very probably a miss, but targeting Pusan was an attack not against Korea's military or government, but against its economic center. Pusan was an international port city, like San Francisco or Rio de Janeiro, situated on a natural and beautiful harbor. Preferred as an international port of call rather than a military port complex, it never had much of a military presence—it was never occupied by the Communists during the war, like Seoul. It was Korea's largest port and second largest city, with a vibrant international trade, over twenty foreign consulates, mild weather, and friendly, hardworking citizens. Its population was packed in between the sea and the mountains, a relatively small area, which made a nerve agent attack that much more deadly. As much as attacking the capital itself, targeting Pusan was a bloodthirsty blow against the people and an attempt to chop off Korea's economic lifelines to the rest of the world.

"This is General Kim," Defense Minister Kim Kunmo said, cutting into the conversation. "I am sorry, sir, but I asked to be patched in by the communications center. Are you safe, sir? Have you taken shelter?"

"I'm fine for now, General," Kwon said. They heard his voice and the background noise change, as if he was maneuvering through a crowded room to a more private place—no doubt his secret service agents were clearing a path for him. "General, do you realize we have almost used up all of our Patriot missiles? We still have Hawks to protect against aircraft, but we are defenseless against any more ballistic missiles. We need to find those rebels. We need to locate all the missing ballistic missiles before the capital is in ashes!"

"Sir, we cannot say for certain whether the missiles were launched from inside our country or whether they were launched by Communist rebels," Kim said. "To me, it appears more likely this is the work of the Chinese. They could have brought mobile ballistic missiles into our country to launch from our own soil, just to confuse us. The threat is from China, sir, not from some ghostly rebels. We should retaliate at once against the Chinese forces arrayed against us."

"Excuse me, General; I was told the evidence suggests that the missiles did not come from China."

"Are we positive of this, sir?" Kim asked excitedly. "Are you sure those were not Chinese rockets? How can you explain a launch against *Japan*? Had you ever heard about the Communists targeting Japan?"

"No," Kwon admitted. The North did once launch one of its early Nodong-1 rockets over Japan, but there had never been any evidence that the Communists ever seriously considered Japan a threat.

"Sir, I suggest we launch an attack that will deter the Chinese from attempting any more missile attacks on Korea: draw a line back along those missiles' flight path into China. Pick a military base or airfield, preferably one where we know missiles or attack aircraft are based. Then attack it with several of the captured Communist missiles with conventional warheads."

"General, this sounds extraordinarily dangerous," Kwon said. "If China should retaliate, the capital could be destroyed within minutes. Chinese troops could easily swarm across the border and occupy the northern half of the peninsula before we could respond."

"Sir, elements of the Eleventh Corps have been deployed to Changbai, just north of the border near Hyesan," Kim said, referring to a map placed before him by his aides. "Approximately thirty thousand troops along a forty-mile front, tank-heavy. Reinforced with air assets from their parent corps at Linjiang, but generally fairly isolated. If they moved south, however, they would be expected to cut off half of Yanggang Do province and all of Hamgyong Pukdo province with ease. The Chinese built a nuclear reactor southwest of Hyesan, and it has long been suspected of being a possible weapons-grade material breeder. This unit lies roughly along the reverse flight path of the rocket aimed at Japan."

"So? What would be the deterrent factor in such an attack, General?" Kwon asked. "Will killing several thousand Chinese troops make our borders any safer? Do you think that China will not be sending in more reinforcements, every one of them howling mad at us for killing their brothers?"

"Sir, the concept of deterrence says you must demonstrate the willingness to use war to achieve your objectives," General Kim said. "Having weapons of mass destruction is not enough—we must demonstrate our willingness to use them. This is our opportunity."

"But against China? If they invaded our territory, perhaps . . ."

"We are not certain they did *not* do this!" Kim argued. "It is more likely than not they did launch this attack, as a probe to test our resolve if nothing else. But even aside from that, China is indeed massing troops on our northern border. That is a certainty. These events may be tied together, or they may not. But one thing is certain: we must act. We have a legitimate target. We should *act*, Mr. President!"

There was a long pause; then: "How do you suggest we respond, Kun-mo?"

"A chemical weapons barrage, sir," Kim replied immediately. "It should be large enough to do great damage, but not enough to trigger a drastic retaliation or risk spreading to Korean territory. No nuclear weapons, unless the Chinese retaliate—we should not show our entire hand right away."

"General Kim," Kwon gasped, "did I hear you say you are recommending a *chemical weapons attack* . . . against *China*?"

"Sir, they have launched a chemical attack on us— we must respond with equal force," Kim argued. "Besides, they have almost fifty thousand troops poised to attack us right now. There are no other weapons we can use short of nuclear weapons to stop them."

"Kim, listen to yourself!" Kwon shouted. "You are recommending *mass murder*! I will never agree to this unless our country is faced with imminent annihilation! Never! Now, give me another recommendation, and do it quickly!"

Kim Kun-mo shook his head in exasperation. "The chances of success are far worse, sir, unless we—"

"General, give me another recommendation *now*, or turn in your resignation!"

Kim swore under his breath, thought for a moment, then said, "Some of our short- and medium-range missiles are armed with fuel-air explosives, designed to clear minefields with overpressure—it creates a devastating punch in a relatively small area. I suggest we use weapons such as these, augmented with high-explosive or cluster munitions."

There was silence at the other end of the phone.

"Sir, we can call an emergency meeting of the cabinet," Kim suggested. "We can do it over the phone, or we can have you transported to the capital. We can wait—"

"We are talking about killing thousands of Chinese troops, General!" Kwon snapped. "Don't you think this requires a little consideration?"

"Sir, killing a few thousand Chinese troops is nowhere near an adequate punishment for the potential deaths of *four million* citizens of Pusan," Kim said.

There was more silence. In the background, Kim could feel the terror permeating the subway station and wondered what it would be like to die by chemical or biological weapons poisoning. Dead was dead, true, but would it not truly be more humane to die quickly, by a nuclear or fuel-air explosive burst, than die slowly, painfully, from the very air you breathe?

"Yes, I want the attack to proceed, on my direct orders," President Kwon Ki-chae said resolutely. "I take full responsibility for the consequences. The attack will commence against the Chinese forces you outlined immediately."

The attack was swift, concentrated, and deadly. A salvo of thirty Scud-A short-range rockets was fired from

Kangwon Do province south of the burned-out area of Wonsan, and Hwanghae Pukdo province near Songnim, south of Pyongyang. Each Scud-A rocket carried a small nonnuclear warhead weighing a little over one thousand pounds—but the warhead was one of the most devastating nonnuclear devices in the world.

Called a fuel-air explosive, the weapon was simply three bomblets filled with high-energy rocket fuel with an explosive detonator. As the warheads descended toward their targets, the bomblets were ejected one by one and descended via a small stabilizing parachute. An electronic fuse cracked them open, allowing the fuel to mix with air and disperse into a fine mist, and then the cloud was ignited by a small explosive charge. The resulting explosion was hundreds of times more powerful than its equivalent size in TNT, creating a fireball, a shock wave, and a mushroom cloud similar to a small nuclear detonation.

Anything aboveground within one hundred feet of the explosion was instantly incinerated; any unprotected human within one hundred and fifty feet was killed or suffered massive burns. The explosions devastated the Chinese forces garrisoned or bivouacked in the Changbai area, and fires broke out in the town itself, sending thousands of civilians fleeing their homes.

Of the more than thirty thousand troops in the area, nearly five thousand lost their lives instantly; another eight thousand suffered massive burns and other injuries. Death would come mercifully only to some of them; for many others, the agony would continue on for weeks, even months. Doctors would soon become mercy killers.

As had been the procedure since the end of the Korean War, either the president, the new vice president, or the prime minister had to man an underground command center during military alerts or times of crisis. Korean Vice President Pak Chung-chu, the former first vice president of North Korea, was in the Osan military command center with Minister of Defense Kim. Pak was watching in fascination and shock as the attack against the Chinese infantry commenced.

"When . . . when will we know how many casualties there are?" Pak asked.

"In Pusan? In Tonghae?"

"Linjiang, the Chinese troops along the border. The ones you are firebombing."

"You care more about the Chinese invaders than you do our own people, Mr. Vice President?" Kim asked derisively. "What is this infection of cowardice spreading through Government House these days? What is going on with you politicians? You all want to roll over and play dead."

"Don't be an ignorant pig-fucker, General," Pak retorted. "I want to see Korea protected from invasion as much as you!"

"Then why don't some of you damned politicians ever show it?"

"If this politician recalls correctly, you *are* a damned politician," Pak pointed out.

"In name only, Mr. Vice President—in name only." Kim looked at Pak for a moment, then nodded as if recognizing something in the vice president's face. "You were a military man yourself, if I remember correctly—Navy, right?"

"Correct," Pak said. "Moved from commanding a bilge in a little coastal patrol vessel to commanding the Yellow Sea fleet."

"Sent a few Communist commandos into the South, I'll bet."

"Seventeen sorties in two years. Lost only one

minisub and nine men. The Korean People's Army was much better then—and your forces were much worse. What is this all about, General?"

"Then you know what I'm talking about, sir," Kim said. "You know better than all of us that we cannot appear weak to the Communists, or they'll crush us. We have to say what we mean and act on it. Do you agree?"

"I have always said we should negotiate from a position of strength, yes," Pak said. "You have something on your mind, General? Spit it out."

"Do you think we should be tougher on China? Do you think we should be content with firing a few gasoline bombs into their encampments . . ."

"Fuel-air explosives are not exactly gasoline bombs, and you know it," Pak pointed out.

". . . or should we be targeting their air bases, their rear-echelon maintenance and logistics bases, and especially their command and control facilities, with special weapons? That's exactly what they tried to strike in Korea—and then added Pusan for good measure!"

"We still have not proved it was the Chinese who launched those attacks," Pak pointed out. "I agree that targeting the infantry at Linjiang is a good idea and a good preemptive strike, but don't try to paint this as a retaliatory strike. The Chinese probably didn't attack Pusan, and you know it."

"But China is the adversary! They need to fear us as they fear Russia and the United States. And the only way to force that is to strike at them with weapons of mass destruction. Don't you agree?"

"I agree that if we promise to use weapons of mass destruction if we are invaded, then yes, we should use them," Vice President Pak said. "The deterrence factor doesn't work if you don't deliver what you promise or threaten. And if China indeed attacked Pusan and the other cities, then yes, we should retaliate similarly. But President Kwon was correct not to use special weapons now! Why on earth did you push to launch a chemical weapons attack before we have all the facts?"

"Because acting timidly never works," Kim said. "If we are attacked, we retaliate, swiftly and powerfully. We need to be able to do that. But with Kwon, we may never be able to do it. The one problem we military leaders face is that all too often, war is left to the politicians, to men like Kwon Ki-chae."

"President Kwon is a great man, a great leader!"

"But he tempers his military decisions with political calculations that have nothing to do with the strategic or tactical realities," Kim said quickly. "A perfect example is the employment of our special weapons. With one-half of the necessary execution codes in Kwon's hands, we are all but assured that we will never get to use them. That is a monumental tragedy for our country, is it not?"

"I get it. I understand now," Pak said. "You want the codes. If the president balks at giving you authority to launch the next time, you want to be able to do it anyway. Correct?"

"If I did truly believe that Kwon would launch a nuclear attack against China if the time came, I would never suggest such a thing," Kim said. "But I cannot say that. I truly believe Kwon would hesitate—in fact, I think he has absolutely no intention of ever firing or even testing a special weapon. He would call an emergency cabinet or National Security Council meeting, perhaps even put it before the leadership in the legislature—but in the end, he would never do it."

"But you think I would."

"I know you would," Kim said resolutely. "Look what you have sacrificed to be standing here now. You would not want to see the Chinese march through

Pyongyang or Seoul again, as I'm sure you have seen once before. I don't think the Chinese would deal with you very gently."

"How perceptive of you," Pak said with an exasperated grumble. But he knew it was so. Pak Chung-chu had been a trusted member of the Communist Party in both North Korea and China. He had burned a major bridge behind him when he burned that party identification booklet. It was a formidable act not just of defiance, but of treason to the state—the Chinese would never let him live to forget it. "So. What is it you want to do? Assassinate him?"

"Don't be an idiot," Kim said—but Pak could see his eyes burning with excitement, and he thought, Yes, that's exactly what you want me to do. "But you can get the codes from him. You have joint custody of the codes."

"I only have them if the president is incapacitated, out of the country, out of communication with the command center, or voluntarily chooses to turn responsibility over to me for whatever reason," Pak said. "I do not 'jointly' control them.

"Nonetheless, you want me to march into Kwon's office someday—perhaps someday *soon*—and get the codes from him using whatever means or justification I care to invent or use. Correct?"

"You act so damn self-righteous about this," Kim said irritably. "I am not talking about treason—I'm talking about defending our country, our *homeland*. You certainly understand that."

"And because I betrayed President Kim Jong-il, I am somehow predisposed or more willing to do it again to President Kwon Ki-chae, is that it?"

"Dammit, you are impossible!" Kim exploded. "You know what I'm saying!"

"I want you to say it, General Kim," Pak snapped.

"Make no mistake—we *are* talking treason. We are talking about a violent, illegal overthrow of the legally elected government. We deserve to die at the hands of the people for what we are talking about doing.

"But it so happens, General, that I agree with you. Kwon will never use the weapons we possess. We would then all be overrun and crushed by China, and persons like myself, former citizens of North Korea and especially former Communist Party members, would surely die.

"What I want from you, General, is your word. If it is done, if we betray Kwon, take the codes, retaliate against whatever enemy we face, and somehow survive, I want your word that you will do everything in your power to support me as president of United Korea. I will in turn support you as vice president."

"I'll do better than that," Kim said. He pulled out a sheet of paper from his desk drawer and wrote and signed a message on it. "It's in writing now, Mr. Vice President. Will you do the same for me?"

"Don't you trust me—comrade?" Pak asked sardonically. Kim blanched, then turned angry again. Pak retrieved a piece of paper, wrote a similar message, then signed it with a flourish. "Now we're both condemned to hell, General," he said. "Care to join me in a drink to celebrate?"

THE WHITE HOUSE, WASHINGTON, D.C.
SEVERAL MINUTES LATER

Kevin Martindale was talking with Ellen Whiting when the telephone on his desk rang. Chief of Staff Jerrod Hale went over, looked at the flashing button, then froze. "You better take it, sir," Hale said. "It's Cheyenne Mountain."

"Oh, shit," the President muttered as he dashed over to his desk. "Jerrod, make an announcement, let's get a nose count going, alert the Secret Service that choppers may be inbound—you know the drill." Staff members of the White House and Old Executive Office Building had become well practiced lately in the art of rapid emergency evacuations.

The President picked up the phone, motioning for Philip Freeman to listen in on an extension in his study. He did not need to push a button—it was the most important button on the phone and would select itself. "This is the President. Go ahead."

"Sir, this is Lieutenant Colonel Gordon, senior controller, Space Command Missile Tracking Center. DSP 9 missile-warning satellite has detected several ballistic missile launches originating inside North Kor . . . er, sorry, inside the northern part of United Korea. I am secure."

"Damn it to hell," the President swore. "Korea is attacking China?"

"Negative, sir," the controller said. "The tracks are headed *south*. It appears the launches originated inside Korea and are targeted against the southern half of the peninsula. Fourth Space Surveillance Squadron radars indicate nine tracks total targeted within Korea and three tracks targeted against southern and central Japan." The Air Force Space Command's Fourth Space Surveillance Squadron's radars and tracking sites in Korea were now all manned by Korean technicians. Very few American servicemen still remained in Korea.

"Who the hell is launching those missiles?" the President demanded.

"Unknown, sir," the controller responded.

"Any reaction from China or Russia?"

"None, sir."

"Very well. Please alert me if any more launches occur." He hung up the phone. "Philip?" he called. "Explanation?"

"It's got to be some rogue ex–North Korean missile units," Freeman suggested, coming back into the Oval Office. "Most of North Korea's operational ballistic missiles were mobile. The big ones, the Nodong series, were rail-mobile; the smaller Scud series were all-terrain road-mobile. Apparently, some were able to escape the revolution and transition, find a presurveyed launch point, and fire in a coordinated attack. Mobile missiles are the hardest to find and relatively easy to disguise."

"Get President Kwon back on the phone right away and tell him I want to speak with him at once," Kevin Martindale said. "I don't want him retaliating against the Chinese."

About to call the White House Communications Center, Hale took another incoming call.

"What was that, Jerrod?"

"It's too late," Jerrod Hale said, his anger palpable. "Space Command says the Koreans fired back."

"Damn them all to *hell*!" Martindale shouted. "Where? How many? What kind?"

"Unknown at this time, sir," Hale replied. "I'll get details right away."

"Shit. And we're as helpless as we can be," the President said. "Jerrod, make sure Space Command notifies the Japanese government. I want to talk with the Russians, Chinese, Koreans, and Japanese ASAP. Everyone has got to back off, or Asia is going to blow up in one big red fireball."

Another call came in: "Reports coming in, sir: Chemical weapons attacks against Kunsan and Pusan. Vx nerve agents. Very high casualties. And State's also issued an emergency report, saying that a thermonuclear warhead exploded at high altitude a hundred miles north of Osaka, Japan," he said. "Japanese Self-Defense Force authorities claim the warhead was large, over three hundred kilotons. An evacuation of the entire area is under way."

"My God," the President said. "What about the Korean retaliation? What about the Chinese?"

"Stand by, sir, we're checking . . ." It took several minutes for further reports to come in. "Looks like Korea launched a small retaliatory strike against some Chinese armored and rocket divisions stationed along the China-Korea border," Freeman finally reported. "Short-range ballistic missiles only, a salvo of about twenty rockets, probably Scud- or FROG-7-series rockets—high-explosive, very high-powered, perhaps incendiary devices. No reports of . . . stand by . . . Now receiving reports of mushroom clouds . . ."

"*Mushroom clouds!* You mean the Koreans attacked China *with nuclear weapons*?"

"I'll get clarification of this, sir. Usually, we get more reliable reports than this of nuclear detonations. We also sometimes experience blackouts of nonhardened communications facilities. We got none of that this time."

"What could that mean?" the Vice President asked. "Did they try to hit the Chinese with nuclear weapons, and they didn't go off?"

"Or they weren't *supposed* to go off," Freeman suggested. "It could be a dangerous game of brinkmanship—threaten China with a nuclear retaliation without producing a nuclear yield."

"But why China?" the President asked. "Did China launch those missiles against Korea? The guy at Space Command I just talked to said the missiles came from inside Korea."

"The Korean military could have made a mis-

take . . . or Kwon did it deliberately," Freeman offered. "We know China had massed several thousand
troops along the border, and there were intelligence reports saying that Chinese air forces were conducting
more cross-border flights, perhaps probing Korea's air
defenses."

"So you think it's possible that Kwon was sending
China a message—stay away or else?" the Vice President asked, astonished. "How suicidal can you get?"

"Suicidal, yes—but he succeeded in getting *my* attention, all right," the President said. "I don't see Kwon's
hand in this—this smells like Defense Minister Kim's
handiwork. If we had to set up an antiballistic missile
system over the Korean peninsula, it looks as though
we'd not only have to try to protect Korea from China,
but protect *China* from *Korea*. There will be no winners
in this game."

He turned to Freeman and motioned to the thick
document they had been discussing earlier. "Green-
light this project, Philip. What is he calling it?"

"General McLanahan calls it Operation Battle Born,
sir," Freeman replied. "That's the Nevada state motto, I
believe."

"I saw something in the daily report from Chastain's
office about a Nevada bomber unit, Air National
Guard, I believe, being decertified following some
crazy-ass stunts they pulled during an evaluation," the
President remarked. "This plan wouldn't happen to
have anything to do with them, would it?"

"I think General McLanahan was conducting an
evaluation at that very same unit to determine the suitability of their bomber unit to accomplish his operation," Freeman said. "Given the nature of it, I think the
general was looking for a very aggressive, rather unconventional fighting force to implement this plan."

"In other words, he was looking for a bunch of military barnstormers—and he found them," the President said with a smile. "Shades of Brad Elliott, all right. I just hope there's an Asia left to implement the plan."

"Unfortunately, that aspect of General McLanahan's project may not be implemented," Freeman said. "The Air National Guard unit has been decertified and disbanded."

"Can he do the job with a single bomber?"

"I think so, sir," Freeman responded uneasily. "We still have a constellation of those small reconnaissance satellites—the ones we know as NIRTSats. At the very least, we can still evaluate the plan with one bomber, add a second when it comes on-line, and then perhaps add a frontline unit or another Guard bomber unit later, if things heat up. Admiral Balboa hasn't signed onto the plan, but he has suggested some alternate strike units from the Navy's weapons and aircraft research labs at Patuxent River and China Lake that can assist if it gets too much for HAWC. But HAWC is ready to go now, so I think it's a good idea to get the plan under way and the forces set up as soon as possible."

"Then let's do it," the President said. "Let's make it happen, and hope to hell it's not too little, too late."

MINISTRY OF DEFENSE,
PEOPLE'S LIBERATION ARMY,
BEIJING, PEOPLE'S REPUBLIC OF CHINA
THE NEXT MORNING

The photographs were the most terrible thing Chi Haotian, minister of defense of the People's Republic of China, had ever seen in his life. Even though they were taken from a helicopter more than a hundred meters above ground, the human carnage was clearly visible and dreadful.

"What was the casualty count again?" Chi asked his aide. The aide looked at the final report and murmured a number. "Speak up, damn you."

"Four thousand eight hundred thirty-one dead, sir," the aide replied. "Eight thousand forty-four wounded, two hundred missing."

"And every death should be avenged threefold, sir!" Chief of Staff of the People's Liberation Army General Chin Zi-hong said angrily. "It was a dastardly sneak attack, the most heinous I have ever witnessed in my life!"

"Our president has stated to the world that he will never use weapons of mass destruction again unless we ourselves are attacked with such weapons," Minister Chi said. "We will no doubt be world outcasts for an entire generation for what we did to Taiwan and the United States, and we have no wish to extend that one day longer."

"So we become the world's whipping boy now?" Chin shouted. "Do we now roll over and play dead and watch as country after country around us arms itself with weapons of mass destruction and uses them against us without provocation?"

"Calm yourself, comrade Chin," Chi said. "All I am saying is that the president has warned us not to present a plan to him or the Politburo involving first use of special weapons—nuclear, chemical, or biological—unless we are attacked first. I expect you to have contingency plans available in case we are so attacked by the United States, Taiwan, Japan, or Korea. But in response to this unholy atrocity, the president will not accept a plan that uses nuclear weapons. Now speak: tell me what our response to this tragedy should be."

General Chin took a deep breath and thought for a

moment; then: "Our major concern, sir, is the Koreans' nuclear, chemical, and biological weapons," he said. Chi nodded, urging him to continue. "We know where the major bases are located in North Korea, and we can predict with great certainty where most are located in the South—only a few bases, mostly ex-American bases, have the apparatus to handle them."

"Full invasion of the South will not meet with approval, comrade General," Chi said. "Although the president and the Politburo support President Kim Jong-il, they will not authorize an invasion of the South below the thirty-eighth parallel. Such an action will certainly create additional world condemnation and action by the United States."

General Chin shook his head in exasperation. Chi glowered at him. "You need to understand, comrade, that the world is enchanted by a united Korea. That is a very, very powerful force. Our country is trying to regain its rightful place as a world power. As much as we may believe that the fall of Communist North Korea is a disaster to the people and our way of life, we must accept it because the world embraces it. Half the world even believes that the rocket attack against our troops on the border was justifiable; the other half believes it was wrong but nonetheless understandable and excusable. Simple retaliation will not be effective.

"No. We need a plan to strike at the heart of what is *wrong* about United Korea. Tell me: what is wrong with United Korea?"

"Its nuclear weapons, of course."

"Of course," Minister Chi said. "The world loves United Korea because they won their reunification, but they hate them for not giving up the captured nuclear weapons. We can therefore take away Korea's nuclear weapons and not suffer world condemnation, yes?" A nod of heads around the conference table. "We have already determined that we cannot hope to take all of the weapons, but what is it we can easily take?"

"Kanggye," General Chin said.

"Not just Kanggye," Chi said with a pleased smile. "Ten years ago, perhaps, before we put the North Korean missile development program into full worldwide production. But today? You are now permitted to think bigger."

"The entire province?" Chin asked excitedly. "Do you think the president will approve an operation to take Chagang Do province in its *entirety*?"

Chi Haotian smiled. Kanggye Research Center was one of the former North Korea's most sensitive weapons research centers. Only twenty miles south of the Chinese border, it was originally the site of a Russian-built nuclear reactor, similar to the doomed Chernobyl reactor in Ukraine, constructed shortly after the end of the Korean War. The plant produced some power for North Korea and Manchuria, but its primary purpose was as a uranium-processing plant. The plant had been built in North Korea so Manchuria could take advantage of Soviet nuclear knowledge while the dangerous reactor itself was in North Korea. When the China-USSR split occurred, the facility was taken over by Chinese engineers, with cooperation from Iranian and Pakistani weapons scientists.

Soon, most of Chagang Do province was converted to weapons research, development, testing, and construction. Chagang Do was the second largest province in the old North Korea and the most sparsely populated. Like the state of Nevada in the United States or Xinjiang province in China, the land was large and inhospitable enough and the population small enough so as to escape attention or scrutiny. Over twenty research centers, test sites, manufacturing plants, and dump sites made Chagang Do province almost totally uninhabitable and unusable except by the military—and a prime target for any power wishing to capture valuable nuclear, chemical, and biological weapons data.

Kanggye became one of Asia's top weapons-grade plutonium-producing facilities. The plant was expanded to eventually include building nuclear weapons, from the massive three-megaton WX120 to the artillery-shell-sized ten-kiloton W18. Dozens of weapons had been built at Kanggye and exported all over the world. Brazil, South Africa, Indonesia, and Pakistan all had weapons or components bought from Kanggye's laboratories.

"Of course," Minister Chi said. "Not just the research facility, but we take the production facilities, all the laboratories, the processing centers, the test facilities, and the launch pads, and we capture and hold whatever bases the capitalists still occupy. We will have to secure these areas, of course, so the capitalists do not use them again to build more weapons of mass destruction—that means troops, at least three brigades, I'd imagine, for a province that size and with that terrain. We will need to strengthen the air support, set up air defense and surveillance sites, to supply all of our peacekeepers.

"Then, if Chagang Do province naturally becomes the center for anticapitalist groups forming in Korea—well, I would think that is part of the trials of any government," Chi said, smiling. "After all, the proliferation of opposition groups, some armed, was bound to happen in a societal, governmental, and ideological transition that occurred so quickly and so underhandedly. Who knows? Perhaps a group strong enough and well armed enough will emerge from the wastelands of Chagang Do. Perhaps it will be President Kim Jong-il, perhaps someone with a little more backbone."

The minister of defense looked around the conference table, his eyes deadly cold. "That is the plan I want, comrades. I want it on my desk before the midday meal, ready to present to the president and the Politburo. And I want you all to remember that thousands of our comrades have died at the hands of the capitalists, and we will do everything in our power to stop this cancerous growth on our frontier before any more of our comrades-in-arms perish."

SOUTHERN CHAGANG DO PROVINCE,
UNITED REPUBLIC OF KOREA
(FORMERLY NORTH KOREA)
TWO NIGHTS LATER

The lone soldier advanced quickly but carefully down the railroad tracks. The weather was the worst in days, with a freezing, driving rain and fifty-mile-per-hour winds. The weather made movement almost impossible, but it also provided excellent cover—because he knew the South Koreans were still looking for him.

It was actually only a matter of time before he was discovered, since there was only so much track in all of North Korea. The question was: could they launch their missile and then make it into northern Chagang Do province, at least another eighty kilometers, before being discovered by the capitalists? It was a race he could not afford to lose.

Kong Hwan-li, who still proudly considered himself a captain of artillery forces of the People's Army of North Korea, stopped to hide and rest. He then scanned the railway ahead of him with his infrared nightscope, a combination of a high-intensity infrared searchlight and a monocular night-vision scope. It was difficult to do in this weather—he could see reliably only a few dozen meters ahead in the rain—so he scanned as best he could, moved a short way forward to a new hiding place, and scanned again.

The pride of accomplishment he felt had long since washed away in this cold, driving rain. Two nights earlier he had accomplished an important objective: he and several other Scud and Nodong units had launched an attack on South Korea. Kong had to launch from an unsurveyed site, which meant the accuracy was probably poor, but the launch itself went well and he had managed to escape before being detected by capitalist patrols.

Now, after two hellish nights on the move, he was ready to strike again.

He could see the situation didn't look promising long before he reached his objective, but he had to check it out anyway. It was a rail siding about fifteen kilometers southeast of the town of Holch'on. The siding, disguised with maintenance inspection towers and even an old-style coal and water tower for aged steam engines, was a presurveyed missile launch point for the rail-mobile North Korean missiles. The presurveyed points made launching a ballistic missile fast and easy. Instead of having to mensurate geographical coordinates, elevation, and determine where true north was, all the launch officer had to do was pull onto the siding and punch in the launch point number—the computers would do the rest. The launch point coordinates and elevation had been measured down to the nearest meter, ensuring the best missile accuracy. The siding had thick concrete walls surrounding it to provide some security and protection.

The South Koreans obviously knew this too, because the siding had been destroyed. Demolition charges had been set under the tracks leading into it, and more charges had been set on one of the concrete walls, toppling it onto the tracks. The main rails were still open—after all, Kong thought, the capitalists still needed them to carry out their invasion—but the presurveyed launch point was useless. He had found this to be so throughout his dangerous trek north toward the safety of China—this was why his first launch had been from an unsurveyed point, guaranteeing a much-degraded launch circular error—but finding this one was doubly disappointing.

But the second missile was on the erector-launcher, fully functional and ready to go. This one had a 350-kiloton nuclear warhead, targeted for Osan. Fused for a groundburst, it would easily dig out the still-functioning Osan Master Control and Reporting Center, the heart of South Korea's military. He had a third missile as well, fully functional and ready to load and fire. His plan was to try and deliver his third missile intact to Kanggye, hopefully under a Chinese military umbrella, and use it as the basis for reconstituting the Army of Free Korea in Chagang Do province and fighting the invaders from the South.

Kong still refused to call the abomination created by the capitalists the United Republic of Korea. As far as he was concerned, it was still South Korea. And it was not a popular people's revolution that had brought down the Communist government in Pyongyang. The capitalists had perpetrated some kind of elaborate mind control process that made most of the people, including the military, go crazy and turn against their leaders. How else could anyone explain the pockets of resistance still in the North? How else could anyone explain the government-in-exile in Beijing? Thank the stars the Glorious Leader, Kim Jong-il, and most of the Politburo had managed to get out and organize the resistance.

Kong made his way back through the driving rain to

the Nodong missile unit and joined his partner, Lieutenant Kim Yong-ku. Kim had commanded another missile unit, but all of his men had deserted shortly after firing their last missile, so Kim joined up with Kong—which was fortunate, because Kong's crew had also deserted soon after firing the first missile. Being on the run for so long was more than they could take, and it grew harder and harder to forage for food or find sympathetic civilians who might help them. The brainwashing of North Korea, Kong thought, was almost complete. Put a little food in their bellies and blast them with propaganda and some people will believe almost anything.

Most of the Nodong-1 missile unit was under a maintenance enclosure, but they had still taken the time to put together some simple camouflage. The loaded erector-launcher was covered by corrugated tin and timber as if part of the shelter had collapsed on it, and they piled debris around the engine to make it appear immobilized. Kong met up with Kim in the command car. With the engine shut down to conserve fuel and avoid detection, the command car, with its own self-contained jet power unit, was the most comfortable place on the whole unit. If faced with capture, Kim could also quickly and easily disable the missile from there.

"Any luck, sir?" Kim asked after double-checking Kong's identity with their own invented tap-code and letting his commander into the cab.

"Yes—but all of it bad," Kong admitted with a wry smile. "The launch point has been destroyed. Completely unusable." He wiped rain from his poncho. "Any contact from our other units?"

"Unit Twenty reports ready—that was the only contact, sir. There were propaganda broadcasts on the strategic message net, urging us to surrender. They addressed us by name."

"By name?"

"By name, rank, and unit number," Kim said. "They even knew that you had promoted me to lieutenant."

"Bastards!" Kong shouted. "Cowardly spineless traitors!" It was obvious that some of those who had deserted them had reported extensively to the capitalist intelligence officers. This was the worst form of human refuse—not just a coward and a traitor, but an informant too. "Did they say anything indicating they know where we are or where we're heading?"

"No, sir," Kim replied. "It appears your plan not to reveal any other unit's firing positions has paid off well." He looked proud of Kong, but very worried. "What do you want to do now, sir?" he asked.

"We are going to launch as scheduled, Lieutenant," Kong said resolutely. "My first impulse is to remain here, mensurate coordinates using the GPS, and launch. We have a good hiding place here, and the missile is ready. But this may be our last opportunity to strike hard at the capitalists. Our assigned target is an underground command complex, and we need a direct hit to disable it—missing by even a kilometer may be unacceptable." Kong started doing ballistic calculations in his head: "Our missile flight distance is over seven hundred kilometers. This means if our gyro heading is off just one degree, every meter our launch coordinates are off means our missile will miss by seventy meters, even if the missile gyros run perfectly. That's too many variables. It is unacceptable inaccuracy.

"Our most accurate shot will be if we march to the spot right beside the launch point. We can hand-measure the distance to update the launch coordinates, and we can use the same heading for gyro alignment and it will be almost perfect." He paused for a moment, then added, "We are three hours to the scheduled coordinated launch time. I think we can start up the engine, march to the siding, elevate, align, and launch our missile right on time.

"If we stay here, it is doubtful we can cross-check the GPS geographical coordinates with any landmarks in time. That means we launch on handheld GPS coordinates alone, and those could be off by five hundred meters. We'd be safer here and we could do a successful launch, but its accuracy would be very poor. I think we should take the risk and march to the track adjacent to the presurveyed launch point. What do you think, Lieutenant?"

"I agree completely, sir," Kim said. He motioned to a map on the console. "Unfortunately, this maintenance shed did not have surveyed coordinates listed. I have a few possible bearing swings we could take on terrain features to refine our GPS coordinates, but in this weather it would be impossible to see them. We should march to the launch point as you suggest, sir."

"Very good," Kong said. "Help me remove our camouflage, and we'll be off."

It took only thirty minutes to remove the debris from around the train, start up the diesel engine, and get under way. It took less than an hour to reach the section of track near the launch point. Kong, acting as train engineer, slowed down so he could double-check that the switch signal was in the proper position, indicating that he would stay on the main track and not switch to the damaged siding, and so he could stop as soon as he was aligned with the siding.

But something happened. As he reached the switch, the train veered right onto the siding. Kong throttled back and hit the brakes, but he could not stop in time—even traveling less than ten kilometers per hour, such a large train needed a lot of time to stop. The engine plowed into a pile of concrete and debris lying on the tracks, and he heard a loud crunching sound from under the wheels that ran along the entire length of the engine until the train finally came to a halt. He shifted into reverse and tried to move—nothing. He went as high as 80 percent power, loud enough to be heard all the way to Holch'on—still nothing. They were stuck fast.

Damn, damn, *damn*! He cursed at himself as he leaped from the engine to inspect the damage. He knew he should have visually inspected the switch. It had obviously been damaged, or else deliberately sabotaged to turn any unsuspecting train into the defective siding. Now he was trapped.

"I will curse my own incompetence from now and for eternity!" he shouted as he joined Kim beside the engine. "How does it look? Do you think we can move?"

"I think we can move if we clear some of the concrete from around the axles," Kim said. "It might take full throttle, but I think it can be done."

Kim got up to retrieve some tools from the engineer's locker in the engine, but Kong stopped him. "We don't have time," he said. "We're less than two hundred meters from the presurveyed launch point. All we need is a single transit shot to update the launch point coordinates, and then we need to start the heading alignment. We can use the gyro platform heading calibrator at the presurveyed point to cross-check the heading alignment. If we hurry, we can make the launch time."

OVER THE SEA OF JAPAN, OFF THE EAST COAST
OF THE KOREAN PENINSULA
THAT SAME TIME

"Feet dry," Patrick McLanahan announced. "We actually made it."

"Amen," Nancy Cheshire, the aircraft commander aboard the EB-1C Megafortress, said, echoing Patrick's relief. They had just completed a nonstop eleven-hour flight from Dreamland to Korea, without seeing any land whatsoever since leaving the United States coastline near Big Sur.

"I hear ya, guys," Dave Luger added. "Good job. Now the fun starts."

Dave Luger was not onboard the modified B-1 bomber—he was more than a thousand miles away in the Megafortress's "virtual cockpit" on Naval Air Station Adak in the Aleutian Islands. The HAWC teams had quickly deployed the ground support equipment to Adak while the EB-1 was made ready for its first mission.

The virtual cockpit, or VC, provided Patrick and Nancy with an extra set of eyes on their instruments and on the tactical situation around them. It was like a miniature mock-up of the EB-1 Megafortress cockpit, using computer monitors in place of aircraft gauges and instruments. Several other screens on the side of the module allowed extra technicians to monitor aircraft systems, and to monitor other sensors and displays and pass along their observations to the crew in real-time. The largest screen in the VC, atop the remote cockpit displays, was the "God's-eye" view, or what the crews called the "big picture," which combined all of the external and mission-specific sensors available into one big chartlike display. The God's-eye view combined civilian and military radar information, satellite imagery, shipborne and aircraft radar data, and even information broadcast from ground forces all on one map.

The most important system adding its information to the God's-eye view was a string of satellites in low earth orbit called NIRTSats, or "Need it right this second" satellites. Four small dishwasher-sized satellites had been released just hours earlier aboard a booster rocket launched from a converted DC-10 airliner and placed into a one-hundred-mile circular orbit, positioned so that each satellite was over the Korean peninsula every twenty minutes. The satellites had been launched and positioned specifically for Patrick's EB-1C Megafortress mission. They used thrusters to precisely position themselves in space but did not have enough fuel or power to keep themselves in orbit very long or allow themselves to be repositioned into another orbit. Within three or four weeks, their battery power would run out and they would burn up in earth's atmosphere.

During its pass, each satellite would take a stream of radar images of broad areas of Korea and China and transmit the images to earth. Within seconds, the images would be processed and sent to the virtual cockpit at Adak and to the crew on the Megafortress. The radar images could see objects as small as an automobile and were precise enough to measure the dimensions of a target, compare it to a vehicle database, and actually try to guess at what the object or vehicle might be. Over time, the images would show trails of moving vehicles, vehicle concentrations, and even vehicles that had traveled off known highways or were trying to hide to escape detection.

Coverage was not 100 percent—each satellite was only in the sky over the Korean peninsula for about twelve out of every ninety minutes. But since most ground vehicles didn't move very fast anyway, it was very good information. The data from the satellites combined with the Megafortress's laser radar system allowed the crews both on the ground and in the air to see all ground activity for most of the northern Korean peninsula and the border region of China, and all air activity within fifty miles. It was truly a God's-eye view.

Patrick activated the laser radar system and got his first look at the Korean peninsula from the Megafortress—a five-second LADAR shot was all that was necessary to get a detailed view of everything around them for fifty miles. The LADAR could detect small vehicles on the ground and aircraft at any altitude, map terrain, scan for weather, and identify ships at sea; it could even detect satellites flying overhead in low earth orbit. Patrick could manipulate the LADAR image to zoom in on the smallest return or out to take a look at the entire tactical situation over a span of 100,000 cubic miles around the aircraft.

The EB-1C Megafortress was loaded primarily for ballistic missile and launcher hunting, but it also carried a big self-defense weapons package. In its forward bomb bay was a rotary launcher with a total of sixteen AIM-120 radar-guided AMRAAMs (advanced medium-range air-to-air missiles). The AMRAAM was a "launch and leave" antiaircraft missile: each missile was programmed right before launch with the target's position, heading, and speed, which meant that the launch aircraft did not have to stay locked onto the target. But since the Megafortress's laser radar could stay locked onto a target even while maneuvering, the AMRAAM received updates on the target's flight path until it got close enough to use its own onboard radar to home in on the target and complete the intercept. The Megafortress's laser radar system could simultaneously track three dozen air targets in any direction and could attack six of them at one time.

The center bomb bay contained a rotary launcher with eight Lancelot antiballistic missile missiles, two of which were armed with plasma-yield warheads. The aft bomb bay had another rotary launcher with eight Wolverine cruise missiles, all with conventional warheads.

The EB-1's "supercockpit" display, the large computer screen on the right side of the cockpit, was showing the God's-eye view of the area within Lancelot missile range of the bomber. The NIRTSat radar data showed positions of ground vehicles, making identification guesstimates when the radar got a clear measurement of the target. The laser radar data displayed data on aircraft and ground and sea targets, and the bomber's electronic warfare suite displayed early-warning radars throughout Korea. As the bomber flew farther inland, it came closer to Seoul, Ch'unch'on, and Kaesong radar coverage, which was displayed as green circles. The size of the circle was a measurement of the strength of the radar signal and the estimated detection threshold of the bomber itself. If the bomber's radar cross section was larger because bomb doors were open or communications antennas were extended, the radar circles became larger; if the Megafortress was in full "stealth" configuration, head-on to the radar and running completely "stealthy," the circle would become smaller, indicating it was safe to fly closer to the radar if necessary.

"Muck, looks like we picked up a newcomer ground target," Dave Luger radioed. With a flashing pointer, he indicated the new NIRTSat radar return on Patrick's supercockpit display. "Appeared on the last satellite pass. Slow-moving, big, long. Take a look."

"Got it," Patrick said. He zoomed his display in closer, then overlaid topographic and highway charts over the sensor display. "Looks like the newcomer is right on a railroad track. We might have ourselves a missile train." He zoomed in on the digital display again. As he did, the targeting computer rendered its best guess on what the radar return was. "Computer says it's a train, all right. Chinese gauge, seven cars. Could be a Nodong missile unit." Patrick entered commands into his laser radar system and bombing computers, preloading a Wolverine missile with the train's coordinates. "Looks like it's parked close to a North Korean missile launch point," he said.

"I'm relaying the find back home," Dave said, entering the information into a secure datalink back to Dreamland. "I think Korea's been looking for this baby."

"Dave, see if the NIRTSats came up with any other trains on previous passes," Patrick ordered.

"Already done," Dave said. "We've actually got seven other likelies." A few moments later several radar returns flashed on Patrick's supercockpit display. "You're within LADAR range of two of them."

Patrick directed a slight turn north toward the two closest radar returns, then activated the laser radar again. Taking LADAR shots from several different directions was the way to get ultradetailed three-dimensional images. These shots were combined with earlier shots and with the NIRTSat radar images to further enhance the target. "No go on target one," Patrick said. "The computer says it's a bus or truck—too small for a seven-car Nodong unit. But target number two could be another player. It's a seven-car train, Chinese gauge, moved into its current position just an hour ago."

"Two Nodongs at presurveyed launch points?" Nancy Cheshire asked. "Sounds like a lot more than coincidence to me."

"Same here," Dave said as he relayed the new information back to Dreamland. "This could be the prelude to another rebel missile launch."

"Hey, we've got an air target behind us!" Patrick said. He had just completed another LADAR sweep all around the Megafortress. It was flying at about thirty thousand feet over the Sea of Japan, heading toward them from the southeast at over five hundred knots. "No ID yet, but it's gotta be a fighter."

"But we didn't pick up any radar indication on him," Nancy said. She continued a moment later: "A MiG-29. It's gotta be a Japanese MiG-29, using GPS for navigation and his IRSTS for targeting." The IRSTS, or infrared search and track system, was a sophisticated Russian-designed heat-seeking sensor that allowed a MiG-29 to scan large sections of sky for enemy aircraft without being detected. Used along with GPS satellite navigation, the MiG would never have to use his radar except for very long-range attacks—most enemies would never know he was there until he fired his missiles. "Are they still patrolling the peninsula with the Koreans?"

"I'm sure the Koreans are happy to have them up here," Patrick said. "Korea might be providing the ground control information for the MiG. I think that as long as we stay farther than twenty miles from that MiG and we don't aim our exhausts right at him, he won't spot us. Dave, why don't you drop a note to General Samson and ask him to ask the White House to find a way to tell the Japanese we're up here. I'd hate to be jumped by a Japanese MiG. Maybe we can exchange Mode Two codes or something."

"You got it," Luger said. "I should be able to find out what his interplane or command frequency is too, so if the shit really hits the fan you can talk to him. You can . . . Hey, looks like fighters launching from Korea." When Patrick expanded his supercockpit display to a full God's-eye view, he saw the new information: relayed from Korea's own air traffic control radar system, two high-speed aircraft were climbing rapidly through the night sky, headed northeast. "Two fighters off from Seoul, headed your way."

"Getting crowded up here," Nancy said. "Maybe we should go low and hide in some . . ."

Just then the LADAR system issued a shrill warning tone, and an icon began blinking near one of the suspected Nodong missile units. *"Launch detection!"* Patrick shouted. "Missile in the air! Left forty and full blowers, Nance!"

Nancy Cheshire shoved all four throttles to max afterburner and yanked the EB-1 Megafortress to the left. They could see the missile launch clearly: a tiny sparkle of light on the horizon, followed by a bright yellow column of fire rising rapidly through the atmosphere. Patrick's turn pointed the nose in precisely the right direction to lead the missile as it climbed.

"Bomb doors coming open! Wolverine away!" Patrick had immediately launched one of the powered glide bombs at the Nodong launcher. "Bomb doors closed! Okay, Nance, follow that missile!"

Nancy raised the nose only slightly to start her tail-chase climb. At first it seemed as if they might overfly or pass the missile—the Nodong didn't look as though it was accelerating so fast, while the Megafortress was rapidly picking up speed. But this was an illusion. Seconds later it was obvious how fast that ballistic missile was traveling. In the blink of an eye the Nodong was above them, accelerating rapidly on a tongue of fire. By this time, Nancy had the speed built up to almost Mach 1 and she easily kept the nose aimed at the missile. They never reached the Mach, however, and the higher Cheshire pulled the nose up to point it at the Nodong missile, the quicker the airspeed bled off.

"Punch it out quick, sir," Nancy urged him. "Airspeed's falling way off already. You got about six seconds . . ."

"Stand by . . . doors coming open . . . missile away!" Seconds later they heard a loud thundering rocket blast, and one of the Lancelot missiles shot past their windscreen on its own plume of fire. "Clear to unload, Nance! Doors closed!" Nancy released back pressure on the control stick, lowered the nose to the horizon, and pulled the throttles out of afterburner. They were rewarded by a spectacular multicolored globe of sparks and fire in the sky as the Lancelot intercepted its quarry.

"Ya-*hoo*!" Nancy shouted. Both crew members had to turn away from the brilliant flash of light and shower of sparks. "Man, did you *see* that! Was that a nuclear detonation?"

"Could have been," Patrick said. "Maybe a partial yield, five or ten kilotons. Lancelot intercepted it about fifty-one miles downrange, eighty thousand feet altitude." Then a heavy rumble of turbulence rocked the Megafortress. "Yep, maybe a nuclear burst, all right. All our systems look okay." Patrick switched to the imaging infrared view from the Wolverine missile, only long enough to clearly see the outline of the Nodong missile train. He had just enough time to roll the aiming cursor onto the car with the erector-launcher still extended in firing position before the missile hit.

Then came another warning message blinking on the supercockpit display. "Another missile launch! Left ninety, max AB, *now*!" Nancy followed Patrick's instructions. This time Nancy kept the Megafortress's nose down until Patrick had launched another Wolverine missile and the Nodong missile crossed the horizon; it was enough to accelerate past Mach 1. The nose lifted quickly, it felt much steadier, and the airspeed drop-off was less drastic—although the fact that they were six thousand pounds lighter on weapons and four thousand pounds lighter on fuel certainly helped too.

"Stand by . . . doors coming open . . . missile away!" Patrick shouted. Nancy shielded her eyes from the bright glare of the Lancelot missile's first-stage rocket motor as the big missile streaked into the night sky. "Doors closed, clear to—"

"Warning!" Dave Luger shouted on the satellite commlink. *"Bandit at seven o'clock ten miles! Get out of there!"*

He was interrupted by a high-pitched *deedledee-dledeedle* and a large MISSILE LAUNCH warning on the supercockpit display. "Break left!" Patrick shouted. Nancy yanked the Megafortress to the left—it was already in a slight left turn—and pulled hard right to the stall warning stick shaker. At the same instant, Patrick ejected several TALDs from the bomber's right ejector racks, then quickly reeled out the first towed decoy and activated it. The tactical air-launched decoys immediately deployed their radar fins and activated infrared and radio emitters—to an air-to-air missile they were hundreds of times larger than the escaping EB-1. Both enemy missiles hit the TALDs without a single look at the Megafortress.

They saw another explosion in the sky, not as big as the first one, but spectacular nonetheless. "Looks like we got the second Nodong," Patrick said, "but I don't know what happened to the second Wolverine. It might've been shot down."

"By who? Who is shooting at us?" Nancy shouted.

"That motherfucker Japanese MiG-29 sneaked up behind you when you plugged in your 'burners and shot two missiles at you!" Dave replied.

"Why would he do that—other than the fact there are missiles flying everywhere and he might've thought we launched all of them," Patrick declared. "You got his frequency yet, Dave?"

"I'm getting it now," Dave replied. "He's talking to Seoul GCI and those two Korean fighters. I think they're going to try to box you in . . . I got it. I set the freq in radio two. They're unsecure."

"Let me talk to 'em," Nancy said. She moved her comm switch to radio number two and keyed the mike button: "Hey, boys, we're on your side. Stop shooting at us!"

"Unidentified aircraft, this is the United Republic of Korea Air Force," a voice replied in a thick Korean accent. "You have violated Korean airspace. Roll wings level, slow down, and lower your landing gear immediately or you will be shot down! This is your final warning!"

The supercockpit display showed the deployment of the air targets. "Looks like those Korean fighters are F-16Ks, judging by their radar signature—they don't have us on radar yet," Patrick said. "We are well inside Seoul radar coverage, but we can be out of it in less than two minutes at mil power. The MiG-29 might still have us on IRSTS. There's squat we can do to escape him unless we get beyond his sensor's max range, which is about ten miles. That's pretty unlikely—he can fly just as fast as we can up here."

"Unidentified aircraft, this is your final warning!" the Korean voice repeated. "Slow and lower your landing gear now or we open fire!"

"Warm up a Scorpion missile, Patrick," Nancy Cheshire said. "We've got no choice—it's him or us."

"I'd rather not shoot the bastard down, Nance—he may have shot at us, but he's a good guy." Instead, Patrick activated the laser radar once more, got a fix on the MiG-29, then designated a Wolverine cruise missile against it. "Doors coming open . . . missile away! Get ready for a mil power TERFLW descent, Nance!"

"You got it, boss," Nancy said happily, quickly configuring her autopilot switches. Patrick opened the bomb doors and commanded the ground-attack cruise missile against the MiG-29.

The Wolverine-powered cruise missile normally had a fifty-mile range, but this time it was heading up against a MiG-29 fighter, so its range was considerably less. But it was enough. Patrick and Nancy watched on the supercockpit display as the Wolverine missile flew closer and closer to the MiG. About two miles away, the MiG's infrared search and track system must have detected the missile on a collision course, and it did a spectacular snap-turn to the right, followed by a roll and a steep dive away from the missile. The little cruise missile tried to follow, but it quickly lost track of the MiG and crashed harmlessly into the Sea of Japan.

At the same instant the MiG-29 did its wild evasive maneuver, Nancy rolled the EB-1C inverted and pulled. The bomber plummeted toward the sea in a steep thirty-thousand-foot-per-minute dive. She pulled the power to idle to keep from overstressing the plane. At five thousand feet above the ocean, she rolled upright, engaged the terrain-following system, and pushed it to full military power. They leveled off smoothly two thousand feet above the ocean, accomplished a systems check, then stepped it down until they were two hundred feet above the dark waves.

Nancy made a turn south to parallel the Korean coastline, in case the MiG tried to pursue them along their last known track, while Patrick scanned the skies around them with the laser radar. "The MiG is fifteen miles at our five o'clock, heading southeast," he reported. "I don't think he's got us. Good job, Nance.

Let's work our way back to our patrol orbit and see if we can catch any more Nodongs tonight!"

"It stinks that we had to take a shot at a good guy and waste a perfectly good Wolverine just so we wouldn't get shot down ourselves," Nancy said. "But I guess he's just doing his job. And we actually got two missiles tonight! Awesome!"

The rest of the evening was relatively uneventful. The Megafortress crew stayed in their patrol orbit over central Korea for another hour, easily skirting all of the search radars and fighter patrols over Korea. By this time there was a general air defense alert over the entire region, but the Megafortress crew was easily able to evade all searchers. There were no more missile launches from either side. They then broke off and hooked up with a KC-135 tanker over the Sea of Japan, 150 miles west-northwest of Kanazawa, Japan. With full tanks, they returned to their patrol orbit until an hour before sunrise, then headed back toward Japan and terminated their first successful night of antiballistic missile patrol.

They refueled again with the tanker, then flew to their "due regard" point, the coordinates in their military flight plan where they would again be back in radar contact. The Japanese military air traffic controllers on the island of Hokkaido, where the Megafortress crew checked in, might have suspected that the unidentified aircraft near Korea was this mysterious B-1 with the "Fortress" call sign, but there was nothing they could do but let the plane go on its way unmolested. Once it crossed the "due regard" point outbound outside Japanese airspace, its business was its own. As long as it crossed the proper point inbound at the proper time and squawked the proper transponder codes, it was a legal return flight and could come back without question with a valid flight plan and full air traffic control service.

With their identity confirmed and their flight plan reactivated, they continued on uneventfully and a little over two hours later set down in Adak, Alaska. Total flight time: twenty-one hours. They had taken off from Dreamland just after sunset and were landing just before arctic sunset—the sun would be up again in a couple of hours.

The ground crews immediately prepared the Megafortress for relaunch, while the flight crew made their way to the hangar where their new headquarters had been set up. David Luger himself picked up Nancy and Patrick from the plane, fed them sandwiches and drinks, escorted them to maintenance and intelligence debrief, and then to the conference room where they could sit and relax and talk about the sortie.

Waiting for them on a secure satellite videoconference hookup was Lieutenant General Terrill Samson, calling from Dreamland. "Helluva job, you two," Samson said proudly. "Congratulations. How do you feel?"

"We need to get some more-comfortable chairs in that plane," Nancy said. "And we need to get the microwave oven and hot cup working again too."

"Why bother, Nance? You never unstrap or even lower your oxygen mask anyway," Patrick said with a smile. To Samson, he said, "What's the word from Korea, sir?"

"The word, thank God, is 'what the hell happened?'" Samson replied. "Both China and Korea observed the exact same thing: two ballistic missile launches originating in southern Chagang Do province, followed by two large explosions, one a nuclear burst, high in the atmosphere. Very little damage and few injuries to anything or anyone on the ground. No response from China this time, no further action by

Korea except to declare an air defense emergency. Japan claims it intercepted and attacked a bomber over the Sea of Japan and chased it away. Officially, they did not speculate on its identity. Unofficially—well, my phone's been ringing off the hook. State Department. Pentagon. Gold Room. Oval Office. They all wanted a briefing."

"And?"

"And I told them we had a winner on our hands, and we needed to fully implement it." Samson beamed. "They virtually handed me a blank check. We got tankers, manpower, weapons, whatever we need ready to go. It's our show too. No argument this time—Pacific Command was never even considered. The operation stays black all the way—we still don't want to send any more carriers or combat aircraft into the region until things cool down. Except for the two carriers already stationed around Korea, we'll be the only other combat unit in the entire northern Pacific. So just tell me what you need, Patrick, and it'll be on its way."

"The first thing I'll need, sir," Patrick said, "is the 111th Bomb Squadron, Nevada Air National Guard, and their planes, modified and flown up here as quickly as possible."

"What?" Samson asked incredulously. "After what you went through with that bunch, you still want to use them? You can have their planes, Patrick—that'll be a no-brainer. But the Nevada Air National Guard?"

"Sir, they are still the best Bone drivers in the business," Patrick insisted. "When I did my evaluation of that unit, I was thinking like a BUFF or B-2 bomber guy—low, slow, and fly the blue line. I realized that once we got over Korea, Operation Battle Born won't work if we fly that way. This mission calls for crews who can think and react like close-air-support attack planes, not bombers. They have to drive down the enemy's throat to do this mission. Those guys are the best because they fly like that all the time—they don't know any other way."

"Then you got 'em," Samson said. "What else do you need? Tanker support, AWACS, fighter cover?"

"We need Takedown," Patrick replied.

"You need who?"

"Takedown—that's the Navy version of Coronet Tiger," Patrick said. "Brad Elliott originally got Coronet Tiger from the Navy, and they still have patrol planes modified with the system—on P-3 Orions, I believe. We need that plane, plus its support teams. I also need the *Grand Island*."

"You mean the USS *Grand Island*? The cruiser we almost fried testing Lancelot?"

"Yep," Patrick said. "We need someone to watch our backsides and to provide some air defense support. Besides, they know a lot of our secrets anyway—might as well make them part of the team."

"Well, that might be a tough sell, but I'll do it," Samson said with a smile. "What's the plan?"

"I plan on flying missions or manning the VC with other crews flying the EB-1 until someone orders me to stop," Patrick said. "I'll send Dave back to base to supervise the retrofit of the four Bones at Dreamland, and I'll send Nancy and Wendy out to Patuxent River to supervise the Takedown flight crew setup. In less than seventy-two hours, we'll be fully operational here. I just hope this region doesn't blow up in our faces before then."

111TH BOMB SQUADRON HEADQUARTERS,
RENO-TAHOE INTERNATIONAL AIRPORT,
RENO, NEVADA
THE NEXT DAY

The news about Korea was so nonstop and so shocking that, even after just a few days, it seemed as if it was already old news. Rebecca Furness was hardly paying attention to the TV tuned to CNN in her office as she took pictures, plaques, and other assorted memorabilia off the walls and stacked them neatly in boxes.

At first, it did appear as if the Korean people's revolution was going to hold. Led by the United States, foreign troops started moving off the Korean peninsula within hours of the formal request. At several times, Russian, Chinese, and American transport and cargo vessels shared the same waters, packed full with troops, dependents, and equipment. In fact, it appeared as if all three nations had actually *increased* their naval presence in the region—given the opportunity to sail plenty of vessels into Korean waters, all nations did so with gusto. All of the ships operated near each other without protest or problems. It all led the world to believe that a peaceful transition to democracy was actually possible in Korea.

But then the missile attacks and the destruction of a major Korean city reportedly by a Chinese ballistic missile snapped the world back to reality. Tensions were high again in the blink of an eye. American military forces, already at a high state of alert, were placed on an even more advanced stage of readiness, as far advanced as possible without actually flying aircraft or sending ships to Korea or appearing as if they threatened China or Russia.

There was little talk from China—all of the bellicose

language coming from Asia was from the Korean Communist government-in-exile. President Kim Jong-il was on CNN almost hourly, loudly proclaiming that President Kwon of United Korea wanted nothing more than to precipitate a superpower conflict so Japan and Korea could emerge as leaders of a new Asian power bloc.

All the other noise on CNN came from President Kevin Martindale's critics, who slammed him mercilessly. He was not tough enough with the Chinese or Koreans; he should never have relinquished the lost Korean or Japanese bases; he should send more troops or more aircraft carriers into Asia; and on it went for a dozen other perceived deficiencies. Half his critics wanted war with the Chinese—the other half wanted Martindale out of the White House and *then* war with China.

When the news came over CNN that China and Korea had exchanged missiles, Rebecca thought the world was going to end in the next thirty minutes—about the time it would take long-range sub-launched ICBMs to fly from Asia or Siberia to North America, or vice versa. She had never in her life felt so powerless. She stopped her packing and watched, mesmerized, as the reporters and anchors tried to keep on reporting developments in northeast Asia, even as they, too, knew that their planet could be on fire at any moment.

When the thirty minutes came and went, Rebecca felt enormous relief. Maybe cooler heads were going to prevail here. Maybe everything would be all right. But then President Kim or some Chinese government official would get on the air and promise death, and her panic would start all over again.

"You know," she heard a familiar voice say, "this is a really shitty office." She turned and saw Rinc Seaver standing in her doorway, watching her.

Rebecca looked around, then nodded. Her office was

a former storeroom on the top floor of the General James A. May hangar at Reno-Tahoe International Airport. It wasn't the normal unit commander's office, but she chose it and fixed it up because it overlooked the flight line and had better access to the maintenance teams downstairs, which were the lifeblood of any flying unit. "I've had bigger ones, nicer ones," she said. "But it's not the size that matters, it's what you do with it."

"Are we still talking about offices, Beck?" Rinc said with a smile.

"I don't know," she said. "Maybe not."

"I would certainly prefer to talk about us."

She favored him with a smile in return, then motioned to the TV. "Have you been watching this? It's incredible. One second I feel okay, and the next I think I can hear the nukes flying in."

"I can't watch it anymore," Rinc said. "It's driving me nuts, especially since I can't do anything about it. Besides, I'm concerned about other things—other *persons*." He stepped over and kissed her lightly on the lips. "Hi, stranger," he said.

"Hi yourself."

She did not exactly return his kiss, and he could feel the tension in her body. His shoulders slumped as she turned away and began packing boxes again. "Either I'm losing my touch, or I'm losing *you*," he said.

"I'm just distracted . . . pissed off . . . frustrated . . . take your pick," Rebecca said. "I'm a full-time guardsman, Rinc. This was my job. I've never been fired from a job before in my life. And this was my first combat-coded command, something I've wanted since I started pilot training."

"I know," Rinc said. "What's more, we lost our unit when we were doing our jobs better than anyone else. It sucks."

Rebecca looked at Rinc. "You seem in a pretty good mood. Oh yeah, that's right—you still have a job."

"You can have one too, if you want," Rinc said. "The company is thinking about putting another plane on the line. I talked to them about splitting hours. They provide decent benefits, we get the use of the planes at cost in case we set up some type of rating instruction, and we get to stay in town and . . ."

"I tried that once before—I found I didn't like it," Rebecca said. "I like military flying better. I like command even more."

Rinc shrugged. "Why not accept the offer while you look around for another position?" he suggested. "We could use you, and we'd still be together."

"I don't think so."

"You don't think so, which? The 'we could use you' part or the 'we'd still be together' part?"

"Rinc, sometimes you . . . dammit, sometimes *men* can be so frustrating," Rebecca said. "I just lost my job. I'm hurt. You just lost your job. You don't seem to care. I don't see you for weeks after your accident. I'm hurt. You don't see me for weeks after your accident, and it's no big deal. Does it ever become a big deal for you?"

"Beck, we got tossed out of a job—we didn't receive a death sentence, we didn't get a red 'A' painted on our foreheads, we are still breathing," Rinc said. "We can overcome everything else. Life goes on. We press on."

"Well, I lost some things that were special to me," Rebecca said. "My command, my career, my future."

"But you can have that again. I'm offering you all of it. My bosses want you. I want you. The business is expanding, and there's a future for you there if you want it."

"Pushing another flying service? Forget it. I did that, back in New York. It wasn't for me. I've worked hard to get my light colonel's leaves and my own command,

Rinc—I can't just leave it and go to work for someone else." She reached out and held his hand. "The California Air National Guard tanker wing is looking for a commander down in Riverside. They want to interview me. I think I've got a really good shot at it. KC-135Rs, maybe KC-10s in the future. Lots of missions, high visibility, lots of money."

"And what do I do? Fly Stratobladders? No thanks," Rinc said. "I've put in my time in support squadrons. I'm part owner of a good business here in Reno, and I get a stick and throttles and windows in my planes, even the little piston-powered ones. Why would I give that up?"

"How about for me?" Rebecca asked, a little crossly. "Do it so we can stay together. Start a branch of your flying service down there. Fly for the airlines—you have lots of experience, a commercial license, an Airline Transport Pilot rating. Get a corporate position. Or just come down and be with me. You're a young guy. You can do anything you want. I don't have as many opportunities as you, Rinc. When I find a good one, I have to go for it." She could tell that not only was he *not* considering the idea, he was decidedly uncomfortable even thinking about it. "Or does the idea of following a woman's career totally gross you out?"

"It's not that . . ."

"Bullshit. What is it, then? My age?"

"Hey, I've never thought of you as an 'older woman,'" Rinc said angrily. "You know that. You're as sexy and vibrant and hot as any college hard-body."

"Then what's the problem?" Rebecca asked. "C'mon, Rinc. Give it a try."

"I don't know," Rinc said. Rebecca sensed that he was wrestling with an even greater dilemma than just their future together. "It's just . . . well, I was getting a little tired of the Air Guard scene. I was looking forward to settling down and taking it easy with this little flying service in Reno."

"Well, don't fly for the Guard," she said. "Do other stuff."

"But I'd be exposed to it all the time, being with you. I'm not sure if I want that."

"Why, for Christ's sake? You don't have to have anything to do with the Guard, except maybe a few social-type functions. You can handle that. Besides, if you're doing your corporate or airline thing, you'll probably be on the road most of the time anyway."

"Yeah, but I'll be involved because *you'll* be involved."

"So? I still don't get it." She looked at him for several long moments; then: "What is it, Rodeo? Tell me." He remained silent, his eyes darting back and forth as if reliving some horrible event in his life. Now she studied his face intently, reading the thoughts and emotions that seemed to cross it—and not liking what she was sensing. "It's not that you don't want to be around *me,* Rinc," she said in a quiet, strained voice, "is it? You don't want to be around the Air Guard. Why?" Still no response. "Rinc, you gotta tell me. It's about the accident, right?"

"No."

"Tell me, Rinc. Get it off your chest. It's all history now, lover."

"Forget about it. It's nothing."

"I can't forget about it until you do," Rebecca said. "It's obvious that whatever is bugging you is standing between us. I need to know. Please."

Rinc started to pace the office. Every step he took seemed to cause him immense pain, but Rebecca knew the true pain was in his soul. "You lost it that day, didn't you, Rinc?"

Rinc's eyes were fixed on the floor. "Yes," he said in

a low, barely audible voice. "It was nuts on that plane, Beck. It wasn't recovering. We were practically upside down. I thought I could recover it. Mad Dog had his fingers on the PREPARE TO EJECT switch, and I told him no. I kept on saying, 'I got it, I got it.' I suddenly realized I was going to fly it all the way into the ground, and I didn't issue a command—I just went."

"Rinc, it's all right," Rebecca said, going to him and taking his hand. "The important thing is, you got out alive . . ."

"Like hell it is!" John Long shouted. He was standing in the doorway of Rebecca's office, his eyes bulging in fury. "So you finally admit it—you *did* screw up!"

"John, get out," Rebecca said. "This is between him and me."

But Long had already sped into the office and he shoved Seaver back against Rebecca's desk. Rinc made no attempt to resist. Long pinned him against the desk and started pummeling him with his right fist. "You bastard!" he shouted. "You cowardly bastard! You caused that accident! You caused that crash! You killed those men! *My friends are dead because of you!*"

Furness had no choice—she jabbed her right elbow back into Long's face, then pushed him away. He flew backward, blood spurting from his nose.

"So that's why you've been protecting him—you two have been screwing each other all this time," Long said, holding his nose to try to stop the bleeding. "God damn you . . ."

"That's enough, Colonel!"

"I'm not your subordinate anymore, bitch!" Long snapped. "And even if I was, I call 'em like I see 'em. You covered up for him even though you suspected something was wrong. How can you do that, Furness? How can you cover up for a piece of shit like that, over the rest of your unit? There's no dick or piece of ass good enough for anyone to turn on their own!"

"*Shut up!*" Rebecca shouted. "Just shut the fuck up, Long!" He finally stopped and glared at them both. Seaver picked himself up off the desk, not bothering to cover up a cut lip and bruised cheek. "Both of you, knock it off. This is getting us nowhere. What's done is done."

"Not for me it isn't," Long shot back. "Not until Seaver admits what he did in front of the squadron and to the adjutant general. Then I want to see him drummed out of the Guard."

"Go to hell, Long," Seaver said, his voice defiant but his eyes and expression showing the pain and hurt he was feeling. "Yes, I jumped out without giving a command. Yes, I was too aggressive down low while TF'ing. Yes, I relied on the automatic system to punch everyone out. But my crew didn't die because of me! Those smoky SAMs hit us, we couldn't recover . . ."

"You piece of *shit*!" Long shouted. "You're still blaming something else for what you did." Long took a threatening step toward Seaver.

Rebecca got up to block Long's path again. "I said, knock it off!" Then she realized that someone else was standing in the doorway to her office. It was none other than Lieutenant Colonel Hal Briggs and another lieutenant colonel whom Rebecca recognized as General McLanahan's deputy and one of the members of his inspection team. The way Briggs's field jacket bulged, it was obvious he was still wearing the little submachine gun she remembered seeing at Dreamland.

"We interrupting something here, Colonel?" Briggs asked with his seemingly ever-present smile. He nodded at John Long and added, "Looks like you got blood on you again, Colonel Long, except this time it's your *own* blood."

"As a matter of fact, you *are* interrupting something," Rebecca replied testily. "Can you guys wait for us downstairs?"

"No, we can't," the other man said. "I'm Lieutenant Colonel David Luger, General McLanahan's deputy. We'd like you all to come with us right away. We've already got Captain Dewey with us downstairs."

"It's going to have to wait a few minutes," Rebecca said. "We have something—"

"You don't understand, Rebecca," Dave Luger said. "You're coming with us right now. General McLanahan's orders."

"McLanahan doesn't have any authority over us," Long said irritably, his anger from being elbowed in the face by his ex-boss welling up to the surface.

"You're wrong, Colonel Long," Luger said. "Those wristbands mean he has *total* authority over you."

"What's he going to do if we tell him to go piss up a rope?" Long asked. "Kidnap us?"

As if he were talking only to the cool alpine air, Dave Luger said, "Lieutenant Colonel Luger for Gunnery Sergeant Wohl . . ." There was a brief pause; then: "Chris, come give us a hand upstairs, please."

"Who the hell are you talking to?" Rebecca asked.

Luger did not reply. Moments later the biggest, meanest-looking man any of them had ever seen came into Furness's office. He was the archetypical commando—square jaw, piercing eyes, huge hands, tight, muscular frame, some broken bones in his face and nose that made him look even meaner. He looked at the three guardsmen with undisguised hostility, as if he had been personally insulted or inconvenienced by them.

"This is Gunnery Sergeant Chris Wohl, guys," Luger said. "He's our noncommissioned officer in charge of ass-kicking at HAWC." As he said that, Chris Wohl reached inside his field jacket, grasped the pistol grip of his MP5K submachine gun, and gave it a tug. The little weapon snapped free of its harness, and in the blink of an eye the stock had extended and the big ex-marine had it at port arms. In another instant he had withdrawn and attached a sound suppressor.

"What are you going to do, asshole?" Long sneered. "Shoot us?"

"Yes, sir," Wohl said, smiling. And at that, to the complete astonishment of the three guardsmen, he leveled the MP5K and fired a round right into John Long's chest from less than twenty feet away.

"Jesus! Are you nuts?" Rebecca screamed. Long fell backward, his eyes staring straight ahead, clutching his chest. He went down so fast that Rinc and Rebecca had to scramble to catch him. There was no blood. They quickly found that he was not dead because there was no hole in his chest—just a patch of light brown dust on his shirt. But Long was out of it. One moment he was awake and wondering why his legs and arms wouldn't work—the next instant, his eyes rolled up into his head and he was fast asleep. "What in hell did you shoot him with?"

"A very mild nerve agent crystalline needle," Hal Briggs explained. "The needle is about the size of a human hair and can penetrate several layers of clothing, very much like a bullet but with none of the tissue trauma. It contains a nerve agent that paralyzes all voluntary motor functions. He can breathe, blink, his heart will work okay—he just can't move. He'll be out for about an hour or so." He motioned to Long's crotch and added with a grin, "He can't keep from peeing and shitting on himself either."

"Are you absolutely insane?" Rebecca cried. She checked for a pulse and breathing and found both were normal—but Long was indeed out. Not just asleep, but completely limp, his limbs as mushy as a half-filled water balloon. She got the first whiff of relieved bowels and bladder too, which made her even angrier. "You can't just drag us out of here like criminals . . ."

"We can and we will," Hal Briggs said calmly. "Rather, you two will drag Colonel Long downstairs and into our waiting car, which will take us over to our waiting jet, which will take us to Elliott Air Force Base. If you give Gunnery Sergeant Wohl any more grief, he will shoot both of you, and he and his men will drag you however way they find most convenient to the van."

"By accepting those bracelets, guys, you agreed to be part of Dreamland and HAWC as long as they exist and as long as you exist," Dave Luger said. "I'm sure General McLanahan made that clear to you before you landed at our base. We don't allow visitors, and there's no such thing as a TDY into or a PCS out of Dreamland."

"Just like 'Hotel California' in reverse, guys," Hal added with a big smile. "You can leave anytime you like, but you can never check out."

"This is ridiculous!" Rebecca exploded. "You're taking us back to Dreamland? *Now?* No orders, no prior arrangements, no warning? What about our lives, our families, our careers?"

"All three of you have been federalized," Dave said. "Major Seaver just left a message telling his partners that he's on extended leave of absence—actually, we took the liberty of leaving the message on his behalf. Colonel Furness, you and Colonel Long both are still full-time Nevada Air Guard, even though your unit has been deactivated. The Nevada adjutant general has agreed to allow you to go on extended active duty. We'll see to it that someone looks out for your house or apartment and pays the bills and feeds your dog."

"Which sucks big-time," Briggs added. "Didn't you

guys know enough not to have pets if you're single in the military? Who'd you think was going to take care of them if you had to deploy? Shame on you. Colonel Long needs some serious pet care counseling."

"Later, Hal," Luger said. "Any other squawks, folks? If not, or even if you do, save it for when we get on the plane. Grab an end and let's get Long downstairs." With the big, mean-looking gunnery sergeant standing guard—the guardsmen could see that the spare magazines he carried were all loaded with real bullets, not paralyzing crystals—they carried Long down the flight of stairs to the hangar floor below.

A waiting unmarked blue windowless van was waiting, with Annie Dewey inside. Her eyes got round with worry as she watched Long being carried into the van. "What happened to Long Dong?" she asked.

"He opened his yap one too many times," Rinc said.

A few moments later the group arrived at the other side of Reno-Tahoe International Airport, where an unmarked Gulfstream IV executive jet was waiting inside a hangar with two plainclothes guards standing watch. Out of sight of any curious onlookers, they loaded up, got towed out to the ramp, and took off minutes later. In less than thirty minutes, they were on the ground back at Dreamland, and they pulled into a different set of hangars than the ones they'd seen when they first arrived at this haunting, desolate place.

"I want to talk with General McLanahan right away," Rebecca demanded. "Just because he stuck those microchips in our arms doesn't mean he has the right to yank us out of our homes and drag us here."

"Go ahead," Dave Luger said matter-of-factly.

"What?"

"Go ahead and talk to him."

"How?"

"You're wired for sound now, remember?" David

said. "We can hear everything you say. The microchip is a transceiver too—not just GPS or physiological data, but two-way communications."

"He can hear everything I ever say?"

"Try it and see. Announce who you are and who you want to talk with."

Rebecca looked at Rinc and Annie, shrugged, and then said aloud, "Colonel Furness to General McLanahan. Come in, please." There was no response. At a nod from Dave Luger, she tried again: "General McLanahan?"

"Patrick here, Rebecca. Welcome back."

"A computer analyzes your request, pages the other party, and makes the connection—sometimes it takes a moment," Dave explained.

"How can I hear him without headphones or a speaker?"

"It's a little complicated, but the microchip reads and translates nerve impulses associated with speech and hearing," Patrick explained. "When we say your whole body is wired for sound, we mean it. On a very rudimentary but very real level, we can even read your thoughts."

Rebecca gulped in astonishment—the idea was too wild to even comprehend right now. "Can my crew members join in the conversation?" she asked.

"Sure," Patrick said. "Conference in Major Seaver and Captain Dewey with General McLanahan, please." Patrick paused for a moment, then asked, "Can all you guys hear me okay?"

The startled expressions on their faces answered that question. "Hol-ee shit!" Rinc exclaimed. "This is unbelievable!"

"I take that as a yes," Patrick said. "Listen up, everyone. We don't have time to waste. We have some academics to start with today and tonight. You deploy day after tomorrow."

"Deploy? Where?"

"Your Bones are being modified with a few improvements," Patrick replied. "We're working round the clock to get them ready."

"Where are you, sir?" Dewey asked.

"I can't tell you, not just yet," Patrick said. "Once you're under way, you'll be fully briefed."

"Listen, General," Rebecca interjected. "I wanted to talk to you about the tactics you used to bring us here. I don't like your men barging in on me, and I sure as shit don't like your commandos shooting my guys up with nerve agents. We want an explanation. You can threaten us all you want, but you can't force us to fly your planes or perform any missions for you."

"Fair enough," Patrick said. "Conference in Colonel Luger and Colonel Briggs, please . . . Dave, Hal, can you escort the crew to Foxtrot row? Take them through the Corridor."

"Yes, sir," Luger acknowledged. "Follow me, everyone." He escorted the three guardsmen to a waiting van—Long was still out cold, but now being monitored by an emergency medical technician as he started to come around—and a few minutes later they arrived at Foxtrot row, the place where the Nevada Air Guard's B-1 bombers were being hangared. As when they first arrived, they had to pass through another series of security checkpoints, including a handprint and retinal identification analyzer and an X-ray corridor to check for implanted listening devices, weapons, or recording devices.

"What a goatfuck," Rebecca said. "All to see our own planes."

"They're *our* planes now," she heard Patrick say in her head.

"Is that you, General McLanahan?" Rebecca asked, shocked to hear that voice come out of thin air. "Are you still listening to me, General?"

"We're still connected until you disconnect," Patrick said. "Your planes are through that corridor ahead of you. We have some techs and engineers waiting to start briefing you on the modifications."

"What do you mean, they're yours?"

"Governor Gunnison and General Bretoff have leased the planes to us for an indefinite period of time," Dave Luger replied. "Actually, ever since you flunked your pre-D, we've been modifying them. You need to learn how to fly them right away. You start action in the forward area in two days."

"You're still assuming we want to be a part of any of this," Rebecca said. "Judging by the treatment we got this morning and the support we've received from you and your organization, I vote we tell you to go to hell."

"It would be a shame to lose you, but at the end of our little tour here, if you don't want in, I'll cut the bracelets off and send you home," Patrick's ethereal voice in their heads said. "We can't take the chip out without a surgeon, but it's completely safe and quite inert without the bracelet, I promise. I've had one in for years. Deal?"

Rebecca still looked skeptical and did not reply, but something on the wall caught her eye, and she went over to examine it. It was a series of photographs, memorabilia, charts, and other items, including a control wheel from a B-52. Rinc and Annie went over to look at the items as well.

What riveted Rebecca Furness's attention was the big WAC chart and a remarkable pencil and paper re-creation of an old two-page SAC Form 200 flight plan next to it—describing a B-52 bomber flight from Dreamland to Kavaznya in the Soviet Union, with a final stop in Anadyr near the Bering Strait. The chart had the triangle fix position marks on them, along with the old-style cross data blocks with Zulu time, track, groundspeed, and winds or drift angle. The Form 200 was filled out in meticulous detail with precise architect-like printing. It was dated 1988 and even had the headings filled out—it was as if whoever drew this thing up wanted to duplicate a standard Form 200 exactly, from memory.

Rebecca's mouth opened in surprise as she read the names of the crew members on the flight plan: Brad Elliott, pilot; John Ormack, copilot; Patrick McLanahan, radar navigator; David Luger, navigator; Wendy Tork, electronic warfare officer; and Angelina Pereira, gunner. Most of those names were legends in the Air Force, pilots or engineers or weapons designers known the world over—and here they were, all on one mysterious hand-drawn flight plan.

"Kavaznya—that was that antisatellite laser site in Siberia, wasn't it?" Rebecca asked. "The one that had the accident? I remember the Russians claimed we bombed it, but everyone said its reactor had a meltdown." She looked at Luger in complete surprise. "You . . . *you bombed it*?"

"With a damned B-52," Rinc said breathlessly. "Here's a picture of it . . . I *think* it's a B-52, with the long pointed nose and the stealth fighter tail. This is the control wheel off it. You flew a B-52 bomber all the way inside the Soviet Union at the height of the Cold War and bombed its most important secret military site?"

"I see you've noticed our little display," Patrick said. "Be careful what you ask me, you two—you may find yourself sinking deeper and deeper into the mysteries of Dreamland, and once you're in, you can *never* return.

"We can end the tour right here. Colonel Luger

won't show you what's inside. You've seen more than anyone else not part of the program has ever seen before, and you are the first nonactive-duty military types to ever set foot in here. But once you step inside, I can't take you out again. The bracelet stays on forever. You may get your life in the Air Guard back again, but you will always be tied into the high-level security and scrutiny of this place. From the moment you step through that door, somebody will *always* be listening."

"I . . . I'm not sure if I want to do it," Annie Dewey said, twisting the vinyl-covered bracelet absently, then rubbing the spot where the microchip was injected. "I don't know if I want to be part of all this intrusion into my life."

"She's being honest with herself and with me," Patrick said. "All of you better do the same. Like General Samson said, the life you'll live sucks. You may get to return to Reno and fly for the Nevada Guard, but Big Brother will still be watching. You'll always be under scrutiny, you'll always be watched. Not only you but your families, your friends, your coworkers—anyone who comes in contact with you.

"But you'll be a part of something extraordinary, exciting, almost mystical. We get to fly the hottest jets, test the hottest weapons. We're not on the cutting edge here—we're a generation or two *beyond* it already."

Patrick meant to say it with great excitement, as he did to so many other newcomers to the base. But he knew what it was like in that corridor back in Dreamland, with the faces and memories of old friends staring back at him from many years and many adventures—and he couldn't do it. Working here, living here, making the commitment to be part of this place, it wasn't at all about excitement. It was about doing a terrible job against even more terrible odds—and winning with the fewest number of losses.

Patrick, sitting alone back in the conference room at Adak Naval Air Station, thought about the stuff back on the wall at Dreamland with his somber "thousand-yard stare," as if his friends and partners, both living and dead, were waving to him from somewhere on the horizon—which they were. They were telling Patrick to let go of his feelings, share his fears with these people. The shadows of the dead had accepted these strangers—now Patrick had to do the same.

He paused, mentally touched the photograph of Brad Elliott, and said in a quiet voice, "Maybe you'll save some lives; maybe you'll get to see your friends die horrible, slow, agonizing deaths. Maybe you'll save the world from going up in flames; maybe you'll be forced to do some illegal or immoral things, because the consequences of failure are too grave, and you'll hate the world you live in because you've ruined it. Maybe you'll make a little history; maybe you'll die alone, fighting a battle your country will deny ever happened. If you're lucky and your remains are recovered, you'll be buried in a desert cemetery that no one will ever visit, because officially it doesn't exist. Most times, *you* will just cease to exist."

As they listened to the disembodied voice in their heads, Furness, Seaver, and Dewey looked at each other with a mixture of surprise and sadness. It was like staring into a dark cave and deciding whether or not to go inside. That simple door at the other end of the corridor seemed like the portal to another world. The three guardsmen looked at each other, silently querying themselves and each other. This time Rebecca was not going to make the decision for them.

Finally, Rinc Seaver shrugged. "Well, jeez, General," he said, "when you put it that way, how can we refuse? I'm in."

"Oh, hell—I'm in," Rebecca said. It made her feel

good that Rinc Seaver committed first—she was afraid that revealing his weakness to her might have dulled his fighting edge. It was good to see him want to get back into action once again.

"I'm in too," John Long said. He had quietly entered the Corridor, escorted by Hal Briggs, as they stood and thought about their futures. He glared at Seaver. "As long as I don't have to fly with that piece of shit."

"Fine by me," Rinc shot back.

"Don't argue in this place!" Patrick snapped, jumping to his feet in the conference room nearly three thousand miles away, eyes blazing and neck muscles taut. "Don't you dare even raise your fucking *voices* in that hallway, or I will come back and kick both your asses out into the desert *myself*! That place is as sacred as a church. The floor you stand on is hallowed ground. You will goddamn learn to respect that! Do you understand? *Do you understand?"*

"Yes, sir," Long mumbled.

"Yes, sir," Rinc said. "Sorry, sir."

"You fly with whoever we *tell* you to fly with, both of you," Patrick said. "I think it's time you got your heads screwed on straight, both of you. Colonel Long, Seaver didn't cause the accident. He saved himself. He's a good stick. Let him do his job.

"Seaver, you're busy chasing ghosts that don't deserve chasing. You've got to get your mind properly focused on your crew and your mission before we go flying. You think you have something to prove. You don't. You just need to do your job and back up your teammates. That's what's important. Stop worrying about what others think or feel. Your life will be miserable if you don't—and it won't just be because of us here at Dreamland. You copy me?"

"Yes, sir," Long and Seaver replied quietly.

"Captain Dewey? Are you in? You can go outside

and think about it, give Tom or your folks a call if you'd like."

"You know about Tom, do you, sir?" Annie asked the thin air, as if talking to an invisible friend.

"Hey, he's a nice dude—for an urban cowboy wannabe," Hal Briggs chimed in.

"Hell, Heels, we knew about him too—and we didn't need any spies or listening devices to find out," Rebecca said with a smile. "He looks real fine, but he doesn't have a brain cell in his poor peanut head. Stay with us. We'll have a good time as long as we stick together."

"Then I'm in," Annie said.

"Good," Patrick said. "Colonel Luger, escort the new Megafortress crews into hangar one, please." He visualized the photos, charts, and other memorabilia on the wall, gave the photo of Brad Elliott a light, warm touch with his fingertips, then gave his new air combat team a thumbs-up from three thousand miles away. "Go look at your new ride, Aces."

CHAPTER SEVEN

Reports coming in from Chagang Do province, sir," General An Ki-sok, chief of staff of the United Republic of Korea armed forces, reported as he hung up the telephone. He was in the office of the minister of defense, retired general Kim Kun-mo. "Our infantry and artillery battalion at Pyorbai is under attack. At least two, possibly three battalions of light infantry and armor coming across the border. Kanggye is already surrounded and Chinese troops are in the city. We lost contact fifteen minutes ago—the Pyorbai barracks could already be overrun."

"A Chinese invasion?" General Kim exclaimed. "So *fast*?"

"Yes, sir," General An said. "Here is an update from reconnaissance planes, sir: at least two armored battalions and one infantry battalion against Kanggye itself; three, perhaps four more armored battalions and two infantry battalions moving south from J'an and Waichagoumen. Mostly light armor and infantry, moving very quickly, but they have substantial air defense, attack helicopters, and heavy armor backing them up."

"Do you suppose the Chinese are assisting rebel Communists inside Korea?" Kim asked. "Perhaps this attack was timed to correspond with those two rebel missile launches that aborted themselves over Hwanghae province last night."

"Very possible, sir," An replied. "Kim Jong-il's rhetoric coming from Beijing is more bombastic than ever. He congratulates whoever launched those missiles, and he has promised help from the Chinese to anyone who takes up arms against us. If he was going to mount a counteroffensive with China's help, Chagang Do province would be the best place to start."

"They're going after the weapons labs," Kim said as he picked up the telephone that connected directly with the Blue House, the presidential palace in Seoul. "If they capture the facilities intact, they'll capture a large number of special weapons warheads and prevent us from developing any more of our own."

"We cannot let that happen, sir!" An retorted. "We fought too hard to lose it so quickly and so suddenly like this! We must act!"

"President Kwon here," the president of United Korea answered a few moments later.

Kim raised a hand to silence his chief of staff. "Mr. President, General Kim here. I'm at the Ministry of Defense. Chinese troops were reported invading Chagang Do province. It appears they've taken Kanggye."

"What? Chinese troops? How many? Where?"

"Apparently, two brigades entered Kanggye and took over the Army barracks at Pyorbai," Kim replied. "We've had no contact from the province within the last half hour." Kim read a report handed to him, swallowed hard, then said into the telephone, "Sir, photo and electronic reconnaissance planes report massive Chinese ground movement across the border. In addition to the estimated two brigades that took Kanggye, there are reports of two more full brigades crossing the frontier at Linjiang and Dandong, including aviation units. No reports from Seventh Battalion stationed at Pyorbai—obviously our units were overwhelmed by Chinese forces." The Seventh was called a battalion, but in fact it was a hodgepodge of several partial infantry and light-armored North Korean companies, augmented with former South Korean men and equipment. Up until very recently, the men in this unit were mostly concerned with foraging for food—they were no match for any regular combat force even half their size, let alone two battalions of seasoned Chinese border troops.

"Where are they concentrated?" President Kwon asked. "What could their objective be?" He paused for a moment, then added softly, "The nuclear research facilities? The weapons laboratories?"

"That would be my guess, sir," Kim responded. "Sir, we need a way to stop those troops from taking Kanggye and the weapons labs. If Korean Communist rebels seize any special weapons and are able to use them against us, the loss of life could be staggering. But we cannot sacrifice those weapons labs. If we try an aerial or artillery bombardment, we could damage or destroy them—or the Chinese will do it for us." There was silence on the line for several long moments; then in a low, stern voice Kim said, "This is the time that we must use a weapon that can kill the enemy but not harm the buildings or equipment."

"What are you talking about, Kim?"

"A subatomic or chemical weapons attack against Chinese troops, sir," he said ominously. "Precisely what these weapons were designed for, exactly why North Korea had them in their inventory—to wipe us out without destroying our cities, our factories, our military or civil infrastructure. We have no choice, sir. If we lose Chagang Do province and all of its military facilities to the Chinese and to the Communist rebels, we will eventually lose our cities to attack."

"I am not convinced an attack like this is necessary, General."

"I believe it is necessary now more than ever, sir," Kim said emphatically. "We were not sure if the Chinese had launched an attack against Seoul and Pusan—this time we're sure the Chinese have invaded. They've attacked our aircraft and overrun our army outposts, and they are apparently trying to capture our weapons research facilities. We cannot allow that! We need to keep those facilities intact. The only way to do it is to use special weapons.

"The effects of both a chemical weapons and a neutron weapons attack will be confined to a very small area," Kim went on. "Vx nerve gas is potent but nonpersistent, meaning our forces can safely move in within days of the attack; the chemical disperses when exposed to wind or moisture, so danger to surrounding areas is minimal. The subatomic weapons create great destruction within a few hundred meters of ground zero, but virtually no destruction outside that radius. They kill within two miles of the blast and injure within four miles, while leaving our facilities intact. We can—"

"I do not believe we are even discussing this!" President Kwon shouted. "This is insanity! This is foolishness!"

"Sir, the Chinese knew the risks when they staged this invasion," Kim said. "If we do not respond immediately with overwhelming force, we stand the risk of losing our weapons facilities, Chagang Do province entirely, and perhaps our entire nation to the Chinese. What will you do, sir?"

President Kim hesitated. "Is there any word from our forces in Kanggye?" he asked. "Have they been captured? Killed? What is the extent of the Chinese incursion?"

"There is still no word from Kanggye, sir," Kim said, "only reports of massive numbers of Chinese armored forces heading south from all across the frontier. The longer we wait, sir, the harder it will be to uproot those troops."

Kim heard Kwon loudly swear to himself and pound on his desk as he tried to sort out the jumble of fears and emotions swirling inside. The attack on Pusan had forced him to agree to a massive bombardment of Chinese forces near Changbai—but this was different, completely different.

"I . . . I must consider this," Kwon said uneasily. "I must have more information. Call me as soon as you know more about the status of our forces near Kanggye and more precise numbers of Chinese troops in Chagang Do province." He hung up before Kim could say anything else.

"Damned coward!" Kim swore as he slammed the receiver down. "We took such enormous risks in reuniting the peninsula, we have the power to hold it or punish any who try to take it from us—but now Kwon grows weary and afraid. What a time to grow chicken feathers." He got up from his desk and started to pace. "If Kwon allows the Chinese People's Liberation Army to gain a toehold in Chagang Do province," he said to General An, "with American military forces all but gone, it would only be a matter of time before they would control the entire peninsula."

"Doesn't he realize how precarious a position we are in right now?" An asked rhetorically. "Those two aborted missile launches we saw last night, the unconfirmed report of a bomber over central Korea, and now fighters and armor south of the border—the Chinese are undoubtedly beginning an invasion campaign." He looked at Kim and said, "Sir, I think it would be worthwhile to pay a visit to the prime minister and the minister of foreign affairs. Perhaps we can convince them how necessary it is to act right away."

Kim stopped pacing and looked searchingly at General An. "Interesting," he said after a moment's careful pause. "And what if they agree with us, General? What if they feel as we do that a massive response is necessary?"

"Then . . . then we should act, sir," An replied. His words were straightforward but noncommittal—but his eyes spoke much more strongly, more forcefully. "We should do whatever is necessary to protect the republic."

"And what of President Kwon?"

"The president is a true patriot, a true visionary, the embodiment of the spirit of the Korean people," An said. "I bear no malice toward the man who has engineered the revolution and led the long-awaited reunification. But if he does not have the stomach for battle, he should be willing to step aside and let the warriors decide the fate of United Korea for him."

"I can see you are speaking from the heart, General," Kim said. "I share your thoughts completely. But what if he will not step aside?"

"Then," An said plainly, as if stating an obvious fact, "it is our sworn responsibility to *take* command."

THE WHITE HOUSE OVAL OFFICE,
WASHINGTON, D.C.
SEVERAL HOURS LATER

This invasion was completely unprovoked, unwarranted, and could touch off an all-out nuclear exchange!" the President of the United States thundered. In the Oval Office with him were Philip Freeman, Secretary of Defense Chastain, Chairman of the Joint Chiefs of Staff Balboa, and Vice President Whiting. He was speaking with the Chinese ambassador to the United States, Zhou Chang-li. "We're very fortunate that President Kwon of Korea didn't retaliate."

"Indeed," Ambassador Zhou said. The diplomat, young for a senior member of the Chinese foreign ministry at age sixty-one, seemed bored and distracted. "It would have meant the end of United Korea once and for all, I think."

"Is that supposed to be humorous, Mr. Ambassador?"

"No, sir. I am just stating a fact," Zhou said evenly. "The illegal government of the Republic of Korea agreed to terms of withdrawal of foreign forces. One part of the agreement was that our personnel not be detained or searched. Korea broke their part of the bargain. Second, we agreed that neither side would initiate hostilities against the other. Korea broke that bargain . . ."

"Korea thought that China launched that attack against them," Philip Freeman said. "It was a tragic error, but only an error, not a deliberate act of aggression."

"We respectfully disagree, General Freeman," Zhou said. "Kwon lashed out at our troops merely as a show of force. He knew full well that those military units he attacked had no ballistic missiles—our ballistic missile forces are located far from the border, even the mobile ones. He shows little regard for human life. It was a despicable act, and he deserves to be punished for it."

Martindale shook his head. "The old saying goes, 'Two wrongs don't make a right,' Mr. Ambassador," he said. "I'm talking about Kanggye, about Chagang Do province. Chinese troops have swarmed across the Korean border in several places by the thousands. They have occupied several parts of three provinces and have cut off highways and communications from three major Korean cities. It appears as if China is breaking the reunification agreement and is intent on invading Korea—or destroying it. What's the justification for this?"

"We are of course concerned about retaliation from South Korea," Zhou said plainly, as if the answer was obvious to everyone. "President Kwon and his advisers are plainly insane. He has launched an attack against peaceful Chinese ground troops, obviously using the unfortunate attack against his cities by some rebel soldiers as an excuse to lash out against our forces on his border. The entire world knows that his rocket attack was completely unwarranted. The rockets that hit his cities did not come from China. Yet he launched a rocket attack against my country that killed thousands of troops, most of whom were asleep in their beds. It was an incredible act of barbarism that Kwon must answer for! We are understandably concerned that he will next launch a missile attack against our civilian population."

"So in retaliation, you've decided to occupy three entire Korean provinces?" Secretary of Defense Chastain said. "You have over thirty-five thousand troops in Chagang Do province alone, and more crossing the Yalu River by the hour. This looks like an invasion force, Mr. Ambassador. It's 1950 all over again. After what you've done in the Philippines and to Taiwan, sir, the world naturally is afraid China wants to take the entire peninsula. Is this true?"

"It is a security force, nothing more," Ambassador Zhou said. "Quite frankly, sir, we fear the Koreans. We fear President Kwon. We think it is very possible that he could precipitate a thermonuclear war in northeast Asia."

"That's nonsense," Chastain said. "Kwon says he wants peace. He wants Korea to be left alone, without outside intervention."

"And he is willing to risk the lives of millions of innocent persons?" Zhou asked. "Mr. President, what would you do in our situation? Would you stand idly by and watch an unpredictable nuclear power spring to life overnight in your backyard? Or would you fight for peace at any cost? We chose to fight for peace."

"By invading a sovereign country?"

"It is well known that Chagang Do province was the seat of North Korea's chemical, biological, and nuclear weapons testing programs, and also where they conducted many of their rocket tests," Ambassador Zhou said. "The province has nine weapons facilities, several rocket testing facilities, four intercontinental-class launch facilities, and three nuclear reactors, all of which are capable of producing weapons-grade nuclear material. It has an extensive underground military laboratory, storage, staging, and security complex. This was too important a target to risk being left to a foreign power and obviously insane adversary such as Kwon Ki-chae.

"The safest alternative was to retake the military facilities, remove the scientific and manufacturing data, destroy the facilities, and then depart. This is our intention." Zhou fixed the President with a sincere gaze. "It is the truth, Mr. President. China only desires peace. It is true we assisted North Korea in its development of weapons of mass destruction. North Korea needed our economic assistance, and we wanted to ensure that our influence exceeded that of the Russians. Setting up weapons laboratories was a simple and effective way of making sure North Korea stayed in our sphere of influence."

"And what about the other invasions along the border?" the President asked. "*Four brigades* on the march in the first hour alone?"

"I am a bureaucrat, not a soldier," Ambassador Zhou said. "I do not understand military tactics. But I assure you, our only intention is to disable or destroy the nuclear, chemical, and biological labs in Chagang Do province. Perhaps the other moves are feints to divide and confuse the Koreans. If they launched nuclear weapons against our forces in Chagang Do province, perhaps the other units could accomplish the mission. We know what secrets those weapons facilities hold, sir. If United Korea was allowed to use those laboratories to develop new weapons or to repair its existing arsenal, the threat against our country would be absolutely intolerable."

"You mean, the risk of Korea's revolution spreading to China would be intolerable?" the President asked knowingly. Zhou seemed to squirm uncomfortably and he averted his eyes as if he had just been discovered in a lie. "You know as well as we do that Korea is not a threat to China or anyone else, that even a nuclear arsenal doesn't make Korea's threat any greater. But China can't allow a successful revolution on its borders because it might spark a similar revolution in *China*."

"That is hardly the issue, sir . . ."

"Oh, but I think it is," President Martindale said. "A few provinces in China think they have a shot at autonomy. If Beijing doesn't do anything against a nuclear-armed Korea, maybe they won't do anything against Inner Mongolia, or Xinjiang, or Tibet. Maybe you thought you needed to show Vietnam or the Philippines or Taiwan that you are still the big kid on the block. Maybe with democracy breaking out in Asia, Beijing is finding it more difficult to deal with protests and insurgency without using military force!"

"This speculation is pointless!" Zhou interjected. "Mr. President, I have stated my government's position as openly and honestly as possible. China is concerned about United Korea's development of more weapons of mass destruction using captured Chinese technology, so we have taken steps to prevent the technology from falling into their hands.

"I assure you, this is a peaceful undertaking," Zhou went on. "We desire nothing but peace. Our intention is to transport sensitive weapons technology and information out of Chagang Do province, then make sure that the Koreans cannot use the laboratories, and test and manufacturing facilities. We will destroy only military facilities. My government is even willing to reimburse United Korea for damage to civilian and nonmilitary properties we may cause. But we *will* do this. Kwon says he will go to war to remove us. We say we will go to war to prevent any more weapons of mass destruction from falling into Kwon's evil hands. I think we all know who would win such a confrontation."

"Mr. Ambassador, listen to me very carefully," President Martindale said. "The United States was more than willing to give peace a chance when the bloodless revolution took place and the peninsula was reunited. We did everything asked of us: we vacated the country, abandoned our bases, and pulled out. We did this because we wanted to show China and the world that we could trust and be trusted. As long as the conflict in

Korea was between Koreans, we were willing to stand aside.

"But with Chinese troops on Korean soil, it's not an internal matter anymore. I feel betrayed. The American people trusted me to keep Korea free. My duty was to the thousands of Americans who died trying to defend freedom and democracy in Korea in the 1950s. I trusted you, and now China has broken that trust. My people, and the shades of the men and women who died in the Korean War, are ready to turn their backs on me."

"Mr. President, I . . ."

"Be quiet and listen, Mr. Ambassador," Martindale went on angrily. "As long as Chinese troops are on Korean soil, my promise to stay out of Korea's affairs is ended. I now promise the complete opposite: I now promise that I will strike with all the power at my command any foreign military forces in Korea. The life of every soldier your country has sent into Korea is in my hands right now, do you understand?"

"You dare threaten the lives of Liberation Army soldiers so casually, sir?" Zhou asked, trying to inject as much indignation as he could into his voice. "My country has fought wars that have lasted longer than your nation's entire *existence*!"

"Mr. Ambassador, we have spent the last two years since the Taiwan crisis examining your nation's military," Secretary of Defense Chastain said. "We know your strengths and weaknesses, probably better than you know them yourself. China is a formidable adversary. But we stopped you from taking Taiwan, and we'll stop you from taking Korea—any way we can."

Ambassador Zhou gathered his briefcase and headed for the door but stopped and turned. "Mr. President, Madam Vice President, gentlemen. I implore you one last time: do not interfere in this. We have no intention of precipitating or fighting a war with United Korea.

But if China is faced with the prospect of a nuclear-armed Korea on its front doorstep, inciting revolution and insurrection and supporting Chinese dissidents with its nuclear weapons, we will act. And we will consider any nation that aids the Koreans to be our sworn enemy as well."

"We do not appreciate your threats, Mr. Ambassador," the President said. "Tell President Jiang and the Politburo that China first made the mistake by arming North Korea and building those weapons facilities. You do not have the right to interfere now that those facilities are not under your rightful control, no matter what your rationale is. Peace begets peace, Mr. Ambassador, and conflict begets conflict. Chinese troops are on Korean soil and have killed or captured thousands of Koreans. If it's peace you're working for, you're not going about it the right way.

"My demand is simple: Remove your forces from Korea immediately. If we see China's forces moving north at great speed within the hour, we will speak with President Kwon and compel him to stop any offensives against your retreating forces. If you do not begin withdrawing your forces within the hour, they will be destroyed. Plain and simple."

Zhou said nothing. He hid a deep scowl by bowing deeply, then departed.

The President returned to his desk and took a moment to collect his thoughts and try to unwind. "Well, that went *swimmingly*. China has come right out and admitted they're taking a Korean province for an indefinite period of time."

"What is Kwon going to do?" the Vice President asked. "He's shown us he's capable of anything. He's likely to level everything inside Chagang Do province with whatever weapon he can."

The President stared out the window, lost in

thought. "And I can't blame him," he said finally. "If it's proved that Kwon launched those rockets against China even though he knew China didn't attack, his actions are unconscionable. But he's also demonstrated his resolve to defend United Korea using every tool at his disposal. I believe Zhou when he says China is afraid of Kwon. *I'm* afraid of Kwon, and I don't think he has any missiles pointed at us. China might very well do as Zhou says they will: destroy the nuclear weapons labs, burn everything down, and get out."

"And that wouldn't make me unhappy either," Philip Freeman admitted. "The question is, who's going to step over the line next? Will Kwon back off? And if he doesn't, how much force is he going to use?"

"And what the hell do we do in the meantime?" the President asked. "Do we risk an escalation by sending in more aircraft carriers? What do we do if China and Korea start an all-out missile exchange? Do we dare even put our forces at risk?"

"Our best shot right now is McLanahan and his Coronet Tiger antimissile technology," National Security Adviser Freeman said. "If he can keep everybody's head down and prevent any more mushroom clouds from going up over Korea or China, we may have enough time to defuse this matter."

"What's the status of McLanahan's deployment?" Chastain asked.

"The support teams were dispatched right after you gave the order, while the Nevada Air National Guard crews were recalled and the bombers got ready to deploy," Freeman replied. "The bombers launched late last night." He glanced at Admiral Balboa. "Unfortunately, because of what the Guard troops did during their evaluation, Admiral Balboa ordered the Coronet Tiger program halted and all the funding pulled. McLanahan has a substantially degraded force."

"But I notice McLanahan and Samson disregarded my orders and went ahead anyway," Joint Chiefs of Staff Chairman Balboa said. "I ordered the program halted and the planes to be returned to the Guard until I could conduct a full investigation—instead, they convinced the state of Nevada to turn the planes over to them for a dollar each per year! A fucking *dollar*!"

"Those planes do belong to Nevada, Admiral . . ."

"And Samson dumped a quarter of a billion dollars of unauthorized funds into modifying them, against my orders," Balboa went on angrily. "When are we going to stop rewarding these HAWC guys for disobeying orders? This Lancelot thing has only undergone limited testing and only one live launch—illegally, against Navy ships, I might add. And what about those Air National Guard crews? I briefed Arthur and Philip on what they did during their predeployment exercise. They're dangerous as hell."

Balboa glanced at Freeman. He knew that Philip Freeman had the President's ear much more often than he did; he knew the President liked to use secret programs to avoid a lot of public or congressional scrutiny. But just because he knew what the President preferred didn't mean he had to recommend it to him, as Freeman was apt to do: "Sir, I have great respect for Generals Samson and McLanahan, and I know you do too. They're true patriots. But they operate well outside an established chain of command. Even I do not have full authority to interfere with a HAWC project because of all the security involved. If they don't answer to me, whom do they answer to? Will the President of the United States have to issue orders directly to a couple of Air National Guard pilots thousands of miles away? That's not how it's supposed to work, sir."

Balboa paused, considering his next words—he knew full well how the President respected Samson's predecessor—then said, "I truly believe, sir, with no disrespect, that Brad Elliott's don't-give-a-shit attitude has carried through to Samson and McLanahan. Their unauthorized and potentially disastrous plasma-yield warhead test near our Navy support ships, and their tacit approval of that Nevada Air Guard's actions in the bombing ranges, bear this out. I believe that once those two get into it, they'll disregard any plan of action or lawful order if it doesn't fit in with their own agenda. And if they start lobbing plasma-yield missiles into China without proper authorization, they could single-handedly plunge the world into nuclear war. I believe we can't take the chance."

"I think that's unfair, Admiral," Freeman said.

Balboa ignored him. "Mr. President, I know how much respect you had for General Elliott and his men. But they haven't proved themselves in combat conditions yet. All they know is what Brad Elliott taught them years ago, which was, 'it's better to ask forgiveness than ask for permission.' "

The President had a serious, somber expression when Balboa began speaking, but as he went on, the President let a hint of a smile spread across his face. When Balboa finished, he shook his head, the smile on his face now broad.

"Admiral, I am convinced now that you are mostly full of shit," the President said. Balboa's own expression went from surprise to shock to red-faced anger. "But you weren't around for the early years, when Brad Elliott and HAWC were just getting started. Yes, they were unconventional, shot from the hip, even insubordinate at times—no, *most* of the time. But to say these guys don't have combat experience shows how little you've learned and how little you know."

"That's not a fair assessment, sir, but I'll accept your criticism," Balboa said, his face pinched and uneasy.

"But if I may ask, sir: what's the chain of command? Who gives those crews their orders? And who takes responsibility for them when those nutcase Nevada Air Guard crews crash themselves into Korea or China?"

"As always, Admiral, *I* take full responsibility," the President said. "That should come as an immense relief to you—unless you already found a way to distance yourself from them. Now, get out of my office before I remember that my senior uniformed military officer just wished the worst on one of his own flying units."

OVER SOUTHERN CHAGANG DO PROVINCE,
UNITED REPUBLIC OF KOREA
(FORMERLY NORTH KOREA)
EARLY EVENING HOURS

Contact!" the observer/weapons officer of the *Han-Guk Kong Goon* (United Republic of Korea Air Force) A-37B Dragonfly close-air-support and observation aircraft shouted on his intercom. There was certainly no reason to shout; his pilot was less than ten centimeters to his left in the tiny side-by-side cockpit. The observer put his left hand on the glareshield and pointed at the target. "Two o'clock. A Chinese ML935 locomotive pulling six cars."

"Can you see the engine crew arrangement?" the pilot asked, making a slight turn to the right.

The observer strained to look through his field glasses. "I need a closer look," he said finally.

"C'mon, we don't want to get too close to those guys," the pilot said. "They have antiaircraft guns."

"But we gotta try to identify them before we call in a patrol," the observer said. "Let's get down in the weeds. Keep the smash up." Like most Korean fliers, they liked using American military aviation slang.

"Okay," the pilot said. "Here we go." He shoved the throttles to full military power, rolled the little Cessna twin turbojet on its right wing, and made a diving right turn toward the locomotive.

It appeared that a section of track ahead was partially broken, and the train was stranded. The crew of men working around the break scattered and ran when they heard the loud high-pitched whine of the Dragonfly's tiny General Electric turbojets. "That looks suspicious already," the observer said. Automatically, he checked weapons status. The A-37B, a Vietnam War–era veteran close-air-support plane, was armed with a 7.62-millimeter Minigun with three hundred rounds of ammo in the nose, two "Mighty Mouse" folding-fin attack rocket pods, two target-marking rocket pods, plus four huge fuel tanks, making the little Cessna look ungainly and slow—which it definitely was.

"Fingers off the arming switches," the pilot warned him. "The last thing we need to do is fire a rocket at a noncombatant."

"Nose is cold," the observer acknowledged.

But not for long. As they careened closer, they could see that the men working on the track had retreated back to one of the cars—and soon the roof of the car opened, revealing a single-barreled antiaircraft gun. "Look out!" the observer shouted. "It's a Type-93! Break left!" The Type-93 was a Chinese-made 37-millimeter antiaircraft gun, murderous to any slow, low-flying aircraft. The pilot yanked his Dragonfly into a tight left turn and pulled until right at the verge of a stall, then relaxed the back pressure until he rolled out heading the other way. He immediately started a climb to get out of the 93's lethal range.

"Call it in, dammit!" the pilot cursed.

"How do we know they were Communists?"

"We don't for sure—but they were ready to blow us out of the sky," the pilot said. "We need backup on this one. Call it in." The observer got on the UHF radio and called in the position and description of the train.

"Orders are to mark the target for inbound paratroopers, disable the locomotive by any means possible to keep it from moving, and eliminate any heavy weapons that might endanger inbound troops," the observer reported a few minutes later. "A security paratroop squad from Sunch'on will parachute into the area by cargo plane, ETA thirty minutes."

"We've got an hour before we bingo, so it looks about right," the pilot said, checking his fuel gauges. "I don't think we need to worry about disabling the locomotive—that train's not going anywhere with a torn-up track. Let's see what we can do about that Type-93." The pilot started a left turn back toward the train and leveled off at twelve thousand feet. "Give me some markers first and let's see what they do."

"Roger," the observer said, flipping his arming switches. "Target markers armed, your trigger is hot."

Seven miles from the train, the pilot started a dive at seven thousand feet per minute, accelerating to 420 knots. Winds were mostly calm and the visibility was good, so it was simple to put the aiming pipper right on the car with the antiaircraft gun, and he squeezed the trigger. One target-marking rocket shot out of pods on each wing.

"Guns! Guns!" the observer shouted. "He's firing!"

The pilot squeezed off two more rockets, then rolled hard left away from the train. "I'm off! Safe 'em up!" he said through his antiblackout straining. The observer clicked the target-marker pods' safety switches to SAFE.

"Nose is cold!" The observer strained to look behind them as they rolled out of the escape turn. "No damage, no flak," he said. "They missed us that time." He checked the target area. Mixed in with the bright yellow target-marking smoke were streams of black smoke, pouring out horizontally as well as vertically. "I see black smoke. Looks like we might've hit something."

"You get a look at that gun mount?" the pilot asked. "It looked to me like the gun was mounted close to the top of the car—almost down inside it."

"That means they might not be able to lower the barrel too much," the observer said. "You want to try a low pass?"

"Affirm," the pilot said. "Give me rockets."

"Roger . . . Mighty Mouse is armed, your trigger is hot."

The pilot started a steeper descent and leveled off barely one hundred feet aboveground. Even so low to the ground, it was easy to locate the train. The terrain was rolling hills, but visibility was good from several miles out. Guesstimating the range, the pilot put the smoky car on the bottom range marker on his calibrated gun sight and fired. The spin-stabilized folding-fin attack rockets flew straight and true, hitting the car square on. "Two good hits!" the observer crowed. Now the car was burning fiercely, with black smoke billowing out. "Nice shooting! You want the Minigun?"

"A-firm. Arm up the Minigun," the pilot ordered.

"Mighty Mouse safe . . . triggers clear . . . Minigun armed, your trigger is hot."

"Roger," the pilot said. The Minigun was his favorite weapon—close-range, powerful, exciting. The cannon itself was mounted right below him, with the chamber practically in his crotch—it felt like a massive orgasm every time he fired it. The gun didn't bang—it hummed. It was the world's best hum-job.

Same pipper, same range marks . . . he had to

get a little closer, but it was no problem. Even if the Type-93 could fire that low, the gunner couldn't see anything because of all the smoke. But the Dragonfly pilot could see his target very clearly. A little closer . . . closer . . .

Suddenly, the A-37 shuddered and decelerated, as if they had just landed wheels-up. Warning lights snapped on everywhere, including the red FIRE lights on both fire extinguisher handles.

"Double compressor stall!" the observer shouted, quickly scanning the engine instruments. "TOT redline . . . fuel flow max . . . two fire lights! We've been hit by something! We've been hit!" He didn't think to look out the cockpit canopy, but if he had he would've seen both engines on fire.

There was only one line, one word, to the emergency checklist for two FIRE lights on. The pilot favored his observer with a "Prepare to eject!" command before slapping himself back into his seat, giving the control stick one last pull to try to gain a little more altitude, reaching between his legs, shouting "Eject! Eject! Eject!" and pulling the thick oblong handle. The canopy unlatched itself and lifted up an inch, enough for the slipstream to blow it up and away. Two seconds later the ejection seat rockets fired, blasting the pilot clear of the burning aircraft. A second and a half later the observer jetted out.

They were just high enough to get a fully open parachute and one swing before hitting the ground, with nothing that even remotely resembled a parachute-landing fall. But somehow both United Korea pilots picked themselves up off the ground without any broken bones or other serious injuries. They had landed about two miles from the burning train cars, just behind a tiny hillock.

Both men sprang into action without a word between them. They released their parachutes, wadded them up as fast as they could, then stuffed them under rocks and in dirt crevasses. They then retrieved their seat kits, which were tethered to their ejection seat harnesses. The seat kit was also a small backpack. Each took only three items from the backpacks—the survival rifle, spare ammunition clips, and a can of water—before throwing the kits over their shoulders, stuffing the ammo and water into their flight suits, and running for the nearest cover they could find.

Once they reached cover, they took a quick heading with their wrist compasses, then took a few moments to rest. "What happened?" the observer asked. "What hit us?"

"I don't know," the pilot responded. "Must've been rebels, maybe a detached security unit with a shoulder-fired antiaircraft weapon." He nodded resolutely toward the south. "We need to get as far away from here as possible," he said. "The transport carrying our commandos will be arriving soon."

"We've got to warn them off!" the observer said. "Whatever shot us down will take them next!" He pulled out his survival radio and clicked it on. His pilot looked at him wordlessly, and the observer nodded. They both knew that the minute they activated the radio, the enemy could triangulate their position. But if they didn't make the call, the deaths of thirty commandos and a C-130 Hercules flight crew would haunt them forever.

"Samtek Seven, Samtek Seven, this is Patrol Three-Four on the ground, over."

"Patrol Three-Four, this is Samtek, we read you loud and clear, authenticate one-Zulu."

"Charlie," the observer responded, referring to a tiny authenticator card. He accomplished another authentication routine with the transport pilot; then:

"Samtek, we have been shot down by unknown hostile forces, possibly hostile AI or SAMs. The LZ is hot, repeat, LZ hot. Remain clear of the area and go get help. Do you copy?"

"We copy, Three-Four," the transport pilot replied. "Air cover and strike forces are on the way, ETA four. If you can make it to extraction point Lotus, repeat Lotus, help will be waiting."

"Roger," the observer said. There was nothing that made a downed aircrew feel better than to know there were friendlies in the area who were willing to risk their own lives to rescue them. "Our ETA to Lotus is three." They used a simple code for time—multiplied the number by the day of the month—to avoid giving the enemy an idea of when and where to find them.

"We copy, Three-Four," the transport pilot said. "Good luck. Samtek is clear."

"Now let's get out of here," the pilot shouted, and they took off running to the next bit of cover they could see, about two hundred yards off.

They were halfway to their next hiding place when they heard it—a deep, loud, screeching roar, coming toward them. They looked up—and realized immediately that they were dead men. It was two Chinese Q-5 light jet fighter-bombers, careening down on them in a shallow dive.

"It's Chinese," the observer said. "We're well inside our own borders! China is flying attack jets over our territory!" No doubt that's who had shot them down—and now they were coming in to finish the job.

The pilot frantically got on his handheld radio again. "Samtek, Samtek, this is Three-Four. We spotted a Chinese Q-5 fighter-bomber, repeat, a Chinese fighter-bomber, at our location. Recommend you get as far away from here as possible and send help! How do you read?"

"Loud and clear, Three-Four," the transport pilot acknowledged. "Thanks for the warning. Get off the air and take cover!"

But it was far too late. The United Republic of Korea crew members' last thought was that the stupid Chinese bastards sure were wasting a lot of bombs on them—both Q-5 fighters dropped cluster bombs on their attack pass. All that ordnance just to kill two arrogant Dragonfly crew members who were too stupid to check their six for signs of threats. It was an impressive attack, very accurate—but one bomb would've done the job just as easily.

With the cluster bombs gone, the Chinese Q-5 fighter, a copy of the old Soviet MiG-19 fighter-bomber, now flew like a jet fighter instead of like a wallowing pig. Both Q-5s climbed up from their attack pass to four thousand meters. The leader checked his wingman over and noticed he had dropped his bombs too. Well, now they were both fighters again.

"Han-301, this is Control," their ground controller radioed. "We have detected an airborne target, slow-moving, altitude unknown, twenty-three kilometers south of your position. You are directed to intercept and destroy. Acknowledge."

The Q-5 flight lead checked his radio range from the controller's position beacon, cross-checked his position with some prominent landmarks, then checked his chart board. He was about thirty kilometers inside United Korea, what was once free-flying airspace of North Korea. Technically, this was a violation of UROK's airspace, an act of war. But since China had not yet recognized the United Republic of Korea, it still considered this airspace as belonging to its ally the Democratic People's Republic of Korea, whose president and government just now happened to reside in Beijing to escape political persecution. Besides, when UROK fired those missiles against Chinese troops in Yanggang Do province, they technically started a war. So flying another twenty-three kilometers or so inside Korea was no big deal.

"H-301 acknowledges instructions," the flight lead responded. He turned south and activated his ranging radar. The tactical controller, based in a mobile radar trailer just north of the Korean border, kept feeding him a constant stream of position updates until it became apparent that the target had descended low enough to escape his radar.

But soon the Chinese fighter pilots didn't need the controller's help. Just a few minutes later the Q-5 fighter lead spotted the big transport. It was an American-made C-130 transport in black and brown camouflage, hugging the rolling, rugged terrain, flying barely a hundred meters aboveground. "Control, H-301 has visual contact on aircraft, proceeding with intercept." There was no response—he was flying too low and too far from the radar controller now to maintain good radio coverage.

No matter. He had the target visually, and it would be an easy kill. He deactivated his range-only radar, selected his 20-millimeter cannon, armed his trigger, dialed in the proper settings on his mechanical heads-up display—no fancy electronic HUD on this thirty-year-old bird, nor was one required—double-checked his switches, and began to slide into firing range. When the C-130's wingtips began to touch the edge of the aiming reticle, he slid his finger down to the trigger and . . .

"Lead!" It was the wingman frantically shouting on the interplane radio. *"Incoming missile! Break left! Now!"*

The Chinese pilot ignored the warning—he was exactly at firing range. But in the blink of an eye his instruments began rolling, warning lights flashed, and his tiny cockpit immediately filled with dense black smoke. He was momentarily distracted by another flash of light—the fireball of his wingman exploding in mid-air—before he reluctantly released the grip on his throttle and control stick and pulled his ejection.

The Q-5 slammed into the ground in an inverted dive traveling almost the speed of sound. He had made the decision to eject just three seconds too late.

"Splash two," Brigadier General Patrick McLanahan radioed. "Good shooting, Rebecca."

What a weird feeling, Rebecca Furness thought. She had of course launched missiles and killed the enemy before—her RF-111G Vampire bomber carried Sidewinder air-to-air missiles for self-defense, and she had to use them during the Russia-Ukraine skirmish. But that was self-defense, a means to help blow past area defenses or put a fighter screen on the defensive long enough for her to get to the target. This was different. They were the hunters this time.

Rebecca and three other crews loaded EB-1C Megafortress battleships at Dreamland and flew them to Adak, Alaska. After crew rest, the crews were briefed, and three Megafortresses launched together to take up combat air patrols over Korea, with the fourth and fifth planes launching later to begin an eight-hour rotation schedule to try to keep as many planes up over Korea at once as possible.

"You okay, Colonel?" Patrick McLanahan asked Furness. Patrick was back on the ground at Adak Naval Air Station, commanding the virtual cockpit. He and Nancy Cheshire would spend four hours in it, then man Fortress Four and relieve Rebecca on patrol in northern

Korea. Four hours later another crew would launch in Fortress Five, and the rotation would continue until they were ordered to stop.

"I . . . I think so."

"It doesn't get any easier after the first or the second or the fourth kill," Patrick said, expertly reading her mind. "In fact, it only gets more nightmarish. Probably because the technology gets so swift, so efficient. Those Chinese Q-5s were seventeen miles away. We could've been another ten miles farther away."

"I guess we're not into fair fights anymore, are we?"

"Fair fights? That *was* a fair fight, Colonel. That's about as close as you want to get to a fighter, even a thirty-year-old clunker like a Q-5. If you missed and he turned around and got close enough to get a visual on you, you'd have maybe a fifty-fifty chance of making it out over the Sea of Japan and over to friendly air cover before he blew *your* shit away. If both of them came at you, I'd lower our odds to twenty-eighty. Fifty-fifty is generous—I'd like at least ninety-ten on our side."

"Hey, lighten up, everybody," Nancy Cheshire, the senior pilot back in the virtual cockpit, interjected. "Rebecca, I say, You go, girl! First air-to-air shots in anger for the Megafortress, and she scores two hits! Oh, sure, Scottie might have had something to do with it."

"Thanks a bunch, Chessie," said Major Paul Scott, Rebecca Furness's mission commander in the Megafortress's right seat. Like Cheshire, he was a longtime veteran of the High Technology Aerospace Weapons Center and had flown many sorties in the old EB-52, the B-52 version of the Megafortress. He double-checked that his weapons were safed and added, "Maybe a little—but I'll still give all the credit to the Megafortress."

"You're allowed to show a little pleasure now and then, Scottie," Cheshire said. "Just a little 'hot-diggetydamn'? We just saved that Korean cargo plane and probably a few dozen of their commandos."

"I'll take that under advisement, Nancy," Paul said. "Scope's clear. Give me forty left and let's get back in our patrol orbit, Rebecca." Their assigned orbit was over Kanggye itself, monitoring the movement of Chinese forces across the border into Chagang Do province.

"Fortress, Fortress, this is Iroquois," a call came in moments later. "Bogeys at one-one-zero at one-one-zero bull's-eye, angels thirty, heading northwest toward Fortress One at four-eight-zero knots." "Iroquois" was the call sign of the EB-1's "back door," the USS *Grand Island,* a 9,500-ton *Ticonderoga*-class guided missile cruiser, escorted by the USS *Boone,* a *Perry*-class guided missile frigate, in a patrol position about fifty miles off the Korean coast. "We count eight, repeat eight, bogeys. They are going to cross south of SAM range."

The *Grand Island,* named after the large island just south of Niagara Falls that was the scene of Revolutionary War and War of 1812 battles with the British Army, guarded the Sea of Japan and the Megafortress's exit path. It used its long-range three-dimensional SPY-1B radar to scan the skies from the surface into near space for two hundred miles in all directions. Its surface-to-air weapons included SM-2MR Standard antiaircraft missiles and Standard Block 4A antiballistic missile interceptors; it was the first Navy warship to carry these weapons. The cruiser also carried Tomahawk land-attack missiles and Harpoon antiship missiles. The *Boone* carried Standard and Harpoon missiles, but it was along as an antisubmarine warfare vessel, carrying two ASW helicopters and a total of twenty-four air-launched and six ship-fired torpedoes.

"Looks like the Japanese are coming back to play," Patrick commented.

"Hey, guys, I got something," Patrick reported. "Aircraft lifting off from Pyongyang North airfield, heading for Kanggye. Low altitude. Probably attack jets. I'm picking up a formation of fast-movers lifting off from Seoul as well. Looks like the two formations are going to join up."

"And here's their target, I'll bet," Paul Scott on Fortress One reported. He had just updated his own laser radar scan with recent data from a NIRTSat reconnaissance scan. The scan detected a long line of heavy vehicles on the principal highway between Kanggye and Anju. "The Chinese tanks are moving fast. They're twenty miles south of Holch'on, almost at the southern edge of the province. They're . . . wow, the computer says they're main battle tanks. A line of tanks probably three miles long on the principal highway. I've also got main battle tanks going cross-country along a ten-mile-wide front on either side of the highway. At least two hundred vehicles spread out over twenty miles."

"Can the system identify them?"

The LADAR ran the laser-derived dimensions through the computer's large database of vehicles, but the results were inconclusive. "We got everything in the book out there: Chinese Type-59s and -69s, ex-Soviet T-53s and BMPs, self-propelled artillery, the works. I'd want to get a little closer. Ten miles the other way should do it."

"I'll pass the contact along to HAWC and to NRO anyway," Patrick said. "It looks like you picked up something else on that last LADAR image." Patrick had expanded his virtual cockpit display to show the entire fifty-mile LADAR image. Sure enough, it had detected several Chinese fighters heading south. "Computer identifies them as a large flight of J-6s, heading across the border too," Patrick said. The J-6, a copy of the old Soviet MiG-19 "Farmer" tactical fighter, was the most numerous attack jet in China's large aircraft arsenal. "Looks like four flights of four. China is definitely looking for trouble."

"If those units on the ground aren't firing up antiaircraft systems," Nancy observed, "we can assume that either those vehicles don't know they're there—in which case they could've been bombed pretty easy—or the vehicles on the ground are Chinese as well."

"Good point," David said. "Looks like we got a Chinese ground invasion under way, supported by some air cover. We might get some action tonight, after all."

"Great," Rebecca said, tightening her straps even more. "I felt pretty good up here—until now. I feel totally naked now."

"Your fuel looks good—about an hour before you bingo," Patrick said. "Electrical, hydraulics, pneumatics, CG in the green. Looks like the fighters are going to stay at midaltitudes. Want to go up high?"

"Sounds good to me," Rebecca said.

"Let's do it," Patrick said. In less than five minutes they had climbed up to thirty-four thousand feet, at least ten thousand feet higher than the Chinese fighters. The Japanese MiG-29s had descended below the Megafortress bombers as well. "HAWC has acknowledged our data transmissions and passed along a tactical alert to Space Command and Pacific Command," Patrick went on. "We saw it first—good work, guys. The *Grand Island* and the *Boone* are listening in with us on real-time and have gone to general quarters." Patrick and Nancy looked at each other at the exact same moment. They could both feel the excitement and tension running hot.

"Okay, we're picking up a full-scale air defense alert being broadcast in the clear to all Korean military units," Patrick reported. "Air defense radars are lighting up . . . we should be able to tap into them any minute. We'll have peninsula-wide radar coverage pretty soon."

As the battle developed, it was obvious the Korean defenders were on the defensive all the way. Even combining the old North Korean air assets—a mixture of a few modern MiG-23 attack jets and MiG-29 fighters and many more older, obsolete ex-Chinese aircraft—with South Korea's Western-designed aircraft, the Korean forces were at least numerically outgunned.

The Korean F-16CJ aircraft led the main attack group. They stayed at fifteen thousand feet, flying high enough to stay away from antiaircraft artillery, presenting themselves as inviting targets. The idea was that they should have drawn fire from Chinese surface-to-air missile batteries, at least a squeak on radar, enough so that they could open fire on any enemy search or tracking radars with their AGM-88 HARMs (high-speed antiradar missiles).

But the Chinese armor and infantry units were smart enough not to take the bait. They knew that if they didn't activate any radars, the Korean F-16CJs did not have anything to shoot at. The Korean F-16s flew right up to the Chinese tanks—and never even received a rifle shot in their direction. They could do nothing but orbit over the area and wait for targets to pop up. A few tried to go low to drop cluster bombs on tanks and self-propelled artillery, and those planes were hit by optically and low-light TV-guided antiaircraft artillery and heat-seeking surface-to-air missiles. The Koreans lost four aircraft to enemy fire before being forced to retreat.

The F-16 Block 52 attack jets went in next, armed with infrared-imaging AGM-65D Maverick antitank missiles, followed by MiG-23 fighter-bombers carrying gravity bombs and target-marking rockets. But the Chinese J-6 fighters had arrived over the battlefield by now, outnumbering the Korean fighters by six to one. Even with those odds, the Korean jets were racking up impressive kills, but soon they began to run out of missiles and the numbers of Chinese jets just didn't seem to be diminishing. Before long the Korean jets were on the defensive and forced to run south. Several formations of Korean F-4E Phantom II bombers tried circumnavigating the entire Chagang Do battlefield and tried to cut in from the west, but they were intercepted by Chinese fighters out of Dandong and chased off as well. Both sides lost a handful of planes, but it wasn't a stalemate or tie—every plane Korea lost composed a major percentage of the fleet, while four fighters could replace even the most obsolete Chinese fighter.

Even though both the Koreans and the Chinese lost a fairly equal number of planes, the first Korean counteroffensive was a complete failure. The massive numbers of Chinese armor and mobile infantry units in the three Korean northern border provinces were barely scratched.

MASTER CONTROL AND REPORTING CENTER
OSAN, UNITED REPUBLIC OF KOREA
(FORMERLY SOUTH KOREA)
THAT SAME TIME

Five F-16s and six F-4s lost or damaged, sir," the command operations officer summarized. "We have reports of confirmed hits on just thirteen Chinese main battle tanks and nine artillery pieces. Our weapons list was in excess of two hundred Maverick missiles, forty antiradar missiles, and over one hundred sticks of gravity weapons. Our surviving forces are rearming and refueling."

"Those losses are completely unacceptable!" Minister of National Defense Kim Kun-mo shouted. "Five percent! Five percent of our strike fleet was destroyed or damaged *in just the first wave*! How can we expect to drive out the enemy with losses such as this?"

"Sir, we are gathering more tactical reconnaissance and rebuilding the target list," General An Ki-sok, chief of the general staff, replied. "But the Chinese Air Force has simple numerical superiority over Chagang Do province right now. The Chinese fighters do not engage our F-16 fighters—they merely shoot and run, shoot and run. They do this because they know there are four or five more fighters entering the battle for every one that retreats. Why risk being shot down in an engagement with a superior force?"

"What are you planning on doing about it, General?" Kim asked.

"We can do little at night without better photo intelligence," General An replied somberly. "Only one-third of our F-16s can carry Maverick missiles, and they cannot do their job very well if we do not control the skies. In daytime, we can use the F-5 *Chegong-ho* fighters for air defense and the Hawks and Mohawk planes for attack." He paused, then looked at his commander with a painful expression. "But it will do little good, sir," he admitted. "China's Air Force is qualitatively far inferior to ours, but they will have the numbers on their side no matter how good our pilots are. We may never get control of the skies over Chagang Do province."

"This is unacceptable! Completely unacceptable!" Kim shouted. "We have struggled too hard and have come too far to be turned back. If we cannot defend our own land from attack, what good are we as a nation?" The hot line phone began to ring. Kim ignored it for several long moments, and a stern glare warned General

An not to touch it either. Finally, Kim answered it: "What is it?"

"This is the president," Kwon Ki-chae said angrily. "What is going on? My staff tells me we are attacking the Chinese troops!"

"I had no choice, Mr. President," Kim said. "I assembled a strike package and executed a conventional weapons attack against the spearhead of the Chinese armored units. I also conducted a probe to try to determine what kind of air defenses they had set up in Chagang Do province."

"This was completely without authorization!" Kwon shouted. "You will launch no more attacks tonight! Is that understood?"

"Sir, we lost eleven aircraft to the Chinese," Kim said bitterly. "They continue to move south and are threatening to break out of Chagang Do province. By this time tomorrow they can have four brigades of tanks on the outskirts of Pyongyang. If we do not stop them, they will be knocking on your door at the Blue House in three days."

"General, don't you realize we cannot hope to defeat the Chinese People's Liberation Army by military means?" President Kwon asked incredulously. "Don't you realize what happened here? We achieved a major victory over the Communists not by the use of force, but by the use of reason and truth. North Korea fell because the people threw off the dictatorship that was slowly killing them, not because we used our military might to subdue them."

"I am well aware of how we defeated the Communists, sir," Kim said, his voice a low monotone.

"Then under what delusions of grandeur are you suffering, General Kim?" Kwon asked. "Did you think that just because we captured some jets and artillery pieces and nuclear weapons we can scare China? The smallest military district in China has twice as many men, planes, and tanks as our *entire country*!

"We are a nation of peace, Kim, not because we are small and defenseless, but because we are Koreans, bred for peace," Kwon went on. "We do not have an offensive striking force because we never wanted one! We should have given those special weapons away. We never should have kept them!"

"And let China overrun us again?" Kim asked. "Did we fight to win reunification, only to roll over and die just a few short weeks later?"

"This is a different world than that of 1895 or 1945," Kwon said. "Don't you realize this? The conquest of land is less important than technological and economic competition. China never wanted our land. But you—we—acted as if the Ming dynasty ruled China, or the Imperial Japanese warlords wanted to annex us again. The Chinese would have been perfectly happy to wait and watch to see if stability and peace would take over the Korean peninsula—as long as they were not threatened by nuclear weapons. When we kept those weapons, we became a threat to them."

"Sir, we kept those weapons because they were to secure our borders and guarantee our security against the Chinese People's Liberation Army," Kim retorted. "We knew we could not defend ourselves against China's overwhelming numerical advantage. China is stupid enough to risk the lives of millions of its citizens and soldiers just to take Chagang Do province—well, that was their mistake. We have no choice now, sir.

"We have to back up our threat to use weapons of mass destruction to stop the Chinese. I am requesting your launch codes for our nuclear, chemical, and biological weapons force."

"You . . . you are insane, Kim . . ."

"I am *realistic,* sir!" Kim exploded. "I am trying to

save Korea, not watch it destroyed! I am in the command center directing our troops to try to drive the invaders out, not sitting in my cozy office or in some underground secret bunker wringing my hands and hoping for peace. I have ordered twelve Scud-B and six Nodong-1 ballistic missiles targeted against the Chinese brigades in Chagang Do province and inside Jilin province in China. I have also targeted air bases in Dandong, Fushun, and Shenyang, the tank base at Linjiang, and the naval bases at Luda and Qingdao. In addition, I have targeted two Nodong-2 missiles at the People's Liberation Army command center . . ."

"Beijing?" Kwon said in horror. "You . . . you have targeted Beijing with *nuclear weapons?"*

"I know this seems a drastic and inconceivable act, sir," Kim said with amazing calmness, "but if we have any hope of stopping the Chinese war machine from sweeping across Korea, we must do this. I need your execution codes, sir, and I need them now. You must read them off to me over the phone—I can send someone over there immediately to help you compute the codes if you wish. The senior controller here will copy them down and authenticate them. Combined with my codes, we can proceed with the attack."

"I will *never* agree to give you those codes, Kim!" Kwon shouted. "Do you honestly believe I would authorize an attack that could kill hundreds of millions of persons? You are insane! I order you to leave that command center immediately, or I will have you placed under arrest! I am dismissing you from your post."

"You cannot do that!"

"It is done already," Kwon said. "You are no longer minister of defense. I will issue the order immediately." And the line went dead.

Kim Kun-mo's head was spinning as he hung up the telephone. The bastard, he thought angrily, he actually *fired* me? We are in the middle of a war with Communist China, and he *fired* me? "He can't do that!" he shouted. "I can't let that happen." He picked up the telephone to the senior controller.

"Sir?"

"Seal up the command center, General," Kim said. "Go to full nuclear-chemical-biological protection mode. Full EMP protective measures. Hard-wired analog communications only."

"Yes, sir," the senior controller responded. "Switching to internal power, canceling digital and high-gain communications inlets."

Moments after an announcement was made, the lights flickered, then died except for a handful of battery-powered safety lights. The air also smelled different—mustier, dry like the inside of a coffin. They were on the air recirculators now, completely cut off from outside air; they were also on internal batteries that would be recharged as long as outside power was still available, but would instantly switch over to internal-only power if a nuclear blast erupted outside.

Kim got up from his desk and looked down below to the floor of the command center—it was almost completely dark, with only a few consoles illuminated. But the activity did not cease. Technicians started carrying out sound-powered communications systems, simple Korean War–era field telephones, and old-style greaseboards to replace the now-dark digital information screens. Using hard-wired analog communications systems instead of digital or broad-bandwidth systems reduced the likelihood of total destruction in case of a nearby nuclear blast . . .

. . . but it also isolated them from President Kwon Ki-chae, at least for a short time. The question is, would it be long enough?

. . .

Vice President Pak Chung-chu trotted into the president's office then. "I was just notified!" he shouted excitedly. "General Kim and General An attempted a counterattack and were swept aside, and now Chinese troops are swarming across the border!"

"General Kim seems to have gone insane," Kwon shouted. "He requested—no, he *demanded*—I give him the execution codes so he can launch a special weapons attack against China. He has already targeted several Chinese cities, *including Beijing*! Can you believe this? He wants to drop two three-hundred-and-fifty-kiloton nuclear warheads on *Beijing*! He must be crazy!"

"What did you order him to do instead, sir?" Pak asked.

"I ordered him to get out of the command center because I have removed him from his office!" Kwon shouted. "I don't want that madman in my military command center! I will find a replacement for him right away."

"But what about the Chinese, sir?" Pak asked, the panic rising in his throat. "The report said that three brigades of tanks are on the highway from Kanggye heading south toward Anju—they say Anju could be captured in three days! They have total air superiority above the fortieth parallel. What are we going to do?"

"We negotiate with President Jiang," Kwon said. "Trying to fight the Chinese People's Liberation Army will only result in more casualties on our side. Besides, reports from the Americans say that China only wants to destroy the nuclear weapons labs in Chagang Do province, and they will withdraw once that mission is accomplished. To tell the truth, I am not unhappy about that plan."

"Mr. President, you cannot allow this to happen—

you cannot simply let the Chinese march into Korea unopposed," Pak said. "It is an act of war already for China to step across the border, no matter what we've done to them. But for us to do nothing and simply let them destroy our military facilities and labs and take whatever they please is not right! They must be stopped!"

"And how can we do that, Mr. Pak?" Kwon asked.

"I have already appealed to the United Nations. The United States has asked for a special emergency meeting of the Security Council to discuss the invasion. The United States has again asked us to remove all of our weapons of mass destruction, and has agreed to set up a border monitoring system—without using American troops on Korean soil. I am going to ask the legislature to approve this measure . . ."

"That is all well and good for the future—if the Chinese Army will allow us to *have* a future!" Pak interjected. "Sir, you must *retaliate.* You promised the Korean people—*my* people, we from North Korea, the people that you promised would be safe from tyranny and dictatorship—that you would protect them. You have no choice but to act. Even if you fail, as General Kim has tonight, you must act."

"But what if Korean soldiers and airmen are killed trying to stop the Chinese horde?" Kwon asked. "Their deaths would be needless and tragic. They—"

"You are wrong, Mr. President," Pak told him sincerely. "Those soldiers and airmen are there because they want to be there, fighting for their country. They trust that we will direct them in defense of their homeland. We cannot, *we must not,* abdicate that responsibility, not to the United Nations, not to the United States, to no one. You have to give the order, sir."

"What order? I have been in contact with the service

chiefs and the director of National Security Planning. They offer no solutions other than appealing for aid."

"You know the order that must be given," Pak said in a low voice. "You know. You must attack with special weapons." Kwon's eyes bugged out as if he had just seen a ghost rise out of a grave. "You have to target China's war machine, both on Korean soil and on Chinese soil. General Kim is not crazy. He knows we must act. You are the only one . . ."

"I will not!" Kwon shouted. "I will never give those codes! I would rather die than let myself be responsible for the deaths of hundreds of thousands, perhaps *millions*, of souls."

Pak stared at Kwon for a moment, then slowly shook his head. He stepped over to the telephone on Kwon's desk. "Send in the attaché, please." A moment later, an Army officer entered the president's office, carrying an average-looking black briefcase. He set the briefcase on Kwon's desk before the president, turned it to face him, withdrew a key on a band around his left wrist, then stepped back a pace. "Mr. President, open the briefcase," Pak ordered.

"I will not," Kwon replied. The Army officer looked puzzled, looking at both leaders in growing confusion.

Pak Chung-chu reached into his jacket and withdrew a North Korean Type 64 automatic handgun with a six-inch sound suppressor attached. The Army officer gasped and tried to reach for his own sidearm, but Pak turned and fired a single round into his heart from ten feet away, killing him instantly.

"You . . . you killed him!" Kwon exclaimed. "You bastard! He was innocent! He was a courier . . ."

"Many will die tonight—he was just one more," Pak said coldly. He went over to the body, picked up the key, and inserted it into a lock on the briefcase. "Now you, Mr. President. Unlock the briefcase."

"Or you will kill me too, Mr. Pak?" Kwon asked. "You seem to be in the mood for killing tonight."

"I suppose I am," Pak said—and he shot Kwon Ki-chae in the heart. After the initial pain of the 7.65-millimeter slug, Kwon's face actually looked peaceful, relieved, as he collapsed to the floor and died.

Pak retrieved the second key to the briefcase from Kwon's wrist and unlocked it. There were a series of twenty-five cards inside. Pak searched Kwon's body until he found a small card with a series of instructions on it. Whoever was responsible for the briefcase was given a code number at the beginning of the day; his task was to apply the day's code number and the current date-time group and come up with a code corresponding to one of the twenty-five cards in the briefcase.

Kwon had never taken this exercise too seriously—after all, the minister of defense had to do exactly the same procedure, and then it had to be entered into the computers in the command center; enough checks and balances were involved. So when he was assigned the day's code number, he usually wrote it right on the day's decoding instruction card—a serious violation of security procedures, since anyone with the code number could issue the execution code. But that was Kwon Ki-chae, unconcerned about such details. Sure enough, the code number was right on the card. Kwon, Pak decided, just didn't have the intestinal fortitude to play this game.

After selecting the current date-time group, applying the numbers to the instruction card, and coming up with the correct execution code card, Pak had to contact the command center and give them the execution code and the date-time group he used to choose the card. The minister of defense then had to use the same date-time group to come up with his execution code. Then both codes had to be relayed to the command center senior controller, who entered them into the prearming computer. If the codes matched and were within six minutes of the original date-time group, the computer would allow launch commands to be issued on the special communications network to all missile units.

Pak dialed the direct line to Kim Kun-mo's office in the command center. "It is done, General," he said solemnly. "The execution code follows . . ." and he read off the execution code and the date-time group.

"You have done the right thing . . . Mr. President," Kim said excitedly, and he hung up the phone to get to work on his own decoding task before time ran out.

The right thing . . . Mr. President. The right thing . . . Mr. President. Pak Chung-chu smiled at the words. They sounded good. They sounded very good. He had a lot of work to do, a lot of pieces to pick up, a lot of promises to fulfill, a lot of fears to dispel.

His first official act was to kneel beside the body of the brave visionary Kwon Ki-chae, first president of the United Republic of Korea, put the muzzle of his Type 64 pistol into his own mouth, and blow his brains out.

OVER CENTRAL KOREA
THAT SAME TIME

Hey, boss, why don't we go down there and do something?" Rinc Seaver asked. The Americans had been watching the air battle unfold below them on their supercockpit displays, amazed at the waste of men and equipment in such an incredibly short period of time. "Let's lob a few Wolverines in there—that'll stop that Chinese armor cold."

"I agree, Major," Patrick said. "Genesis, this is Fortress Zero, how do you read?"

"Loud and clear, Fortress," Lieutenant General Terrill Samson responded. Samson was listening and watching the patrol on his own office-sized version of the virtual cockpit system from back at Dreamland. "Just about to call you guys. You got the green light, repeat, green light. Stand by." As they watched, one by one small triangle target symbols appeared on their supercockpit displays and on the virtual cockpit displays at Adak. Each target symbol represented a column of vehicles within the kill pattern of a Wolverine cruise missile. The computer quickly calculated the proper attack axis of each target so the warheads in each Wolverine had maximum effect, and then the target list was divided by aircraft. All of this flight planning was done in a matter of moments, then presented to the crews.

"Looks like we're putting rocket-killing on hold for a while," Rebecca said.

"Just remember, you need to high-tail it out to air cover as soon as you release," Patrick told them over the virtual cockpit communications net. "You guys are fairly undetectable, even with your bomb doors open, but Wolverines are not, and it'll take over half a minute to pump out your missiles. The bad guys will be on you like stink on shit."

The Wolverine runs were all done from high altitude. Seaver and Long had to fly north to catch up with the others, and Furness and Scott had to fly eastbound, then back around to the west, to coordinate their release as well; but all three EB-1 Megafortress bombers reached their release points within ten seconds of each other. They unreeled their towed emitter arrays from each Megafortress's tail just before reaching the lethal range of the mobile surface-to-air missiles below them.

At the optimal range for the attack profile, the bomb doors opened, and they started raining Wolverine cruise missiles down on the Chinese armored columns rolling across southern Chagang Do province. Each Megafortress released six Wolverine missiles every nine seconds from a rotary launcher in the aft bomb bay, leaving two Wolverines each for reattacks or for rocket-hunting.

Each AGM-177 Wolverine cruise missile steered itself slightly away from the target as it descended and started its small turbofan engine. As it got closer to its first target, it leveled off less than a hundred feet above the terrain, guided by a satellite navigation computer, a terrain-comparison computer, and a millimeter-wave radar. Thirty seconds before impact, the missile's radar took a snapshot of the target area, refined its steering, then began transmitting pictures of the target back by satellite to McLanahan and two other Megafortress bombardiers in the virtual cockpit at Adak Naval Air Station. This way, the flight crews would not have to divert attention between helping to fly the aircraft and finding targets. If the missiles needed a slight aiming tweak, the techs could do it right from their control consoles at Adak.

The Wolverine missiles each had three bomb bays. Each bomb bay was loaded with the same weapon—ten BLU-108/B "Shredder" sensor-fused weapon submunitions. Each Shredder had four projectiles that, once released, would search out their own target and shoot a slug of molten copper into it with enough force to pierce even heavy armor.

As the Wolverine approached each column of ground vehicles, it made a slight climb, then ejected the submunitions one by one from about three hundred feet above the column before descending back to treetop altitude. The ten submunitions would spin as they were ejected, extending four skeets with tiny heat-seeking sensors, which would lock onto a vehicle below. At the right moment, the skeets would detonate, sending the molten copper slug at the target at twice the speed of sound.

The effect was devastating. Each slug had a range of one-half mile, so the submunitions did not have to be directly over a target to hit it. Any vehicle smaller than a tank within a half mile of the projectiles was destroyed. The molten copper slug easily penetrated metal up to an inch thick, but after it cut through the metal, it had cooled enough so that, once inside the vehicle, it couldn't act as a penetrator again. When the still-molten copper slug hit the next piece of metal—usually the floorboards—the molten copper spattered into a thousand tiny hot copper bullets traveling at the speed of sound. Anything inside the vehicle would be cut apart in the blink of an eye. Tanks fared a little better. Unless a slug hit the very top of the tank, which is usually made of thinner metal and is more vulnerable, the copper slug simply bored through the outer armor plating and stopped—usually causing fuel tanks to explode, setting off ammunition magazines, or turning transmissions into twisted blobs.

The death dance was repeated over and over again as the Wolverine missiles flew down the long columns of tanks and infantry support vehicles. Little escaped their detection: Jeep-sized four-wheel vehicles were hit, along with mobile antiaircraft weapons, supply trucks, and troop transports. A Shredder skeet hitting a diesel-powered vehicle's engine compartment instantly turned the engine and its fuel supply into a gigantic white-hot fireball, engulfing it and its occupants within seconds.

When the last bomb bay was empty, each Wolverine missile located one last large target using its millimeter-wave radar. The techs back in the virtual cockpit got a last look through the imaging infrared camera, made minor course adjustments if necessary, then flew the missile into the last target. Even empty and without an exploding warhead except for a small amount of unexpended jet fuel, a nine-hundred-pound Wolverine missile traveling at over three hundred miles an hour packs a devastating punch.

The Megafortress bombers all performed a semi-"scram" maneuver after launching the last Wolverine missile—power back to idle, a hard turn away from the concentration of Chinese ground vehicles, decelerate to cornering velocity, then gradually push the power back in to maintain cornering velocity until the turn was completed.

The flight crews couldn't see the Shredder sensor-fused weapon effects on the supercockpit display—all they could see was the Wolverine's final impact. "Looks like those things work pretty well," John Long commented. "How come we don't have them in the inventory now?"

"Because we can buy four conventional air-launched cruise missiles or seven SLAMs for what it costs to buy one Wolverine," Paul Scott replied. "I've got a pop-up threat, combined Golf-India-Hotel-band tracking radar, four o'clock, twenty miles, looks like an SA-6 . . . Shit, Hotel-band height finder up . . . trackbreakers active, let's get the power back in and start a descent, Rebecca, and get the hell—"

At that moment, they heard a high-pitched *DEEDLEDEEDLEDEEDLE* warning tone. "Missile launch! Chaff out! Engage TERFLW, break right!" Rebecca immediately engaged the terrain-following system, and the Megafortress started a thirty-thousand-foot-per-minute dive for the ground. At the same time, Rebecca started a hard right turn and pushed the throttles to military power. She stepped the clearance plane right down to two hundred feet to get below the SA-6's minimum altitude capability. The towed emitter immediately started sending out both jamming signals and tiny fins that enlarged its radar cross section to ten times the size of the Megafortress itself.

They felt a shudder run the length of the Megafortress, then quiet. "Shit, that was close," Paul said. "They got the towed emitter. I'm reeling out number two."

Suddenly, just as the cockpit got quiet again when the SA-6's radars went down, it seemed as if the ground all around them illuminated in pinpricks of light. "Triple-A!" Paul shouted. "Climb! Any way out to the left?"

"More triple-A out this way!" Rebecca shouted. There was no way to turn to get around them—everywhere they looked, another stream of lights arced up to meet them. The only way to go was straight up. Rebecca paddled off the terrain-following system, shoved the throttles to max afterburner, swept the wings forward to thirty-six degrees, and pulled the nose skyward. "Fortress One is defensive, climbing to get away from triple-A around us!"

Just then it felt as if they hit a stretch of gravel road racing down the freeway at eighty miles an hour. For a brief instant, the vibration was so bad that Rebecca couldn't see the instrument panel. She leveled off at fifteen thousand feet. The rumbling subsided but didn't stop. "I'm hit! I'm hit!" Rebecca radioed. "I'm not accelerating . . . Shit, I just lost my number one engine! Fire lights on! Shutting number one down!"

"Fly the airplane, Rebecca, just fly the airplane," she heard Nancy Cheshire's voice say. "I'm on your gauges. Get your nose up . . . there you go. Let me check your systems. Scottie, back me up." After a few moments, Nancy said, "Okay, it looks like you got hit in the left wing. You've still got a hot exhaust, so you still might have a fire back there. You're losing fuel from your left wing, and I think that flutter might be from some damaged flaps, so it looks like you're stuck with thirty-four-degree wing sweep for now. I've initiated fuel transfer out of the left wing to the forward intermediate and forward fuselage tanks; you're going to have to use manual CG management, but we'll help you watch the center of gravity. We will . . ." There was another radar warning, another SA-6 at their three o'clock position. "Left turn to one-six-zero, Rebecca, let's get away from that SA-6 that just popped up! Use afterburners if you need to."

"C'mon, Long Dong, fire up one of those things and let 'em have it!" Rinc shouted. John Long activated the laser radar, and the positions of the mobile 27-millimeter and 57-millimeter guns around Fortress One appeared. Rinc turned toward the nest of antiaircraft artillery while John selected three of the road-mobile artillery units, with the mobile SA-6 launcher as the final impact target, and launched one Wolverine missile. Less than a minute later two antiaircraft artillery units were destroyed, pierced through and through with deadly molten copper, and a mobile SA-6 surface-to-air missile launcher was burning fiercely.

"You're out of there, Rebecca," Patrick ordered. "Fly heading zero-eight-five, climb to one-niner thousand, vectors to the *Grand Island*. We'll have you orbit inside his SAM coverage until we get a tanker out here to pump you up and assess the damage."

"I'm rejoining on her," Rinc said.

"Negative. We need you back on patrol, Rinc . . ."

"I said, *I'm rejoining on her*!" he shouted. "We don't leave our wingmen. I don't care if the whole fucking Korean peninsula goes up in flames—I'm not leaving her."

A few minutes later Rinc eased his Megafortress

bomber in tight to Rebecca's left wing. "How does it look?" she radioed. "I still feel a vibration. Feels like it's coming from that side. Roll control is sluggish too."

"It looks like shit, Go-Fast," John Long said, studying the bomber through a set of night-vision goggles. "A spoiler looks like it's partially up or bent up, and you have a section of flap sticking through the wing gap seal. You might want to consider landing at a longer runway than Adak—you'll be doing a thirty-four-degree wing sweep no-flap no-slat approach with three engines."

"We're already getting Kadena cleared for recovery," Patrick radioed. "Twelve thousand feet usable. It's supposed to be closed to attack aircraft, but I don't give a shit—we're landing there anyway. If we have to, we'll—"

"Hey—do you guys see what I see?" Nancy Cheshire radioed. "What are those tanks doing down there?"

"Holy shit—it looks like they're turning around!" Dave Luger aboard Fortress Two said gleefully. "Those Chinese tanks are heading north again! Genesis, you see this? Are you seeing this?"

"That's a big roger, Fortress Two," Terrill Samson said happily. "I'm on the phone to Washington right now. I see them pulling back all across northern Korea."

"The mobile search radars are down too," John Long verified. "Looks like they pulled in their claws. Man, this is incredible. They . . . wait. I've got a fighter radar up . . . India-band 'Flash Dance' radar . . . Shit! They're MiG-31 Foxhounds! Two of 'em!" The Russian-designed MiG-31 Foxhound was one of the fastest and most deadly interceptors in the world, designed from the outset to destroy low-flying supersonic bombers and cruise missiles. "The war seems to be over—but it looks like someone forgot to tell the fighters!''

HIGH TECHNOLOGY AEROSPACE
WEAPONS CENTER, GROOM LAKE, NEVADA
THAT SAME TIME

Sir, what do you mean, no one can get hold of the Korean leadership?'' Lieutenant General Terrill Samson thundered. ''You mean we can't talk to anyone in the Korean military chain of command?''

''Terrill, we can't talk to anyone in a leadership position in Korea at all,'' Chairman of the Joint Chiefs of Staff Balboa said. ''All communications have been cut off to their command center—they sealed it up tight, full EMP, nuclear and bio-chem protection. And when we contact the Blue House or someone in the capital, everyone's mum. No one will talk to us.''

''Sir, it's confirmed—the Chinese are pulling out of Korea,'' Samson said. ''We need confirmation from President Kwon that he has his finger off the red button and that he's not going to try any more retaliatory strikes against Chinese forces as they're retreating.''

''We're trying our best, General,'' Balboa said. ''I suggest you get your people out of there fast. If the Chinese see you up there, they're likely to think you're part of a Korean counterstrike. You'd better . . . Stand by one.'' The line went quiet for several long moments; then: ''More shit hitting the fan, General. President Kwon and Vice President Pak were found dead in the president's office.''

''What?''

''Looks like some kind of murder-suicide thing,'' Balboa said. ''And it looks like the execution codes for

Korea's nuclear missiles may have been compromised. Aides found the code briefcase open, the president's decoding card filled out, and the right execution card retrieved from the briefcase. They checked the phone log and found that Pak called the Osan command center shortly before the MCRC went off the air."

"That means that whoever's in charge at the Osan command center has one-half of the execution codes," Samson said. "If the minister of defense is at Osan too, then he has the other half—and they can launch fully prearmed nuclear weapons anytime they want."

"Looks like the balloon's going up any minute, General," Balboa said grimly. "Are your people in place over the peninsula?"

"Yes, sir."

"Well, let's hope to God your plan works and they can stop any missiles Kim wants to cook off," Balboa said. "I better notify the President. Balboa out."

Terrill Samson hung up the phone, deep in thought. What in hell was going on out there? Would Minister of National Defense Kim actually launch a nuclear attack against China?

Well, Samson thought, I wonder if anyone tried the direct approach. If only hard-wired communications were going through, why not try a simple phone call? The Osan Master Control and Reporting Center used to be a joint American and Korean facility, so I must have the phone number for it somewhere. He started a computer phone directory search, and sure enough found the number. The Defense Satellite Network number did not work—that was pure digital, vulnerable to EMP, or electromagnetic pulse, the damaging surge of energy during a nuclear blast—but when he tried the commercial number, a man answered in Korean.

"I want to speak with the senior controller," Samson said.

The same man switched from Korean to English without hesitation: "Who is this? How did you get this number?"

"This is Lieutenant General Terrill Samson, United States Air Force, calling from Elliott Air Force Base in Nevada. I want to talk with the senior controller on duty right away."

"Communications are restricted. The facility is under full combat conditions."

"I know. I have spoken with Washington and with Seoul. You have sealed off the Master Control and Reporting Center even though the Chinese forces are pulling back. I want to know why."

"Pulling back?" the man said with obvious surprise. "The Chinese are pulling back?"

"All of them, as we speak. You didn't know?" There was no response. "Who is the senior controller?" Samson racked his brain for a name. "Colonel Sung Hye-gu was on duty just after reunification—I would like to talk with him. Or General An, or General Kim, if they're on duty. It's urgent."

"This is Colonel Sung," the man said. "I remember you now, sir. You are the black general they call Earthmover. I did not recognize the name of your base."

"Colonel, what is going on out there?"

"General Kim cannot speak," the man said. A few moments later he added, "The Chinese are withdrawing? Full withdrawal?"

"As far as my reconnaissance assets tell me, yes—full withdrawal," Samson said. "Do you require authentication? Do you need me to send you proof? Tell me what I need to do to convince you, Colonel."

"Sir . . . General, Minister of National Defense Kim has ordered a full missile attack on China," Colonel Sung said.

"A *what*?"

"A full nuclear and chemical attack," Sung repeated. "Targets in China—including Beijing. He received full authorization from President Kwon—rather, from Vice President Pak . . ."

"President Kwon and Vice President Pak are *dead,* Colonel," Samson said. "They think Pak forced Kwon to give him the execution code, then killed Kwon and himself. Kim's attack is unnecessary, and it's probably not legal—Kim may have engineered this just to lash out at China or grab the presidency for himself. He has got to stop this attack."

"I . . . I do not know what to do," Sung said.

"Listen to me, Colonel," Samson said. "You must stop Minister Kim or General An from launching any more missiles against China. I have special aircraft in the vicinity, heavy stealth bombers that are armed with highly effective weapons that can destroy the MCRC. Their mission is to destroy any ballistic missiles launched by either Korea or China, but they can attack heavily defended ground targets as well. They successfully attacked the Chinese armored brigades and caused them to turn back.

"I have authorization to attack the Master Control and Reporting Center with any weapon in my control to try to stop any more missile launches. If I don't get a response, Colonel, I will have no choice but to attack. You must try to stop Minister Kim any way you can. Do you understand?"

But the line had gone dead—Samson didn't know how long he had been talking to no one.

What could he do? He had some of the world's most potent weapons at his fingertips, but he was powerless. He could not do . . .

He couldn't do anything . . . but the Megafortresses could.

Terrill Samson called up a digital map of Osan Air
Base in Korea and studied it. It had been well over four
years since he'd visited Osan, but he didn't think it had
changed that much.

It was in a remote corner of the base, far from the
runway, far from Seventh Air Force headquarters.
There were no other structures nearby except for a
plain two-story military-drab building, surrounded by a
tall barbed-wire fence. Zooming in, he could see a lone
tree about fifty yards in front of the building.

That was it. He had heard of the famous lone cherry
tree, the rumors that it was the most heavily targeted
tree in the world. They said the North Koreans had
targeted ten thousand bombs, rockets, and missiles on
that cherry tree—because a hundred feet below it, under layers of soil, rock, steel, and Kevlar armor and
suspended on shock absorbers, was the Osan Master
Control and Reporting Center, the military heart of Korea. Terrill Samson rolled a set of electronic cross hairs
on that cherry tree and ordered the computer to mensurate its exact geographical coordinates and elevation.

Now there was going to be one more weapon
targeted against that little tree.

ABOARD THE EB-1C MEGAFORTRESS BOMBERS
THAT SAME TIME

Fortresses One and Three, you've got bandits at five
o'clock, fifty miles, angels . . . shit, angels forty-
five, speed seven hundred knots and closing fast. 'Flash
Dance' radar . . . damn, it's a pair of MiG-31s," Dave
Luger shouted. "Notch left, Fortress One. We'll try to
break that Foxhound's pulse-Doppler radar lock . . ."

But before the two Megafortress bombers could even

begin to make any defensive maneuvers, they got a verbal "Rocket launch detection" warning through their intercom systems. "I'm picking up ballistic missile launches—from Korea!" John Long shouted. "Korea is launching missiles!"

"Rebecca . . . those fighters . . . I'm staying with you in case they—"

"Go after those missiles, Rinc! Nail those bitches!" Rebecca shouted. She knew she could not use afterburners for fear of igniting a fire in her engine compartments, and because she could not sweep her wings past thirty-four degrees, she would not have enough speed to make steep pursuit climbs. "I'm heading out to the *Grand Island*! I'll be all right!"

The two undamaged Megafortress bombers advanced their throttles to full afterburner and maneuvered to intercept the missiles. With fuel more than half burned off and all but a few Wolverine missiles expended, the Megafortresses climbed skyward like angels from hell.

"Good maneuver, Annie," Dave Luger said. "Little more right . . . little higher . . ."

"You've got about fifteen seconds, David!" Annie Dewey shouted. She had the Megafortress climbing at ten thousand feet per minute, aiming the nose at an expanse of stars she guessed the Korean missiles would fly toward. "Airspeed's down to four hundred . . . three-fifty . . ."

"Missile one away . . . launcher rotating . . . missile two away . . . missile three away!" Annie swept the wings forward as she slowed, trying to decrease her stall speed as much as possible until she saw the third Lancelot missile race ahead on a column of fire. She immediately shoved the nose down and swept the wings back to regain speed—just two more seconds and they would have had to fight off a full stall.

Rinc and John were able to punch out four Lancelot missiles—one while a missile was still below them, and three in the tail-chase aspect. But Rinc wasn't thinking about the success or failure of this attack—all he could think about was leaving Rebecca with two MiG-31 Foxhounds closing in on her . . .

"We missed two missiles!" Patrick McLanahan shouted over the virtual cockpit circuit. "We missed two! Take-down, Takedown, you copy?"

"We copy loud and clear, Fortress," the crew of the U.S. Navy NK-135 "Cobra Spear" aircraft radioed back. The NK-135 was an airborne laser flying laboratory run by the U.S. Navy's Air Weapons Research Center at China Lake, California. "Takedown has the strays in sight, and we're getting the lassos ready. Stand by."

"Takedown" was the code name of the original Lancelot antiballistic missile program begun by the U.S. Navy. The first missile-targeting lasers were mounted on a modified Boeing 707 airliner, the NK-135, for testing. In addition, the original Lancelot missiles—not modified Air Force AGM-69A short-range attack missiles, but modified Navy AIM-54 Phoenix air-to-air missiles—were mounted on P-3 Orion patrol aircraft. The program was never completed, but the aircraft and weapons were still in the inventory—and now they were going to be put to good use.

As the Korean ballistic missiles rose through the atmosphere, the NK-135 Cobra Spear aircraft locked onto them with their laser radar. Since the Navy's LADAR was mounted on an airliner instead of a strategic bomber, it had much more power and much longer range than the LADAR mounted on the EB-1 Megafortresses. As soon as the ballistic missiles were detected, the tracking information was passed to the P-3 Orion, and it released four ABM-54 missiles from wing hard-points.

The first operational launch of the Navy's ABM-54 antiballistic missile missile was a success—two Nodong-1 missiles targeted for Beijing were intercepted and destroyed.

As soon as the last Lancelot missile blasted clear, Rinc lowered the Megafortress's nose and turned toward the incoming Chinese MiG-31 Foxhounds.

"Arm up the Scorpions, Long Dong," he shouted. "We've got to get to them before they attack!"

But before the two Megafortress bombers could even begin to make defensive maneuvers, the MiGs had opened fire with long-range R-33 radar-guided missiles. "Missile launch! Amos missiles in the air! They fired from about forty miles away . . . Two more missiles in the air! They targeted both you guys. Fortress Three, break right!"

"Rebecca!" Rinc shouted on interplane.

"Get the hell out of here, Rodeo!" Rebecca shouted. "I'm maneuvering as best I can! Get going!" Rinc had no choice but to execute a steep turning dive for the ground.

The one not-so-cool thing about the Megafortress's laser radar system was that it showed everything in stark, cold detail—including their time to die. The LADAR tracked the big R-33 Amos missiles with ease, even projected their flight path and time to intercept—which, at their speed, was in about seventy seconds. No matter how tight they turned, how fast they flew, or how low they went, the R-33 stayed right with them—their projected flight path line always intersected the middle of the screen.

"Kill those sons of bitches, Long Dong!" Rinc shouted. Long quickly armed up the AIM-120 Scorpion AMRAAM missiles, and as soon as the R-33 missiles got within twenty miles, he fired two against each missile, then two at each MiG-31 when they got within range seconds later . . .

. . . but even though the R-33 missiles were big targets, they maneuvered quickly and were too fast for the AIMs, which were designed for aircraft less than half their speed. All of the Scorpions fired against the R-33s missed. Their last chance was the Scorpion missiles fired against the Foxhounds themselves—if they hit, or if the MiG-31s were forced to turn away and break radar lock with the bombers, the R-33 missiles would simply fly their last assigned heading and turn on their onboard radars. If they saw a target, they would kill it—if not, they would self-destruct. It was their only . . .

Suddenly, a tremendous globe of brilliant silvery light appeared in the sky above Rinc and John, then disappeared—it went away so fast that they thought they imagined it. Rinc made another hard jink to the left and pumped out more active decoys to try to lure the R-33 missiles away—and this time it worked. The R-33s continued on their last course and exploded harmlessly several miles away.

"Rebecca! Are you all right?" Rinc shouted.

"We're okay!" Rebecca replied. "The R-33s missed! They stopped guiding on us! What happened?"

"Hey, you know, these Lancelot missiles make fine air-to-air missiles too," Dave Luger radioed from Fortress Two. "And that last one just happened to have a plasma-yield warhead on it. Wonder where you go when you get hit by a plasma-yield explosion?"

"To plasma hell, I hope," Rinc said. "Hey, Fortress

Zero, can we escort Fortress One out of here now? We'll all be running on fumes pretty soon."

"Not quite yet," General Terrill Samson's voice broke in. "This is Genesis. Check your targeting displays. I've got one more target for you guys to attack . . . and may God have mercy on my soul for doing this."

"None . . . of . . . them?" Minister of National Defense Kim gasped. "*None* of them hit their targets?"

"None of them even began reentry toward their targets," Colonel Sung, the senior controller in the Master Control and Reporting Center at Osan, said. "They all either reported malfunctions . . . or the telemetry simply ceased."

"How is this possible?" Kim shouted. "How can this happen?" He was almost crazed with blinding anger— but he forced himself to be calm. "I want a second salvo readied immediately!" he shouted. "This time I want it doubled! I want every target on the original list targeted with two warheads! No . . . no, better make it three."

"Three? Three nuclear warheads on every target?"

"If they are malfunctioning or sabotaged, we need at least three to ensure the targets are destroyed once and for all!" he cried out. "Now get to work! Put three . . . no, four, *four* missiles on every target! Do it! *Now!*"

"Sir!" a technician shouted. "Enemy aircraft inbound! Patriot and Hawk batteries are responding!"

Kim dashed over to a radar screen, one of the old-fashioned twenty-four-inch cathode-ray tube displays— the old vacuum-tube radar displays were less vulnerable to EMP effects, so some were still in use in the MCRC. Several blips appeared on the screen with data blocks beside them indicating speed and altitude. "Fast-moving target inbound from the southwest at very low altitude, range seventy miles. They are not maneuvering . . . they are coming straight in."

"Then it will be that much easier to destroy them," Kim said. "Commit every available unit on—"

"Sir! More targets inbound from the southeast! Very low altitude, six hundred knots, range sixty miles."

"It's a massive Chinese attack," Kim shouted. "Get those ballistic missiles launched now, General! Get them—"

"Sir! More inbound targets, slow-moving, low altitude . . . I have another target, high altitude, sixty miles to the east, four hundred knots."

"A command or surveillance aircraft," General An said. "Possibly directing the attack."

"No—they are American attack aircraft, Minister!" Colonel Sung shouted.

"What are you talking about, Colonel?"

"I received a phone call from Lieutenant General Terrill Samson," Sung said. "He is the commander of the United States Air Force's secret air weapons center. I know of him. He told me that he had stealth bombers in the area armed with special weapons that were capable of destroying both ballistic missiles and the MCRC. He warned me that his aircraft will attack if they do not get a response from us."

"What in blazes were you doing on a telephone in the middle of a battle?" Kim Kun-mo shouted. "I can have you shot for that!"

"You've been fooled, Colonel," General An said. "That call could have come from anyone. The Chinese certainly can look up an American general's name and base of assignment and make up a tale like that."

"I know that, sir," Sung said. "But he also told me that his bombers attacked the Chinese armored forces and caused them to retreat."

"*What?* The Chinese are in retreat?"

"It must be verified," Sung said, "but I think we should wait on our second missile attack until it can be verified."

"Nonsense!" Kim shouted. "We are not stopping any attack to verify anything, especially not based on information you received on an unauthorized, unsecure telephone call!"

"Sir, he also told me that his bombers carry weapons that can destroy ballistic missiles in flight, and that his orders were to use them against missiles fired from either Korea or China . . ."

"Ridiculous! I've never heard of anything like that before!"

"He also said that—"

"Colonel, you are relieved of command," Minister of National Defense Kim said. "Get out of my command center. General An, designate a new senior controller, and proceed with the launch immediately! Security, escort this gullible, incompetent officer out of here!"

"Sir, he said that his bombers have weapons that can destroy the MCRC," Sung shouted as two security guards stepped over to him and reached for his arms. "If we do not establish contact with his aircraft, we will be destroyed!"

"Get him out of here!"

The two guards grabbed Sung's arms, but he twisted away, grabbed a rifle that was slung from one of the guards' shoulders, turned, and aimed it at Kim. "I won't let you kill us all, you maniac!" he shouted, and pulled the trigger.

General An raced forward to tackle Kim just as a line of bullets stitched across his back and left side. Sung swung the gun around and aimed it at the launch control console, but he was gunned down by another security guard before he could open fire.

"Fortress Two is defensive Patriot!" Annie Dewey shouted. They were penetrating from the southwest of Osan, the most heavily defended sector. She suddenly found herself bracketed by two Patriot missile batteries that had opened fire simultaneously.

"Fortress Two, Fortress Two, be advised, I show a fault on your defensive system," Patrick McLanahan radioed. "Decoy launchers, towed decoys, all jammers are faulted. Get out of there!"

"We've got two Patriots opened up on us!" David Luger shouted. "We're trying to get away!"

"Annie, break right, let me have a shot at them!" Rinc shouted on interplane frequency.

Rinc Seaver and John Long had released all of their Wolverine cruise missiles from maximum range, but they had not hit their targets yet. Seaver started a fast climb. "What are you doing?" John Long asked.

"Just get a fix on those Patriots, Long Dong!" he shouted.

Long zoomed the supercockpit display out, and sure enough the laser radar was tracking the inbound Patriot missiles. "Bring it all the way around to the north, Annie," Rinc said. As they watched Annie make her turn, the incoming missiles started a right turn of their own. The missiles flew a ballistic flight path and aimed not for the aircraft itself, but for a "basket" of airspace where they predicted the aircraft to be when they arrived.

"What in hell are you doing, Seaver?" Long repeated.

"I'm going to shoot down those Patriots and get them off Annie's tail," Rinc said. "Get a couple Scorpions ready!" The supercockpit display showed Annie's predicted flight path as well as the Patriot missiles' predicted path. As the Patriots turned, Rinc pointed his Megafortress's nose at the intersection of the two flight paths, waited until they were within AIM-120 Scorpion missile range, then shouted, "*Shoot!* Annie, break left, *now*!" John Long fired their last four Scorpion missiles at the Patriots.

Annie turned hard left. At that exact moment, the Patriot missiles had activated their own onboard terminal guidance radar and began tracking. All four Patriots made a direct hit—right on the Scorpion missiles.

"Got 'em!" John shouted. "Nice going! Now let's get this attack under way and get the hell out of here!"

"Fortress One, missiles away," Rebecca said, and Paul Scott launched their last two remaining Lancelot missiles—not at any ballistic missiles, but at the set of coordinates for the Osan Master Control and Reporting Center that he had received from General Samson at HAWC.

"Fortress Two, missiles away," Dave Luger radioed.

"Fortress Three, missiles . . ."

At that moment, they received a MISSILE WARNING advisory on the supercockpit display and a slow-paced *deedle deedle deedle* warning over the intercom. "Missile tracking and height finder pop-up threat!" John Long shouted. "Looks like an I-Hawk, eleven o'clock, six miles, within lethal range! Hold heading! Hold heading! Missile counting down! Jammers active, towed decoy is alive."

"Withhold the launch! Withhold!" Rinc shouted. "Let's get out of here before that I-Hawk tags us!"

"Hold heading, dammit!" Long said. "Twenty seconds and we're outta here! That's an order, Seaver! Hold heading!"

The rotary launcher had moved the first Lancelot

missile into launch position and was counting down to release just as they received a MISSILE LAUNCH indication and a rapid-fire *deedledeedledeedle* tone. "Missile launch!" Rinc shouted. He looked out the left cockpit window and could see the first Hawk missile, an American-built air defense system, lift off on a column of fire and speed toward them. It looked so close that he thought they had flown right over it, although it was over five miles away.

The Lancelot missile left the bomb bay, ignited its first-stage motor, and pulled ahead of the Megafortress. *"Now! Break right!"* Long shouted.

But it was too late. The Hawk guided unsteadily on the tiny radar cross section of the Megafortress until the Lancelot missile left the bomb bay, and then it guided on that larger target. When the Lancelot was only a thousand yards in front of the bomber, the Hawk hit. The plasma-yield warhead did not detonate, but the nine hundred pounds of solid rocket fuel did . . .

. . . and the Megafortress flew directly through the fireball.

"Shit! We've been hit!" Rinc shouted. The cockpit seemed bathed in fire, and it quickly started filling with smoke.

"Rinc! Can you hear me?" It was Patrick McLanahan. "If you can hear me, break left now! Another Hawk missile launched! I'm activating your countermeasures! Turn left *now*!"

Rinc started his turn—but then he noticed the supercockpit display. The Korean Patriot missile systems had successfully attacked and destroyed every other Lancelot missile launched against the Osan command center. Rinc had the last one.

Fire lights started illuminating on the instrument panel one by one. "Two . . . no, three fire lights!" John Long shouted.

"Eject, Long Dong," Rinc ordered. "Get the hell off my ship."

Long looked at Seaver through the thickening smoke. His eyes widened, as if to apologize—then he straightened in his seat and pulled his ejection handles.

Rinc twisted the knob on his ejection mode switch from AUTO to MANUAL just before Long ejected. He wasn't going anywhere until the last Lancelot missile was gone.

At that same moment, the I-Hawk's tactical control officer saw the target still flying after missile detonation and immediately commanded a second launch.

Rinc watched as the attack computers commanded the bomb doors to open partially—since the Lancelot missiles launched one by one from the rotary launcher, the doors did not need to open fully—and the last Lancelot missile was ejected into the slipstream. It dropped away from the bomber, its fins unlocked and stabilized the missile in the slipstream, the first-stage motor ignited, and the missile shot past the bomber and flew off into space on a ballistic trajectory.

"Rinc!" he heard a voice call out. It was Rebecca. "Get out! Eject!"

"I still show you in there, Rinc!" Patrick radioed. "Get the hell out, now! *Eject! Eject!*"

The smoke in the cockpit had cleared as soon as Long's ejection hatch blew off, so now he could see everything clearly. He saw the second I-Hawk lift off—and this one began tracking the last Lancelot missile too.

Nuts to that, Rinc thought. He started a rapid climb, swept the Megafortress's wings full forward, dropped the gear, and lowered full flaps and slats, instantly destroying all the bomber's stealthy characteristics and increasing his radar cross section about 10,000 percent.

He couldn't see the I-Hawk missile anymore, but it didn't matter—he had done all he could.

"Rinc, what are you doing?" Rebecca called out. "Eject! What are you waiting for?"

The mission was over. Time to get the hell out. "I'm with you, sweetheart," he radioed back. "Pop open a cold one for me." He reached down to his ejection handles . . .

The I-Hawk missile hit the Megafortress's vertical stabilizer, blowing it and most of the tail section off. The bomber nosed over into a gentle descent, then started a slow roll.

Rinc was halfway through his second roll when he saw a shining silvery globe erupt just a few miles in front of the Megafortress. The inside of the silver orb looked like swirls and billows of liquid fire, but the surface of the globe was perfectly smooth, flawless. He pulled the ejection handles and shot out of the stricken bomber, out into the artificial marblelike sun growing before his eyes.

He expected to feel a volcanic heat and hear thunder, something to demonstrate the horrible violence he was witnessing. Instead, it felt more like falling onto an infinitely soft pillow. He felt the silver orb surround him, caress him, welcoming him into the alternate dimension within . . .

EPILOGUE

Rebecca Furness's Cessna P210 squeaked to a halt onto the cracked concrete runway. As usual, she landed right on the faded white runway numbers, but there was hardly any reason to do that—she still had over eleven thousand feet of concrete ahead of her. She turned off at the first intersection and taxied toward the weather-beaten old hangars and base operations building across the huge expanse of tarmac ahead of her.

"I didn't think this place was still open," John Long remarked. He still wore a neck brace and bandages over one elbow as a result of his ejection, and it would be several more weeks until he was back on flying status. He had a copy of the Airport/Facility Directory open in his lap. "Says here there's a Department of Forestry squadron here, and one card-lock fuel pump." He looked over at Rebecca when she didn't answer. She was handling the little single-engine Cessna okay, but her mind was a million miles away . . .

. . . or, more precisely, eleven thousand miles away, in Korea.

Rebecca taxied over to the unattended credit-card-operated fuel pump, shut down, and they stepped out into the brilliant sunshine and cool, fresh air. The airport was in a valley between two mountain ranges, with the biggest peak rising over five thousand feet above the airport only ten miles to the southeast. There were a few private planes parked here and there, a few cars parked beside the old base operations building. But the place looked deserted. A sign on the base operations building read, "Welcome to Tuscarora Army Air Corps Base, Battle Mountain, Nevada, elevation 4532 ft." "I guess this used to be an old World War Two bomber training base," John said. He looked around. "Must've been hairy flying around all these mountains, but it sure as hell is pretty secluded."

Rebecca still wasn't saying much—in fact, she had hardly talked at all since picking up John at Reno-Tahoe International Airport and flying him in the rented Cessna to Battle Mountain. She was going to head into the base operations building, but she looked around and noticed that the old wooden hangar on the northeast side of the airfield had its doors open, and wordlessly she started walking in that direction. Long followed.

It was soon obvious that the doors were open because there was an aircraft inside—the same Gulfstream jet that had picked her and her squadronmates up in Reno and taken them back to Dreamland. Inside, she found General Terrill Samson, Patrick McLanahan, Dave Luger, Nancy Cheshire, Hal Briggs, and, to her surprise, Annie Dewey.

"Nice P210," Patrick said as she and Long entered the hangar. "I was thinking about getting one myself. Do you like them?"

Rebecca shrugged. "They're okay," she said as she shook Patrick's hand.

"Nothing like a Bone, huh?" Patrick said with a

smile. Rebecca didn't return the smile. "Is it yours?" he asked.

"It was Rinc's," she said woodenly. "I'm . . . borrowing it."

Annie walked over to Rebecca and gave her a warm hug. "Are you doing okay, boss?" she asked.

"Not really," she replied. She looked over at Dave Luger, then back at Annie and gave her a shy grin. "You and Colonel Luger?"

"Hey, love strikes at the weirdest times and in the weirdest places," Annie said. "Looks like we were meant to be 'crewed-up' after all." Rebecca gave her a congratulatory squeeze of the hand.

"Welcome, Colonel," General Samson said. "Glad you could make it." She shook hands with him and the others. "How are you doing, Colonel Long?"

"Much better, thank you, sir."

"Good," he said. "Well, I'm sure you heard the good news by now: China and United Korea finally began formal diplomatic relations and exchanged ambassadors. What you may not have heard is that China has decided to pull all of its troops away from the border. No troops on either side. Same with the Russia-Korea border area." No reaction from Rebecca.

"More good news: they held peninsula-wide elections, and the prime minister, Lee Kyong-sik, was elected president. They elected an ex–North Korean as vice president. That country might actually make it, even after everything it's been through."

"Any noise about the . . . er, aftermath at Osan?" John Long asked.

"Lots," Patrick said. "But, as always, the answer was 'no comment,' except to the President, of course. But he's all worried about reelection and politics, so he didn't ask too many questions."

"What happened to Osan?"

Terrill Samson shrugged. "The Korean Master Control and Reporting Center was destroyed. The initial reports said that part of Osan Air Base just . . . disappeared. Of course, that's *impossible*." He gave a smile that made him look like a big black crocodile about to have dinner. "Later on, they found nuclear material in the area and evacuated the base. The word now is that it was a subatomic blast. It's under investigation by a joint American-Chinese research team. One of the guys on the team is a friend of ours. There's no telling how long it will be before any concrete information is available . . ."

"Your 'friend' will see to that."

"Good to see you're starting to understand how our little world works, Colonel," Samson said. "It so happens that the Chinese did end up destroying most of United Korea's nuclear, chemical, and biological weapons labs in Chagang Do province on their way out of the country, so Korea's special weapons capability has been all but eliminated. The new president has vowed to destroy the rest of the weapons. We'll see.

"Well, let's do some business here. I heard you turned down that assignment offer from the Air Guard at March Air Reserve Base, Rebecca. Mind telling me why?"

She shook her head, then lowered her eyes. "Didn't feel like going for it, that's all, sir."

"You done with flying, then?" he asked. "Done with the military?"

"I think so."

Samson shrugged his shoulders, then looked around. "Too bad," he said. "It's a shame to lose good, tough, aggressive commanders."

"Being tough and aggressive didn't get us much, did it, sir?"

"It brought victory, and it brought peace," Samson

said. "You taught it well to your troops, and you did the job and conquered. For a warrior, that's the best reward there is. You should be proud." No reply. "The 163rd Air Refueling Wing is still looking for a new commander, Rebecca. I'd be happy to put in a good word for you."

"No thank you, sir."

"Plenty of other good units out there need commanders," Patrick McLanahan said. "In fact, I've heard of a Nevada Air National Guard unit that needs a commander."

Rebecca looked up at him—she knew there was only one Nevada Air Guard unit, her old one in Reno, and it had been disbanded. "What did you say, sir?"

"I heard of a plan to put twenty Block G B-1B bombers at a new base to be built in northern Nevada," Patrick said. "Specifically, right here at Battle Mountain Airport. I heard this new B-1B unit, the 111th Bombardment Wing, Missile, will be training down in Tonopah Air Force Base until the new base is built and the planes are modified. They wouldn't be Megafortress aircraft, but they'd be primarily deployed for suppression of enemy air defenses, antiballistic missile defense, and standoff attack."

"What do you think about that, Rebecca?" Samson asked. "It would mean lots of headaches: lots of deployments, training new instructors, setting up a new base, setting up a new wing, congressional wrestling matches . . ."

"I . . . I think it's great, sir," Rebecca said, her eyes lighting up. "Where might an interested party sign up for this assignment?"

"Why, I think the general is taking applications right now," Hal Briggs said with his famous smile. "And I do believe you're first in line."

ABOUT THE AUTHOR

DALE BROWN is a former captain in the U.S. Air Force. He lives in Nevada, where he can often be found high in the sky, piloting his own plane. He is the author of eleven previous novels, all of them *New York Times* bestsellers.